The Evening Blade

Edge of

Awakening

By
Kyle K. Oates

Book cover design and layout by,
Ellie Bockert Augsburger of Creative Digital Studios.
www.CreativeDigitalStudios.com

Cover design features:
Archaic Tunnel: © Sondem / Adobe Stock
beautiful woman red cloak in the woods: © bereta / Adobe Stock

Editing Services provided by,
Ellie Bockert Augsburger of Creative Digital Studios.
www.CreativeDigitalStudios.com

To my wife, Andrea, who helps me find the energy and motivation to try new things. Thanks to my family who support me and my editor who catches my mistakes and offers helpful advice.

CONTENTS

PROLOGUE

Echoes of pain scream forever within my mind. Why do they cry out against their bonds? I am right there with them. Trapped for all eternity within the Eye of the Gods. I miss the feel of the wind against my skin, the scent of a freshly bloomed meadow, the sight of Soleanne setting in the west, and the sounds of birds in spring. I yearn for the warmth of a lover's embrace. My pain is no less than theirs. Yet I chose this willingly. Why did I choose this?

I see now I was mistaken. The Gods tricked me. Please, someone, free me from this torment.

- Passage from *Whispers in the Void*
Unknown Speaker

I

THE ORPHAN

Three dolls rested on top of an old, battered dresser. They were not the finest crafted dolls. In reality, they were far from it. The patchwork cloth, carefully stitched together with tediously hoarded spare threads, the random frayed and faded strands of yarn for hair, and the strategically packed straw stuffing designed to give the impression of humanity to the dolls were perfect to the young girl who had painstakingly assembled them. The girl who currently sat with knees pulled up to her chest on the only windowsill in the room, watching the rain run down the window as if it were the only thing in the world deserving of her attention.

A light knock on the worn, abused door drew her attention. The tear hanging onto the corner of her left eye rolled down her bright red cheek. Fear of an unknown future made her cry. Not sadness. She had been sad far too often to cry from that anymore.

"Anara?" A gentle, elderly woman's voice called through the thin wood. "Anara, it's Sister Dawn. Are you awake?"

"Y-yes," Anara answered, choking on her sobs. "I'm awake." The door opened, revealing a Priestess of Fiel standing in the doorway. Anara had known her since before she could remember. Sister Dawn was her protector. The closest woman Anara considered as a mother.

"Are you feeling well, Anara?" Sister Dawn asked, crossing the room and taking Anara's face gently in her hands. She frowned at the trails left by tears.

"I'm fine, Sister Dawn," Anara said, lithely sliding down from her perch. "I will just miss you, is all," Anara looked away in a

2

poor attempt to hide her grief. She *would* miss Sister Dawn, but that was only a small part of it. This was her life—a life amongst other children without mothers or fathers. A life that no longer belonged to her. It was also a life she no longer desired, yet had no path to follow away from it. Shadows seemed to grow darker with each passing year inside these walls. The world outside of them was pitch black. "I'm too old to stay here, anyway," Anara bitterly mumbled to herself.

"If you're certain? We could at least wait for the weather to clear up," Sister Dawn said, hesitating by the window as Anara gathered her satchel and the best of her dolls from the dresser.

"That isn't part of it, Sister Dawn," Anara said, forcing a smile. "There are rules we must all abide by. You taught me that."

"Rules I recall you've conveniently broken in the past. Many times, if I'm not mistaken," Sister Dawn stated with hands resting on her hips.

Anara laughed. It felt tense. It should have been genuine as the truth of Sister Dawn's retort was just right for the moment. Simultaneously, it was also far from it and their chuckling ended abruptly.

"That's also Wentworth's excuse to throw me out nearly a year early," Anara said, gently sliding the fraying straps of the satchel over one shoulder. The pouch had once been a deep red, but now appeared more like a pinkish-gray. "I'm ready."

"That's all you're taking?"

"This is all that's mine," Anara frowned as Sister Dawn refused to move. *Why is she making this harder than it already is?*

"What about Claire and Cindy? Won't they miss you?" Sister Dawn asked about the other two dolls.

"They'll be loved by the next girl to live here. I want to leave them for her."

"That is generous of you." Sister dawn smiled, *finally* starting towards the door again. Sister Dawn was delaying her. Anara's discomfort at not knowing *where* she was going drove her towards it. It felt foolish. Rushing to the unknown instead of clinging to the familiar was unnatural. If she did not go now, though, she would be forced to later.

"Not that generous," Anara briefly smiled. "I'm taking Cassie with me, she's the best of them."

"Only right, of course. After all, you *were* the one who made them," Sister Dawn said, circling an arm around Anara's waist. The priestess really *was* short. "I'll never get over how tall you've grown. I remember carrying you in my arms nearly seventeen years ago. You were such a small thing back then. And *I* was much younger. Nearly all my life has been spent at *Wentworth's Home for Wayward Souls*, and you were the most beautiful child I ever held. You've always had such brilliant blue eyes." Sister Dawn spoke tenderly, gazing at Anara with nostalgia.

"Everything changes, Sister Dawn," Anara sighed as they walked out into the hallway.

The hall was in as much disrepair as Anara's room. The wallpaper peeled back from the boards where leaks in the roof stained the walls. Loose floor boards creaked beneath their feet as they walked. Some even bent beneath their weight. Others were splintered where the years or idle hands had worn away at them.

Dozens of doors similar to Anara's ran along each side of the hall until it made a right turn towards a much larger room. Each doorway marked a room for a younger girl; each one blissfully cocooned in ignorance of what the world had in store for them when they came of age, as Anara had been when she lovingly crafted her dolls.

"Not everything," Sister Dawn said as they made their way into the atrium of the orphanage. "You're still beautiful, and your azure eyes are just as kind and trusting as they were back then."

"I wouldn't say that," Anara said ruefully, receiving an elbow in her ribs. Unjustly, of course. Anara knew plenty of girls from around Barrowton and even at the orphanage who were prettier than she was.

"You don't give yourself enough credit," Sister Dawn said. "Fiel teaches us to love who we are."

Easy for Fiel to love himself. He's a bloody *god.* Keeping her thought to herself, Anara smiled back at the priestess with a nod.

Anara no longer blindly trusted her elders. Not that Sister Dawn wanted to hear it. Not that *anyone* wanted to hear what she really thought.

The atrium was much more elaborate than the hall and had been carefully maintained. Anara secretly suspected all orphanages were intrinsically similar with a beautiful façade and tarnished interior. Across the room from them was another hallway where the boys' rooms mirrored the girls' wing. To the right was Wentworth's office behind a richly carved, mahogany door. To their left was the entrance marked by four glass doors displaying the dingy gray of the gathered thunderstorm, and a black carriage at the gate. Anara had never seen *that* carriage before. Normally it was a simple wagon from the workhouse, but this one had an enclosed cabin. The finer details of it were obfuscated in the black paint from this distance.

"Best hurry up; it wouldn't do to have Overseer Wentworth wait on you."

"Thank you," Anara said, pushing down her anger and fear for her future in the presence of the old priestess. Sister Dawn would be even more devastated if Anara let any of that show. "Thank you for all you've done for me, Sister Dawn."

"You're most welcome, Anara," Sister Dawn responded, pausing at the mahogany door. She looked at Anara, her lips turning into a frown even as her eyes glistened with growing tears. "You're sure you don't want to wait until the storm passes?"

"Rules, remember?" Anara forced a smile and gently brushed her fingers down Sister Dawn's arm.

Sister Dawn sighed but gave up her protestations. She lightly knocked on the thick door and the two waited.

"Come in," Jeremy Wentworth answered. Sister Dawn opened the door for Anara to step through. The priestess curtsied before leaving Anara's side to return to her other duties. "Well, are you coming, Miss Swift?" Wentworth barked at Anara's slight hesitation once the door was open.

"Yes, sir," Anara said, entering and bobbing unsteadily in an unpracticed curtsy. She felt the tattered edges of her skirt with her fingertips; the dress was of appalling quality compared to the luxury of Wentworth's office. Anara felt so out of place among the bookshelves of tomes, bound in fine leather, and the massive desk that *had* to be larger than her previous room. A single glow lamp, an enchanted device with an eternal flame, was all that served as the room's dim illumination. The air smelled thick with musky incense, which smoldered with an orange glow at the edge of the desk; the scent masking all but a hint of something putrid. Anara gently shut the door while Wentworth ducked beneath the desk; his muttering interspersed amongst the sounds of parchment snapping as he thumbed through a disorganized filing system. The searching stopped as parchment brushed against parchment behind the monumental desk.

"Ah, here it is," he gleefully said, slamming the drawer shut with emphasis, causing Anara to jump slightly. Anara felt her heart racing, Wentworth's clear enjoyment from this adding to her anxiety. "Anara Swift arrived on the first Fillesdahd of the Second Month of Gathering, unknown age. Abandoned on the steps outside the home in the year of thirty-one sixty-three." Wentworth spoke dramatically, a piece of parchment obscuring his face from Anara as he reclined lazily in his monolithic, brown leather chair behind the table. His left hand was wrapped in dirty gauze, stained yellow and pink from whatever he was hiding beneath it. "Given that today is the same Fillesdahd of the year thirty-one eighty, that would make today your seventeenth birthday, would it not? Nearly a woman grown now, aren't you?"

"Yes, sir, it would," Anara answered, feeling uncomfortable as she remained standing before his inquiries. "I guess I am, sir." The enormity of Wentworth's chair made him appear minuscule from her elevated vantage point. Only a man of opulence could afford a chair with such intricate embroidery and finely carved woodwork. It was beautiful and fit seamlessly within the room. Anara felt out of place. The contrast of how she must look with the belongings around her would draw anyone's eye if they could see.

"Which means..." he slowly put the folder down and leaned forward to look at Anara. Anara blanched as the man's disfigured face came into view from the light of the single glow lamp. The steady orange glow illuminated Wentworth's rotten skin. "Today is the last day you can remain here. Establishments such as *Wentworth's Home for Wayward Souls* cannot cater to those who have outgrown youth. You have failed to attract anyone to adopt you through your consistent disobedience and failed to conform. It is time you were sent off to learn a valuable trade." Wentworth's sneer made it worse, and the glee in his voice showed he enjoyed this but Anara could only focus on the scars. Anara recoiled, wanting to flee. *Thade's Grasp*, Wentworth's affliction, was the source of the stench of rot. She had heard it was bad from Sister Dawn, and the other priests of Fiel when they thought no one was listening. Nothing like this.

His left cheek was nearly gone, exposing teeth and tongue behind it every time his mouth moved up and down. As he continued to drone on her mind was transfixed by the face, the words vaguely registering as some speech of the pride she would obtain in service to Iliona.

The part of his gums she could see were gray with black blotches instead of a healthy pink. One eye was dead; the pupil and iris were covered with a filmy haze that dulled any color it might have had. The left half of the jaw was lopsided with bone cysts and pits beneath the repugnant flesh and what hair Anara could see on his head was a mess of matted clumps. The rest of his left side, hidden by ornate silk clothing, was likely to be as wretched of a sight as well. A few patches of silk were darker than the rest where his wounds had seeped through his bandages to stain the cloth.

Anara could remember six years ago when it first started. The flurry of healers who had come to see Jeremy Wentworth about his ailment had been exciting. Anara was still young, and to see so many people from towns far away was a rare treat for the orphanage.

Overseer Wentworth had been strikingly handsome back then. A chiseled jaw, penetrating, dull green eyes, and shoulder length lustrous black hair had even caused Anara to fancy him as some sort of knight in shining armor who would free her someday. Not to mention his captivating smile. That had all changed, along with his demeanor toward his charges, when the tips of his left fingers had gone numb and turned black. After that, they started coming.

First the priests from Aederon City; not the ones from the orphanage, as they were hardly equipped to handle the affliction, but real healers who practiced their craft behind closed doors. It had worked to a certain degree, buying the overseer time and keeping him free of deadly infections, but Wentworth had sought a cure. His need to be rid of the disease consumed his mind while the disease greedily devoured his flesh. He sought aid from all of the realms

Only the Dristelli answered.

Anara had marveled at the initial sight of the Dristelli. She had never seen anyone from beyond Ashfall before. The Dristelli were both beautiful and scandalous at the same time. They were long limbed, slender of build, and all of them—men and women alike—wore loose dresses that hung from one shoulder and left the other side of their chest completely exposed. Their eyes were large, like birds of prey, and instead of hair they had plumes of feathers that grew from their scalp and down their back. The plumage was more colorful and longer on the men than the women.

By the time the Dristelli physicians had arrived, Wentworth no longer resembled a hero from a story. Instead, he was the villain. His face had become pitted with scars, yet still whole, and his hair had thinned considerably. They left soon after with Wentworth screaming at them for wasting his time because they had refused to bond him, whatever that meant. So, with Ilionans unable to do anything to cure him, Wentworth had slowly rotted. His mind had turned inward. His life now revolved around *Thade's Grasp* except for the little pleasure he got from making others miserable.

It was singularly revolting. Even so, Anara could not rip her eyes from Wentworth's visage. His undulating throat and jaw as he spoke caused the scraps of flesh on his left jowl and neck to shudder and sway. His dead eye only closed half-way with a ragged eyelid. The milky, green eye always stared outward next to the yellowing bone of his eye socket. Despite the damage, there was very little blood. Green ooze, so dark it was nearly black, leaked from the wounds as cracks formed in the dried layers of decayed flesh. Had a quick wound done this much damage, Wentworth would have been dead. *Thade's Grasp* worked slowly. Slowly enough for the wounds to try to heal, even as the foundation of those scars were eaten away.

"...perhaps you will learn respect in your new life!" Wentworth snapped and Anara realized she had been staring.

"My apologies, sir," Anara curtsied, averting her gaze from the man. If his disfigurement had not been enough to keep even the bravest of men's eyes from him, the burning rage in his good eye would have. Wentworth frightened Anara. "I did not mean to stare."

"No one *means* to stare! *You* unabashedly gawk! The sooner this place is rid of your rebellious and insubordinate behavior the better," Wentworth spat as a light knock sounded. "A wretch like you should know better, *Miss* Swift. You should know your place. You are nothing. An insect on the heel of a peasant's boot." The knock came again more persistently. "Come in!"

Anara glared at the man, biting her tongue to stop the tears burning in her eyes, as the door to Wentworth's study opened once more. Clicking sounds drew Anara's attention from the horror of Wentworth's face to a woman as she gracefully swept into the room. She was easily as beautiful as Wentworth was ugly. Her skirt teasingly revealed flashes of her legs with each step that landed with a saucy click from her high-heeled shoes. Her sleeveless bodice was even tighter than the skirt. The woman was certainly as old as Wentworth, but in much better care than Anara had ever seen a woman.

She had only the faintest of wrinkles at the corners of her eyes, as if her life had been void of any real mirth to smile from, and the pale complexion was proof enough her skin had been sheltered from *Soleanne*'s light. Her stunningly red hair was pulled back into a tight braid that fell to the small of her back and her eyes flickered with the minimal lighting of Wentworth's office. Her lips were just as vibrant as her hair, obviously painted, and a light blush gave color to her cheeks. That was fake, too, as the woman probably had very little to actually blush about. She seemed worldly and confident in the way she carried herself despite the revealing dress that she wore with a straight, hourglass posture. Anara enjoyed how the strange woman looked, she had never seen someone dressed so enticing and exotic before.

"Jim!" The beautiful woman exclaimed as she walked up to the desk, brushing past Anara as if she were not there, and took his hands into her own. The woman wore long gloves that came up above the elbow, leaving her shoulders bare. "It has been too long since I've had the pleasure of visiting your home. I had heard about your affliction but had no *idea* it had progressed so far. Is there any hope of a cure?"

"The Order of Light does not seem to think so. Even their best healers are confounded," Wentworth said, smiling the most genuine and repulsive smile Anara had ever seen. "And the Dristelli have refused my petition to perform a bonding to preserve what little is left of me."

"I never trusted them anyway. Perhaps it is best if you see to your affairs within the realm before reaching outside of it for aid. Surely the other orders may have proposals to consider," Mistress Adair said. "Perhaps if you prayed to Malef instead of Fiel."

"The Order of Flame wants to burn it off, Erin, as if that wouldn't kill me faster. No, I'm afraid the God of Fire's answers are only helpful in battle or in bed." Mistress Adair smiled at that.

"And the others?"

"Ezebre teaches to accept life as it is — a fat lot of good her advocates in the Order of Wind were. The Order of Stone says death, in all its forms, is the natural order of things and should not be opposed. An individual cannot oppose a mountain."

"So, no aid from Duloreb. What of Mertas?"

"The priests of the Order of Streams make useless tonics—all of them," Wentworth finished his list of the five orders that followed the five gods of Iliona.

"That is unfortunate. Though if I might change the topic to one of a less unsavory nature, why have you sent for me? It was an uncomfortably hasty three-week journey here from Aederon City. I certainly hope my travel has not been just to hear such disagreeable news. Especially since I will no doubt miss the majority of this year's Harvest Festival as a result."

"Of course not," Wentworth said, motioning to Anara. The woman's eyes followed. "I have a ward who is of an age that might interest you."

Anara clenched her fists under the weight of Mistress Adair's gaze. She had a sudden sensation of being a slab of meat before a butcher as the woman looked her up and down.

"Really, Jim, I thought you'd stopped sending your girls to establishments such as mine," Mistress Adair said, slowly walking around Anara.

"I changed my mind concerning her," Wentworth grumbled and rubbed his right temple out of irritation.

"She isn't much to work with." Mistress Adair tsked as she paced. She shot a sideways glance at Wentworth, clearly picking up on his tone as well.

"I have a name!" Anara blurted out, thinking how hypocritical it was for Wentworth to talk about showing respect. Both of them were speaking to each other as if she were not even there. It was rude.

"Willful," Mistress Adair smiled, ignoring the outburst. "I take it she's a problem child," Mistress Adair sighed, glancing at Wentworth.

"Not too horribly," Wentworth weakly countered, half laughing like a child caught in a lie. "She's broken a few rules during her stay, but what child doesn't in sixteen years?"

"You used to lie better, Jim," Mistress Adair said, pushing Anara's shoulders back. "Stand up straight, girl. Let me get a real look at you." Anara obeyed, her fists clenched.

"Long blonde hair, arrow straight too," Adair noted, running a hand through Anara's locks from the top of her head to the small of her back. "Dirty," the woman wrinkled her nose and wiped her hand on Anara's back. "Beautiful if she took care of it."

"I only get..." Anara started, feeling embarrassed.

"No talking," Wentworth barked.

"She is a little behind on maturing," Adair leaned back and tapped her chin with her right hand while the other held her elbow as she looked Anara up and down from head to toe. "Obviously from malnourishment. Pity, Jim. You used to feed your girls."

"What has that got to do with anything?" Anara squeaked, crossing her arms over her chest, self-conscious of her lack of bust.

"She's too skinny and tall—nearly five-nine despite the malnourishment. Men don't like women taller than them." Adair said and shook her head. "A few years in a corset should fix her silhouette, not that it's horrid but it could be tighter in the waist than it is. Her face is a bit wide, but not so much it appears manly. Though that could just be from the dirt and sweat on it coupled with your office lighting. Full lips balanced by the width of her face, which is good. Still... I don't know, Jim," Adair shook her head with a long sigh. She took Anara's chin in her hand and turned her face side to side.

"So, wash her and feed her, she'll be pretty enough for your requirements," Jim said, waving a hand apathetically even as his brow furrowed with worry.

"She has a pretty nose. I'd wager silver that she is from the Eastern Coastal Region given her features. And I presume, with eyes as vibrant and exotic as those, most men might look past her height and strong jaw line. What did she do to warrant your ire so suddenly, Jim?" Adair folded her arms beneath her bust, giving Wentworth a stern look.

"Nothing to worry about," Wentworth demurred.

"Remember how your lies used to be better?" Adair asked. "Put your arms up." Anara complied and was suddenly aware of just how short her dress was. She was seventeen now, yet still wore the same outfit from three years ago. Adair ran her hands down Anara's sides starting from her elbows and pressing harder as they neared her ribs. "Be straight with me Jim, no more dancing around it. The truth."

"She attacked a priest," Wentworth said. Adair paused, her hands stopping at Anara's waist.

"I never attacked..."

"I said be quiet," Wentworth barked. Mistress Adair frowned at the disfigured man.

"A violent girl is far worse than an insolent one. You want her to come to *my* establishment and attack *my* employees? Or worse, my *patrons*?" Adair asked, glaring at Wentworth. "I should not have come. Just to satisfy my curiosity may I ask whom she attacked?"

"Brother Mitchel," Wentworth said and Adair frowned again before going back to her examination. She lowered Anara's chin to look into her eyes again. Even wearing such tall heels Anara was taller than Mistress Adair. Like most people, Anara had bothered looking at so closely, Mistress Adair's eyes were as brown as they came. Lighter than usual, but still brown.

"I'm certain that old lecher deserved what he got. You still keep him around, knowing how severely he punishes rule breakers? How badly was he hurt?"

"Not so bad. It was an emotional shock more than anything. His methods worked, usually," Wentworth admitted. "Brother Mitchel never was able to make this one comply, though. He has grown old, and the girl is too old for that kind of scolding anymore. He left for the Fertile Vale."

"That bad? How long ago? Has she attacked anyone else since then?" Adair quickly rattled off, causing Wentworth to pause and consider his words carefully. The way Wentworth's expression changed clearly showed he did not enjoy being put on the defensive.

"No other incidences in the past month worth noting. Honestly," Wentworth said and Anara clenched her jaw. Wentworth was lying; she never attacked Brother Mitchel, no matter how much he deserved it for his method of punishing the younger children.

"Don't grind your teeth," Adair scolded offhandedly to Anara. "She's passable, Wentworth. I'll admit as much. Barely more than skin and bone, but I can work with that."

"Then we have a deal."

"I did not say that," Mistress Adair said, turning away from Anara. "I said passable, but the work to get her ready will be costly. More than just money, but time as well. The price point still needs to be discussed."

"You're selling me!" Anara protested angrily. First Wentworth *lies* about her and now they're discussing fees for taking her. Her eyes widened as she glanced back and forth between the two with a strong urge to flee and the dull warmth of anger. "Slavery is illegal in Iliona, everyone knows that!"

"A finder's fee, dear," Adair said, placing a hand on Anara's shoulder as she moved to stand behind her. "Not a slaver's fee. Once you reach the age of citizenship in a year you'll be welcome to forge a different path if you choose. I'll merely provide you with some skills to fall back on should you need them."

"Which you most likely will," Wentworth grumbled under his breath.

"You aren't helping your case, Jim. You're supposed to tell me her *redeeming* qualities. Slothfulness will not be tolerated, and only decreases her value to me," Adair said, her voice sweeter than honey. "I'll pay a quarter what you want for finding her."

"Three-quarters."

"Perhaps if you had taken better care of her," Adair said. Anara *really* felt like a slab of meat now. *Do they have to do this with me present*, she thought. "Look at her, she's half starved, half covered in mud and half naked. I'm surprised the realm lets you keep your orphanage. You *used* to take better care of your wards." Anara clenched her teeth together again, she was not *that* dirty and it stung a little that the strange woman offered so little. Anara almost laughed at the irony of feeling ashamed of being worth so little to the woman. "Don't grind your teeth, dear, they're one of your better qualities."

"Half," Wentworth said coldly. "But if she recoups your loss within two years, I get a small percentage of that." He might have cared about such an insult to his reputation once; before *Thade's Grasp* started destroying his mind. He might have been angered by Adair's claim that he did not take care of his wards. Then he would have puffed out his chest, daring them to prove his lax attitude towards the welfare of his wards.

But not now.

"Three-eighths and you can have that percentage," Mistress Adair said, smiling as if she had bested some indomitable foe.

"Deal," Wentworth said, holding out Anara's custodial form. Mistress Adair signed with large, flowing strokes and the two shook hands to finalize the deal. Mistress Adair linked her left arm with Anara's right and turned to go.

"Nicholas will be in to pay you and to see to gathering any medical or personal documents you may have on the child. Oh, and include any records of her other infractions so I may be well informed," Mistress Adair said as she opened Wentworth's mahogany door.

"Of course," Wentworth said, sounding relieved.

The door shut behind them and Mistress Adair shuddered. Her composed and shrewd demeanor melting away in a heartbeat. She let go of Anara and practically clawed her gloves off, taking care to turn them inside out, before balling them up.

"Vile man, he should have just let *Thade's Grasp* kill him," Adair hissed. "Pay him three-eighths what he suggested in the letter, Master Brenton," she said to the man who opened the glass door for them. He was considerably older and taller than Mistress Adair but Anara recognized the boyish grin on his face as she addressed him. He was enamored with the younger woman even though he could have been old enough to be Mistress Adair's father.

"Who's the new gir'?" He asked in a heavily rural accent.

"This is..." Mistress Adair started, pausing to blink long eyelashes at Anara a few times. "What *is* your name?" Before Anara could answer, the man let out a deep, rumbling laugh.

"Jus' like you 'rin, to care more about the barter than the gir'," Brenton said holding out his hand towards Anara. "Name's Nicho'as Bren'on," he said.

"Anara Swift," Anara answered, taking his hand which he shook so vigorously that her arm felt more like a wet noodle than a limb with bones in it.

"Pleased ta meet ya, 'nara!"

"*Uh-nar-uh*," Anara enunciated.

"Tha's wha' I said, 'nara," he only grinned back at her.

"Don't bother," Mistress Adair sighed. "Our driver has known me nearly twenty years and still refuses to say mine correctly. Which, need I remind you, Master Brenton, you should not be using at all. I am Mistress Adair to you and all others outside of the temple. This young woman will be Mistress Swift from now on."

"Wha'ever you say, 'rin," Nicholas said as the two of them stepped out into the drizzling weather.

"One more thing, Brenton," Adair said and the driver stopped half-way through his turn to go back towards Wentworth's office. "Burn these as soon as you get a chance," she said and tossed the balled-up gloves to the driver.

"Will do, 'rin," Nicholas said, nodding his head very slightly.

The two of them waited on the steps of the orphanage, keeping just out of the rain from an overhang above them. Anara shifted uncomfortably. The entire world seemingly hushed by the steady downpour just a few feet away from them. Anara shivered. She had no coat to speak of and the waiting just stretched on as Adair kept her attention on the carriage. Anara looked around, wondering why they were just standing there. She was alone with a complete stranger. Someone who had just judged her based solely on her appearance. An appearance Anara had never really enjoyed and to have the woman voice so many of her self-critical thoughts renewed the grief she felt from earlier.

Anara caught herself from letting tears flow down her face. She looked around to bring back better memories from growing. Memories of splashing in mud or playing in snow. Memories of the other orphans that would become her friends only to be taken in by a childless family, leaving Anara behind year after year. Each year growing older, each year becoming more and more of a woman and less of a child.

"Where are we going?" Anara asked, realizing her reminiscing had spiraled down towards despair. "Mistress Adair," she added, unsure of how to address the woman.

"Please, Anara," the woman smiled warmly at her. "Call me Erin. We are sisters now. As for your question, didn't Wentworth tell you?"

"He might have," Anara hesitated, remembering Wentworth's half-dead face and the lecture she was supposed to be listening to at the time.

"But you didn't pay attention, and I cannot blame you for that, dear," Erin said, gently patting Anara's arm as she spoke. "He really has become a shut-in since the last time I came through here if *his own wards* are shocked by his appearance. If not for my training I probably would have stared at him with a blank expression as well. As it was. I did not even notice you were in the room when I came in. If you'll forgive my oversight."

"Of course," Anara said, slightly annoyed the woman had not answered her. Nicholas returned, opening an enormous parasol and Mistress Adair instantly started walking beside the large man. Anara followed a few steps behind, getting hit with a brisk splash of rain before taking refuge under the cover. "But where are we going?"

"*Lussena's Temple*," Erin answered as they walked down towards the carriage, avoiding puddles and as much mud as they could.

The carriage was well maintained, of course, but as they drew closer Anara noticed it had very little embellishment. The dark paint, unfortunately, did not obscure any potentially intricate details from her first glimpse. After Wentworth's office and Adair's fine, albeit revealing, dress Anara had expected more extravagance. Adair's dress probably cost a significant percentage of the carriage's. *Why would a woman with such wealth travel in such a common carriage?* she wondered as Nicholas helped them up and into the cabin. The carriage door latched shut as Anara sat down across from Mistress Adair.

"I'm to become a priestess? To Malef?" Anara asked. Anara had never considered the life of a priestess. Let alone devoted to the Order of Flame, but Lussena was one of Malef's wives, if her memories of Sister Dawn's theology classes were right. *Who pays finder's fees to hire a priestess?* The absurdity of the internal quandary made her blush when Mistress Adair started laughing. It was the same sort of laugh as Nicholas's, the kind Anara had not heard for a few years now, but completely different as well. Where Nicholas had nearly shaken the building, Mistress Adair's was airy and light, delicate even, but was one of honest humor.

"Far from it, in fact," Mistress Adair sighed, touching her bare sternum with her fingertips as if to catch her breath. "*Lussena's Temple* is a courtesan house." Anara felt her stomach drop and she felt tears welling up in her eyes.

"I'm being..." Anara started but she could not finish. *Sent to a whore house*, she wanted to say, but the words got caught on something in her throat. Of course, this would be where *he* sent her. She had no *why* Brother Mitchel left for the Fertile Vale. Anara did not even remember attacking him. Mistress Adair had paid too much. Wentworth would have done this for free. He may have even gladly *paid* Mistress Adair to take Anara. Mistress Adair sighed, moving to sit beside Anara.

"Poor child, he really *didn't* tell you, did he?" Adair said, gently placing her arm around Anara. Anara reflexively leaned against the warmth of Adair's shoulder as all the tears she had held back for Sister Dawn cascaded down her flushed cheeks.

Mistress Adair began to sing a soft lullaby as Anara cried. Anara barely noticed when the carriage shook and they started on their journey away from *Wentworth's Home for Wayward Souls*. Sleep came to her as Mistress Adair's melody mixed with her tears.

Anara stood at the edge of a cliff, staring across a valley of nothing. Pure black seemed to consume the world beneath the precipice but somewhere in that abyss, she knew someone was in pain. Anara tried to reach out to them, tried to help them, but something stopped her. *Hush, Swiftling*, Brother Mitchel cautioned. *You brought this on yourself.* Anara clenched her fists and screamed at the priest, rage filling her because she knew he was the source of her anger. A bright flash of orange was followed by searing pain and Anara woke up.

"NO!" she screamed, batting at the arm around her shoulders and pushing away. She needed to do *something*, it was unfair. She was powerless to help them.

"Be still," Mistress Adair's sweet voice cut into the dark as the carriage continued to shake. The soft hand of a woman pulled her back towards that warmth and Anara trembled. Her hair was damp with sweat and cold against her scalp as Mistress Adair gently placed Anara's head back against the older woman's shoulder. "Thade's veins," Adair cursed. "You've taken with fever, so quickly!" She knocked on the carriage wall and the swaying slowed to a stop.

"Mistress Adair?" Anara asked, her mind felt fuzzy and her whole body ached. It ached like it did the night after... It was lost to her: the dream, what really happened a month ago. All of it was gone, blocked behind a wall of nothing in her mind. "What's wrong with me?" she cried.

"It was time to make camp for the night anyway," Mistress Adair said. She sounded concerned. Whether that was regarding the price she paid for Anara, or for Anara's health was something she could not discern within the turmoil of her mind. Her thoughts felt like they were behind a sheet of obsidian held up to the light; form without substance. Outlines of thoughts formed but they had no clear pattern to them.

"Wha' is it, 'rin?" Nicholas asked, but Anara could not remember him opening the door. The chill of the night came next, followed by the sound of the door. Everything was all out of order. The only constant was the pain and her shivering.

"Anara's taken fever." A more calloused hand fell across Anara's forehead. A hand like Brother Mitchel's and she screamed, clawing at it and feeling skin tear beneath her fingernails.

"Ack, 'nara, calm down, it's on'y me," Nicholas said, finally grabbing Anara's wrists together in one massive hand as he felt her forehead. "Teethed slit of Thade's whore!" Anara would have blushed if she did not feel so weak. She had never heard *that* curse before. "What happened? Does she have... Did Wentworth give her?"

19

"No, *Thade's Grasp* starts in the extremities with a blackening of the digits. I don't know what happened, Nicholas, I've never seen a fever come on so suddenly or so fiercely," Adair said. "I had drifted off to sleep and next thing I knew she was fighting to get away from me and I felt like I had fallen asleep too close to a hearth. Set up camp, and fetch some water," Mistress Adair ordered. "We need to bring this fever down."

"Yes, ma'am," Nicholas said, shaking the carriage as he stepped down. "Gerrol," he yelled. "Water!"

"You'll be all right, Anara," Mistress Adair said and Anara felt the other woman hold her tight before her mind slipped into the embrace of unconsciousness.

II

THE SQUIRE

Joshua grabbed the hilt of the dueling sword and inwardly sighed. It was typical of Sir Echton to forget such an important piece of equipment; he left his sword in the ready room moments before the first duel of the Harvest Festival but. Then again, it was Joshua's job to make sure Sir Echton had what he needed. The dueling sword was heavy. Nothing like the one Joshua wore on his hip. His father's sword, an enchanted short blade, was like wielding a delicate long feather compared to the longsword. Still, the larger sword was not *that* heavy. Joshua had, after all, trained with a similar blade since he turned fourteen three years earlier. Next year he could enter the tournament to try to win a knighthood. One more year and he could realize his dream.

Joshua carried the sword out into the arena where Sir Echton waited, pacing up and down the packed dirt, eyes seeking his squire. The aging knight tightened the straps on his dented right bracer as he stared across the field at his much younger opponent. Sir Wallace Stanson, a knight who was recognizable everywhere by his polished black armor and arrogant gait, stood impatiently as he leaned against his own dueling sword across the arena.

"Thank you, Joshua," he said, taking the dueling blade and giving it a test swing. Sir Echton was more accustomed to his own sword, as all knights were, but the dueling swords were dulled to level the playing field against a knight who might normally wield an enchanted blade. "What can you tell me of Sir Stanson?" Sir

Echton asked. He constantly quizzed Joshua about the other knights of Iliona. "It is all well and good to know how to fight," Sir Echton had explained when Joshua first asked *why* he needed to know the fighting styles of other knights. "But more importantly is how your opponent fights. Knowing that can save your life."

"He favors a swan stance," Joshua said, tightening the straps on Echton's cuirass. "Which means most of his strikes will come high, intending to score the most points on your helm or chest. Though, if pressed, he will switch to a more solid boar stance to keep his center protected." Where a man was struck in a tournament during the sword competition resulted in various awarded points; one for a leg or arm, two for the chest, and three for the head.

"Good," Sir Echton said, tussling Joshua's hair as if he were still a lad ten years old. Joshua frowned at the knight since Echton was old enough to be Joshua's grandfather. Normally he would protest the treatment as he was seventeen years old, but he remained silent. Just before a match was not the time to distract his tutor. "And how should I counter?"

"Match him in swan stance," Joshua said. "Then when he switches to boar, go with wolf to draw his defense away from the center."

"Excellent," Sir Echton said. A horn blared, signaling the start of the match, and Sir Echton slammed his visor down. The crowd cheered and jeered for the knights as they stepped forward and took their place.

They both turned to King Aegen the Third, a man even older than Sir Echton, and his three queens who were all closer to Joshua's age. Despite having had fifteen wives, three at any given time in his life, the king had never produced a single heir. The competitors saluted King Aegen, crossing both arms over their chests, and turned to face each other while drawing their swords.

The cacophony of the crowd doubled with the first ringing of blade on blade as Joshua watched. Sir Echton had slowed with age in the time Joshua had known him. He used to be the best back then. Now the knight lost more often than he won. Yet Echton held his own the way only an expert swordsman could. As

Joshua had predicted, Stanson started high and Echton matched the stance to keep their swords entangled instead of leaving an opening for quick points. A few lesser strikes to the arms and legs exchanged between them and, seeing them tied so late into the match, Stanson switched to boar, as Joshua had anticipated. Sir Echton drove forward with wolf, dancing and dodging out of Stanson's range to attack from the sides.

The wolf would tire Echton out, as any stance would, but before he fatigued it would allow the old knight to gain a sizable lead over Stanson. A solid thud echoed in the arena. The strike—initially telegraphed to Stanson's right—had quickly changed to the left, leaving a dent in Stanson's armor where it hit. Stanson fell back, abandoning boar and switching to dragon, transitioning to one the older knight, without full use of his joints, could not perfect. Stanson spun, bringing his blade around so fast that Echton's blade snapped out of his hand. In mid spin Stanson's sword deftly changed hands, whipping around and crashing into the side of Echton's helm. Echton staggered to the side as the crowd cheered. As an observer, Joshua admitted that dragon stance's quick spins and exaggerated flourishes were entertaining for the crowd. In a real fight, it was ineffective since it left a knight vulnerable against multiple enemies and was easy to block with a shield.

Echton stumbled against the wall of the arena and slowly lowered to the ground. He fumbled with the buckle under his chin. Stanson turned around slowly, holding his sword up for the benefit of the crowd in a jubilant victory stance. All of Aederon City could hear the roar of the crowd.

Joshua ran to Echton's side, helping the old knight remove the freshly dented helmet to check for any serious wounds. The old man blinked his dark blue eyes—the old man was one of the few people Joshua had seen with any color other than brown—as he focused on Joshua.

"Gave him a good fight, didn't we," Echton bellowed as he clapped Joshua on the shoulder. Blood left a triumphant mark down the side of his face from the blow, coloring his silver stubble red. "Probably expected an easy win against a knight over three times his age." Despite the loss, Echton was grinning from ear-to-ear as he stared at the score. Eight flags flew on Echton's side. Nine were needed to win. "What was my tally?"

"One chest, two arms, and four legs," Joshua answered. "Stanson's were one head, five arms, and one leg."

"Bloody good fight," Echton bellowed again as he allowed Joshua to help him back to his feet. Echton groaned as his exhausted leg muscles strained to support his weight. "I might be too old for this next year, Joshua," Echton said over his shoulder, walking towards Stanson to congratulate the younger man.

Joshua watched, absentmindedly running his hand over the dented helmet, as Echton held up Sir Stanson's gauntleted hand before bowing to him. Stanson nodded, acknowledging the congratulation but not admitting to the close match. Joshua sighed. Most of the knights treated Sir Echton so apathetically, even though Sir Echton still showed unrivaled skill for his age.

"He's old blood," the other knights would say. "Young is what Iliona needs! Young will crush the Raykarn skirmishes once and for all."

They just did not understand.

It enraged Joshua to hear. Not just for how the others belittled Sir Echton, but their ignorance as well. Only those who had *lived and fought* in the Borderlands could comprehend. The skirmishes with the Raykarn would never end. Nearly ten years of Joshua's youth had shown that truth to him. Joshua puffed out his chest as he watched his mentor, remembering when they had first met. He poignantly recalled the horror of it and how Sir Echton's true character unfolded before him.

"Josh," his mother called out to him as he tossed the hay in the barn. The Borderlands often had swiftlings—cat-sized lizards similar to the massive dragons of myth—that liked to hide in the hay. They would set it on fire when they shed their skin if the hay was not tossed regularly. "Dinner be ready."

"I'll be there in a minute, mother," Joshua called out, looking at his mother standing in the doorway. "I just have another stack to toss." His mother was beautiful that day, like every day he remembered, as she stood with the setting light of *Soleanne* at her back. She was a native Borderlander, with dark skin, narrow eyes, and her head half shaved per their religion. Borderlanders believed in the same gods as the northerners, but elevated Thade among them. His father believed as those north of Ashfall did, in only five gods. "It be balance," his mother said when he asked about her beliefs. "Night," she motioned to the shaved side, and then the other, "and day. Fiel, Ezebre, and Mertas be day. Thade, Duloreb, and Malef be night." It was as simple as that. The Borderlanders did not rank the gods. There was no right or wrong, no good or evil gods; they were just gods. Which made sense at the time. Day or night, it did not matter. The Borderlands were always dangerous.

"Okay, but be hurrying up, father be coming home soon and Elisa be growing impatient!" his mother called out before disappearing back into the house.

Joshua sighed, turning back to his work. Elisa was *always* impatient. *She'll live for a few more minutes*, he thought as he plunged the pitchfork into the hay.

Something hissed and slithered out of the haystack. The serpentine lizard flared its wings at Joshua for disturbing its sleep. It hissed again, letting its forked tongue dance towards him, before it took flight and disappeared out the back window of the barn. At the same moment, Joshua's eyes fell on the Raykarn as it menacingly slipped in through the large opening the swiftling had just exited.

The Raykarn looked like a twisted form of an Ilionan man. The red scales that covered its body from head to toe were so minuscule they appeared like coppery skin at a distance. Joshua observed the pronounced musculature rippling beneath the scales, indicative of great strength. The creature wore only a loincloth and baldric that held its greatsword on its back. Fangs the size of kitchen knives appeared as it hissed at Joshua. The Raykarn started forward. The face was the least Ilionan characteristic, with no hair and only vertical slits in the absence of a nose. The eyes, bright orange and burning with inhuman hatred, were the worst. Hatred for Joshua even though he had never done anything to warrant it. The Raykarn just hated *all* Ilionans. In that instant Joshua knew. The war with the Raykarn clans could not be won. It had nothing to do with possession of land or riches. It had nothing to do with their different religions. It was because the Raykarn hated Ilionans with a deeply ingrained malevolence carried across generations.

"Mother!" Joshua yelled, throwing the pitchfork like a spear as the Raykarn lunged at him. The tall Raykarn blocked the pitchfork easily, cutting the shaft in half with a swipe his sword. It was not an Ilionan sword. Ilionans crafted straight swords, an effective design at punching through armor. This was a heavy, curved, single-edged sword meant for hacking limbs from bodies. The Raykarn stepped forward and Joshua ran. He ran for the shelter of his house. He ran for his father to protect him. He ran from the monster. Somehow Joshua reached the house before the Raykarn and slammed the door shut behind him. A second later the noise of battle erupted all around the small hovel.

"Mother!" Joshua called out as Raykarn hisses mixed with the screams of men outside. "Where are you?" Joshua ducked into the kitchen, yelling at the top of his lungs, as something crashed through the door. Wood splintered, spraying the wall behind him with debris, as the Raykarn continued its pursuit.

The Raykarn lunged and Joshua instinctively rolled beneath the kitchen table just a second before the beast crashed into it. The Raykarn hissed—a curse from what little Joshua could understand of their language—and tossed the table aside as if it were a child's toy. Plates, spoons, knives, and forks flew into the air as Joshua pushed back against the cabinets and the Raykarn stalked forward. His mother's evening meal, a roast he had helped her pick out at the market that morning, slapped against the floor, juices pooling beneath it. Soup splashed against the wall and their weekly flatbread stores broke against the ceiling into dozens of pieces, raining onto the dirt floor.

Joshua panicked, seeing a sword by the door to the front room. *Father's forgotten his sword again*, Joshua thought wildly as he rolled between the legs of the Raykarn towards the blade, just before the Raykarn's weapon crashed into the cabinets. The heavy weapon cleaved the sturdy wood in half like a lumberjack's axe. He had to get the sword to his father. His father could not protect them without it. Joshua reached the weapon and clutched it to his chest as he stood. The Raykarn was there a second later, laughter in its hateful eyes glowed like smoldering embers in the dimming light of evening.

The Raykarn hissed an insult at Joshua, threw its head back and laughed. Joshua roared in defiance. His father's sword sang as the steel scraped against the scabbard's locket and Joshua furiously plunged the too-light blade deep into the Raykarn's gut. It stopped laughing. Its hissing transformed into curses as it grabbed hold of the weapon, and Joshua staggered a step back.

It snarled at him in a blood rage, backhanding Joshua so forcefully he flew across the room and against the broken planks of the door. The Raykarn pulled the blade from its gut as if the wound were a mere scratch and tossed the blade, slick with orange blood, aside. Joshua retreated against the wall in terror. The monster descended on him, wrapping its scaled hands around his throat. It snarled, inches from Joshua's face, its fetid breath rancid with the promise of death, and it raised its massive blade with one hand. Joshua felt the ground disappear beneath his feet and tried to scream. The grip on his throat was so tight nothing came out. Then a flash of silver fell across Joshua's vision and he was suddenly on the ground. His legs crumpled beneath him as he looked up. The Raykarn was making an unearthly noise, an agonized scream commingled with surprise. Its severed arm fell in Joshua's lap, staining his brown slacks dark orange from the oozing stump. The monster desperately swung its blade at a man in armor, painted in streamlets of orange Raykarn blood. The man gracefully deflected the blow with his sword, sending the unbalanced weapon harmlessly into the ground before the knight's sword whipped around, severing the Raykarn's head from its shoulders in one effortless swoop. The last sound of battle was the knight's weapon clicking home in its scabbard.

Just like that, it was all over.

"Momma!" Joshua screamed and ran for the front room but the knight caught him around the waist.

"No, son!" he said as Joshua struggled to get free. "You don't want to go in there."

"Momma!" Joshua screamed at the top of his lungs. "Elisa! Momma!" The man picked him up even as Joshua kicked and punched at his armor in futility. "Momma! Momma! Where are you, Momma?! Where's Elisa?!"

The knight pulled him close in an attempt to keep him still. The knight's strength was greater than Joshua's thrashing could fight against and he eventually gave up the struggle. Joshua felt numb, emotionally spent. His futile screams were replaced with the quiet sobs of grief as the knight gently guided him outside. Joshua knew what had happened to his sister and mother. The stories of Raykarn raids were common in the Borderlands. Night or day they came, it did not matter.

"Sir Echton," a man said, riding up on a white stallion. Orange and red stained the horse's fur and mane. A longsword of living flame flickered in the man's gauntleted hand. His full plate was ornamented with gold filigree, glittering like fire in the sunset. A royal blue cape billowed behind him and Joshua felt a subdued sense of awe as he watched the man. The way he held himself, straight-backed and deservedly proud, created a desire to follow this man inside Joshua he had never expected.

"Yes, Lord Commander," the knight said, saluting with the hand that was not keeping Joshua. Joshua blinked at the man with wonder. He had never met a lord before.

"A splinter of the Raykarn party has fled south. I'm taking twenty of my knights in pursuit. See to the village. Make sure all survivors make for Ashfall," the Lord ordered. "A scout just brought word that the Redclaws intend to push forward."

"Yes, my lord," Sir Echton said solemnly as the Lord Commander galloped south. Joshua was vaguely aware of the dust kicked up as twenty other men on horseback followed their leader. Another man walked up to them as Echton helped Joshua into the horse's saddle. The horse was too big for him, but Joshua felt too tired to protest. Too tired to fight anymore.

"What household was this?" Echton asked the man. Joshua vaguely recognized him as one of the village watchmen. Nothing mattered, though. Why did the knight care?

"The Kentaines," the watchman answered and Joshua sobbed even harder, his insides felt on fire and the world tilted sickeningly. "The father was taken on the road. Have you seen the mother and daughter?"

Sir Echton glared reproachfully at the watchman and the man nodded in grim understanding. He turned away and went back to the house to help clean up.

"Stick with me, boy," Sir Echton said, climbing into the saddle with ease even though he wore plate mail. He removed his full helm and kindly looked down at Joshua. Joshua could not believe the man had fought as well as he did. He appeared much older than his own father, his skin tanned into leather from years of exposure to the harsh elements. The knight's hair was gray with deep, expressive wrinkles crinkling at the corners of his eyes and mouth. "I'll get you safely north of Ashfall. We aren't free of Malef's flames, yet."

"I want to kill them," Joshua said coldly, clenching his fists and glaring southward through his tears. If an old man can fight Raykarn, so could he.

"Hate will drive you to say reckless things," Sir Echton said, his first lesson for Joshua. "It'll drive you to do reckless things, too. Reckless things get you killed, son. Best to avoid them."

"I don't care."

"Someday you will, and I intend to see you live to that day without doing anything you may regret."

"I'm unfortunately not as young as I used to be," Sir Echton sighed, pulling Joshua from his memories. The blow Stanson had given Sir Echton had left him dazed, so Joshua had taken him to the Temple of Light for treatment from a priest. "It used to be I could walk off a slap upside the head and be none the worse for it, son."

"That was hardly a slap, old man," Joshua said, though he *had* seen the knight walk off hits like that before. "You should take better care of yourself. Maybe try to dodge next time?" Sir Echton chuckled wryly at the suggestion.

"I take good enough care of myself, especially with you making sure I'm following all your rules."

"They aren't *my* rules, and your wife would strip my hide if I let you get away with half of the things you want to do still."

"My wife would probably praise you as a god if you let me die, son," Sir Echton laughed, which turned into a cough. "She only married me for my money. I was already old when I caught her eye, as you well know. Sword-master isn't as glamorous as tournament champ, but it sure earns a large amount of gold for as long as I had been winning. You'd be a better match for Cynthia."

"You shouldn't say such things," Joshua said. Cynthia was beautiful, but to be blunt she was a little too old for Joshua since she was twice his age.

"The truth should always be spoken," Sir Echton shook his head. "Doesn't matter anyway, I'll be dead soon enough and she'll be free to find the next plump bag to leech money from so you don't have to worry."

"Cynthia isn't like that," Joshua countered.

"Cynthia's exactly like that. And stop arguing with me. You know I'm right," Sir Echton laughed again, ending with a fit of coughing. The knight *was* right about one thing, he would probably be dead soon enough if he continued to let younger men thrash him in the arena. Sir Echton could not see it. At least from Sir Echton's side of the century. Joshua and Cynthia were still young. But Sir Echton was wrong about why Cynthia had married him, Joshua could tell she loved the old knight. "I'm always right," he stated for emphasis.

Joshua rolled his eyes and shook his head, but let the old man have his victory. He deserved it after the matches he had to forfeit on top of the loss today. Sir Echton was effectively out of the sword competition at this year's Harvest Tournament now.

"It was reckless of me to marry her," Sir Echton continued. "Though perhaps a reckless thing or two is warranted at the end of your life."

"So, I can go to the Borderlands?"

"I said at the *end* of your life, boy," Sir Echton snapped, his voice taking on an agitated tone. "Avenging your family at your age will only end it a lifetime too soon." Sir Echton sighed, stopping to sit down outside the temple. The sigh turned into a groan as bet his knees more to reach the seat. "You're a good boy, Joshua. Always have been, always will be. But you have a bloodlust about you I don't much care for. Too much like the young, pompous fools in the courts today. You know the ways of this world, which will keep you alive if you take what I said to heart. Knights today don't understand that sometimes the wondrous world the gods gave us is just plain cruel. Most have never been south of the fortress, let alone in the Borderlands proper."

"You're not dead yet, old man," Joshua said, sitting beside the knight.

"Close enough, and I want you to know," Sir Echton leaned his head back against the wall. "I have arranged to transfer my knighthood to you when I go. Cynthia can have the gold and riches I've won, or what's left of them after she spends them, but I want to know an honorable man has my title."

"I can't, I'm not your..." Joshua said, feeling a touch of sorrow at the prospect of seeing the old man go. Even if it *did* come with a knighthood, he had no desire to see Sir Echton die.

"Not my what? Son? Boy, you're as close to a son as I ever had. I didn't marry until after my seed had rotted so I never had my own children, not even a bastard during my younger days. Perhaps my seed was always rotted, like King Aegen's. It's only right that my honor lives on in the lad I hold above all others in the realm."

Joshua clenched his teeth together, fighting back the lump in his throat. More frequently Sir Echton had gotten into these sorts of conversations with him. It was unsettling to think that the man who had practically raised him would be gone someday. So much that Joshua tried not to think of it at all if possible, but Sir Echton always seemed to bring it up.

"You can't die yet," Joshua said, his voice wavering with every word. "I won't let you."

31

"I can die when the gods well please, boy. You can't fight off death with a sword or stick, it comes when it comes, as the Order of Stone teaches," Sir Echton shook his head. "And that isn't today. Help me up, I suspect the wife might have prepared us dinner tonight. If she isn't too busy celebrating Stanson's victory. Decent fighter, Sir Stanson is, but a lousy knight." Joshua grinned as he helped the knight back to his feet. "I should stop standing up, my knees tell me that every time I do."

"You can't stay sitting down, or how would you sword fight?"

"I could joust," Sir Echton laughed. "Jousters only need to sit, right?"

"You're no good with a lance," Joshua teased, the idea of Sir Echton on a horse seemed impossible. Even in the Borderlands, the knight preferred to walk as Joshua rode after Sir Echton saved him. "And I was a better rider at ten than you ever have been."

"So what? Being in a tournament is all I care about anymore. Who said anything about winning one? I'll leave that to you and the young pretenders after I go. You're good at jousting *and* swordplay, and would be the best knight in the realm if you had the title."

The two laughed as they continued to make their way to Sir Echton's estate in Merchant's Row. The Orders were located in the center of Aederon City. Each one had a temple of their own, six total, although one had been vacant since the Last Necromantic War a millennium ago. Thade's Temple had no roof as it had rotted away after collapsing a few hundred years prior along with most of the towers. The towers that had fallen outward had long since been cleared out of Aederon's streets, but the rubble of those that fell into the sacred structure could be seen through its broken stained glass windows and between the crumbling exterior. Only one of the other five, Fiel's Temple, was in pristine condition.

"Soon everyone'll be worshipping Fiel," Echton said as they made their way through the plaza of the gods. "And they'll treat the other five just as poorly as they treat Thade now. They'll likely tear down the other five. After High Priest Jensen makes enough stink about the vagabonds that use Thade's Temple as a home spreading to the other four, that is." Echton sighed.

"It's the natural progression of theology, I suppose," Joshua shrugged. "Why worship five or six gods when you can just worship one?"

"I just don't like seeing it, is all. You'd think that if we had six gods they'd still be gods even if no one worshiped them. But no one seems to care. Why not worship no gods if that's your philosophy? Thade take me if it wouldn't be easier to worship no god. There would be a lot less standing and sitting to be sure. Speaking of the gods, you don't still follow..."

"Malef, of course," Joshua said. "The God of Fire approves of revenge."

"Figures, but Malef isn't only about that, son. He's about love as much as hate. Why'd you think the classiest courtesans are typically themed around him?"

"I wouldn't call what courtesans offer love, old man," Joshua countered and the old man laughed.

"No, I suppose not," Echton coughed out. The exertion of his battle had done a number on his lungs today.

North of the temples was Noble District, where a gate and a fortified stone wall separated the highborn from the less fortunate. South and east was Merchant's Row, with their destination to the east. West was Cheapside. It was easy to tell a tourist from a native when they spoke of western Aederon City. Visitors referred to it as its proper name, West End, usually looking for the ferry across Gunthor's Bay.

Heading east the streets grew wider with more landscaping and ornamentation until they reached Merchant's Row. That extra space was suddenly replaced with vendor carts and shop stalls that normally bustled with the city's daily activity. Even now there were dozens of them open, attempting to glean as much coin out of the shoppers as they could during the festivities. However, most were closed as their owners celebrated the Harvest Festival in the numerous taverns and drank away their disappointment or delight at the outcome of the tournament events for the day.

Joshua and Sir Echton circumvented the sounds of merrymaking as those who had bet on Echton winning today would probably have a few choice words, if not fists, for the old knight if he showed his face. Several years ago, Sir Echton would have been welcomed at any tavern, even praised and showered with drinks for his feats, but age had caught up to him quickly since then. Praise turned into "better luck next tournament" as Echton won less and less. Now only the desperate would bet on Echton, and desperation led men to recklessness.

Homesteads were squeezed between the main thoroughfares of Merchant's Row, as far out of the way as they possibly could be, so Joshua and Echton were soon wandering the dark back alleys of the district. Three and four story buildings made the walkways nearly pitch black as they went about. It was a treacherous area to be since the alleys at night were nearly as dangerous as Cheapside. Joshua felt safe wandering them alongside Sir Echton because even despite his aging physique, he was skilled enough to dispatch a group of would-be bandits if the need arose. Not to mention Joshua could fend for himself. Joshua tightened his grip on his father's sword just in case he needed to draw it. Yet, like every night, the two men with swords were left alone in the alleyways.

"I hate the Alleys," Echton muttered, the nickname for these streets. "It reminds me too much of the Narrows, south of Ashfall." Joshua nodded, remembering those canyons from his childhood. They were just as dangerous as the alleys of Merchant's Row. More so given the unpredictability of Trista's land and weather in the area. The cold north of Ashfall and warmth of the Borderlands could cause flash storms that flooded the Narrows faster than a horse could run across open plains. Rock slides could crush a man in a suit of plate armor or block a path at any time. Not to mention just one Raykarn, if trained well enough and in the right spot, could hold an entire regiment of soldiers at bay in those narrow, winding canyons.

"This isn't the Narrows, though," Joshua said as they turned out onto another thoroughfare. There were no shops here because it was too far east. Instead the wealthier merchants, knights, and lower class nobles lived on this road. Sir Echton's estate was the easiest to spot.

Sir Echton, the acclaimed master swordsman, had the most modest estate on the entire road. Where all of them were three to five stories tall, Sir Echton's homestead was an unimposing two stories, including a basement with kitchen and storage, and had the least amount of landscaping and ornamentation. The houses on either side boasted elaborate designs etched into their siding, making them appear like a grid of brown and white, with shrubbery sculpted into exotic animals unknown to Joshua. In contrast, Sir Echton's had simple brick for the first level, a whitewashed second story with a pine tree gracing the front corner of his property, and neatly trimmed grass. The interior was much of the same as the two entered the abode.

The only paintings, tapestries, and sculptures were ones Cynthia supplied, usually depicting rays of sunshine over fields. If they were not scenery, they were images of Fiel, God of Light, in all his glory as he looked over various historical scenes. Scenes the god had never *actually* been present in. The largest one that nearly covered the wall directly across from the entryway had Fiel holding a spear over a shadowy figure. A plaque on the frame called it *Fiel's Victory Over the Undying*, a reference to Ulgrin the Undying who had thrown all of Iliona into chaos during the Last Necromantic War. Of course, Fiel had not conquered Ulgrin. It had been Gunthor with the legendary blade *Solaris*, but the Order of Light seemed not to care for actual details. Luckily the crown did, as Joshua learned training as a soldier in the legions. In fact, the crown had more proof of the events than the Order of Light because *Solaris* still decorated the king's hip.

"Cynthia, dear," Sir Echton called out, his voice sweeter than honey. For all his complaining about his wife, he acted the fool around her. "Where are you?"

"In the study," Cynthia called back, just as fondly. Despite being married three years the two still acted like newlyweds. "We have guests."

Joshua and the knight made their way to the room and stopped short. Lord Commander Ackart, the leader of the Crown's

Legion, stood gazing out the enormous bay window. There was no grass or lawn on that side of the house, nor for any of the houses on this road. On that side was only a cliff. The sharp drop fell precipitously into the flat horizon of the Crystal Ocean.

The Lord Commander was an impressive man, roughly thirty years Sir Echton's junior, yet old enough to have adult children of his own, and held himself with a superiority befitting one of the wealthiest nobles in the kingdom. He was dressed in his formal, black uniform. It was an impressive sight with pressed lines and numerous badges decorating his right breast. The Lord Commander held his hands clasped at the small of his back. His sword, an enchanted blade that he used on the battlefield named *Heartflame*, rested against his left thigh. His face was clean shaven with a strong chin and single scar across the left cheek that enhanced, rather than detracted from, his proud appearance. His hair was kept short by Legion standards. He was a man always ready for battle, a man Joshua had been trying to emulate ever since his family's death.

Lord Commander Ackart's son and daughter were seated across from Cynthia. The twins, Eric and Cordelia, were the same age as Joshua. Eric was the ragged, mirror image of his father with long, curly brown hair. The way he was dressed suggested he had been celebrating in a tavern only to be dragged out of it. Eric glared at his father as he pinched the bridge of his nose, a burgundy wine stain decorating the young man's upper lip. Cordelia was as radiant as ever, sitting up straight as she delicately held a teacup between thumb and forefinger. Her long, wavy brown locks shimmered in the dancing light of the fire. Her blank expression suggested she was a little disappointed, possibly even bored, by the lack of decoration as she surveyed the room. Only Sir Echton's own enchanted blade, *Desertfrost*, stood over the mantle.

"Lord Commander Ackart," Sir Echton said, saluting with both arms across his chest as he fell to a knee. Joshua was a split second behind his mentor with the same salute.

"Stand up, Sir Echton," Ackart said, turning around. Sir Echton rose slowly, but he did not groan or complain. "You too,

Kentaine. Take a seat, both of you." Joshua sat in the corner, furthest from the nobles and knight. Sir Echton sat down beside his wife, who shifted so that she was practically sitting in his lap since the chair was only large enough for one. Lord Ackart left the remaining seat empty.

"What is this about, my lord?" Sir Echton asked. His wife bit her lower lip and pressed her head against her husband's.

"I have need of your sword arm again, old friend," Lord Ackart said, standing in front of the fireplace, staring vacantly into the flames. Their proximity to the Crystal Ocean meant it was always cold at night, especially as winter approached.

"My lord?"

"My greatest fear has come to pass. The Ironeyes, the largest Raykarn clan, are marching north," Lord Ackart said, and the night seemed to grow quieter. Even the crackling and popping of the fire was subdued. Joshua felt himself nervously grinding his teeth. The Redclaws had been bad enough nearly eight years ago. The Ironeyes, the so-called peaceful clan, would be worse. "You know what that means, then?"

"Yes, my lord," Sir Echton nodded, lowering his head solemnly. "The Ironeyes are ten times the strength of the Redclaws. They must be marching to war."

"It is considerably worse than that. The advance parties have been kidnapping women to draw our forces deep into the Endless Waste. Despite my orders to stand firm, the ploy is working. We've lost eleven regiments to the tactic already," Lord Commander Ackart sighed. "I wouldn't be asking you to come out of retirement if it weren't dire, Sir Echton."

"I'll gladly serve my kingdom once again," Sir Echton said proudly, raising his head. Joshua felt his own chest swell at the strength in his mentor's eyes and voice.

"Malcolm, no!" Cynthia pled, tears streaming down her face. "You can't, you're too old."

"The Lord Commander has requested my aid, Cynthia, and I dare not refuse," Sir Echton said, wrapping his arms around his young wife. "Joshua will make sure you're taken care of."

"I am going south, with you, I can't stay here!" Joshua demanded, jumping out of his chair, ignoring proper respect for the Lord Commander. Eric grinned, nodding slightly in approval, and Cordelia snickered. He did not care, he wanted to kill the Redclaws. He wanted to kill the Ironeyes. He wanted to kill *all the Raykarn.*

"Quiet, boy," Sir Echton barked. "You'll keep my wife safe, understand! Reckless acts get a young man killed. Only the old can afford them." Joshua clenched his fists and jaw, trying to see reason but all he could feel was a red veil of rage surrounding him.

"You'll do as your master says, Kentaine," Lord Ackart said calmly, and suddenly Joshua felt the fool. "I need knights in the Borderlands, not squires. Squires are just easy targets for the Raykarn. We've seen as much of that as I care to. They swarm them and ignore the experienced warriors, driving our armies into bloodlust as they prey upon the weak. They're doing so now with our women. Your time will come soon enough, and if what Sir Echton says of your skill is true I suspect you'll claim your knighthood in next year's tournament. Until then, Lady Echton *will* need a protector and, above all else, someone she can rely on."

"Is there any word on *what* has caused the Ironeyes to head north?" Cynthia asked through silent tears. Joshua felt his stomach lurch. He *was* a fool. Cynthia knew her husband's duty came first. She recognized it and, though she hated it, she supported him nonetheless. Joshua should do the same thing for his mentor, but a majority of him found that too difficult to do.

"Troubling news has been arriving from all the other kingdoms if even half of the rumors are true. I'm afraid that very little has been mentioned of the Endless Waste. We don't have very reliable sources from there, given the number of their clans and innate hatred of our people," Lord Commander Ackart stated as calmly as he had said everything else.

"What sort of news?" Sir Echton asked, though he was staring out over the ocean now.

"Vindi fell," Lord Ackart said. "That is a fact. One of my men has seen the destruction with his own eyes."

"Fell, how?" Sir Echton asked. "How could an army even *reach* Vendi? It's one of the Dristelli's floating fortresses."

"I didn't say it was attacked; I said it *fell*," Lord Ackart repeated and Joshua's eyes widened. It had literally fallen.

"That's impossible," Joshua muttered, falling back into his chair. The Dristelli cities were held up by infinite sources of mystical energy. They did not just fall out of the sky.

"One of the daughter trees of Miandrelle has rotted from the inside out as well. An entire city of Tulien died with no wounds or sickness because of it," Ackart continued. "A black tide has killed thousands of Xulesi as well, and the N'Gochen hives seem to be at war with one another. How much of this is true, I cannot be certain. I cannot confirm anything other than Vendi's fall. I don't even dare mention the rumors from the Endless Waste as each of the possibilities is as improbable as the next, though all seem possible given what is happening."

"Is it another Necromantic War?" Cynthia asked.

"I don't know," Ackart shook his head. "I would think that sort of thing would start in Iliona, as it has in the past, but I can't be certain. I can't even be certain about what's happening in our own kingdom. The Order of Light's campaigns to silence all news they don't deem appropriate is strangling my network of scouts and spies. For all I know there could already be another necromancer sect rising to power, tapping into new ways of ruining the world and driving the other realms into chaos. I wouldn't even recognize the signs of it if it was necromancy. History, in a large part due to the Order of Light, has been forgotten and changed since Ulgrin's reign of terror."

"Fiel protect us," Cynthia prayed and Joshua could detect Ackart's annoyance at the statement by the slight raise of his eyebrows and flare of his nostrils. The Order of Light, Fiel's most devoted, were hindering Ackart's defense of the realm. Even though he practically flat out stated as much Cynthia still refused to hear any of it.

"When do we leave?" Sir Echton asked, gently pushing Cynthia aside so he could stand.

"Tomorrow morning," Lord Commander Ackart said, turning to look directly into his friend's eyes. "I'm afraid *Desertfrost* will see battle after all." Sir Echton nodded, and Joshua understood what that meant. Enchanted blades were valuable to most Nobles and priceless to a knight. Lord Commander Ackart was in dire need of anything he could throw at the Ironeyes, especially the powerful gift Echton had received for his involvement in the skirmishes seven years earlier.

"By your command," Sir Echton saluted again. "My lord."

III

The Heiress

The needle—coated in a dark yellow ink—bit into the tender flesh of Miranda's left breast, the fresh mark burning even after the steel sliver was pulled free. A single bead of blood seeped to the surface suspended like a jeweled garnet against her luminous, porcelain skin. The rest of her breast ached, smeared with yellow and red from the hours of torture the ordeal had lasted. Her tormentor claimed it was almost over. It had seemed to be that way for ages now. Miranda clenched her fists, tears leaking from the corners of her brilliant, emerald eyes as the cruel needle claimed another mark.

"I'm almost done," the witch snapped as the needle clinked against the opaque ink vial. "Stop fussing, Miranda. I know it hurts, but this must be done before your father returns."

Miranda opened her eyes and looked up at the woman. Like Miranda she was beautiful and the two shared many features, although nearly two decades separated them. The woman had a narrow, oval face, sharp at the chin with a slender nose and shallow bridge. Her eyebrows were thin and highly arched, complementing the fullness of her lips. Wrinkles at the corners of her brown eyes contrasted with Miranda's. Her skin was soft and pale with a perfectly slender hourglass waist and voluptuous bust. Miranda's mother was remarkably beautiful, traits mirrored and inherited by her daughter. Miranda preferred her green eyes, her father's eyes.

Another stab to her already tender, naturally sensitive skin. Miranda pressed her lips together as she fought back another tear. She hurt all over from lying on the stone altar. The tendons behind her knees felt like they were going to rip apart if she had to keep them straight for much longer. Her shoulders and tailbone ached from the cold stiffness of the table. The altar even seemed to drain her warmth despite the enchanted heat boxes at the four corners of the room.

"Why do I have to do this? Why can't I go outside?" Miranda asked, yearning to go outside. She always wanted to go outside. She had never *been* outside. "Why can't I just go to balls and banquets like the other noble children? Ester gets to."

"Hush," her mother said as the needle claimed another spot of unmarked skin. "It is a family tradition," she explained. "I've told you before. Every first daughter in my family receives this mark to show our devotion to one another when they reach the age of twenty."

"But I'm not devoted to you, Cassandra," Miranda snapped and her mother was a little more forceful with the next prick. "Ouch!"

"Of course you're devoted, if not emotionally, but you are my blood child. I cannot accept your sister into this special pact," Cassandra said, her voice as calm as it had been all day. At least what felt like all day. *How many hours* have *I been on this altar*, Miranda pondered as her mother droned on with traditions and ancestry. "Blood is all that matters for this."

"Why is your blood so special?" Miranda asked as the needle rattled in the ink well and Cassandra wiped her hands on a towel. "You weren't exactly wealthy before marrying Father; you weren't even ranked among the high nobility. So why does your blood deserve this grueling tradition?"

"It unites us," Cassandra said. Miranda could not understand why they needed a permanent mark on their breasts to remind them that they were already united by blood. "We are done for the day. I'm certain a bath has been drawn and warmed by now for you. It would be best to make yourself presentable for when Father returns home."

"Yes, Cassandra," Miranda said, sitting up and seeing a flash of anger in her mother's eyes.

"Call me Mother, dear. It'll be a year before I can finish. Lunarin won't be able to come by with more ink until then." Cassandra stated, slipping into a gauzy red dress with black lace on every hem. "You call Ariel 'Mother', why not me?"

"Because I *like* Ariel," Miranda said, slipping off the table only to receive a curt slap on her exposed buttock. "Thade's Abyss, woman, what's wrong with you? I'm *nineteen* now, aren't I too old for that sort of punishment?"

"I am your mother by birth, Miranda! Need I remind you?!" Cassandra reprimanded. "Watch your tongue in my presence! I will stop punishing you as a child when you stop acting the child."

"I'm letting you give me this stupid mark, so you watch *your* tone!" Miranda retorted. Cassandra raised her hand again and Miranda shied away.

"As I thought," Cassandra huffed as if the threat of violence proved something. "Wash up, Father will be home in an hour." Miranda glared at her mother and marched from the room, leaving her dress behind. "Get dressed first, Miranda," Cassandra called out from the small enclave at the back of their mansion. "You cannot walk around naked! Miranda!"

Miranda ignored her. It was not like anyone would see. Aside from Ariel, her father's second wife, and her half-sister, Ester, there was no one else in the massive estate of the Heath family. Ariel nearly dropped a tray of pastries as Miranda marched through the kitchen towards the bath. They had no servants, unheard of for a family of their wealth and probably the source for any number of rumors... at least Miranda suspected. She had never heard any rumors because she could never leave the estate, let alone go outside.

"Damn her to the abyss," Miranda muttered as she marched through the halls. Her chest ached so much she just wanted to cry. "That bitch! Thinks I could ever be devoted to her."

"Language!" Ariel called after her from the kitchens.

"Sorry, Mother," Miranda called back and took a deep breath to calm her nerves. It was one thing to lash out at Cassandra, but

Ariel did not deserve her irate mood. Ariel did *all* the work around the house even though she was nobility now. Until Ester had been born, Miranda thought this had been normal.

"Why don't we have servants?" Miranda remembered her younger sister asking after Ester had come home from a friend's house. Miranda had been stewing all day so Cassandra, as her two mothers enjoyed their afternoon tea, did not notice her pouting in the corner. It was not fair that Ester got to leave the mansion, but she could not. Even worse, Miranda had no friends to go visit.

"Why would we need servants?" Ariel asked her blood daughter. "I manage with all the cooking and cleaning."

"I know, but the Taren's have servants, and they aren't even half as wealthy as we are," Ester stated.

"What's a servant?" Miranda asked and Ester laughed. Miranda felt ashamed, idiotic even, when her much younger sister thought she was making jest.

"What are you doing here?" Cassandra snapped, setting her tea down with a clink of porcelain. "You're supposed to be in your room."

"Mother Ariel said I could come down after an hour," Miranda said, folding her arms as she stood in front of the two women. Cassandra glared at Ariel who in turn raised her eyebrows at Cassandra.

"I told you it was an idiotic idea to let Ester visit the Taren family," Cassandra said, rising and storming out of the room with her elegant gown billowing behind her.

That was five years ago, when Miranda had been fourteen years old. She still had not gotten an answer to *why* they had no servants, though she did learn what servants are supposed to do. They were supposed to do what Ariel did. It hardly seemed fair to Miranda. Ariel was a much better mother, it should be Cassandra who cleaned the house.

Miranda slipped into the bathroom where a steaming tub of water, kept warm by Ariel, was waiting. Miranda steadied herself with one hand on the rim of the enormous porcelain tub, testing the waters with one foot before she stepped in and slowly lowered her body beneath the surface. Her left breast screamed in agony as the warm water washed over it, causing her to take a sharp breath that she slowly released. Excess green ink and blood clouded the water, slowly spreading outward from her chest as she let the warmth relax her sore back and replace the cold of the altar.

Miranda dipped beneath the surface, wetting her hair. She parted the clinging strands from her face as she resurfaced and leaned her head against the tub's rim. A single window of tinted glass gave a dim, amber glow to the room as she felt herself drifting off to sleep.

"Cassandra would be cross with me if I fell asleep," Miranda whispered to herself with a smile. She was tempted to let the warmth take her just to annoy the woman, but her father would be home soon after nearly two months away. She did not want to miss the sweets he undoubtedly had from the Fertile Vale, so she sat up and began pulling rose-scented cleansing oils through her hair. The dark red tresses were black when wet. She wished it would stay that way when dry, or turn brown like Ester's. Anything to make her look less like Cassandra. She sank her body beneath the water's surface and draped her hair over the side of the tub. She listened to the pitter patter of water dripping from the locks that turned into a slow, steady drip as she stared into the murky water of the bath. It almost looked black, the ceiling mural of Saint Driadra reflected on the surface.

Miranda smiled, recalling the fortitude of Saint Driadra when putting up with dissenters of their god. Driadra never put up with nonsense. Cassandra was nonsense, everything about her was. Nineteen years of screaming and switching taught Miranda that her mother was nothing.

Two lights flickered in the water and Miranda sighed. Ariel had forgotten to put out the morning candles. She sat up, preparing to extinguish them, but the candles were not there. Miranda froze. She looked back down trying to make sense of the rippling surface. She held her breath, waiting for the water to calm, and the lights were back.

"Thade take me," Miranda cursed, rubbing her eyes with a shiver down her spine. She wondered just how *long* she had been on the altar, but she felt wide awake. "I'm seeing things." She pulled the stopper and watched the water swirl around the drain which funneled the water out into the creek beside the mansion.

Slipping out of the bath, Miranda stood in front of the mirror as she squeezed the last droplets from her long hair. The mark her mother had made was glaringly obvious against her pale skin. Two rings, both less than the width of her smallest finger, circled her breast. The inner ring was right up against her nipple and the outer was four finger widths further out. Six crescent lines that tapered to a fine point evenly divided the wheel and connected the two rings. It really was identical to Cassandra's, only her mother's had runes in each section of the wheel and at the points of each line. Even in the dim light, the ink had a vaguely metallic, golden sheen to it as she turned her waist back and forth.

"What does it mean?" Miranda asked, gingerly prodding the tender flesh and wincing.

She's hollowing you out, the answer hissed in Miranda's mind and she jumped. Miranda looked up in the mirror and saw the same flickering lights in front of her emerald eyes. *Making room.*

"Making room for what?" Miranda asked anxiously, feeling her flesh crawl as goose bumps rose. The lights flickered as if blinking. No answer, but those lights seemed to be staring at her. Into her. Judging her. "I'm going insane," Miranda laughed to herself, throwing on a robe a before walking out into the hall. Miranda passed through the first floor to the southwest corner where she ascended the wide, spiral stone staircase.

The second floor was heavily decorated. Suits of armor lined the red carpet that ran down the center of each hall. Murals depicting the twelve saints of their family's patron god covered the wall at evenly spaced intervals. Glow boxes emanated warm, steady, orange light from their enchantments every ten feet in the ceiling. Everything was free of dust, a task which probably took Ariel hours every day to complete. Cassandra really should at least help with the chores. Miranda grinned at that idea. The picture of her mother fussing about the mansion with Ariel's apron over a slimming dress was worth conjuring up in her mind, but it would never happen. Cassandra was her father's first wife and employed this position to her advantage.

Every bedroom—and there were many of them—was fully furnished and stocked with clothing for Ester. Miranda's sister liked to sleep in a different room every day and would have if there was enough of them to last a lifetime. Miranda was satisfied with her room, toward the back. Her world was small anyway, so why would she *need* a bigger room? Miranda walked into her private sanctuary where all the paintings were of Saint Driadra. She had taken them from the halls and placed them in her room at the disdain of her mother. "Our god had more than *one* saint," Cassandra had said. "You should revere them all equally."

Miranda had promptly ignored her.

Her bed was at the center. Sheer, black curtains hanging from a canopy obscured the sheets and covers perfectly arranged by Ariel. It was large enough for four people to comfortably sleep side by side. The rest of the furniture was arranged several paces away from the bed, lining the bedroom walls. There were two cherry wood wardrobes full of the latest fashions, a hand carved jewelry cabinet, a detailed vanity desk, and a gilded full-length mirror. At the back, a narrow door lead to her personal powder room. Hers was the smallest bedroom in the house, but she was content with this arrangement.

Miranda opened her jewelry cabinet first and withdrew a golden necklace. The lattice of the necklace clung tightly to her throat, covering from just beneath her jaw down to her collarbone. A large, dark red garnet pendant hung as the centerpiece. It was her favorite necklace, reminding her of a golden spider web wrapped around her neck. Similar pieces decorated her arms, the glittering latticework running delicately from above the elbow and connecting to a ring encircling each middle finger, with a sister garnet to the pendant on each sleeve resting against the back of her hands. Taking a pad of blush from a cabinet drawer, she moved to paint her face, promptly dropping the soft bristled brush when she saw the flickering lights in front of her own eyes again.

"Go away," Miranda gasped, slamming the cabinet shut with a loud snap. The rattling of jewelry sounded from the small, narrow wardrobe as they fell from their precarious perches inside. Miranda took a moment to catch her breath and slowly opened the doors. She bit her lower lip, squeezing her eyes shut as she faced the mirror again. "It isn't real," Miranda nervously told herself. "Just my imagination." She opened them and smiled, sighing with relief when the vibrant green of her own eyes greeted her. Miranda kept watch on her eyes as she braided her hair, making sure they did not revert into twin flaming orbs, and then went to work on her makeup. Subtle pink, which would look as white as snow on Ariel, lightly dusted the apples of her cheeks and a deeper shade of rose on her eyelids drew out the green in her eyes. Her skin was so pale that very little was needed to achieve a striking look. Red lips, as dark as her hair, came next. She smacked her lips together, nodding with satisfaction at the result of her primping. She closed the cabinet, more gently this time, after putting each piece back where it belonged.

Her corset was the first to go on with pre-tightened lacings and a front busque that latched together. It was a design of her father's—as Miranda had found out—since they had no servants to tighten the back of a common corset each day. Then she slipped into a puffy pair of petite bloomers as black as the corset, overlaid by a black dress accented with red and a keyhole that showed a glimpse of her cleavage. The dress had red, lace off the shoulder sleeves and was held up by the tight, form fitting bodice. Miranda spun, letting the loose skirt lift a little before nodding at it as well. Dressed like this Miranda looked *a lot* like Cassandra, but at least Cassandra knew how to dress. It was her mother's only redeeming quality, and something Ariel was lacking in.

Miranda put on her heeled shoes, with a cut out at the toe, and carefully made her way back downstairs. She reached the front room and Ester giggled with joy before throwing her arms around Miranda's legs.

"You look like an evil queen!" Ester laughed.

"What is she talking about, Miranda?" Cassandra hissed.

"None of your concern, just playing with my sister," Miranda shot back through a forced smile. "I thought you said Father was almost here."

"He is," Cassandra said back, through the same forced smile. Ester shifted her weight from one foot to the other and played with the white lacing on her layered skirt.

"You look adorable, Ester," Miranda said, kneeling beside her sister.

"Stand up, Miranda," Cassandra hissed. Miranda ignored her.

"Mommy got this at the market last week," Ester said, spinning for her older sister.

"Wow," Miranda said, ignoring Cassandra's orders. "I'm surprised Mother can find the time to go shopping for you."

"Morgan won't mind, Cassie," Ariel said at Cassandra's fuming. "Let them talk."

"It's pink, and look at all the ruffles!" Ester squealed happily as she swayed the skirt back and forth, the fabric making a soft swishing sound.

"I see that; it's beautiful. A gown fitting for a princess," Miranda said, tapping Ester's nose.

"We should play knights and princesses after dinner! You can be the knight who saves me from the dragon."

"Miranda is too old to play that game, Ester," Cassandra said testily. Ester's lower lip turned into a pout.

"I'd happily play with you, but I'll be the dragon and father can be the knight," Miranda said and her mother clicked her tongue. Ester giggled as Miranda tickled her. The four of them hushed at the sound of the door's latch lifting.

"Papa!" Ester exclaimed and ran for the door even before it opened all the way. Miranda's father, Lord Morgan Heath, caught the little girl as she jumped into his arms, and spun with her as he stepped into the waiting room. "Look at my dress! I'm a princess!"

"That you are," Morgan said and kissed Ester on the cheek. "And where is my *other* beautiful princess?"

"Right here, father," Miranda said, stepping forward and giving her father a hug and kiss on his cheek. "How was it in Solitude this year?"

"Dismal as ever," Morgan said cheerily. "I had to buy new boots before coming home. I didn't want to track any of the Fertile Vale into Ariel's clean home. I swear that place should be called the Vale of Muck."

"I appreciate that," Ariel said in a sultry voice, kissing her husband fully and deeply on the lips.

"And my other queen?" Morgan raised an eyebrow towards Cassandra.

"Welcome home, dear," she said, quickly pecking him on the mouth before stepping back. "How are our friends?"

"Most are doing well, but I'm afraid Warren told me Jeremy hasn't much time before *Thade's Grasp* consumes him."

"He should not have been so greedy, then," Ariel said, laughing lightly as she took Ester from her father. "And how are you, my love? You aren't immune to the blight just as the fool Wentworth isn't."

"It's moved further up my arm, but I'm certain I'll see our plans through to the end," Morgan said, taking Cassandra in his arms and kissing her properly. Miranda wanted to gag as her mother feigned an attempt to get away. It was sickeningly embarrassing.

"Have my daughters prayed to our god today?"

"I did!" Ester jumped up and down. "And he answered them because you came home safely. Well, half of them anyway."

"What was the other half?" Morgan said, kneeling to look into Ester's eyes. Miranda scowled at Cassandra for the noticeable lack of rebuke toward her father's action.

"That you'd bring..."

Morgan pulled a small package from his bag, tantalizingly holding it outside her grasp for a few moments, then placed it mischievously into Ester's hands.

"You did bring them! Vale Chocolates are the best!" she kissed Morgan again, scampering off to squirrel away the box.

Morgan laughed as he stood and held out a similar package for Miranda.

"Thank you, Father," she said, but he held on as she tried to take it from him.

"Did you pray?" he asked, raising his left eyebrow questioningly.

"I will," Miranda promised and he let go.

Morgan rubbed his hands together, the left gloved in white leather, and took a deep inhale through his nose with half-closed eyes.

"What is that celestial aroma, Ariel?" he asked, grinning at his wife.

"Swiftling," she said as Morgan linked arms with her and Cassandra. Cassandra looked aghast with the choice of delicacy for the night's meal. Miranda almost laughed, she knew how much Cassandra hated the little dragons from the Borderlands. It usually meant Cassandra would be more irritable than normal.

"My favorite," her father said as the three went deeper into the mansion's interior.

Miranda walked up to the door and gazed outside. *Soleanne's* light was fading from yellow to red as it lowered on the horizon behind the mansion. Vibrant hues merged with the treetops in the gathering shadows to the east and became fire the further west she tried to look. She sighed, taking in the rolling hills and the distant city of Crossroads nestled at the bottom of the shallow valley to the south. A small forest bordered Crossroads, appearing to Miranda as patches of dark green separated by yellow fields of wild grass, and swaying golden swaths of grain surrounding the city. Some of the fields had already been cut with bales of straw sitting out in the open as they dried. Standing there, inhaling the balmy, early autumn air deep into her lungs, she could feel the earth's energy surrounding her, beckoning her to go out and discover its mysteries.

Miranda hesitated, one hand on the door as she leaned her head against the warm wood. The world was so vast out there, what would it hurt to just go out and see it? Miranda smiled, biting her lower lip with a quick glance over her shoulder before reaching her foot forward towards the rest of the world.

"Miranda!" Ariel yelled, breaking Miranda's daring state. "Are you coming?"

"In a moment, Mother," Miranda shouted back, looking out over the view one more time before shutting it away behind the heavy oak door to the mansion.

Dinner passed by uneventfully as it always did when Morgan was home. Miranda only argued with Cassandra whenever she was not in her father's presence. And Morgan was more than happy to play along as a knight after dinner until Ester's annoyance at them both for playing the wrong way was cause enough to send Ester to bed. Next came her punishment from Cassandra. As usual, Miranda was given a scolding with a few switches of a cane despite her age. Miranda thought it unfair for playing with Ester as if she were still a child, sisters *should* play together, but that did not stop the sting of the switch. After the punishment, she sat on the softest cushions she could find in the study with a half glass of wine in one hand as her parents discussed things she would rather not think about. She would rather think of the world outside of the mansion's walls.

"Wentworth was always weakest of you all," Cassandra said. Miranda had little care for whatever political dealings her family was in, but she was expected as the heir to the Heath Estate to learn of them. "He overextends himself, and his pursuit of a cure is folly. No Dristelli would agree to that. He risked exposing us, and Jensen agrees with me."

"I doubt he let much out. Besides, he only met with those Lunarin suggested," her father said as he swirled his glass of whiskey before drinking from it. It was his third serving. Miranda, who was not permitted to have such strong spirit, took a sip of her wine, the second glass for the evening. She let the sweet notes followed by bitter permeate her mouth before swallowing. It was an aromatic red wine, but she had little to compare it against. The wine was certainly not anything one would consider unpleasant.

"I'm going to bed," Miranda sighed, feeling slightly tipsy.

"But we haven't even discussed what else is happening with the others," Cassandra insisted.

"Let 'er go," Ariel slurred. "Sheesh been through enough today, Cassie."

"So, you marked her?" Morgan asked sternly, glaring at Cassandra.

"Of course," Cassandra said as Miranda stood and unsteadily made her way toward the door. "It is necessary."

"Don't forget to pray, Miranda," Morgan reminded and Miranda slapped her forehead. She'd forgotten. "Why do you feel like it is a necessary precaution, Cassandra? This mark is... wrong."

"You know how she is about our... affairs. I have to ensure..."

"She is *my* daughter as well, Cassie!" Morgan bellowed and the room seemed to grow darker. Seeing her father's disapproval and anger over the mark on her breast shed some light on Cassandra's insistence that the tattoo be done *before* he arrived. He had a short temper when drinking, and Miranda was thankful she was retreating for the night.

Miranda made her way back to the despised enclave and kneeled beside the altar with her arms folded on top of it. She looked up at the obsidian sculpture and closed her eyes. It wasn't a very detailed statue. How could it be? She had never seen a depiction of their god in any of the books she had read, even though they showed the other five any number of times. The jagged, black form merely resembled a human shape, barren of any distinctive features. More a void of a human than anything.

"Thade," she began. "God of Dark, ruler of the abyss, bring a swift end to my witch-of-a-blood-mother so I may be free to live as I want." Miranda smiled, remembering how Cassandra had caught her uttering this prayer once before. She had not sat on her backside for a week after that. Her father's yells echoed through the halls, pulling her back to the present moment, and she heard Cassandra cry out in pain once before she started screaming back. Miranda could not keep the corners of her mouth turning upwards, given the extended pain Cassandra had put her through earlier.

Miranda laughed and thought how ridiculous this was. Praying to a god that had never, not once, answered her prayers was so utterly futile. She opened her eyes and snatched the empty vial of ink from her mother's supplies and threw it at Thade's nondescript face. The vial shattered, spraying glass and obsidian outward.

"Fiel! God of Light, ruler of all creation," she begged, looking up towards Driadra. "Free me from my cursed family." No answer. "Of course not. Gods don't care about their subjects." She stood up, staring at Thade's blank face, and jumped. Thade was staring back at her. No, not Thade. Her reflection in that flat, now chipped, black stone had those flames in her eyes again.

"Are you... the God of Shadow?" Miranda asked and the lights danced with mirth. It was eerie knowing that the shadow creature was laughing but she felt the humor in her own mind.

I have felt him, it answered and Miranda fell to her knees and bowed her head. *The light and dark agree. You must remain in you. In death, the world has opened to me. You will see as well.*

Miranda shivered. She knew everything died, eventually, but the hissing thoughts in her mind made it so clear. She would see, soon.

"Is this how I die? I know I'm like Wentworth and my father. Will I die from *Thade's Grasp* as well?" Miranda asked frightened, suddenly knowing why Wentworth was fighting so hard. She had not even come into her power yet, and she wanted to live. But Wentworth's body had faded so fast in such a short time since he had finally awakened.

Kill her, kill the one who seeks to hollow you out, it answered. Miranda smiled, looking up into the flickering lights. *Kill the one who marks you.*

Miranda raised an eyebrow, pausing at the idea of killing her mother. Cassandra being out of the picture would be much better. Miranda could *finally* leave the mansion and see what Ester can only tell her about. She would see the trees of the forests on their doorstep and the water that she could hear in the stream behind the house. She would see Crossroads, not just from a distance, but walk the streets and smell the bakery Ester always loved to visit.

Without Cassandra, Miranda would be free.

"How?"

In nearly one year's time, you will awaken, it told her. *Steal your mother's ink and I will guide you. Kill her together.*

"One year's time," Miranda said, agreeing, and the lights faded from existence.

"Who are you talking to?" Ester asked and Miranda jumped.

"You should be in bed," Miranda scolded, though she only rumpled her sister's hair instead of raising her voice. She would not treat Ester as Cassandra treated her.

"I heard yelling, and breaking glass," Ester said, frowning as she ran a hand through her messy, auburn hair. "Papa is saying bad words again." Ester's other hand clutched her stuffed, rabbit doll.

"I dropped mother's inkwell," Miranda said, brushing up the glass and obsidian with her hand. "Ouch," Miranda said, gingerly pulling a black shard of the statue from her thumb. She sucked on the wound, tasting her own blood. She swallowed, letting her hand drop to her side as she stood.

"That isn't how you clean up glass," Ester said, disappearing for a moment and returning with a hand broom and pan. "Don't you ever watch Momma?" Miranda blushed as her younger sister cleaned up her mess. *This is what Cassandra does,* Miranda thought and ground her teeth. *She makes messes and expects Ariel to clean them up.*

"Let me do that," Miranda said, kneeling and taking the brush from her sister.

"We both can," Ester said and smiled, holding the dustpan as Miranda swept the pieces into it. Ester had made it look easier than it really was. Pieces of glass kept getting away from the ends of the brush as Miranda tried to sweep it into the pan. The screaming from the study had died down by the time Ester showed her where the trash bin was and they began walking back upstairs.

"Which room are you in tonight?" Miranda asked.

"The thunderbird room!" Ester said. "I like how purple they are." Miranda smiled and escorted her sister to that room. The walls were a pale lilac with large murals of mystical, violet birds of prey. Thunderbirds were large raptors with hooked beaks and impressive talons and their bodies crackled with arcs of lightning. They looked ferocious to Miranda, elegant in their lethality, but Ester only appreciated the brilliant colors.

"Goodnight, Esty," Miranda said, kissing her sister's forehead. "We'll play again tomorrow."

"Goodnight, Miranda," Ester said, hugging her tightly. Part of her never wanted Ester to let go. It was hard having only one friend in the house, but she had her own room to retire to. "Here," Ester said, offering one of her chocolates. "Did you know it's the end of the Harvest Festival?"

"I didn't," Miranda said, taking the offered gift and smiling at the young girl with compassion in her eyes. "Thank you."

IV

LUSSENA'S TEMPLE

"...I don't know, headmistress," a woman said as Anara's mind waded toward consciousness. "She could wake up any week, any day, any hour. Fiel willing she could wake up right now."

"Why hasn't she, Lena?" Mistress Adair asked. Anara quietly propped her head up to take in her surroundings.

Anara was in a room with white curtains for walls similar to the hospital wing at *Wentworth's Home for Wayward Souls*. The differences, though, were vast and obvious. The bed beneath her was soft, supporting and comforting her body with warm, quilt blankets covering her. It was not some lumpy sack stuffed with straw and a threadbare sheet like those at the orphanage. The satin robe she wore was smooth and cool against her skin and the cotton sheets smelled freshly laundered. A bedside table held a glass of milk and a tray of food atop a dark brown, leather folder. She could identify the shapes of two women through the curtain across from her. One tall with a pronounced silhouette, probably Mistress Adair, and the other shorter with less exaggerated curves.

"I don't know," Lena said, the shorter of the two, holding her hands up in a perplexed gesture.

"But you do know she isn't dying," Mistress Adair said, standing still with her hands clasped behind her back.

"She is healthier than everyone in the ward, Headmistress," Lena answered. "Probably healthier than most of the courtesans in the chapters above us. This long without food would have left most people withered, yet her body seems to be sustaining itself on... *something*."

"Then why won't she wake up?" Mistress Adair asked, sounding distressed. "She passed out weeks ago. I missed the Harvest Festival to go fetch her, and I have had nothing but a headache for it. It's just... not natural. What's wrong?"

"I haven't a clue," Lena sighed, folding her arms. "I can't say what's wrong. I've never encountered anything like this before. Regardless, there's no need to fret over the Harvest Festival. Roxanne and the other chapter heads managed admirably without you."

Anara blindly reached towards the tray as she watched the women, accidently bumping it so the glass fell and shattered on the floor, milk spilling everywhere. The two women looked up in surprise. Lena was the first through the door and Anara brazenly stared at her as she cleaned up the mess.

Lena had dark skin, not a tan from *Soleanne*'s light but a naturally dark, olive complexion. Anara had never seen another Ilionan who was not pale skinned with pink undertones. Her jet-black, straight hair was cut strangely; the left half was completely shaved off, exposing a red tattoo of a sinuous heart. The right was so long it touched the small of her back. Lena's eyes were a light brown with thick, long, dark eyelashes and high arching brows. Tight steel bands, etched with the same heart and runes, circled Lena's neck, ankles, and wrists. Her attire of white and red—Fiel's colors—reminded Anara of the priests and priestesses of the orphanage but was cut more closely to Lena's figure. The robe was semi-sheer white fabric cinched together at her narrow waist by a red, satin sash. Beneath the sheer fabric, Lena wore a white dress fashioned entirely from lace that let her dark skin peek through with the floral pattern of the fabric strategically keeping her decent.

"You've woken up," Mistress Adair said. She was dressed similarly to Lena, but instead of white and red her robes were black with an orange sash, Malef's colors. Beneath her robes, Adair wore a skin-tight, black bodysuit that left her arms and legs exposed. Mistress Adair wore a slender sword at her left hip,

Anara's eyes widened at the taboo practice of a woman wearing a sword. Ilionan women were not permitted to touch weapons of war like swords. A woman could have a dagger for self-defense but even that was an oddity. War was not a woman's worry. To see Mistress Adair with one made Anara uncomfortable yet secretly exhilarated. The blade was around three feet long and narrow with a tassel of black and orange string hanging from the silver pommel of the hilt. It reminded her of the rapiers wielded by masculine heroes on the covers of some of Sister Dawn's romance novels but had a hexagonal hand guard instead of the signature bell. "How are you feeling?"

"Rested," Anara said, her voice husky from disuse. "Where am I?"

"*Lussena's Temple*," Mistress Adair said, raising an eyebrow at Anara. "What is the last thing you remember?"

"Falling asleep in the carriage after I found out I was coming to a..." Anara stopped abruptly. She wanted to say *whore house* but thought better of it given her current audience. "When you told me I would be going to a courtesan house."

"You don't remember waking up that night?" Lena asked, standing up with the broken glass tucked into a towel. "Not even attacking poor Master Brenton? He still has scars from that scratch you gave him." The exotic woman smiled at Anara with a flash of excitement in her eyes.

"I attacked Nicholas?" Anara gasped in dismay.

"He should have known better, given your manic state and delirium. You had a high fever, higher than I've ever felt," Mistress Adair glared at Lena, who backed away into the corner. "Given that you are now lucid, I have questions regarding some of your incidences at Wentworth's."

"What?" Anara asked, glancing over at the tray. She really *was* hungry, her stomach rumbling to make that known to the other two women. "Now?"

"I've waited five weeks to ask, and now I'd like some answers," Mistress Adair stated matter-of-factly, sitting down in the chair beside the table and slipping the folder from underneath the tray. "I'll not tolerate rule breaking at *Lussena's Temple*, insofar as there isn't a good explanation, and I would like some insight from your side of the story. Wentworth failed to mention anything leading up to the infractions he detailed concerning you. We'll start with why you instigated a rebellion?"

"What?" Anara asked incredulously as Mistress Adair pulled out a sheet of parchment from the folder.

"Five years ago, I'd not considered a twelve-year-old capable of such a scheme but you, to use Wentworth's words, 'rallied the other orphans to fight against the orderlies in open rebellion' when he wrote of the incident," Mistress Adair said, reading off the paper in front of her.

"Five years ago? You expect me to remember..." Anara trailed off in bemusement, looking down at the white sheets as she thought back. She had no recollection of gathering anyone in opposition to... "Oh! That," Anara blushed and cleared her throat. "He called *that* a rebellion? I didn't even start it!"

"Start what?"

"Charles started it," Anara folded her arms petulantly.

"Started what!" Mistress Adair snapped with a frustrated and authoritative tone that made Anara sit up straight.

"A food fight," Anara explained. "Charles threw his porridge at me, so I threw mine at him. It happened to hit Carol, who threw hers back at me and hit Brother Aldren."

Mistress Adair nodded, noting something on the file. Anara leaned forward, hoping she might get a better vantage point to watch what the woman was writing. "What happened after that?"

"The entire hall erupted into a fight, but not because I said or did anything. Once they'd seen what happened to..."

"Brother Aldren," Mistress Adair interjected. "You seem to have a knack for endangering your stewards."

"He wasn't hurt," Anara blushed, trying not to think of the juvenile incident and fighting to keep the image of Brother Aldren with porridge covering his robes from causing her to snicker. Lena's clearly amused face did not help. "And I didn't ever participate in one after that."

"How about this incident—it says you bit a man named Jake," Mistress Adair said and Lena snickered.

"We were five, so I would hardly consider Jake a man at the time," Anara blushed again. How many of these things had she done? How many would Mistress Adair bring up? Surely Mistress Adair would understand that children just *do* these things. Anara bit her lower lip in worry.

"Punching Brother Escart?"

"He stole my doll, and I wanted it back," Anara shrugged and Lena laughed again. "I was seven."

"Why did he steal it? Adults don't normally take away toys for no reason," Mistress Adair shot a look at the other courtesan.

"I refused to help clean up the halls after tracking mud through them," Anara looked down at the sheets. "I was *only* seven and *everyone* was tracking mud through them."

"Mistress Weston," Mistress Adair turned towards the woman. "If this amuses you so much, perhaps your fellow orderlies could use your assistance instead."

"I apologize, headmistress, I'll not make another sound."

"And the incident with Brother Mitchel?" Mistress Adair asked, turning her attention back to Anara, who pulled her legs protectively up to her chest.

"I was protecting a new girl from being picked on by Charles," Anara said. "Charles has always been the *real* trouble maker."

"I know that you pushed a boy down and were given seven strikes with a switch by Brother Mitchel," Mistress Adair said, shaking her head. "Wentworth said you attacked Brother Mitchel, why? What did you do to him?"

"I don't remember," Anara said quietly, a tear falling from her cheek.

"I need to know what happened," Mistress Adair said sternly. "A priest of Fiel does not just run away to the Fertile Vale because of an insolent girl. *Something* happened."

"I don't want to talk about it," Anara shut her eyes, but a flash of orange filled her vision. "Please, no," Anara gasped, finding it hard to breathe as her flesh tingled with the memory of searing pain. The stench, god the *stench*... it smelled of meat in a fire.

"You should leave, Headmistress," Lena said firmly, her speech had a very slight accent, and Anara felt someone's arms wrap around her. Instantly the anxiety of suppressed memories faded and Anara's pain vanished at Lena's touch. "I've permitted your questions, but can't you tell this one is disturbing her?"

"I will have my answer," Mistress Adair said, sounding disappointed. "But perhaps another time after she has settled in here. Take care of her, Mistress Weston, and when she calms down, see that she is given a proper meal and a tour of the facility."

"Of course, headmistress," Lena said as Anara felt the woman swaying her back and forth like a child.

"Anara," Mistress Adair said softly and Anara looked up. "Whatever you did to Brother Mitchel, I am certain it was deserved." Adair disappeared behind the sheet wall as Lena cradled Anara's head against her shoulder.

"Hush," Lena murmured reassuringly, kissing Anara's forehead before placing it against her neck. The steel band there was cold to the touch and caused Anara to gasp.

"What is this?" Anara asked, touching Lena's collar and feeling her cheeks warm when she realized how forward she was being. Lena did not recoil but instead put her own hand on the back of Anara's.

"It is a Raykarn slave band. I was a pleasure slave since I was five," Lena answered without hesitation. "The Borderlands are a harsh place to live, and Redclaw slavers enjoy taking Ilionan children."

"Redclaw?"

"The cruelest of the Raykarn clans," Lena explained. "Ten years ago, when I was eight years old, I was rescued from a Redclaw camp and escorted north of Ashfall with other refugees. My bands are a permanent reminder of that time," she said, eyes misting over in recollection. "If I were ever south of Ashfall again I would be taken as a slave. Treated as a slave."

"Don't they come off?"

"They're enchanted," she said, pressing a thumb against one. Anara watched as the metal flexed as if it were skin instead of steel. "They *can't* come off, not before it's my time."

"I'm sorry," Anara said, feeling awful for the woman.

"Don't be," Lena shrugged, smiling at Anara. "That was my past, and my life has improved greatly since I became a courtesan."

"But you're still..." Anara blushed as she left the words unsaid.

"Pleasuring men? Yes, and an occasional woman," she grinned mischievously at Anara, "That is mostly what I know, but now it is on my terms. If I do not like a client, in manner or body, I can refuse," Lena said, gently sliding a hand through Anara's hair. "Of course that is not all I do here. I don't know what you're going through—or what caused you to sleep for so long—but I'd be honored if you let me help you adjust to your life here. It's my duty as an orderly to see to your basic needs. But I would also like to help you heal any wounds of the heart you have collected so you are no longer weighed down by the past."

"Thank you," Anara said as Lena slipped out of the bed.

"I'm going to fetch you something fresh from the kitchens," Lena said, picking up the tray. "I'll be back soon."

Anara sat up in bed, using the headboard as a backrest and looked around the room. There really was nothing particularly interesting to focus on since everything was white. She slipped out of bed and stood next to the washstand opposite the table. Anara stared into the oval mirror, touching her neck and wondering how Lena could live knowing she had been violated over and over since she was a child. Anara inwardly shuddered. She did *not* want to know that. Instead, she tried her best to manage the tangled mess that her blonde hair had become in the weeks of sleeping. She winced as a knot caught on her fingers and gave up to search for a brush. She found robes of a solid pink fabric, tailored like Lena and Adair's, inside the table on a shelf beneath her satchel that still held her doll. Another shelf held a few necessary grooming supplies so she was refreshed and dressed by the time Lena returned.

"You look good in novice pink," Lena said as she placed the tray on the table. The food smelled heavenly. A full chicken breast, peppered with black and yellow flecks, still steamed alongside celery, mashed potatoes and a whole baked apple. Anara licked her lips at the feast. "You'd look better in the colors of my chapter, though."

"Your what?"

"My chapter. The courtesans are divided into chapters while we train at the temple," Lena explained. "I'm an orderly, studying medicine and herbs."

"I thought you were a courtesan, why would you..."

"Study that?" Lena interrupted. "I'm not *always* going to be a courtesan. At least I hope I won't always be one. Once I finish my studies I plan to move to the Fertile Vale where I can help a small village that lacks proper access to the Order of Light. Most of the orderlies have similar goals."

"I don't think that's what I'd like to do."

"Well, you could remain a courtesan and learn how to blade dance like Mistress Adair."

"Blade dance?"

"Fight, but we can't call it that," Lena winked. "Since we are, after all, only women. All of the blade dancers are career courtesans, but they double as our guards inside the inner sanctum where no men are permitted."

"Inner sanctum? What are you..."

"I can explain that better on the tour," Lena said, holding up her hand and motioning to the food. "Eat as I talk and just listen."

Anara eagerly did so. She cut a piece from the chicken and slowly chewed it, involuntarily moaning at the divine flavors of lemon mixed with the spice of pepper. It was the most delicious thing she had ever eaten; unsurprisingly given the gruel and porridge she grew up on at the orphanage. This food, though, was divine.

"I'll let Mistress Graves know you approve of her recipe," Lena said. "Where was I? Right, given you were found out instead of coming here willingly, you're probably not going to want to remain a courtesan. There are three other chapters, though. First, the scribes, composed of women who pursue accounting as well as economics. They wear the colors of Ezebre, white and yellow. Second are those *I* like to call hoarders, though Mistress Adair calls them caretakers. They oversee all the purchases and shipments to the temple and see to the needs of the house. They're sort of the opposite of the scribes so they often disagree, like Duloreb is the opposite of Ezebre, and wear black and violet. Scribes earn money through selling our crafts; caretakers buy and hoard goods. Finally, we have the craftswomen, in the white and blue of Mertas."

"Wait..." Anara interjected when Lena took a breath. It all felt so overwhelming. She decided to cling to the one tidbit of information she could remember from the deluge coming from Lena. "What sort of crafts?"

"Clay sculpting along with painting, drawing, enchanting..."

Anara nearly choked on a bit of potato not quite as mashed as the rest.

"You teach enchantments here?" Anara looked up and noticed that the small room was lit with not one, but *three*, glow lamps set into the ceiling.

Lena bit her lower lip, slowly wiping some potato from the corner of Anara's mouth. Anara felt a pleasing shiver down her spine at the woman's touch. The sensation startled her but ended before she could recoil away. "I was hoping you'd study medicine with me, but I could use a glow lamp or two to read by just as much." Anara raised an eyebrow at the woman as Lena licked her finger clean. Lena sounded playful, but not like any game Anara had ever played before.

A game Anara was not entirely comfortable playing with a stranger.

"Lena..."

"Sorry," she cleared her throat. "Habits, you know." Anara did not. "I couldn't help it, seeing the excitement in those beautiful eyes of yours. Yes, we offer that as an option. Of course, our resources are rather limited. It isn't like our enchantment library is as extensive as *Aederon's Enchantorium*, but you'll probably figure out how to make a few simple things. Nearly unbreakable glassware, glow lamps, uh... let's see. What else do we use? Oh, yeah, heat boxes in the baths. Those are rarer than glow lamps. I don't know why, but they're supposed to require more talent or something, or was it more valuable ingredients?" Lena tapped her lips as she thought for a moment, her dark eyes darting back and forth as she sorted information in her mind. "Either way, the few we have that don't heat the courtesan bath go quickly in the winter months."

"How can that be paid for? Enchanting is expensive, and to learn would be..."

"Worth a noble's estate?" Lena interrupted, again. "Well, yes, but we sell or appropriate—a hoarder's word not mine—pieces. Three of every four enchanted pieces a courtesan makes are sold. Of course, courtesans who have no skill in the magecraft are quickly placed somewhere else since *Lussena's Temple* can't afford to let a girl keep trying with *that* type of art. Are you ready for the tour now?"

"What?" Anara asked, looking down at her plate. It was empty except for a few black and yellow flecks of the spices. "I guess I am."

The hospital ward turned out to be *three* stories underground. Anara had no idea a building could be constructed lower than one level beneath the earth.

"The temple was built on an old mine shaft," Lena explained as they walked through painted halls lit only by glow lamps that felt like any other Anara had been in except for the distinct lack of windows. "I suspect there's some secret place where it goes deeper. Or rather, I hope it does. I'd love to find some hidden chamber that no one knows about. I'd tell you, of course," Lena batted her eyes at Anara. "It could be *our* secret place, but I haven't found it yet."

The next floor housed an enormous pool for bathing in. They stopped here and Anara, disrobing, slipped into the warm water to bathe. Lena joined her, staying closer than Anara entirely felt easy about. Their robes, hanging up on two of the twenty-nine silver pegs lining the room, were as solitary as the two young women.

"Don't touch the heat boxes," Lena cautioned, pointing out what looked like a metal plate built into the pool's wall between two glow lamps. Anara could barely detect what looked like some sort of script engraved onto the steel beneath the surface of the rippling water. "It won't do any lasting damage, but it hurts like touching a hot kettle. Believe me; *I* know. I tested one the first day I was here, blistered my palm and had to put this nasty smelling paste on it for two weeks. But look," she held up her hand, "See? No scars. It's why I decided to become an orderly when I turned eighteen. That's the age we choose what you will study. If you change your mind about being a craftswoman you still have a year to decide what you'll do."

Lena helped Anara wash her hair with cleansing oils, something Anara had never used. Lena massaged the lavender scented oil into her scalp with gliding strokes, slowly drawing oil down the length of her hair.

"It was silly of me really, touching the heat box like that. I'd seen enchantments before, *lots* of them growing up amongst the Raykarn where the magecraft originates from. I just had never encountered a heat box before, it would be kind of pointless in the Endless Waste given how hot it gets. Then again, the nights *are* unusually cold down there, I recall more than often wishing I had something to keep warm."

Anara let Lena drone on, her topics fleeting back and forth between her life with the Raykarn and her dreams for the future without a pause of painful memories. It impressed Anara that Lena could have overcome her troubled past so easily. The entire time Lena slowly worked Anara's scalp and shoulders in the warm water. By the time they left the bath Anara felt deliciously pampered. The tour soon continued with the storage areas across from the bathhouse. The first room was full of necessities. Food, wines, spices. An unusual amount of brushes.

"They break a lot more often than you'd think, but probably not for you since you have straight hair. Just ask Mistress Daisy... I mean Mistress Delayne how many she's broken this month. Poor girl has hair like a bird's nest," Lena explained and Anara actually giggled at the mental image. She could picture a woman with the head of a brush broken off at its handle and stuck in a mess of frizzy curls with a little blue bird poking its head out from inside the tangles. "This is also where you'll get a packet of Moon Tea the day before an engagement."

"Moon Tea?" Anara had learned to keep her questions short. Lena liked to interrupt her.

"Makes you bleed, like when it's that time," Lena said and Anara blushed a deep red. "It prevents pregnancy."

"You can do that?" Anara asked, looking back into the room as they left.

"We have to do that," Lena said, taking on a pretentious tone as if she were imitating someone. Anara assumed it was probably Mistress Adair. "A pregnant courtesan is a worthless courtesan. Also, bastards are *not* what our clients expect from us. If they wanted that, they would pay a common whore's prices."

"Our clients?" Anara followed Lena to the next storage room.

"The nobility, or wealthier knights and merchants... I love this room," Lena said, changing topics as fast as Anara could keep up on the tour. "If you're looking for artwork, you'll find no better selection than what *Lussena's Temple* has to offer." Anara blushed once she realized what was mixed in with the hundreds of paintings. Paintings depicting a sexual act were plentiful enough amongst the displays of shorelines, forests, random fruits, and any number of innocent displays that Anara felt like she should avert her gaze. Despite some of the subjects, they were all surprisingly well done.

"Do the... hoarders... sell these?" Anara asked, nodding towards some of the scandalous art.

"No," Lena said and Anara sighed. "The scribes do, remember? Scribes collect money, hoarders spend it to hoard stuff. You'd be surprised how much gold comes into *Lussena's Temple* from these. If you'd like you can take one for your room."

"I'd prefer something not so..." Anara stopped as she lifted a canvas of a woman in bed with another woman. "Uh, daring?"

"Of course," Lena said, waving her over. "The enchanted items are back here. The heat boxes look like they've already been given out now that the colder months are approaching." Lena sighed, shaking her head. "Best become a master enchantress soon, so I can finally get a heat box for my room."

Anara ignored the enchanted items, though she really wanted to focus on them. She started to sort through the paintings, her eyes wandering across the lavish scenes until one caught her attention. She pulled the canvas out. It was a forest along the seashore and the brilliant blue of the sky, broken by white and silver clouds, was a breathtaking display against the unbroken royal shade of the horizon beneath it. It was so detailed, with even the way the beams of light caught dust in the air to give it a diffused glow, that Anara would have sworn she was seeing the real place frozen in time.

"Where is this painting supposed to be?" Anara asked, wanting to touch the scene but the crests and valleys of the thick paint looked too delicate to disturb.

"Oh, that," Lena laughed. "That's outside."

"What?" Anara asked, turning to the woman.

"I'll show you," Lena said. "Take the painting if you like, and we can drop it off in your room on the way there. Your room is in one of the courtesan chapters. The novice rooms are full since we did not expect to take on another so soon."

The next two floors went by quickly.

Above the bath were the novice quarters. The first floor, above the novices, was the orderly chapter and gardens. There were no flowers in the gardens, it was too late in the year, and all the seasonal trees had lost their leaves. The gardens were fenced in by high walls and another separate structure called the Outer Sanctum, blocking the view from any passersby. The Outer Sanctum's wall that faced the garden was a lattice of large glass panes where Anara could see men and women speaking to one another as they ate from silver bowls of fruit. The men would let their eyes wander over their companions as well as the women that walked the stone paths through the maze of shrubbery. They returned to the Inner Sanctum, the larger structure where the courtesans actually lived, and up a flight of stairs to the craftswomen's chapter.

"I guess it was fate," Lena sighed as Anara placed the framed painting on the wall of her new room. It was easily twice the size of her room at *Wentworth's* with a bed, even softer and more spacious than the hospital bed, up against the wall. A wardrobe twice the size of her old one stood empty. "Tina actually wed a blacksmith not long ago, so that's why this room is empty. She was an expert with needlework, so she's probably helping that man's business with a side business of tailoring or embroidery now. We're not *supposed* to fall in love, but Tina had been a courtesan for ten years and was looking to get out. Anyway, it's fate because you're so obviously going to join this chapter anyway." Anara tossed her satchel onto the bed as Lena pulled her out of the room.

Each chapter was split in two by the bulk of the structure. The dining hall was between the orderlies. A full ballroom was between the craftswomen, where Lena playfully pulled Anara onto the dance floor.

"I absolutely *love* this room. Not as much as the art storage of course, but I just feel so..." Lena sighed as she took Anara's hands and spun around with her. The spacious area was the largest room Anara had ever seen. Tables lined the outside on a raised platform and a stone column supported the floors above at each corner of the dance floor.

"I don't know how," Anara protested but Lena paid no mind. It was not much of a dance, really, just spinning that quickly made Anara dizzy, and there was no music to keep rhythm to if Anara even wanted to try. Yet, as Lena and she spun around in the empty chamber Anara found herself laughing.

"Your first lesson," Lena said as they went back and forth across the room. "Look at me, not the walls." The dizziness was lessened, but not entirely gone as she focused on the other woman. Lena smiled as Anara blushed when their eyes locked together. "Up above here are the three classrooms where you'll learn about Aederon's history, which goes into great detail concerning the accomplishments of our clients, a musical skill and how to finish a man. A good way to leave a man satisfied is to stroke his ego—both of them." Lena laughed at the renewal of

Anara's flushed cheeks and they slowed to a stop. Anara stood unsteadily for a moment as she caught her breath. "And above *that* is the library. Your painting was done above that, on the blade dancer balcony. We'll go straight there since it is getting late."

Anara shivered as she walked out of the cover of the northern blade dancer chapter and onto the open balcony. The Third Month of Gathering was in its second week and the chill of winter was already strong this far north. The southern blade dancer chapter completed the view of the five-story tower across from them. Lena linked arms with her as they both gazed reverently at the night sky, clear and lit by countless, glittering stars.

"You woke up just before the evening meal," Lena sighed as they walked. "A good time to get a tour. I love coming up here after *Soleanne* has set and *Luminara* has risen to chase her lover across the sky. Especially with someone to keep me warm."

Anara shuffled uncomfortably. "Lena, I..."

"Teasing," Lena laughed and looked up. Anara doubted that was entirely true. "I love the stars. Have you ever wished you could be up there with them, shining down on this world like a brilliant jewel for all to admire?" They stopped at the railing on the eastern edge of the balcony. "When I was little I would pretend I was there. Far away from everything, seeing Trista in all of her glory instead of the confines of a stuffy tent, or the imaginary borders of the kingdoms."

"Trista's a woman?"

"Of course she is," Lena laughed. "Only women could be as beautiful as the world is. What do they teach up here in the north?"

"I can't really say," Anara said. "Mostly I only ever learned about Fiel. The priests at *Wentworth's* had nothing much to say about the other gods or the world they created."

"Askialla," Lena said and Anara raised her eyebrow at her. "The Great Dragoness," Lena said. "Raykarn believe in only two gods. The Great Dragoness, Askialla, is the name they give to Trista and The Great Dragon, Askarenesh, is the name they give the sky."

KYLE K. OATES

"How do you know that?"

"I already told you, silly," Lena elbowed Anara in the ribs. "I spent several years in Raykarn clans."

"Raykarns have a language? But I heard they..."

"The soldiers only kill Raykarns, and your stories come from them," Lena shrugged. "Not all of them are evil, you know. Some even speak Ilionan fluently," Lena said. "Esuesialle, the Ironeyes, are peaceful. They can afford to be, of course, since not even the Exsishkar, the Redclaws, are strong enough to stand against them."

"Does it hurt to talk about your time there?"

"Sometimes," Lena said, leaning her head against Anara's shoulder. Until now the Borderlander had seemed taller than she really was. "It used to all of the time."

Anara looked out over the world below her. It *was* where her painting had been done. The shoreline was visible as a shifting line of white that ran along the beach in the crescent light of *Luminara* and the stars. The forest was there too, just as it was in the picture, but the horizon blurred with the night sky. The only feature that separated the two was the stars.

"I don't know if I can be a courtesan, Lena," Anara said after a period of silence, swallowing back the lump in her throat but failing to hold back the tears. She wanted to scream, but at the same time, her heart felt lighter just having Lena beside her. Anara still could not understand why Brother Mitchel had fled from *Wentworth's*. Mitchel was a priest in the Order of Light, it seemed impossible that Anara could have done anything to humble such a proud man. After getting in trouble, all she remembered was waking up several days later from a feverish sleep. "I don't have your strength; I can't even remember my past to put it behind me."

"You'd be surprised," Lena said.

"I'll try," Anara said, more to the night sky.

"Askarenesh hears your vow," Lena said as if she were performing some ritual. She may have been, but Anara had no idea what the religion of the Raykarn was like. "And Askialla will help you lift your burden. And so will I." Lena kissed Anara's cheek. "We should go down. It wouldn't do to have you catch a cold after you slept for so long."

V

COMPETING AGE

Joshua stared up at the soot-stained ceiling of *Mathews and Son's* blacksmith. He squinted at the swirls of ash that had accumulated over the years, letting his mind conjure up a landscape of images from them. It was a lot like cloud gazing, though he would never announce any of the things his imagination manifested. He was not a boy anymore. Today he was eighteen; the youngest age a man could participate in a tournament.

Further inside the shop, Joshua could hear the steady ringing of Cole Mathews hammering away at some slag of metal that would turn into a beautiful sword. Or it would be another horseshoe, Joshua thought with a smirk as he looked around the walls where hundreds of horseshoes hung.

Gabriel, Cole's son, leaned with his back resting against the wall near the door as he polished a massively impractical sword. The claymore was even oversized by two-handed sword standards but fit Gabriel's impressive build perfectly. He was much taller than Joshua, who was already tall among Ilionans, with a broad and heavily muscled build, except for his midsection. He had an impressive gut to match the muscles of his arms and chest above it.

Tina Mathews, Gabriel's stepmother, hummed softly to herself as she sewed lining to a chainmail shirt. Her voice was beautiful as the humming turned into incoherent syllables that followed the melody. Her compassionate demeanor warmed the room but her presence always reminded Joshua of Gabriel's birth mother who died from winter flu two years prior. Tina's age was between Gabriel and his father, somewhere in her thirties, but Joshua would not ask for the specific years. "A gentleman does not ask the age of a woman older than himself," Sir Echton told him when speaking of women. It made little sense to Joshua as he mused, *how could I tell if I didn't ask? Especially if she was close to my own age.*

The bell rang at the front door of the shop and Joshua propped himself up on his elbows.

"There you are," Eric said as he strode across the large room. His boots thumped against the heavy beams of the floor until he stood over Joshua. "Mrs. Echton is having a litter of swiftlings since she hasn't seen you all day."

"So, what?" Joshua shrugged, leaning back on the counter with hands behind his head.

"You're eighteen years old today, Joshua. She's throwing you a celebration party. You're finally of a competing age."

"And I still have to wait nine more months before I can claim a title in one of the competitions."

"Still, there's the Tournament of Ice in a week, and the Planting Festival when the snow melts. Why does it matter if a knighthood is only offered at the Harvest Festival? You *need* to compete to prove that you're a force to be reckoned with next year."

"And give my opponents the opportunity to know of my abilities before a fight, allowing them a chance to train for it? I won't be caught off guard like I was with Stanson last harvest." Joshua shook his head. "*That* would be reckless."

"So, win them as well."

"I need to be certain I'll get a knighthood for winning," Joshua persisted. "I can't let the other knights and swordsman know how good I am."

"They *already* know how good you are," Gabriel laughed.

"In practice," Joshua corrected. "A squire is not allowed to actually *beat* his opponent in practice, poor training if you ask me. I doubt a real opponent would hold back. They won't think of me as real competition until it's too late. They already doubt I'm any good since I'm Sir Echton's squire."

"So why not prove them wrong, Joshua?" Eric urged. "Prove them wrong for your and Sir Echton's honor."

"You want to teach them a lesson, Eric? Go right ahead." Joshua shrugged off the goading. "I intend to win my first tournament, and I intend to do it for a knighthood."

"Just like Sir Edwin?" Eric asked, rolling his eyes.

"I'm nothing like him," Joshua said defensively, sitting up. Sir Edwin had won his knighthood in the lists instead of battle as well, but he had never learned to be humble in victory. "Ideally, I would earn my knighthood, not win it like Edwin. But since there aren't any hordes of bandits in the kingdom that we're aware of, that is out of the question for me." The ringing turned into a hiss as Cole submerged his work in a bucket of water. "What *is* your father making, anyway, Gabriel?"

"I can't tell you," Gabriel said. "It's supposed to be a surprise for your birthday."

"Gabriel!" Eric snapped. "Now he knows about it."

"I didn't tell him what it was, milord," Gabriel's brow furrowed as Eric sighed. "And pap is in the back, so it isn't like he can see it."

"He's got legs, hasn't he," Eric said as Joshua moved away from the counter. "No," Eric moved to block Joshua. "No, no, no. No peeking."

"I'm not going to look. I'll let you two have your surprise," Joshua groaned. "Like you said, Cynthia has been looking for me."

"Ah, good, so you'll go let her know where you are." Eric's triumphant grin turned upside down when Joshua shook his head.

"I think I'll pay a visit to Cordelia at her school first," Joshua stated, and Tina laughed lightly from where she worked in the corner.

"Joshua," Eric whined, trailing behind him as Joshua quickly marched from the blacksmith shop. Gabriel quickly caught up a few moments later with his beastly sword strapped to his back. "I don't think that's a good idea either."

"Of course you don't. She's your sister," Joshua laughed. "What's the harm? The girls will all gawk at you if you're with me anyway."

"All while sneaking glances at you," Eric said. "They only want me for my title."

"And they want me for my lack of gold?" Joshua joked, and Eric rolled his eyes.

The *Academy of Enlightenment*, where all highbred noble girls went for their education, was just east of the temple plaza at the edge of Merchant's Row. It was a brief walk from Gabriel's smithy. Before long the three of them were standing at the edge of the school grounds. Boys were not permitted beyond the low wall built of mortared river stones. Joshua sat down, using the gatepost to support his back as he surveyed the beautiful ladies in waiting and their handmaidens.

The academy was an impressive sight, closely resembling a keep, like the *Tower of the Watch* in Crossroads if the tower had been built to be pleasing on the eyes instead of for tactical use. The crenellations of each tower level were abundant and painted a light blue. The paint was simply for aesthetics as it would have added no real benefit against a stone launched from a trebuchet. The stained-glass windows with their intricate designs were too large to provide an archer adequate cover. Still, it was a marvelous feat of castle engineering.

"*Really*, Joshua?" Eric sighed as a few groups of ladies noticed them and instantly started giggling, coquettishly fanning themselves. Given the chill weather they wore full dresses and some even wore thick fur coats that obscured their feminine curves. "You should just go to a whore house or something."

"I'll leave that to you, my friend," Joshua said, laughing as Eric glared at him.

"I only do that to annoy father," Eric protested. "Mostly."

"I'm well aware of what a chore it must be to bed so many women all for the sake of annoying the Lord Commander,"

Joshua teased. "Hence, it is the main source of jest between Gabriel and me."

"Like how many women does it take for Eric to mount a horse?" Gabriel grinned, speaking as he often did without thinking. "None," Gabriel laughed. "He's already mounted it!" Joshua snickered, but Eric was *not* amused.

"I could have you in the stocks for less, Gabriel," Eric growled, quickly killing the merriment.

"Sorry, milord," Gabriel muttered, kicking at the dirt as Cordelia and her friends wandered over to them.

"I see you're skipping your studies again, brother," Cordelia sighed. She was always a pleasure to see, but particularly today in her pastel yellow winter gown. Winter gowns were more decent than those meant for warmer months, but the embroidered designs were more elaborate and usually intended to draw the eyes right to... "And stop staring at my tits, Joshua."

"Begging your pardon, my lady," Joshua said, looking up towards the steeples of Fiel's Temple. "I was merely lost in thought of how much Fiel has blessed you in your life. For only the God of Light himself could grant a woman with such radiant beauty." The girls all started smiling at that, even Cordelia before she caught herself and just glared at him.

"Honestly, Joshua," Eric growled. He could be so defensive of his sister sometimes. The girls behind Cordelia giggled again. Girls did that a lot whenever he and Eric were around. "I've not smelled sappier words in a syrup mill." All to more tittering.

"How does one smell words, I wonder?" Joshua said, grinning at the young lord.

"Have you seen Cynthia, Joshua? I heard she was looking for you," Cordelia interrupted, ending her cohorts' laughter.

"You too? Who told *you* Cynthia was looking for me?" Joshua asked, leaning hard against the gate post and folding his arms.

"When isn't she looking for you?" She grinned at him manipulatively.

"Thade take me," Joshua cursed under his breath and the girls blushed, fanning themselves to hide their grins. "That woman will be the end of me. I'm not her bloody son! I'm her husband's squire."

"You could at least show *some* gratitude. It isn't like you get a party thrown for all of your birthdays by a woman who is practically nobility. She probably *will* be nobility after the skirmishes with the Ironeyes cease no matter *what* happens to Malcolm," Cordelia scolded.

"You aren't my mother either," Joshua pointed at her, poking her sternum three times. The girls all gasped, aware of the social difference between him and Cordelia. As Eric had so bluntly put it to Gabriel, he could be thrown in the stocks for less.

"Really, Joshua, act your age," Cordelia sighed, swatting Joshua's hand with her fan and stamping her foot. "No wonder Cynthia treats you like a little boy."

"Good advice, sister. Perhaps you should follow it too," Eric snickered and the girls giggled again. Cordelia glared at her brother; her stare as sharp as daggers. Eric flinched back.

"That's what I thought," Cordelia held up her nose and began walking away. The group of women behind her moaned in drawn-out disappointment as they were forced to follow, leaving Eric and Joshua to themselves. Gabriel was there, too, not that they noticed since the blacksmith had not spoken up.

"I don't understand women," Gabriel muttered as the three of them walked away from the *Academy of Enlightenment.*

"I don't think a creature on earth does, Gabriel," Eric agreed. "You really should head to Echton's estate."

"Yes, *Mother*," Joshua groaned, but Eric was right. He should really check in on Cynthia. It had been three months since Sir Echton left and every day she still had worry-fueled nightmares of her husband's death. Joshua didn't care what his mentor said, Cynthia was genuinely in love with Sir Echton.

When they arrived, the estate was... different. Streamers draped across the yard from the house to the lone pine tree in the corner. Flags, lining the stone path up to the door, fluttered and snapped in the light breeze coming over the cliff behind the house. Several tables, probably purchased that day, dotted the expansive front lawn with miniature ice sculptures of a lance and sword crossing at the center of each table. White linen, hemmed in red satin, covered the round surfaces that were already set for the night's festivities. For the occasion, Cynthia had even splurged on serving women who wore low-cut, identical gowns. They looked young as they skirted around the tables making sure they were all set properly. A pair of them, a Borderlander and a taller blonde, caught Joshua's eye. The Borderlander, with half of her head shaved just like his mother, was escorting the blonde and gesturing at the placements as Joshua approached.

"May I be of any assistance?" Joshua asked with his best grin when they turned at his approach. "I was unaware such beauties would be attending this event." The Borderlander grinned, batting her long lashes at him and the blonde blushed. Joshua's eyes fell on the exotic girl's neck and his grin faltered. The Borderlander wore Raykarn slave bands. "I am sorry," Joshua clenched his fist as he stared. He wanted to say *something* about the cruel devices but found his mind blank.

"For what, my *lord*?" she asked, glancing at the other woman as if unsure about the title, and Eric laughed. "I fail to see any amusement in my question, my lord."

"I'm a lord, yes," Eric said, placing a hand on Joshua's shoulder. "Forgive my friend here. It is his birthday today and I'm afraid he may have already dipped into a keg of ale or two."

"I have not," Joshua said, rolling his shoulder to force Eric's hand off.

"I am Mistress Weston, and this is Mistress Swift," the Borderlander said as the two women politely curtsied. The blonde's movements were considerably more awkward than Mistress Weston's. "And, I'm afraid the young Lord Ackart has betrayed you to be Master Kentaine given it is *his* birthday we are here to serve."

"My reputation precedes me," Eric gloated, grinning sideways at Joshua. Cocky, of course. Most servants in the entire kingdom would know the Ackart family line by portrait alone.

"That it does," Mistress Weston said, briefly touching Eric's shoulder. "It is not very often one such as myself stands in the presence of such an important man as the future Lord

Commander of Iliona's Legions." Joshua rolled his eyes at Eric. It was obvious what the woman was doing. Worse, it was working perfectly as Eric's chest was puffing up even larger by the second.

"Where did Cynthia find such knowledgeable caterers?" Eric asked, practically gawking at Mistress Weston.

"It would bore you, I'm certain, my lord," Mistress Weston said, pulling away from them and returning to Mistress Swift's side. "I'm afraid I cannot continue to converse with such fine gentlemen, as you see I am training a new recruit in the ways of a hostess. If you'll excuse us." With that, the two walked away but not before Mistress Swift looked up, flashing Joshua with startlingly blue eyes. Not just muddy blue like he had seen before, but pure azure, brighter than a cloudless, summer sky. Even Cordelia's lovely eyes paled in comparison to Mistress Swift's beauty. He stared at the blonde, watching her hips sway with each unsteady step across the lawn and realizing Mistress Swift was the first woman he *wanted*. Cordelia was beautiful, but he had grown up with her and could remember her as a spoiled child. Mistress Swift was a very desirable woman.

"Did you see her eyes?" Joshua whispered in awe, watching as the pair of women went about their tasks. This time Mistress Swift was gesturing to the placements and Mistress Weston nodded or shook her head with each right or wrong answer.

"I know, Borderlanders," Eric sighed and Joshua followed his gaze. He was staring intently at Mistress Weston's backside. "Aren't you half Borderlander? Do you recognize her?"

"Not her, the blonde!" Joshua playfully smacked Eric on the back of the head. "And I lived in a small village, so I don't know her."

"Ouch," Eric said, punching Joshua in the ribs. "What about her? So, she has eyes. Everyone has eyes. But did you see that *hair*... Who wears their hair like that? And the tattoo on her scalp..."

"They were blue, and my mother wore her hair like that. Don't bring up the tattoo either, it's a Raykarn slave mark," Joshua snapped. Eric frowned and shrugged.

"I've seen colored eyes before. Thade's Abyss, Morgan Heath has green eyes."

"Look at the *food!*" Gabriel exclaimed as more women, in the same gowns and equally as beautiful and refined in posture as the Mistress Weston, brought out plate upon plate of delicacies and placed them on the banquet table that ran parallel to the front of the home. Joshua sighed in bewilderment. Presented with a choice between beautiful women and food, Gabriel was always sure to pick food. It was no wonder he had not been courting much. Taverns had food and beautiful women, but Gabriel could only focus on one thing at a time. Food always won.

"There you are, Joshua!" Cynthia called out, crossing the lawn as quickly as she could manage in heels. "I've been looking for you all day. This party was *supposed* to be about you. How are the hired hostesses supposed to show you off if they don't know who you *are?*"

"Speaking of these hostesses, where did you find them? Especially so many on such short notice?" Eric asked, still staring at Mistress Weston.

"That doesn't matter, Eric," Cynthia said, batting him with her fan. Joshua grinned. Not only did those contraptions hide inappropriate grins but they doubled as an effective tool to snap Eric out of his gawking. "Come with me, Joshua. I have to introduce you to the head hostess so at least *she* can let our guests know who you are." Now that Eric mentioned it, however, Joshua did not recognize any of the women from his time spent in Merchants Row where hostesses were normally found. And they *certainly* did not have the air of Cheapside about them given the way they held themselves.

"Shouldn't our guests know who I am already?"

"Most, yes, but a few of Malcolm's old friends are coming to meet his young prodigy as well. Now come inside. Mistress Adair is waiting in the kitchens."

Cynthia pulled Joshua past the line of women carrying food and into Sir Echton's home. Toward the back of the house were stairs leading up to the second floor and down to the kitchens and storage. Joshua, who had rarely been in the kitchens as Cynthia insisted guests did not belong there, was surprised by what he found. Upstairs may have appeared barren, but Sir Echton's kitchen rivaled any noble's. A lavish array of meats hung against the eastern wall, where the chill of the ocean would help keep them cool, and bread loaves of various sizes covered an entire counter. He had never seen so many brightly colored vegetables gathered in one place outside of a market; fruits, nearly impossible to keep fresh, looked like they had all just come off the tree or vine on which they grew.

All around him the hostesses went about their work gracefully in beautiful, silver serving gowns despite the multitude of rather demanding tasks. Some cooked and cleaned while others carried out food and—as if he had arrived late to his own party— some returned with trays that were already empty. Wines were being opened and casks were being tapped. It was chaos. In the middle of it all stood a tall, well-endowed woman who barked orders like the best taskmasters at the *Academy of Tactics* where Joshua had spent a few years training. Joshua fancied what it might be like to sneak off with one of these women. Any one of them would have been more enjoyable than the women he passed when fetching Eric out of the red-light districts, much more enjoyable.

"Mistresses Tasha and Sasha! Open those ones *away* from each other," she said and two women, looking exquisitely *identical* in figure except for their hairstyles, opened bottles of champagne. The corks popped and slapped against the wall and ceiling before landing behind the girls, who jumped in surprise and giggled at the show. "Ah, Cynthia, there you are. Is this why you called us in? I'm always grateful to be contacted by one of my past mistresses, and even more so to offer help when they need it, but I really expected the man to be here sooner."

"Wait, you're from *Lussena's Temple*?" Joshua asked, looking around at the women. His eyes widened. Now that he knew *where* they were from he *really* considered taking one aside since it would not be more in line with their regular duties. Mistress Swift would be his first choice. They were *all* courtesans. How could one house have so many? "*All* of you?"

"He knows?" the woman asked, raising an eyebrow. Cynthia blushed.

"Of course he knows, Erin," Cynthia said. "He's practically Malcolm's son. Closer actually, like soldiers who fought beside each other. I doubt the two of them have a secret between them. Plus, I met and courted Malcolm years after Joshua had been training with my husband."

"Just so you know, boy," Mistress Adair said, holding up a finger as Joshua couldn't help but gawk at the women around him. "We are not here for *that* type of pleasure tonight, so keep your hands to yourself. Understood?"

"Yes, ma'am," Joshua said, still grinning at the women.

"And you'd better hold your liquor. I don't want the other young men of your acquaintance to find out. I have more than one novice here tonight, and I'll not have them defiled before they come into their own competing age, so to speak." She sounded like a stern taskmaster again as she spoke, her tone forcing Joshua's grin away.

"Yes, of course," Joshua said, straitening his posture and fighting the urge to salute her.

"Good," she smiled and her tone softened considerably. *How can women flip emotions on a copper wyrm like that?* "You may call me Mistress Adair," she motioned back toward the stairs, "If you'll allow me?"

Joshua nodded and the older woman took his arm and let him guide her back upstairs and out into the party which had filled with guests. He had arrived just in time. Eric and Gabriel were engaged in animated dialog with a few of his old sparring partners at the academy, Terry Isaacs from the Fertile Vale and a Borderlander named Yondel. Like many Borderlanders Yondel had no last name. Among them was an old man, Vheng, dressed in dark blue robes and closer to Echton's age. Vheng was an enchanter, the one who created both *Heartflame* and *Desertfrost*. He was also a Borderlander, a native given his dark skin that made his long, white beard prominently stand out. He was bald, making it seem as if his beard was trying to pull him down by the chin. Cordelia, plus her flock of giggling girls, had arrived as well.

Cordelia smiled at Joshua as if his disruptive visit at her school was already forgotten.

"Welcome," Mistress Adair said. "As you all know, Sir Echton's wife, a very dear friend of mine, has gathered you all here to celebrate the journey of one individual from a boy," she said, pausing as everyone turned their attention towards the house. "To a man. Today, Joshua Kentaine is eighteen years old," she said, guiding Joshua down onto the lawn as she spoke.

At that moment, Mistress Swift, with her captivating eyes, stepped forward bearing a tray with two slender glasses that stood on tall, fluted stems. *How can someone so beautiful have become a courtesan?* Joshua thought as he watched her. She bowed her head, her golden locks braided tightly to keep them out of the way. A yellow liquid bubbled in the glasses as Mistress Adair handed one to Joshua and took one herself.

"What many of you don't know," Mistress Adair said, raising her glass in a toast as Mistress Swift bowed away. No one watched Mistress Swift go as they were all looking at Joshua. "...is the trial it has been for *this* boy to come *so* far. Born a Borderlander who saw the cruelty of this world at too young of an age," she continued and Joshua felt himself choking up to the memories of his family and the day Sir Echton found him. "His own family, taken by the ruthless clans of the Raykarn. Saved by a man whose honor is without question, Sir Echton, and raised as the knight's own son. He survived the campaigns eight years ago, though barely a boy of ten, dutifully serving Sir Echton as a squire through every step of those bloodied sands and into the safety north of Ashfall. I present to you Joshua Kentaine. No longer a boy, but a man who will exceed all expectations."

Joshua half laughed out of relief when the crowd cheered. Mistress Adair gently tapped Joshua's own glass with hers to a chorus of ringing crystal as everyone else did the same.

"Did Cynthia, or Sir Echton, tell you all of that?" Joshua asked as Mistress Adair took a sip from her glass and untangled her arm from his. She slyly smiled at him but didn't speak a word as she walked away to mingle with the crowd and observe her hostesses.

"Bloody good hostess," Eric said, as he reached Joshua and clapped him on the shoulder. "I should get her for *my* birthday when I'm of a competing age."

"You're already of a competing age," Joshua laughed before taking a drink of the golden champagne.

"She doesn't have to know that," Eric said, finishing off his own.

"I'm pretty sure she already does," Joshua said as he let his friend pull him into the midst of the crowd. Yondel and Terry were there, dressed in the uniform of the Watch with swords at their waists. The two soldiers saluted Joshua with one arm and he returned the honor.

"It's been too long, Joshua," Yondel said in his quiet voice. The hair on the left side of his head had been growing for a few days and was a dark shadow against the skin. "You should have joined us at the Watch, my friend. The realm could use more good men such as yourself protecting her."

"He had his sights set higher," Eric interjected. "Joshua will be a knight someday."

"Of course, my lord," Yondel nodded.

"Though I agree," Joshua said, shaking their hands. "The realm does need more good men protecting her, and I'm looking at two of the best. I'm glad you followed through with joining the Watch instead of going back home to your father's plantation, Terry. And you, Yondel, you are just as worthy of praise as I am. If not for you I would not have made it north of Ashfall eight years ago." The two men beamed as Joshua was ushered on to the next group by Eric.

"You have to speak with Vheng," Eric said, pushing Joshua from behind.

"Why? I don't know the man; he was one of Sir Echton's friends."

"You just do," Gabriel appeared out of nowhere, making Joshua start. For such a big fellow, he did manage to sneak about. "It's a surprise."

"No," Joshua shook his head and stopped, putting Cole's work and Vheng's presence together. "An enchanted sword? I can't accept that, especially not one from a *master* enchanter."

"Not just *any* master," Eric grinned and pulled on Joshua's free arm. Joshua placed his empty glass on a tray as one came by, though unfortunately not carried by Mistress Swift. "Vheng is *the* Grandmaster Enchanter of the realm." Eric stopped Joshua in front of a table where Vheng sat between two others, a man and woman the same age as Joshua, with a long parcel in front of him.

"So, this be the boy," Vheng said, his accent very thick and one Joshua had not heard for eight years. "The man, as the fine lady did say, in truth. What be the name of the man before me?"

"Joshua Kentaine," he answered, shaking Gabriel and Eric off him.

"Aye, that be truth as well," Vheng said smiling as he stood. "These be Young Lord Jacob Barnum," Joshua saluted the young man who nodded back. "And Lady Jocelyn Chase," Joshua bowed, kissing the back of the young lady's hand. Jocelyn grinned, blushing as she lifted her glass of wine. She batted her eyes, flirtatiously complimenting her own beauty, but Joshua could not help but feel the urge to find Mistress Swift within the crowd instead. "It be very seldom that I have the honor of meeting a man Sir Echton be holding in the highest esteem. In fact, I be able to count those times on this hand." He said, holding up a hand that had its last two fingers cut off. Joshua noted the sword hanging at the enchanter's own waist. The sheath was covered in protective runes, necessary to shield it from the blade inside, and the leather was well worn.

"This be *Blizzard*," Vheng said, motioning to his weapon. "As a spellsword, it has seen many battles with me. I trust your own blade will be with you," he said as he threw aside the thin parchment covering the weapon the table. He drew the blade and the longsword sprang to life with the flickering of an orange flame. The crowd backed away from the table with gasps of amazement as they looked up at the enchanted weapon. Every guest but one seemed to shy away from the blaze. Mistress Swift stood, an empty tray in her arms, staring at the weapon. Her blue eyes captivated by it. Joshua blinked at the courtesan, enthralled by those azure eyes full of wonder and desire at the sword he held aloft. Mistress Swift was not like all other courtesans, except perhaps Cynthia, but she had a strong mind of her own that stood and fought as others recoiled. Joshua smirked, feeling warm under his collar as he thought of the mistress and fighting the urge to approach her. He *had* given his word to Mistress Adair, after all.

"What be its name?"

Joshua turned back to the sword as Vheng held it out for him. It was lighter than he had expected, but certainly heavy enough that it was not aeromantically enchanted like his father's sword. The leather of the hilt had recently been stained and creaked beneath his hand as he pointed the blade towards the darkening sky. He knew *exactly* what the weapon was meant for. It was meant for killing Raykarn.

"*Vengeance,*" Joshua said in a deep, hushed tone that everyone could hear in the silence around him. The blade was Malef's gift to him, a sign that his family would *finally* be avenged. Joshua took the enchanted sheath and snapped the blade home, silently vowing to himself that it would not be drawn again until he was in the Endless Waste.

"And so shall it be," Vheng nodded, spreading his arms in the informal salute of the Borderlands. "I knew your mother, Joshua," Vheng said solemnly. "She would be proud of you today." Joshua raised one fist to the opposite shoulder in salute to the enchanter. Vheng clapped once and stepped away from his table to let the gawking onlookers rush forward, Terry and Yondel at the front.

Nine more months and a tournament were all that stood in his way to find his revenge in the Endless Waste.

VI

ENCHANTING

"Did you *see* that sword?" Anara asked for what must have been the hundredth time since leaving Aederon City, the tails of her robe lifting slightly as she spun across marble flagstones through the garden outside the Inner Sanctum. The path glowed dimly from the shaded lamps along the edge and she knelt down to get a closer look, trying to see the runes etched into whatever made them burn through the blue fabric and flames.

"Yes, I saw the sword," Lena rolled her eyes, pulling Anara back to her feet. "*Everyone* saw the sword. But I'm tired, we should go to bed." Anara took Lena's hands and began dancing with her towards the Inner Sanctum. It was quite late, but this fact did not matter to Anara. It was three leagues from Aederon City to *Lussena's Temple*, not to mention a ferry ride, but she still could not believe how wonderful that sword had blended with the fiery orange of the clouds at sunset.

"I want to do that," Anara said, watching the other courtesans slowly exit the Outer Sanctum after changing back into their robes. "I want to be an enchantress and make things of beauty like that."

"Swords are for killing," Lena said with decisiveness as they stepped into the hall that connected the two towers. "Not for looking at."

"I don't care," Anara sighed, ignoring Lena's disdain. "I feel like I have a *reason* to keep going. This is how I'll be able to do what I must as a courtesan. Knowing someday I'll be able to become an enchantress."

"Then you should get started," Lena said with interest, and Anara grabbed her hand. She had to take Lena with her to the library. "*You*, Anara. Right now, I'm going to bed," Lena yawned, pulling her to a stop. "Get started *tomorrow*."

"Right," Anara blushed and let go of her friend's hand. "Tomorrow," Anara agreed, kissing Lena on the cheek. Lena blushed, touching where Anara's lips had been. "Good night," Anara said, trying to hide the realization that it was the first time she had returned Lena's usual affection. Anara felt her cheeks growing warm. The few months with Lena had been enjoyable as friends, but this was the first time she felt... more. She wanted to kiss Lena again, her heart raced at the idea but Sister Dawn's voice—and Fiel's teachings—in the back of her mind made her feel ashamed of it even though she no longer followed the Order of Light. Anara looked away from Lena, thinking the other woman might see the conflicted excitement inside her.

"Good night," Lena murmured, smiling coyly at Anara. She *looked* tired now that Anara had slowed down enough to take notice. Lena's eyes were half closed, and she yawned as she turned to go find her own room. Even Lena's posture was slumped over, something Anara had rarely ever seen. Anara smiled, spinning around twice before heading up the stairs to her room.

Her doll, Cassie, rested atop the vanity desk, across from the shoreline painting that Anara could view as she readied herself in the morning at the vanity's mirror. She had chosen another portrait, one of two women intertwined even though it made her blush every time she looked at it because Lena complained her room was too dull every time she visited. The Sapphic art piece ended those complaints. That one was above her bed so she only saw it before crawling onto the feather mattress. Sheer blue curtains framed the window and a blue rug stretched out from beneath the bed so she did not step out onto the cold wood floor in the mornings. Anara undressed and slipped into bed as her mind raced about the night.

The sword had been the highlight, of course, but the evening had actually been quite pleasant. Mistress Adair had kept her word that the night would only be about catering the party. Which Anara appreciated since she was not *technically* a courtesan yet. She was still too young, but that would change before the next Harvest Festival. She had eight months in preparation to prove herself as an enchantress. Her thoughts of the night swirled around her head from the lessons she was given by Lena and the other more experienced courtesans but they would all circle back to the sword. She wanted to jump out of bed and race to the library, thinking it would be illuminated sufficiently for reading by glow lamps at this hour of the night, but Lena was right. It was time to retire. Anara had no real way of knowing *what* time it was after they returned. It was dark, she knew that, but she was far from fatigued.

"I want to see that sword again," Anara sighed, rolling over in her bed and toying with a lock of hair. The man, something Kentaine, had gawked at her unabashedly. But she had endured it. If she could do that, then why not a few years of similar treatment? Anara frowned. Joshua had not really been attractive, not to her anyway. Some of the other girls at the party had spoken up about him in the kitchens, but Anara could not see what they were so enamored by. Not only that, but he had certainly noticed her. The constant attention he would toss her way, even if he never was so forward as to approach her, was unwanted. Not only did the other courtesan notice, teasing Anara for it, but Anara could see the desires in his eyes. Desires like those Lena had for her.

Anara smiled briefly, thinking of Lena.

Anara turned onto her side and frowned out her window. She could not deny she wanted Lena anymore, not after tonight. She also could not deny that she wanted nothing to do with men. None of them had caught her eye at the party, not even the young Lord Ackart. Even the courtesan who did not gush over Joshua did so about Lord Ackart. All of this made Anara's stomach churn. She was *supposed* to see to the pleasures of men as a courtesan, but she had no taste for them.

Joshua's sword came to her mind. It had been intruding on her thoughts all night. She *wanted* to be an enchantress. It was the first *real* desire she could remember having. More than a desire, it gave her hope for a *real* future. Anara bit her lower lip. She could be a courtesan if it led to becoming an enchantress.

"I can't sleep," she sighed, pulling her legs up and hugging her knees to her chest. She took in a deep breath and slowly exhaled, allowing her limbs to fall back into a more open position. Each day brought the duties of a courtesan closer. A very small part of her felt excited by the idea of experiencing a man, but that small part of her was shadowed by insecurities of her own appearance and guilt from Sister Dawn's teachings at the orphanage. She was too tall, taller than most men now. Fiel did not approve of carnal pleasures outside of a union, with men or women. Not that she believed in those teachings anymore. Still, the way Lena spoke of her duties to the house—and how she seemed to enjoy them—gave Anara pause and questions concerning the truth of Fiel's teachings. The discouraging cycle of her thoughts made it even more difficult to sleep. She slipped out of bed and back into her shoes before throwing on her novice robes and walking out of her room.

The halls were eerily quiet this late as she made her way up the stairs towards the library. It was the first time she had walked them without any other courtesans around and it felt so empty. The large halls echoed with each step as she ascended the spiral staircase at the tower's center and crossed over to the library.

A warm glow emanated from the window set into the heavy oak door, and Anara found herself rushing to enter and escape the emptiness. She sighed when the door clicked shut behind her as if she had just escaped being consumed by the ravenous darkness and made her way to the enchantments section of the shelves. Disappointingly, that turned out to be one book. Lena had not been lying about how small it was. Apparently magecraft was more of a secret than the other arts.

Basic Enchantment Theory was embossed over a green stained leather cover in faded, gold-leaf lettering. She sat down in one of the soft chairs directly beneath a glow lamp to examine it more closely. It was a beautiful book, and Anara hesitated upon opening it, lingering a few moments longer to savor its dusty aroma. She traced her fingers over the title, enjoying the feel of soft leather against cool lettering. Once open, the text inside felt special to her, more than any other book she had held in her life. Especially compared to the tattered tomes of *Wentworth's Home for Wayward Souls.*

> *Enchantments are one of the four material magecrafts of Trista. The others being bonding, alchemy, and summoning. Native to the Raykarn clans of the Endless Waste, enchanting was adopted by Iliona following the Last Necromantic War and cessation of the practice known as sorcery. As such, the very best and complicated enchantments are typically of Raykarn in origin, but in regards to the purposes of this study, it was deemed prudent to focus on that of the less complicated Ilionan enchanting.*
>
> *Ilionans, unlike the Raykarn, value the aspects of their gods above all else and have as such divined the types of their enchantments according to the four lesser gods. Malef, God of Fire, rules over what are known as Pyromantic Enchantments. Duloreb, God of Earth, rules over Geomantic Enchantments. Ezebre, Goddess of Air, rules over Aeromantic Enchantments. And Mertas, Goddess of Water, rules over Hydromantic Enchantments. Each of these groups of enchantments can be further divided into two groups: Auras, which produce a visible outward effect, and Boons, which alter the physical aspects of a chosen material.*
>
> *Concerning material, it is easiest to enchant an object the more solid it appears to be. Metal is easier than stone; stone is easier than animal hides or wood; and animal hides are easier than*

cloth. Cloth being nearly impossible to enchant by any reasonable degree and metal being so welcoming of an enchantment that even the most inept and talentless person could do it if given the proper ingredients.

Anara yawned as she looked at the end of the first page. Whoever the author was they could have used a bit of flavor in their writing. Enchantments were *not* this boring. At least not the ones Anara had seen.

"Can't sleep, Anara?" Mistress Adair asked and Anara jumped.

"Headmistress," Anara said, standing up and curtseying. She dropped the book in the process and Mistress Adair smiled as she crouched to retrieve it.

"*Basic Enchantment Theory*? A good book to put anyone to sleep," Adair said, handing it back to Anara. "I've read it at least a dozen times, and—though finding it disappointingly short—was quick to fall asleep as I thumbed through its pages. The appendix is truly the meat of the tome, and even less interesting than the main section."

"I want to study to become an enchantress," Anara blurted out as she clutched the book to her chest. Mistress Adair nodded as if that was what she expected. "I'm sorry, Mistress Adair. I, uh, I know I'm up past curfew."

"True," Mistress Adair said and sat down on the chair beside the one Anara was using. "As a novice, you'll probably be expected to scrub the pots tomorrow because of it, but seeing as how you've already broken that rule for the night why not sit with me a while."

"Yes, Headmistress," Anara said, curtsying with improved grace, and sat back down.

"I was impressed with your performance at the celebration tonight," Mistress Adair said as she looked over the stack of books left behind by a courtesan earlier in the day. The titles all sounded medical in nature.

"Thank you," Anara said, unsure where the conversation was headed.

"I haven't seen a woman as graceful as you in a long time, especially on her first assignment," Mistress Adair continued.

"But?" Anara had heard this tone before, simultaneously approving yet disproving, from the priests at the orphanage.

"You need to learn to look them in the eyes and *return* the desire," Mistress Adair said. "That young man, Joshua Kentaine, was entranced by you. Couldn't you tell?"

"I'm only seventeen, Headmistress. I did not..."

"He would not have done anything," Adair interrupted, shaking her head even though she had an understanding tone. "And one year's difference is nothing, ten years is nothing, no amount of time between you means anything to a courtesan. Besides, you'll have your own coming of age soon enough. Tonight was more than a test to see if you could perform your expected duties."

"It was to see if I could step out of my cage," Anara said, looking down at the book. "I'm sorry, Headmistress. I just... when he looked at me it felt like... it embarrassed me. I've never thought someone would want to look at me. At *Wentworth's* it was bad if people noticed you, it meant you were probably misbehaving, or someone was blaming you for their own misbehavior."

"I know," Adair said gently, putting her arm comfortingly around Anara's shoulder. "But that is all in here," she said, gently pressing a finger against the middle of Anara's forehead. "Your cage, as you called it, is in your mind. People outside your cage don't see you the way you do. Not everyone judges strictly by appearance."

"How do you *know*?"

"I've been with my fair share," Adair answered, laughing a little. "Even men are at the whims of their emotions, though they will deny it, and troubled by doubts and concerns, though they will deny that as well."

"I know that, but how do you *know* which ones are and which ones aren't judging you by how you look alone?"

"Well, to start with, where did Joshua look at you?"

"What!" Anara's eyes opened widely in protest. He had looked *all* over her.

"Where did he focus his attentions?"

"My... eyes?" Anara guessed. She had caught Joshua's eyes exploring the rest of her as well, he had kept bringing his own brown eyes to look into hers each time, though.

"Correct, and do you know what a person's eyes are?"

She knew they were what people perceived the world with, but probably not in the context Mistress Adair was referring to, so Anara shook her head.

"They're windows to a person's intent," Mistress Adair explained. "If you can see into a person's heart, and learn to read the words unspoken there, it is easy to know who is and is not going to intentionally hurt you. When I met with Kentaine I saw in his eyes loyalty and compassion. True, lust *was* present, but tempered and controlled by empathy; lust by itself should merit caution. When another has seen your heart, and you have seen theirs, you can know that they have seen you as a person. Not as some object of desire to be used and thrown aside."

"That sounds like love," Anara said, raising her eyebrow at Mistress Adair. "We can't afford to love; it is one of the rules of being a courtesan."

Mistress Adair laughed as she had in the carriage. It was so lighthearted that Anara found herself smiling as well.

"True, a burden sometimes, but true."

"Like with you and Master Brenton?"

"Now you presume too much," Mistress Adair failed to hide a quick smile, though she did not outright deny her assumed feelings for the head driver. "Just think about what I said," Mistress Adair stood up, placing a hand on Anara's shoulder. "And don't stay up *too* late. You have dance in the morning."

"Yes, Headmistress," Anara dejectedly said. She had forgotten about dance, bringing her attention to how sore her feet were from being on them all night. Heeled shoes wore out her calf muscles and the arches of her feet, not to mention the way the back dug into her heel. After Mistress Adair disappeared into the empty halls of the Inner Sanctum, Anara opened the book again with a yawn, intending to read and thought better of it. She closed the book before taking it with her to her room so she did not have to find it again. It was against the rules, but who would know? None of the other courtesans were currently studying enchantments.

Anara raced to the bath the following morning before any of the other novices arrived and quickly washed her hair so she could get back to her book before she needed to attend dance. As always, the water was warm from the heat boxes in the walls, even though the air was cold now that winter had truly come. She rushed from the bath without properly drying her hair and up to her room before taking the book back to the library. She settled down with it in the same seat as the night before. Surprisingly there were already a few courtesans in the library studying their own chosen fields and wearing the sheer robes of the stations. The different groups tended to stick together out on the open floor where tables allowed for studying.

"I thought I'd find you here," Lena sighed, sitting in the chair Adair had used and picking up one of the books that had been left in the pile. "You aren't supposed to take books to your room you know."

"How did you..." Anara started and frowned at Lena when the woman smiled. "You didn't know, did you?"

"I won't tell. Your devious plan to undermine the temple is safe with me," Lena smirked.

"I won't do it again, I've grown since *Wentworth's*," Anara said. "I'll just leave them out on the table like you."

"What?" Lena acted aghast at the notion and winked at Anara. "These aren't *my* books; they just happen to be the ones I was looking for is all. I think you should aim better next time, you missed my lips with that kiss of yours."

"Mistress Adair saw them," Anara informed her, shifting uncomfortably from being confronted. Part of her had hoped Lena would let it go. The idea of actually *kissing* Lena, not just on the cheek, lingered. "Last night."

KYLE K. OATES

"Now you're just trying to avoid what happened," Lena laughed. "You'd have to break curfew to know these were here. I'm onto you, Mistress Swift. You won't catch me off guard so..."

"Good morning, Mistress Weston," Mistress Adair interjected as she appeared suddenly from behind a bookcase. "I have been looking for *Herbs and Botanical Remedies for Head Pains*. You wouldn't happen to have seen it lying around the library somewhere, would you? I can't seem to find it in the appropriate section."

"*Maybe*, Headmistress," Lena said and blindly reached for one of the books in her stack. "Oh, would you look at that," Lena laughed nervously. "It seems someone *carelessly* left a book out last night before going to an unexpected assignment in Aederon City."

Anara hid her smirk behind her book.

"I see Mistress Swift's influence is rubbing off on you, Mistress Weston," Mistress Adair said sternly, furrowing her brow and taking the book from Lena. "After midday meal, make sure you join her in cleaning duty for Anara's own lapse of judgment last night with breaking curfew." Mistress Adair slowly walked away as Lena glared at Anara, silently mouthing the words *'you could have warned me.'* Anara rolled her eyes knowing she *had* warned Lena. "Oh, and report after evening meal as well, Anara. Lena is correct, books remain in the library at all times. You would not want the *only* copy of *Basic Enchantment Theory* to be accidentally ruined by someone who spilled their evening wine on it, would you?" Lena grinned as Anara blushed at the punishment.

"Sorry," Anara mumbled once Mistress Adair was out of earshot.

"Well, at least you have double duty," Lena said, looking in Mistress Adair's direction. "And I really needed that book..." Lena sighed and went back to the medicine section. Anara returned to where she had left off the night before.

Much like any art, enchantments can be broken down into base components. Just as a

98

painter needs a brush to apply paint, paint to apply to a canvas, and canvas to use as a medium of their craft so does an enchanter need a medium and tools to apply an enchantment to the medium. In this analogy, the brush is the runes. The paint is the ingredients. And the canvas is the material which is being enchanted.

Runes, as used by Ilionans, are related to the ancient texts of the gods that convey the energy from the elemental planes used in the enchantment. If you refer to the appendix provided within this book you will see some of the most commonly used runes in Ilionan enchanting today. Modern script, though limitless in its descriptors, does not work in crafting enchantments and must instead use the runes of ancient Iliona. New runes, for this reason, are unlikely to exist.

Ingredients are a compound of two miscible substances and a solute. Like the enchantments, the ingredients are divided into the four lesser gods. Water, fresh and preferably as pure as possible, can be used in conjunction with two different salts to fuel a Hydramantic Enchantment. Oil, with two different metals in powder or shaved form, for Pyromantic. Quicksilver, with up to two different gemstone powders for Geomantic. Finally, alcohol, preferably highly distilled, and two different essences of herbs are used in the production of Aeromantic Enchantments. As a side note that must be given, any number of these ingredients are known to be hazards and can result in bodily injury if swallowed, inhaled, or mixed incorrectly.

As stated earlier, an enchanter's canvas is the material to be enchanted and is easier or more difficult to enchant given its composition.

Anara turned the page and found the index of runes. She blinked, trying to determine if pages had been torn from the book or not. She quickly flipped through the last hundred pages or so, only to see more and more of the index before snapping the books shut. Disappointingly short was an understatement. The book was thoroughly underwhelming.

"That's it?"

"Can you believe that?" Lena asked, setting down *Herbs and Botanical Remedies to Head Pains*. "She just took it to put it back."

"There's only *two* pages!" Anara said, showing Lena in exasperation. "How am I supposed to get a basic understanding of *how* to enchant something with only *two* pages?"

"Try reading the other books on it," Lena smirked, frustrating Anara. Lena *had* to know there was only one in the library. Though, as encouraging as she was for Anara to learn, Lena *did* have very little interest in enchantments herself. Perhaps she never actually perused the enchantment section.

"There's only *one* book in the entire library about this! How is this *Basic Enchantment Theory*?" Anara shook her head. "All it has done is tell me enchantments exist. I already knew that! I didn't even understand some of the words. Ezebre's mischief is what this is! How is this supposed to help *anyone*?"

"Let me see," Lena said, taking the book from Anara. Lena turned the page a moment later. "Miscible means it can be mixed into something, and the solute is that something." Anara glared at Lena. That answered at least two of her questions but Lena did *not* have to be so condescending about it. "Well, as I see it, why not experiment yourself?" Lena asked. "Maybe that's why we have so many more glow lamps than anything else? We don't have quicksilver to make what I assume prevents glassware from breaking. Why would *anyone* powder gemstones? But we have oil, used in our regular lamps, and I bet Master Brenton has metal shavings of some kind in his workshop from when he has to fix the carriages."

"Maybe," Anara took the book back and quickly found the appendix section regarding Pyromantic Runes. There were a lot of them, and some looked like those on the heat boxes, but without being able to actually see the glow lamp because of the flames obscuring the metal inside the glass box she could not tell which ones they were.

"Maybe that's why only a few courtesans ever get to practice this art," Lena shrugged. "You have to show natural talent before the Headmistress invests the funds to get you started."

"I need to get to dance," Anara said, feeling terribly disappointed. Only *one* book that ridiculously contained only *two* pages of actual information.

"Don't give up, Anara," Lena said as she gave the book back. "Remember the sword?"

Anara did, and that was part of the problem. How could she start with *nothing* and end up making something like that? Luckily the exertion of dance cleared Anara's mind and she made her way down to the storeroom after. One of the hoarders approached her as she was looking through the different oils.

"Can I help you, novice?" Mistress Caidrill asked. Anara turned around. Oddly, Caidrill's appearance was very plain for a courtesan, but that may have been because Caidrill rarely bothered with makeup as the courtesan did daily. Caidrill probably thought it was wasteful if she was not going out or attending clients in the Outer Sanctum.

"I'm looking for oil," Anara said.

"Vegetable oil, sesame oil, coconut oil," Anara raised an eyebrow at that, she had never heard of a coconut before, "or bathing oils? We have fresh rose oil if you are tired of the lavender that is normally in the bath."

"Oil... er... oil. What is used in lamps?" Anara asked, not knowing what kind it was.

"Whale oil," Caidrill nodded. "Rare, cheaper than a glow lamp to start mind you but consumable. Better requisition a glow lamp since it won't waste anything. Those come and go daily so you'll likely get one within the week."

"I don't want it for lighting," Anara said. *Gods, was Caidrill always so tall?* The woman seemed to loom over her as if she were as tall as a man. Not any man, but someone like the

Kentaine boy. A soldier. She even held a switch like a club, and Anara hoped it was just to scare any courtesan caught stealing supplies. It would probably sting like Thade's touch given the bulge of Caidrill's biceps and forearms. Aside from her masculine demeanor, she was definitely a woman beneath her sheer black robe and the black keyhole dress beneath it, and the shape of her waist was accentuated by the violet sash tied around it. "T-to make a new glow lamp."

Mistress Caidrill looked her up and down, narrowing her eyes suspiciously.

"In the future, ask first," Caidrill said and disappeared behind the shelf. The hoarder returned a moment later carrying a large jar of clear, yellowish liquid. The oil was thicker than the cooking oils familiar to Anara. "Be careful with it. The last enchantress didn't use much more than a few ounces to make six glow boxes. Can't tell you the proper ratio of ingredients and I never bothered asking where she was getting the metal. If you run out before you figure out the ratio don't bother asking for more. Like I said, it isn't cheap. My brother risks his life and limb to go out on the Crystal Ocean to get this stuff."

"Thank you," Anara said humbly, taking the priceless jar and cradling it. Only one jar to get it right. "I never knew you had a brother. What is his name?"

"Bjork," Mistress Caidrill answered, and when she smiled Anara could see how she was beautiful. Any woman would envy Caidrill's straight, white teeth and anyone would find it stunning.

"Thank you again," Anara said, curtsying without letting go of the jar.

"Take care, novice," Caidrill said as Anara made her way back upstairs.

Three months and she still *doesn't know my name*, Anara thought and nearly laughed. She would have if she were not carrying such precious cargo.

Anara sat back down in the library, this time at one of the tables, with a sheet of parchment and *Basic Enchantment Theory*, browsing through the pages of Pyromantic Runes for anything that sounded like it might cause a glow lamp's illumination. She settled on six she would try called *Spark, Cinder, Ember, Fire, Flame,* and *Inferno.* Inferno would be last; it sounded more destructive than the others. After transcribing them she went up to the blade dancer balcony, shivering as she looked out over the snow-covered grounds. Somehow, she had to get to the carriage storage at the edge of the forest and talk to Nicholas. It was the biggest rule she was likely to break while living at *Lussena's Temple* and that did not sit well with her stomach. Courtesans were not allowed outside of the grounds except on assignment. They were picked up just outside of the Outer Sanctum and dropped off at the same place.

"What're you doing up here? It's f-f-freezing," Lena muttered and stepped up beside Anara with her arms tightly around her robe.

"I need to see Nicholas about metal shavings," Anara said, each word bringing a puff of condensation in the light of midday. It really *was* cold but she had been so focused on her target she had not noticed. Lena pulled Anara close to her, shivering like a wet animal, as they looked out over the grounds. "I came up here to see if there was a secret way out of the Inner Sanctum to go visit where the drivers stay. I assume Mistress Adair wouldn't be too keen on the idea of me visiting him. I wonder," Anara said, smiling as she looked at the white snow. It was almost perfectly flat except for an indentation leading from the temple out towards the stables. It seemed... unnatural somehow. "You said this used to be a mine, right? How are you coming along with finding that hidden level beneath the hospital ward?"

"It-t d-d-d-doesn't exist," Lena stuttered through the chattering of her teeth. No, the hospital ward would likely be too deep to cause any evidence to appear at ground level. Anara felt like she could *see* the earth and the tunnel buried beneath it the more she focused on the indentation. She could imagine the ground there settling around the tunnel there over time. There *had* to be something there. The contours of the land around it just ended abruptly along that too-flat path of snow. But if there was one, and it *wasn't* in the hospital ward, then that line should lead directly to the bath.

"Did you check the floor above it for any secrets?"

"Of c-c-course not," Lena's laugh was jittery with her shivering. "It w-was a mine, why w-w-wouldn't it go d-deeper?"

"I don't know. Follow me," Anara said, pulling Lena and almost slipping on the icy planks of the balcony. The two hurried down the spiral stairs, nearly colliding with a few other courtesans, as they raced to the bath house. Anara pushed open the door and looked around. It was empty; a rarity since there were so many novices and courtesan living at *Lussena's Temple*. Each chapter had a turn with the bath, starting with the novices in the early morning and ending with the Blade Dancers at night.

"How many courtesans are in each chapter?" Anara asked, counting the pegs the women used to hang their robes.

"Twenty-eight. We have twenty-nine novices, including you. Which is odd," Lena answered, chuckling at her own unintended pun, as Anara slowly walked around the room.

"Why is it odd? Beyond the obvious, I mean."

"Because we only have room for twenty-eight in the any of the chapters," Lena answered. "That's why you were put up in a craftswoman's room. We already had twenty-eight novices."

"And the chapters have different bath schedules, right? So, none of them overlap, right?"

"What are you getting at, Anara?"

"Then why are there twenty-nine pegs for robes?" Anara stopped at the middle peg at the back of the room. Anara had never noticed before since each peg was taken when the novices bathed. It made sense to have enough for all the *expected* novices but not an extra one.

"So, what? There's an extra peg," Lena laughed. "Maybe it just balanced the room."

"You can balance a room with an even number just as easily, possibly more so," Anara said and pulled on the peg. It refused to move.

"See..." Lena stopped as Anara pulled harder. The silvery pole gave way and shifted down slightly. "You broke it!"

Slowly the wall, or a section of it, appeared to pull back. The seams Anara had assumed were made during the laying of the large stones used to fortify the room deepened with the receding wall. After moving back several inches the stone pulled to the side, revealing a dark passage that led the same direction as the indentation in the snow. It was all surprisingly quiet given how much the stone must weigh.

"It does exist," Lena whispered, looking into the pitch black. "I knew it! I knew it! A secret room! Where does it go?"

"Towards the stables," Anara said, guiding the still exposed peg back into position. When Anara took a step back, the secret door closed in the reverse of it opening until it was flush with the rest of the wall. "I suspect it is an emergency escape."

"What?" Lena asked, resting her hand on the peg. It did not budge, so even if a robe *had* been placed on it nothing would have happened. "Why would we need an escape route?"

"How many entrances does *Lussena's Temple* have?"

"One through the Outer Sanctum," Lena said, and realization lit up her face. "What if we were attacked, or the Outer Sanctum was burning or we couldn't *get* to the Outer Sanctum? Why wouldn't Mistress Adair tell us about this? It seems important to know in an emergency."

"Maybe she doesn't know? Maybe this wasn't always a courtesan house, or she doesn't want us sneaking out. Don't tell me you aren't tempted."

"Of course, I'm tempted. It isn't like the other side isn't being watched, if you're right," Lena said as they made their way back around the bath. "Why aren't you going now?"

"Because I'm expected at *History of Aederon Nobility* soon and *Arts of Seduction* after that," Anara hissed when they stepped out into the hall. "My free day is tomorrow, I'll go then."

"That's too bad, I'm on duty in the Outer Sanctum tomorrow," Lena said, frowning as they made their way up and back to the classes.

VII

SHADOWS

I just want to go outside.

Miranda awoke with a start. The echo of this intimately frequent thought about her own life was unnerving to hear voiced by someone else. She looked around but no one was in the room. She blinked, leaning back slowly as her heart raced and tried to remember if it had been her dream that woke her.

If I go outside I'll feel better again, I promise, the voice continued even though Miranda was fully awake.

"I thought you said you wouldn't talk to me again until it was time," Miranda grumbled. It had been months since the flickering lights had agreed to help kill her mother. It seemed more like a dream than a memory now.

I just want to go outside.

As the voice pleaded with her, Miranda realized it was not the same tone as before but rather that of a young boy. *Tone* was not the right word since there was no voice, but it did not feel like the one before. The pattern was wrong and the voice seemed to have a better understanding of Ilionan language. At the same time, it held a certain briskness of youth. The voice before was more knowledgeable of the world and seemed to choose its words more carefully. Not only that, but Miranda did not *hear* the words. They were thoughts, much like her own, but not hers at the same time.

"Then just go," Miranda said, looking pointedly at the curtained window. It was still dark, but not as dark as night. She approached the opening and peeked through the slit in the curtains. Snow fell lightly, blanketing the grounds of her family's estate. The city of Crossroads was still visible in the light flurry, the inviting glow of fireplaces framed by some of the distant windows. Wisps of smoke curled from chimneys as the city's residents burned wood to keep warm. Strange to think people burned wood when they could just use a heat box. Burning wood had to be a terribly inefficient way to keep warm.

If I go outside I'll feel better again, I promise.

"You already said that," Miranda mumbled, stepping away from the window. It was cold outside, and even the heat boxes below her bed were not enough to keep the windows warm against the encroaching chill.

I just want to go outside.

"Go outside, then! Gods, you sound like Ester when she's ill," Miranda fumed, walking over to her vanity. She began brushing her long hair, using her hand to gather more manageable amounts of it as the fine bristles straightened tangles she had gotten during the night.

If I go outside I'll feel better again, I promise.

Miranda clenched her jaw and slapped the brush down on the table. She leaned over, looking closely into her mirror but all she saw were her green eyes. The flickering consciousness was not there.

I just want to go outside.

"Either go outside or be quiet!" Miranda yelled, looking into her eyes as if she were reprimanding her own reflection. Each thought of the new voice seemed to press on her mind like the headaches she would occasionally get. She waited a moment, realizing she was yelling at herself, and nearly laughed at the absurdity. The rest of the cycling thought did not continue. She breathed out, slowly, and went back to brushing her hair. Miranda stood, slipping out of her nightgown and into a plush robe before leaving her room. Miranda yawned, stretching her arms back, and had to hastily pull the robe back up as she walked into the bath. Ariel was there, filling the large porcelain tub lined with fiery orange copper.

"Miranda!" Ariel stood up, almost dropping her bucket, and looked her stepdaughter up and down. "You startled me."

"I am sorry," Miranda said, folding her arms beneath her breasts. The tattoo still itched a little, but that could have just been in her mind as well. It had been a few months since the Harvest Festival. "Did you wake up late, mother? Are you ill?"

"No, dear," Ariel laughed, pouring out the last of the water. Three other empty buckets stood beside the tub. "You're just up early. Are you feeling well? You look rather pale."

"I... had a bad dream, and I'm always pale. If you'd let me outside, I'd..." Miranda paused to pinch the bridge of her nose as if she were fighting off a migraine. She realized the boy's thoughts were actually her own as Ariel bent to pick up the buckets. "Let me help you with that."

"No, no, I manage quite well, dear," Ariel said, deftly juggling all four. "I don't think Cassandra would much approve of you doing housework, let alone doing housework in naught but a bath robe."

"Then I must insist, Mother," Miranda said, taking two of the containers. "Besides, there is *a lot* that Cassandra does not approve of." Miranda smiled as she followed Ariel downstairs to the well at the center of the mansion's foundation. Like the upper two floors, the basement was well lit with glow lamps but was colder since heat boxes were reserved for upstairs. It took three more trips to fill the deep basin in the bath.

The entire mansion was surprisingly still and quiet this early in the morning, and admittedly more serene without Ester constantly underfoot and Cassandra following her around barking orders. Miranda felt time languidly unfurling instead of feeling an anxious panic to avoid one argument and the next. She wondered if that was a part of why Ariel did not mind doing the tasks normally expected of a servant.

"Where's the heat box for the bath?" Miranda asked as her last bucket splashed into the tub. "I can fetch it for you."

"Better not, dear," Ariel said, patting her on her back. "If not handled carefully you can burn yourself. Cassandra would strip *my* hide and wear it as a coat if you were to get any scars because

The EVENING BLADE - EDGE OF AWAKENING

you were generous enough to help me. Just wait here and stay out of sight while I go get it." Miranda slipped out of her robe and tested the water, instantly pulling back at the chill that ran up her foot. She shivered; now that she had stopped exerting herself, the air felt cold despite the room's warmth as her sweat evaporated from bare skin. Several moments later Ariel returned with a bundle of towels in her arms that she set down with a loud thump on the stone floor of the bath. Ariel grunted, pushing the bundle beneath the tub and uncovering the top. Her stepmother stood up, panting, and leaned against the wall opposite Miranda.

"You know, Miranda," Ariel said after she had a moment to catch her breath. "I've wondered where you learned all the curses you scream at your mother?"

Miranda grinned, testing the water with her left hand. It was *still* freezing cold. Apparently, heat boxes did not warm things instantly.

"Cassandra, of course," Miranda answered. "She has the mouth of a... well, of someone who swears a lot."

"A sailor? Yes, I suppose she does. It is why I tend to drink heavily whenever Morgan is home," Ariel agreed and Miranda smiled even wider. "But you don't really want to be like Cassie, do you? So why use her language?"

Miranda opened her mouth to answer but no words came to her. She had never thought of it that way.

"That is a good point, Mother," Miranda confessed.

"I suggest that next time Cassandra screams at you to just keep your composure. Don't scream back."

"But screaming back makes her even angrier."

"And it makes you even angrier as well. Keeping your wits about you, however..." Ariel winked knowingly and Miranda suddenly realized *why* Ariel only ever answered Cassandra calmly. "She can't escalate her screaming, because you aren't, so she is rather at a loss about what to do, and usually just storms off. You'll win a great deal more arguments that way." Miranda grinned, picturing herself handling the next conflict with her mother using this newfound tactic...

Where is that bloody surgeon!

I just want to go outside. If I go outside I'll feel better again, I promise.

"Not *another* one," Miranda cursed, feeling two migraines echoing against each other with the two voices. "And that whiner is back too?"

"What are you talking about?" Ariel asked, raising an eyebrow at Miranda.

"What?" Miranda asked, trying to focus on Ariel's words while the two, distinctly separate voices were repeating in her head.

Where is that bloody surgeon!

"Are you sure you're feeling well, Miranda?" Ariel asked, placing a hand on her forehead.

I just want to go outside. If I go outside I'll feel better again, I promise.

"I'm... I'm fine," Miranda said. "I just... I could use a moment to clear my head."

Where is that bloody surgeon!

Go away! Miranda thought. *Both of you!* She took a deep breath, expecting them to return but they did not. She smiled and looked at Ariel, who had one of her eyebrows raised, appearing more curious than concerned. Ariel was not nearly as blessed by beauty as Miranda or her birth mother, but she was not homely. Her father's wives were both lovely, but Cassandra was on another plane of existence compared to Ariel. Ariel's eyebrows were a little bushy for a courtly woman and she had a large mole just above the left eye that drew attention despite her generous sprinkling of freckles, and her curves were straighter as opposed to hourglass.

"Should I call a priest?"

"I'm not certain the gods can help me, Mother," Miranda said, testing the water again. *Finally*, it was warm.

"I could fetch a Priestess of Malef if you'd like. I am certain Cassandra would be least likely to approve of that," Ariel suggested as if that were a perfectly acceptable response.

If Miranda's studies of the orders were true. The priestess would be more likely to try to fornicate with Miranda than she was to be of any help. Of course, *that* would probably cause Cassandra to die on the spot. Her blood daughter a vixen who found solace in the folds of other women would be sure to cause Cassandra's heart to fail. Miranda felt the corners of her mouth turning up into a smile at the idea.

"I'll seriously consider that offer, Mother," Miranda said as she slipped beneath the water's surface. It was still a bit cool, but the heat box would warm it up to its usual temperature eventually.

"Morning meal will be ready once you are done here," Ariel said, placing a towel on the table beside the tub and hanging up Miranda's robe on the door.

"Thank you, Mother," Miranda sighed and dipped beneath the surface of the water. When she came back up, Ariel had gone.

Today's cleansing oil smelled of jasmine, a very rare scent since it only grew in Miandrelle thousands of leagues south of Iliona. The maps in the mansion's study put the Tulien kingdom south of the Endless Waste which meant the waste was not actually endless. Miranda frowned, remembering her disappointment at that.

"Why is it the Endless Waste if it ends, Father?" Miranda had asked when she was five. Ariel, the heiress of the Shaw Estate south of Fort Stern, had yet to meet Morgan.

"Because it *is* endless, Miranda," Morgan said, sitting on the floor beside his daughter. "Sand, white as bone from *Soleanne's* light as far as the eye can see. That is what the Endless Waste is like."

"But it ends. See? Right here," Miranda said, pointing to the border between Miandrelle and the Endless Waste.

"Oh, my!" Morgan gasped, taking the atlas from her. "You're right! My little explorer has found the end of the Endless Waste."

"Papa," Miranda giggled as Morgan placed the Atlas down and began to tickle her.

"Miranda, if you've finished your studies and found time to play, it is best you retire for the night," Cassandra said as she sat, staring out the study's window towards Crossroads. "Father and I have a big day tomorrow and can't have you running about."

"But I don't want to, Mommy," Miranda frowned, running her small hand over the still open atlas.

"Mother's right," Morgan said, letting out a long sigh. "It is late, princess, time to go to bed."

Miranda smiled at the fond memory, cut short by Cassandra's interruption. She slipped deeper into the bath until only her eyes were above the water. She blinked, staring at the flat, mirror-like surface from this angle. *Is this what the Crystal Ocean looks like?* she mused, relaxing her arms so they gradually floated to the surface. Ripples radiated outward as her hands broke the surface and threatened to splash into her eyes.

If I die, I won't see Ishan's face again.

Miranda bolted upright with the new pain in her skull, spluttering on water from being caught off guard. The new thought was distinctly female even though there was no real voice to it. The first intruder of her mind had felt like a child; the second, a man older than her father; now, a woman Miranda's own age.

Where is that bloody surgeon! She could almost see the man leaning against a fallen tree, encircled by blurred faces, a lumberjack axe resting nearby. His leg was mangled beyond saving and Miranda felt sick at the sight of so much gore. Strips of tattered flesh clung limply to blood-slicked wood that was splintered at a gruesome angle. No, not wood. It was the bone of his leg that had pushed through his flesh. Blood had pooled beneath him amid his tortured screams, staining the exposed tree roots and snow red before seeping into the ground. It was apparent to Miranda not even a surgeon had any chance of saving him, only one of the Order of Light's healers, but when the surgeon arrived it was too late. The lumberjack was already dead.

I just want to go outside. If I go outside I'll feel better again, I promise. A little boy about Ester's age, broke Miranda's heart to pieces, forcing unwanted tears to fall. She had no idea *who* the boy was, but he suffered up until the moment his voice first appeared in Miranda's head. He was bedridden since the first snow of the season, and deathly pale with matted brown hair against his clammy skin. He was painfully thin with an uneaten bowl of soup beside his bed. Such a small bed, such a watery bowl of soup. *How can people live like that?* Miranda's thought intruded on the scene. Two people sat beside him and Miranda could feel the love the little boy had for them. The love he had for his parents. But love would not save him. Miranda knew he was already dead.

If I die, I won't see Ishan's face again. A young woman, plainly dressed in fabrics so coarse Miranda would have screamed at how they itched, lay in a forgotten alley. Her face, though bruised and bloodied, would have been remarkable. Snow piled up around her exposed legs from a slight breeze. She was savagely beaten just before dawn while walking home from Ishan's birthday, then cruelly discarded in a crumpled heap. Ishan was twenty and one now, and he had proposed to her that night. Her last thoughts had been of him.

Miranda was stunned by how two strange men could be so cruel! She was not dressed like Cassandra, showing off her tits for all men to see! The coarse dress barely even revealed her feminine curves, yet they still had attacked her. Violated her. Left her dazed and bleeding to die from exposure in the early morning as blessed warmth rose with the smoke from the chimneys surrounding her.

"What in Thade's Abyss is going on?" Miranda cried out, tears falling for the strangers' misfortune as much as for the throbbing pain between her temples. Her heart raced in the icy grip of terror at what was happening to her.

I just want to go outside.

If I die, I won't see Ishan's face again. Miranda gasped, trying to catch her breath from their anguish.

If I go outside I'll feel better again, I promise.

"It's getting a little crowded in here," Miranda growled. "Please, I don't want this. I don't want your pain!"

Where is that... Ishan's face again... I promise.... surgeon!... I just want to see Ishan's bloody face again... If I die, I'll feel better again, I promise...

Miranda pressed her palms to her temples and curled up in the tub. *Shut up!* she thought and the voices abruptly ceased. Miranda remained still, panting heavily as if she had attempted to outrun the visions. Despite the warm bath, she felt chilled from the last jumbled words spoken by the young boy and woman. Her throat was dry as she sat, hoping it was done.

"Maybe I *should* see a priest if *Cassandra* would let me. I must be going insane," Miranda said, moaning as she leaned back against the tub. Her head felt like it was trying to split apart. "Please, Fiel, don't let it happen again."

Miranda ached all over and decided to get out. She had hoped to relax in a bath but instead she felt worse than when she got in. Her legs gave out just as she slipped out of the bath, barely catching herself before her knees struck the hard, stone floor. A sudden image of the man's mangled leg filled her vision and she vomited into the water. Miranda rolled onto her back, exhausted, yet wide awake.

"This is all because of Cassandra," Miranda growled, covering her eyes with her right forearm and covering the tattoo with her left hand. "She did something to me. Hollowed me out to make room, like that voice said. To make room for what? These voices?" Miranda sat up feeling the warmth of rage in her gut as she wrapped the towel around her. "I have to stop Cassandra." Miranda quietly made her way through the halls until she was near the kitchen, hesitating outside the door upon hearing conversation.

"... voices, Morgan," Ariel said. "You were right to forbid Cassandra from marking Miranda. The bitch left it unfinished. The gateway to the abyss was left open and she's hearing it. She'll hear *all* of it in time."

"I know what an unfinished bonding does, Ariel," Morgan snapped and Miranda held her fist to her chest.

Father knows, Miranda thought, tears of relief welled up in her eyes. *He'll stop this, he loves me,* Miranda thought, biting her lower lip and clutching the towel to her chest. *Just as much as Ester because he always has presents for both of us.*

"But Cassandra has a point. Miranda is twenty years old now. The ritual may be the only way we can be ready in time." That was not what Miranda expected him to say. *He agrees with whatever Cassandra is doing to me?* Miranda fought back panic.

"Time, you subject your daughter to this for *time*! Time to raise the Undying? He has waited over a millennium, so he can wait a few more years until Miranda comes into her power naturally. Until she is properly welcomed into the sect by the twelve."

"Listening to things you shouldn't be?" Cassandra said from behind. Miranda jumped and yelped out in surprise. Miranda spun to look at her mother's stern eyes with a hint of a smug smile at the corners of her mouth.

"You bitch," Miranda shook her head, glaring at her mother. "You did this to me."

"Is that you, Miranda?" Morgan asked, sweetly as ever. It sounded like sugar coated venom.

"Ariel," Cassandra said, sweeping pretentiously into the kitchen. Miranda followed close behind her. "There seems to be a mess in the bath. I think Miranda may have taken ill. Perhaps she should be confined to her bed for a few weeks to make certain she gets better."

"I'm not sick," Miranda insisted, half expecting another poor soul to barge into her thoughts. "I just slipped."

"And decided to empty into the bath what remained in your stomach of last night's meal?" Cassandra sounded amused.

"I slipped and hit my stomach on the rim of the tub, Cassandra," Miranda said, trying to conceal her irritation. It was harder than Ariel made it seem. "If you had let me finish. I was coming here to inform Ariel of my accident before getting dressed."

"Are you all right?" Morgan asked, standing up as if he really cared. *He might*, Miranda thought, hoping she had judged him too harshly.

"Yes, Father," Miranda said, smiling at him. "Though I am a bit hungrier this morning for it. If you'll excuse me from this embarrassment, I'll go throw on something more suitable for morning meal."

"Of course," Morgan said.

Miranda slipped out of the room and started for the stairs. She paused just around the corner and listened to her parents.

"How much did she hear?" Morgan asked coldly. He seemed as if he had no real concern for Miranda's suffering at all, even if he *had* been displeased with the tattoo a few months earlier. He had accepted what Cassandra had done.

"Too much," Cassandra answered.

"We wouldn't have to do it this way if you had just let her leave the mansion, Cassandra," Ariel said, her tone accusing and argumentative despite the advice she gave earlier. "Miranda would have awoken by now if she had been allowed to experience a real life instead of this pampered fantasy you gave her. I cannot imagine what she must be experiencing. Of course, the girl emptied her stomach. The worst thing she has known in this world is the bloody ordeal you put her through for that mark. The shadows of the recently departed must be terrifying her!"

"What would you have me do, Ariel?" Cassandra asked, her voice shrill and on the edge of screaming.

"Finish the mark."

"I can't, I need another vial of the ink. Bonding is Dristelli magecraft, and only *they* know the secrets of the ink to make it work. Lunarin will not be back until next year's Harvest Festival."

"She will go insane! The echoes will persist relentlessly until the mark is completed," Ariel hissed. "Given how long she has been left open to Thade's Abyss, they may never go away completely. Do something, Morgan. She is *your* daughter."

"What's done is done," Morgan said firmly, and Miranda could not listen any more. She hurried to her room as quickly and quietly as she could.

How could Father be agreeing with Cassandra? she thought as she locked her door and sat down, leaning against it.

"I'll run away," Miranda said, clutching the towel around her torso. *I can't leave Ester*, Miranda thought and she started to cry. *What if Cassandra does the same thing to her?* "I need your help," Miranda said, trying to summon the first voice. "I need to kill Cassandra *now*." No answer. "Please, at least tell me what is happening."

She is hollowing you out, the voice answered. Miranda almost laughed with annoyed relief. The voice seemed more coherent than the newer ones, but it still tended to repeat itself. At least the voice was on her side. *The mark prolongs the life. Vessel of new for soul of old.*

"I don't understand," Miranda said, leaving the towel by the door to slip into her bed.

Hollowing you out.

"Who are you? *What* are you?" Miranda asked, sitting up and idly toying with a lock of hair. "Why don't you just say the same thing over and over again like the others?"

I was K'Rania, she answered. *Queen of the Kanach.* That last part came with a heavy undertone of resignation, resentment, and regret. And rage, a boiling storm of it. Miranda had never heard of a queen named K'Rania, but Kanach was one of the few cities listed deep inside Fathen Forest on her father's maps.

"You're an N'Gochen!" Miranda squealed. She had never met anyone outside of her family, but an N'Gochen! She doubted many Ilionans had ever met an N'Gochen. "What do you look like? How are you talking to me?"

Look into my death, K'Rania answered and Miranda frowned with disappointment. K'Rania was dead, just like the other three voices earlier. Miranda was not interested in seeing someone else's demise, she did not even know how to. Earlier had been a fluke.

"I've seen enough death today," Miranda said, falling back against her pillow. "How come you can talk to me but the others barely even listen?" Miranda crossed to her vanity and sat down. The flickering lights were reflected in her eyes.

N'kesh's secrets are open to me, K'Rania answered. As she spoke the lights seemed to dance and Miranda had a vague sensation of remembering something fondly. It almost felt loving.

"Am I going insane?" Miranda asked simply.

Finish the mark, K'Rania said, but Miranda could sense apprehension.

"Will the voices drive me insane before that?"

See the deaths, know them, K'Rania answered. *Bear the mind's burden.*

"But people die every day," Miranda said, placing her head on the desk.

The dead must be close.

"How close?"

Your power is vast.

"What power," Miranda laughed, believing she must be losing grip on reality.

Stronger than the black one, isolation will ease the burden.

"I'm not isolated," Miranda said. She had been caged all her life but now she felt so exposed. Crossroads, the busiest trade city in Iliona, was not even two leagues away. Given the vision of the woman from the cramped alley of a busy city, instead of a village, she suspected she would feel every death within the distance from her family's estates to the city.

Then do not fight the voices. See them for who they are, keep them separate.

"Thank you," Miranda said and a light knock sounded at her door.

"Morning meal is ready," Ester called through the door. "Father and Mother Cassie already left for the market, so I don't get to go into town today." Miranda looked back at the mirror but K'Rania had gone. Miranda slipped into a violet, silk robe and opened her door. Ester stood there with her rabbit in one arm and a hand covering her eyes. "If you're naked put some clothes on."

"I'm not naked," Miranda said, taking Ester's hand and walking with her towards the kitchen. "What is there to eat?"

"Momma made pancakes and sausage," Ester said. "She tried making shapes with the batter again, but they all look like blobs. Call them cows; I think that was what she was trying to make."

"I'll let you have the cows," Miranda said as they walked into the large kitchen. The air smelled of spices from the sausage and fresh, sweet bread of the pancakes. Ariel was piling the fluffy discs onto the serving plate in the center of the table.

"I'll bring these to the dining hall if..." Ariel stopped, looking down at the floor when she caught Miranda's eyes. Miranda had no idea what Ariel saw in them but her mother's change was drastic. Ariel's usual friendly yet proud demeanor had turned into one of shame and guilt. Her straight back was slumped with shoulders pulled in to appear small. "You're looking more and more like your mother every day, Miranda."

Miranda smiled, realizing whatever Ariel saw was putting her on edge. Ariel had probably not intended the comment to upset her. It may even be as she said, that she looked more like Cassandra, but given Miranda's disdain of Cassandra, she felt the sting of an insult.

"I'd like to think both my mothers equally influenced who I am today, but thank you, Ariel. My mother is a *very* beautiful woman after all, and I am honored you think I can compare."

"More beautiful, really," Ariel laughed nervously, and Miranda knew Ariel understood what she was doing.

"I love the *cows*, Momma," Ester said, smiling and winking at Miranda as Ester took one of the still steaming cakes from the pile and tossed it between her hands to cool it down. "You make the best pancake animals."

"We'll eat in here, Ariel, if you don't mind," Miranda said flatly, watching the woman flinch at her tone. Ariel may not agree with Cassandra's methods, but she was still a part of the plotting. It was a pity that Ariel was now caught up in the war between Miranda and Cassandra. *It can't be helped*, K'Rania thought and Miranda found herself nodding as if it had been her own. *Kill her.* Miranda blinked at that, she had no desire to kill Ariel. Only Cassandra.

"I'm sorry, Miranda," Ariel said, pulling out three stools from the back of the kitchen. She sounded sincere, but all wars had unintended casualties. The lumberjack's war against his tree had shown her that.

"Why are you sorry, Mommy?" Ester asked, pulling a pancake from the stack and stuffing half of it into her mouth.

"Yes, Ariel, why *are* you sorry?" Miranda said, filling her own plate in a more refined manner than her younger sister. Her annoyance with her father and Cassandra was spilling over to Ariel. Ariel had been opposed to the mark from what she heard, but part of Miranda felt her stepmother deserved her cold attitude. Ariel had, after all, not stopped Cassandra while she was being marked. Saying you were opposed to something meant nothing if you let it happen anyway. "I enjoyed my bath this morning. Thank you for readying it for me."

"I... uh... of course," Ariel said, bowing her head. "It was my pleasure."

"You already had a bath!" Ester gaped across the table, her mouth half full of mush. "You never get up before me."

"I think I might get up early from now on, Esty," Miranda said, tapping Ester's nose. "You learn a great many *wonderful* things in the morning."

"Indeed," Ariel said, laughing nervously. "Blueberry syrup?"

"I would love some, Ariel," Miranda said, holding up her plate as her mother poured out a generous serving. The thick, dark-blue liquid slowly seeped into the fluff of her cakes as she stared at Ariel for several moments before cutting into them.

"Me too, me too," Ester said, holding up her own plate. There were already three half-eaten 'cows' on it. "Blueberry is my favorite."

"Of course, dear," Ariel said, her demeanor switching back to that of a doting mother.

VIII

AEDERON'S ENCHANTORIUM

Nothing worked.

"Just glow already!" Anara cried out in frustration, looking closer at her creation. The runes looked identical to those in *Basic Enchantment Theory*, but all the ingredients did was stain the little wooden peg darker. This was not her first failed attempt. Dozens of similar pegs were strewn across her vanity. Wood shavings from carving runes piled on one corner, falling toward the floor like miniature landslides at the slightest bump. All of them had been the same, no matter what ratios she tried. Half oil and half metal, by weight, did not work. Two-thirds metal, one third of each kind, also failed. Nearly nine-tenths metal or oil had produced no effect either. The whale oil was nearly gone, only enough for maybe six more attempts. It frustrated her more than anything in her life. Making her dolls at *Wentworth's* had been simple compared to this.

"Maybe the shavings aren't different metals?" Lena suggested from where she reclined listlessly on Anara's bed. Lena was one of the few women at the temple that often went without something underneath the sheer robe of her chapter. If the stubborn magecraft was not enough, Lena's lack of attire constantly caused Anara's heart to race and mind to go. Fiel taught against flaunting beauty the way Lena did. Anara sighed, glancing at the red bound book at the back of her desk. The scripture of the Order of Flame, a gift Lena gave her, had conflicting ideologies with the Order of Light when it came to sexuality. Anara made a mental note to put more effort into reading the tome. She just had very little time outside of her studies and trying to figure out enchantments.

"I must be missing something. Nicholas said the red was copper and the gray was tin. They *have* to be different metals. Have you ever seen silvery copper?" Anara said, shaking her head and turning back to the dowels.

"No," Lena admitted, fondling the tails of her sash, one leg draped idly over the side of the bed so her robes exposed *everything* she had to offer. It was terribly distracting for Anara. The way Lena's delicate, pink folds glistened likely meant she was aroused, which seemed to be her usual state. Anara felt her face flush hotly with shame from her own excitement at that idea and turned quickly back to her work. Anara suspected the slave bands might influence Lena's state of arousal in some way, but she would never know. Slave bands were Raykarn enchantments, just looking at the runes and trying to compare them to Ilionan ones confused her. If there *was* something, Anara suspected she would need to wear all five to feel it. "It's getting late, Anara," Lena said, gently caressing the sheets. "Come to bed."

"I'll go to bed when you finally make your way back to your own room," Anara said half nervous and half playfully, she tried to listen to the side that wanted Lena but she still felt divided down the middle about the whole situation with the Borderlander. She pulled out a new dowel and began examining her carving. "I'm missing something... that has to be it," Anara sighed, tracing her thumb thoughtfully over the runic grooves she had etched earlier in the day. It looked identical to the pyromantic rune *Fire*.

"Maybe copper and tin don't work for the specific runes you're trying?" Lena suggested.

"It's all I have to work with," Anara shook her head. "These *have* to be the right metals for a glow lamp." Anara pulled the jar of whale oil and pouches of metal shavings toward her to measure out another attempt. *Five more tries after this*, Anara thought with growing anxiety and frustration. She carefully weighed out piles of tin and copper. She had half as much tin as copper. Anara hoped that the two metals would work if they were not in the same amounts as each other. She carefully filled an empty cleansing oil vial with the acrid whale oil. *Maybe the oil has spoiled*, she thought at the stench and dumped the metals and a drop of the orange ichor into it. Spoiled or not, it was all she had to work with. She replaced the cork and shook since stirring or shaking did not seem to matter. They both produced the same result – nothing.

She carefully poured the solution into the grooves—barely more than a drop for each rune—placing the stick down inside a crucible in case it caught fire. Both the scales and crucible had been secretly requisitioned from the hoarders over a month ago after she first used the hidden passage to the carriage barns. Technically she should have returned them, but no one had come looking for them yet so it was safe to assume no one cared; just like *Basic Enchantment Theory,* sitting on the edge of her desk. No one had mentioned the book aside from the first time when Mistress Adair found out.

Nothing happened.

"Teethed slit of Thade's whore!" Anara cried out in frustration. She picked up the dowel and held it between her palms. "Catch on fire, damn you!"

"Where did you hear *that* colorful language?" Lena laughed and Anara glowered at the woman over her shoulder. It was hard to stay angry when Lena was smiling, so Anara sighed.

"Master Brenton, I think... I can't really remember," Anara said, still clenching the dowel in one hand.

"Maybe you can talk to Mistress Adair about going into Aederon City tomorrow with the hoarders and scribes for their monthly resupply?"

"How would that help?" Anara asked, her frustration and annoyance building. The dowel felt warm in her hand but that could have just been because she was clenching it so tightly; the frustrating trinket *would* trick her like that. It infuriated her that she had not figure out *how* to enchant anything yet. *Why is it so hard? The book says this is all you need. I must have missed something.* Anara felt so angry at the little stick, part of her knew that was irrational but she just wanted to take all of her frustrations and disappointments out on it.

"You could use the opportunity to talk to a real enchanter about what might be missing," Lena suggested. "Take a few of your solutions, the more promising ones..."

"What more promising ones? They've all done the same thing," Anara said, wrinkling her nose. "Do you smell something burning?"

"Anara! Your hand!" Lena gasped, jumping up, and Anara looked down. The dowel was not just warm but on fire. She screamed, dropping the stick into the crucible, and watched as fire consumed her work. Green and blue sparks fizzled across the dowel in the shape of runes as fire spread to the grooves. "You did it!" Lena squealed, jumping enthusiastically with Anara's hands in her own. "Is your hand hurt?"

Anara continued to stare at the wood, realizing whatever she had just done was not enchanting. The runes had burned away to ash while the wood continued to smolder as Lena examined her palm. The stick was simply on fire, not enchanted, and she watched as it dimmed, turning to soft embers in the ceramic bowl.

"Not even a blister, but that's impossible," Lena murmured and Anara was suddenly aware of Lena's soft hands holding her own, an eagerness between her legs growing at the tender examinations of the other woman.

"It didn't work," Anara sighed and Lena looked into her eyes. It was incredible how beautiful her amber eyes were. Most people had brown eyes, but Lena's sparkled with a hint of orange glow similar to the carefully contained embers on her desk. "The stick just caught on fire."

"But that's promising, isn't it?" Lena smiled, kissing Anara's cheek. "At least you have *one* solution that produced different results. Did you see those sparks? I had no idea metal could burn." Anara felt her heart racing and pressed her lips together into a thin line. Lena was often so close, but something was different about her tonight.

"It is, I guess. I don't even know−" Anara stopped when Lena kissed her.

It was a quick gesture, only a peck really, but Anara pulled back from the shock of it. It had been soft, and Lena smelled marvelous. Anara took in Lena's scent with a long breath. Vanilla mixed with lavender, where Lena got *vanilla* to use on her skin and hair was one of the Borderlander's many mysteries.

"What are you doing?" Anara whispered, excitement and terror urging her to run even as she felt rooted to the spot. She could taste the sugary paint from Lena's lips as she licked her own. It tasted like honey with a bitter undertone from the dyes, but even that was pleasing knowing it had come from Lena.

"I didn't want to hear you doubt yourself again," Lena whispered back. "I've wanted to do that since I first saw you. I hope I didn't overextend my..." Anara fervently kissed her back but quickly pulled away.

"I shouldn't," Anara mumbled, blushing with guilt.

"Hush," Lena smiled, gently pushing back Anara's hair behind her ear. Lena's feather touch went down to Anara's shoulder and pulled the sleeve of her robe down over her shoulder. "The world won't end because you don't obey the words of a random book." Anara shut her eyes, a shiver of excitement coursing through her as Lena's hands slipped beneath the pink satin of her clothes to expose her breasts. Lena's lips followed closely behind, brushing her skin and stiffening her nipples as Anara felt her loose clothing slip from her body. "I love you, Anara," Lena whispered and Anara's heart raced.

"I love you too," Anara said, gasping as Lena's mouth reached her mound. Anara's legs shook as she fell back onto her bed and her thoughts were consumed by the pleasures Lena provided.

Anara opened her eyes.

She felt a loving warmth around her, but was alone in a courtyard of perfectly level stone. Six statues surrounded her, each one looking down on her as she slowly stood up. Anara half expected to be naked, remembering Lena removing her robe, but instead she wore a suit of plate and chain armor. The steel plates of the cuirass were as tight to her figure as a corset and polished to a mirror-like quality as if by a lowborn soldier who took great pride in his tools of war. Decorative, gold filigree adorned the edges where the plates overlapped and blossomed into a floral pattern that swirled around the steel cups of her breastplate. A skirt of bronze rings rattled against her thighs with each movement, and a sword ornamented her hip. Unsurprisingly, it was a blade dancer sword, but the scabbard was enchanted against pyromantic energies by the runes of hydromantic boons pounded into the leather.

"Who made this?" Anara wondered, pulling the sword free. The blade sprang to life in a white flame with blue linings at the edges. It was surprisingly light – lighter than the real blade dancer weapons she had felt at *Lussena's Temple*. The rune pattern on the blade was Ilionan with not only the pyromantic aura but an aeromantic and geomantic boon given to the blade. She did not recognize the markings that connected the three enchantments. She could feel the heat coming from the weapon and expertly slid it back into the sheath as if she had been born to fight with it. "What is this place?" Anara walked around, looking at each of the statues, trying to take in their detail but only one caught her eye.

The statue was of a woman more beautiful than any Anara had ever seen. She was carved from stone as white and pure as freshly fallen snow, and so detailed she seemed alive. She held both hands up in front of her, palms raised to the sky in a welcoming gesture as if offering something to Anara. Anara glanced at the others but they appeared to be a considerable distance away, making it difficult to distinguish more than a general shape. Three of the blurred statues were men, the other two of women, arranged in an alternating pattern balancing male and female around the courtyard.

At the center of the plaza was a hexagonal obelisk, each side seemed to be made from the same stone as the distant statues it faced with enchanted steel plates fixed to the flat planes. It was pristine except for a black, hairline cracks that extended across each face through the steel and into the stone. Surprisingly each side had the exact same fracture pattern. The crack was so dark it seemed unnatural to Anara given how bright the area was, it seemed as if light could not exist in the fracture.

"Where am I?" Anara asked, walking to the obelisk. As she drew closer to the center a dense fog circled the statues and runes of the obelisk glowed with a brilliant white light. "I'm dreaming, I know that much," Anara said. The ringing of a sword being drawn sounded behind her. She spun around to see a man, dressed in a suit of black armor, wielding an ebony blade encircled by a swirling, dark green miasma. Anara screamed, backing up into the woman with outstretched arms as she reached for her own sword only to find it gone. The armor was gone as well. Instead, she wore her tattered dress from *Wentworth's*, the skirt so short she was practically exposed to the man. He came forward, raising the sword. Anara wanted to fight; she wanted to defend herself from the attacker, but the statue wrapped its arms around her and held her still.

The hour is late, you must awaken, a voice echoed around the plaza.

The dark warrior finally reached her, plunging his blade towards her heart.

"No!" Anara gasped, sitting up in bed as *Soleanne's* light broke over the ocean's horizon and bathed her room in a comforting orange glow. Lena stirred beside her, still half asleep, one leg draped between Anara's. The images of her dream fading to nothingness as Anara gently placed her hand on Lena's leg to free herself.

"Up already?" Lena said, arching her back as she yawned and moved her head to Anara's lap. "What sort of novice gets up at first light?"

"I had... a strange dream," Anara absently began weaving her fingers through Lena's hair, the shaved side was pleasantly prickly against her inner thigh.

"What was it about?" Lena asked, furrowing her brow with concern as she looked up at Anara.

"I-I don't know," Anara shook her head. "I can't really remember. I should go find Mistress Adair."

"Then you'll go to Aederon today?" Lena asked, sitting up with a large yawn and extended stretch.

"If I can," Anara said, slipping out from underneath the sheets and moving to the vanity to tidy her hair. What *was* Lena to her now? A friend? A lover? She looked at her pile of failed enchantments and frowned. That question could wait.

"Don't be gone too long," Lena sprawled onto the bed now that she was alone.

"I'm sure I'll be gone as long as it takes," Anara said, spying Lena's robes and slipping them on when she failed to find her own.

"I knew you'd look good in my chapter's colors, *Mistress* Swift," Lena said, tucking one arm underneath a pillow and tossing it at Anara. "What am I supposed to wear if you take my robes, though?"

"Would walking around naked really be that much different?"

"Well, no, but what if a novice needed an orderly and mistook you for one, or passed me without knowing I could help? What then? Could you set a sprained ankle or apply the right salve to a cut so there would be no scar?"

"I'm sure everyone in the temple knows you by your exotic hair, Lena," Anara said, grinning to herself as she waved over her shoulder. "I'll let you know how it goes in Aederon when I get back."

"Anara!" Lena playfully whined after her as Anara slipped out of the room, making her way towards the bath. "Come back here with my clothing!"

After her bath Anara slipped into a fresh novice gown and robe. She grabbed her satchel with some vials, three etched dowels, and *Basic Enchantment Theory*, and began wandering the halls in search of Mistress Adair. After searching *both* towers, peeking into the storage room, and grabbing a morning meal from the dining hall, she finally found the headmistress crossing the courtyard to the outer sanctum with six women, three each from the scribes and caretakers.

"Headmistress," Anara called, briskly walking across the courtyard. Unfortunately, a light snow had covered it again and she nearly lost her footing several times. She really disliked the shoes of a courtesan; the high heels always made her feel like she was about to fall over as she balanced on the balls of her feet and toes. "I need to go to Aederon with the scribes and hoard...uh-caretakers." *Damned Lena, beating the chapter's other name into my head.*

"Anara, courtesans, particularly novices, are only permitted beyond the Outer Sanctum under strict circumstances," Mistress Adair said, folding her arms sternly beneath her breasts. Little clouds of condensation escaped the headmistress's lips as she spoke; otherwise, Mistress Adair showed no sign of the cold affecting her. "Those circumstances are not for you to choose, so I can hardly see how you could *need* to go to Aederon City."

"I'm sorry, Headmistress." Anara managed to keep her balance while she curtsied, panting slightly after running up from the storage rooms. "What I meant was I would like to request joining the courtesans in Aederon today."

"And why is that?" Mistress Caidrill snapped, brandishing her switch.

"I'm afraid I've gotten as far as I can on my own with understanding enchantments," Anara said as clearly as she could. "And to avoid wasting more of the supplies the caretakers have so graciously permitted me to use, I would like to get input on what I may be doing wrong from an *actual* enchanter in Aederon."

"I'm sorry, Mistress Swift," Adair sighed, shaking her head. "I'm afraid I can't permit a novice outside of the grounds..."

"If you'll pardon me, Headmistress," interjected Mistress Cadence, one of the scribes with bouncy auburn curls that framed her sharp features. "But had I known we had a prospective enchantress in our midst I would have suggested bringing the young novice sooner. It has been awhile since we have seen the funds such a courtesan can bring in through her training."

"And it *is* wasteful to try doing so blindly," Mistress Caidrill added.

"All right," Mistress Adair smiled slyly at Anara as if the headmistress had planned to let Anara go all along if she had only asked. Anara felt foolish for not trying this earlier. The weeks and ounces of oil wasted left a slightly queasy feeling in her stomach. "You've convinced me. You have my blessing, but be careful

Anara. Aederon's streets can be dangerous this time of year when food from the harvest is growing scarce, especially for a young girl... Crossroads is safer than Aederon City and even news of some unsettling deaths has reached me from that place. Take heed, novice."

"Yes, Headmistress," Anara curtsied, barely containing her grin. She shivered against the cold as she was ushered into the changing rooms of the Outer Sanctum by the other courtesans.

All of the dresses had changed since the last time she had been in these rooms. Instead of the white, silk gowns of a hostess they were thicker wool for daily use during the winter, of which she was grateful. The hostess gowns had offered little protection against the cold that night over a month ago. When Anara finished dressing as two blade dancers joined them. She waited with the other seven by the stairs leading up and out onto the roundabout where the carriages dropped off and picked up courtesans. Two spiral staircases at either end of the hall ascended to an area where they attended clients visiting for intimate companionship, as opposed to being summoned to a gala, ball, or a client's personal estate. There was no wall behind them, only columns supporting the rooms above, so a light breeze fluttered Anara's skirts and chilled her ankles. She looked back at the Inner Sanctum and thought of the warmth of her room. She wondered if Lena would be up there tonight, her cheeks flushing from more than just the cold.

"Let's get going," the tall blade dancer, Mistress Ashton, barked when the doors at the top of the stairs opened. She was, for all intents and purposes, the second in command of the courtesan house, but had very little to say to her fellow mistresses. Her fiery, red hair was always pulled back in a tight braid with an orange ribbon at the end. It was a good choice for her since it highlighted the stronger features of her face. Her jaw was wider than most women with a steeply sloped bridge to her nose. Like nearly all the people Anara had met, which was *a lot* since she lived in an orphanage before coming to *Lussena's Temple*, Mistress Ashton's eyes were brown with a very slight hint of color.

"Mornin', 'nara!" Nicholas said, winking at her as they approached. It was a secret between him and her about where she got the metal filings, though Anara suspected Mistress Adair was privy to that secret. Erin Adair seemed to know everything about everyone.

"Good morning, Master Brenton," Anara said, doing her best to curtsy. She had improved a lot in the last few months since she left *Wentworth's*.

"I've not seen you abou' much," Brenton said, his inability to act casual around her was probably enough to raise suspicion in the courtesans nearby but they kept quiet. "How's i' been in the temple?"

"You know I can't discuss what happens inside the Inner Sanctum with you," Anara sighed, following the rules with others present. She may have shared what happened with Lena the night before, at least briefly and without great detail, if she had been at the carriage barns instead of the front steps of the temple. She was excited to tell *someone*, even if the question of what Lena was to her was still uncertain. Of course, she also wanted to keep it a secret. Anara sighed, she was not usually so conflicted about the people she met.

"Tha's good ta hear," Brenton said, helping each of the women aboard. "Good ta see you to Lisa, Roxy, and Helda."

"Really, Master Brenton," Mistress Caidrill said. "It's bad enough you address us so familiarly, so you could at least get Roxy's... I mean, Roxanne's, name right."

"You aren't helping, Helda," Mistress Ashton said. "I don't understand *why* Mistress Adair puts up with you, Nicholas."

"I do, Roxanne," said Mistress Cadence, who by elimination must be Lisa. *I guess it isn't so strange that Mistress Caidrill doesn't know my name as I never bothered to learn hers in full*, Anara thought during the exchange. "I've seen her sneaking out the Outer Sanctum at night. I *wonder* where she's going."

Nicholas turned bright red beneath his winter scarf and wide-brimmed driver's hat, eliciting giggles from the three courtesans. Anara did her best to keep a straight face, but her suspicions about the older driver and the headmistress had nearly been confirmed.

"Best not be spreadin' rumors, girls," Nicholas said, clearing his throat. "You got it all wrong." He shut the door to a stronger encore of laughter, Anara included this time.

The carriage ride felt longer today than it had when she was dressed as a hostess. Looking back on that day, she realized everything had seemed so radiant as the carriage rolled past fields of snow that sparkled in the afternoon sun. Her white gown had been a welcome change after being relegated to only pink.

The carriage swayed with the bumps, rises, and falls on the dirt road as it continued northward. Three leagues was a long way to travel across frozen ground that turned to patches of sticky mud without warning. While they had visitors nearly every day at the temple, Lena said it was *much* slower during the Months of Frost and Anara suspected the state of the road was the reason.

Anara pulled back the curtain to watch the landscape roll by as the older women talked amongst themselves. The open meadows were still mostly covered in a blanket of snow. Patches of mud and dormant grass poked through now that the weather was slowly changing, reminiscent of threadbare blankets she had made her dolls out of. Cassie was stuffed in the satchel alongside vials of solutions to show the enchanters, looking like a proper doll now. Her arms and head were cut from a salmon-colored cotton while her dress was the same smooth, pink fabric as novice robes. Anara had not cut up any of her own gowns to sew it this time as the craftswomen tailors always had plenty of spare scraps. Cassie even had green buttons for eyes and a line of stitching for a mouth now. Her stuffing was raw cotton instead of straw, which was more easily shaped into a human form. Cassie was, in essence, an entirely new doll, the other one's materials having since been discarded.

The meadow turned into a forest, and their progress slowed as the patches of mud became more abundant. Nicholas even had to get down and help push the carriages along a few times, never asking the mistresses for help, which made Anara feel uncomfortable. Nicholas was working so hard to get them to

Aederon, but he seemed to hardly get any reward for it. Unless Mistress Adair saw to that as Anara suspected.

After a few hours, the forest gave way to more fields of snow and mud which would turn into fields of wheat, cabbage or corn once the Months of Growing were over. The road turned from dirt to stone and their travel progressed faster with a steady crackle as the wooden wheels easily cut through the sprinkling of snow from the night before. Anara could hear the horses' hooves on the stones as they clomped up the road towards the ferry.

It was cold on Gunthor Bay. Anara shivered as she tightly wrapped her light shawl around her against the ocean spray as the ferry meandered towards West End. Worse, the large bay was choppy with winds from the east driving strong waves, making the small vessel rise and fall sickeningly. Anara could barely focus on anything other than keeping her balance and the contents of her breakfast down. The ferryman pulled a chain from one end of the shore to the other that carried the boat along. He was not very clean. Anara could smell the rancid stench of excrement mixed with alcohol from their side of the ferry, and he kept leering at the courtesans with a smile missing *far* too many teeth. Anara suspected the only thing keeping him from trying to take advantage of the courtesan was Nicholas's massive build, along with the other driver from the second carriage, standing on either side of the women. Of course, Mistress Ashton and the other blade dancer probably could have taken care of the ferryman. He didn't look very strong to Anara, and if he was he probably did not know anything about fighting, unless his missing teeth had come from practice. Anara almost laughed at the absurdity of that. Even if he had been in a fight to lose them he clearly had not been the victor.

Anara welcomed the sturdy, solid planks of West End's crowded docks where fishermen and their wives peddled the day's catch in loud voices, competing with one another to draw customers. Two scribes and two caretakers, along with the unfamiliar driver and a blade dancer, went to inspect the docks. Fish had become a staple at the temple since game meat was scarce in winter. Anara made her way with the others towards

Merchant's Row where they would find the more expensive needs of the temple like cloth, wood, and various other items requiring replenishment. It was midday by the time they reached the Plaza of the Gods for a break from shopping.

"Where would I even find an enchanter?" Anara asked, throwing up her hands in frustration. In all their wandering of Merchant's Row she had not seen a single stall, cart, shop, or store that looked like it catered to the magecraft. "Isn't there a school here that teaches it?"

"Yer lookin' for *Aederon's Enchantorium*; why didn' you say so before?" Nicholas laughed and pointed towards a structure behind Mertas's Temple. Anara had been looking for something more like *Wentworth's* that might resemble a school – not a bloody palace!

The edifice had two massive stone towers with corridors connecting them to the main structure in between, forming a V-shape. The central structure itself was nearly seven stories tall, competing for the skyline with the steeples of Fiel's Temple at the north of the plaza. The roof of the towers and main building were conical, painted blue, and would have blended in with the sky if it were not overcast that day.

Anara jumped up, ignoring the food they had bought for midday meal, and started for the structure.

"Mistress Swift," Roxanne called and Anara stopped, sliding a little on the wet, ceramic cobblestones. Anara turned as the blade dancer caught up to her, carrying their food. Roxanne was short but still seemed to look down on Anara as she handed over her food. "You are still a novice. Headmistress Adair will hear about your attempt to elude your escorts for the day."

"I wasn't..." Anara started but Roxanne clicked her tongue. "My apologies, Mistress Ashton."

"Please take care of the scribe and caretaker, Masters Brenton, while I escort Mistress Swift to the *Enchantorium*," Roxanne said, turning to the rest of the group.

"O' course, Roxy," Nicholas said and Mistress Ashton started for the building. Anara slipped on the slush as she hurried to catch up; the blade dancer was surprisingly swift on the streets.

As impressive as *Aederon's Enchantorium* was on the outside, it was wondrous on the inside. The first floor of the main structure had to be three stories tall. Six massive, vaulted arches that divided the circular ceiling into identical slices supported the floors above them. A beam circled the edge of the ceiling and another circle was cut out of the center where Anara could see men and women in flowing blue robes and gowns walking around above them. Dozens of people went about the main floor. Most were visitors that stood in lines to talk to a man or woman dressed in blue behind the counters that circled the floor.

"This may take a while," Roxanne sighed, guiding Anara to the back of the visibly shortest line. "You know, you could just become a blade dancer and forget this nonsense."

"I would like to learn how to fight," Anara said, suddenly remembering the sensation of holding a blade dancer's sword bathed in white flame. "But I want to become an enchantress more, Mistress Ashton."

"Pity," Roxanne sighed, shifting her weight to the other foot. Most of the other courtesans preferred to keep straight posture, but there was something alluring about the way Roxanne allowed one leg to stick out just slightly which pulled her skirts tighter against her legs. Anara mimicked Roxanne's contrapposto stance perfectly and the woman smiled. "You would have made a good blade dancer, Anara."

"Thank you, but white and blue are my colors," Anara smiled back. "I haven't really talked to any blade dancers besides Headmistress Adair. Where are you from, if you don't mind me asking?"

"My father and mother live in Noble District," Mistress Ashton said, smiling and instinctively turning towards the north as she tossed her long braid. Outside, behind the *Enchantorium,* was the wall that separated the nobility from the lowborn.

"You're a *lady*?" Anara gasped, looking at the woman in a new light, and hastily added, "milady."

"*My* lady," Roxanne corrected. "We speak properly at the temple when addressing those above us, remember? Yes, I'm a noble, but please call me mistress. I'm not the heir to my family's estates – having four other brothers ahead of me. I was not likely to be married off to secure or advance my family's standing. Unless it was to the king as he's had plenty of wives, but he's too old for my tastes. And I did not want to become a lord's second or third wife either, my only purpose to produce more heirs to ensure the survival of *his* line."

"But still," Anara lowered her voice since they were *supposed* to be shoppers today, "a *courtesan*?"

"Where else can I bed as many men as I want? I joined the temple because I wanted many men instead of being one of a man's many. Women cannot have two husbands in Iliona, no matter what her station is; be it servant, lady, or queen. But any nobleman, even the poorest of them and no better than a common merchant, can have up to five wives. Were you aware of that?"

"I knew about the men, but not the women, I'll admit," Anara said, looking around and furrowing her brow nervously. *Is this suitable for a public discussion?* she wondered, trying to tell if anyone was eavesdropping. It certainly felt like a topic best left back at *Lussena's Temple.*

"Isn't that unfair to you, to all women?" Roxanne asked, placing her hands on her hips as she shifted again.

"It does seem unbalanced," Anara agreed. "I would rather just be with one, and be their one as well," Anara blushed, her mind wandering to Lena again.

"I abandoned my belief in Fiel's teachings and took Malef's to heart. My family disowned me. Now they pretend I don't even exist if I happen to be called upon to attend one of the balls or events that they also attend."

"That's awful!" Anara gasped. "To be abandoned by your family."

"I abandoned them, Anara," Roxanne said, standing taller. "I hated being pampered so much anyway. You can't do anything yourself if you're nobility. There are servants who cook your food, who make your bed and wash your clothes. Servants who comb your hair and powder your nose. Even worse, it is expected of you to *let* them do their work. Doing anything yourself is taboo. I'm sorry if you feel they abandoned me, because of where you grew up, but don't pity me for it. I am myself now that I can do all those things with my own power. Understood, Mistress Swift?"

"Yes, *my* lady," Anara curtsied and Roxanne rolled her eyes. "You know I grew up in an orphanage? We've never talked."

"Mistress Adair keeps me updated on those inside the Temple," Roxanne paused, tapping her lips with a finger. "Would you keep that story to yourself back at the temple? As open as we are about some things, others we tend to be a bit more secretive," Roxanne laughed as the line *finally* started moving forward. "I don't even know *why* I told you. You certainly managed to catch me off guard. You *really* should have been a blade dancer."

The wait went by quickly as Roxanne spoke of her various escapades as a courtesan, not caring who might hear. Anara wondered what those around them thought of the blade dancer. No one ever said anything, but more than a few men with grins on their faces, and women with furrowed brows and narrowed eyes looked her way. Anara blushed furiously when Roxanne smiled back whenever she caught them looking. To Roxanne, all men were conquests to be, as she put it, "sheathed as deep, hard, and fast as they could." Anara was mortified to be in public with the blade dancer, but Mistress Ashton shrugged it all off as if *all* women should freely speak like her.

"Nothing is quite so satisfying as a strong man between your legs," Roxanne confided as they walked up to the counter.

"Please stop," Anara whispered and Roxanne laughed.

"I could hear a bit more," the enchanter behind the counter said, giving Roxanne a half smile. It was charming, but Anara could not have cared less about his interests. "Though maybe it could be more than just heard?"

"Maybe it could, for the right price. You're Lord Barnum's boy, right?" Roxanne said and she laughed as the man turned red. "Tell your father you want to visit *Lussena's Temple*; I can see to your desires. Just ask for Mistress Ashton."

"Mistress Ashton, please," Anara rolled her eyes at the woman. "This isn't why we came here." Roxanne smiled but said nothing more.

"How can I be of service to such fine women?" the enchanter said, clearing his throat and giving a brief smile at Anara.

"I've been trying to make a glow box for my mistress's estate, but I think I haven't gotten the ratios of my solution correct," Anara said, opening her satchel and laying out the five remaining vials she had.

"Ah, right," the man said, rolling his eyes. "One of *those* questions. Jocelyn, could you come take care of this pair? I haven't the patience to deal with peasants trying to enchant today. No matter how," he looked Roxanne up and down, "provocative they are." Roxanne batted her eyes, barely taking notice of the enchanter's tone of superiority. Anara knew she was a peasant. She had thought her new life might have raised her a little bit, feeling the sting that in the eyes of a highborn she was still just a lowborn. To people like the enchanter there were only two types of people. Highborn and peasants.

"One moment, Jacob," a woman several stations down, with a box wrapped in paper between her and another customer, answered. Jacob yawned, leaning back against the wall behind him as he continued to gawk at Roxanne.

A little while later, after Jocelyn finished attending to her patron, she came walking over with the same dignified air as Mistress Adair. She closely inspected the vials on the counter, shaking each one in turn and holding them up to the light.

"These two have ratios that would do in a pinch, shavings are a bit crude. I would suggest powder or granules, those work better for weighing out," Jocelyn said, laying down the two vials where the ratios of metal were equal but, when combined, were no more than the oil. "If you're making a glow lamp, which I assume you are considering the use of tin and copper, this would be the best. Two parts copper for every part tin. One part oil for every metal. Again, powder and granules work better, they get a more uniform coverage of the rune as well."

"Then why don't they work?" Anara asked, fishing the *Basic Enchantment Theory* from her satchel and turning it to the pyromantic section of the index. "I tried all of these but none of them worked."

"Thank the gods that one did not!" Jocelyn exclaimed when Anara pointed to *Inferno*. "I've yet to see an Ilionan use that rune and not blow themselves up. The only enchanted pieces I know of that use something similar to that are Raykarn channeling rods."

"So why didn't the others work?" Roxanne asked, trying to get the woman to focus.

"That's simple," Jocelyn said, turning to the front two pages of the book. "Alastair Lorne forgot to mention the binding ichor when he spoke of the ingredients. It makes sense you would have troubles as you couldn't even get a spark out of a pyromantic enchantment without it."

"But I did," Anara said, furrowing her brow. "One of the sticks I practiced on burst into flames."

"You're mistaken," Jacob laughed dismissively. "You probably held it too close to a candle or something. The oil *is* flammable. Why were you trying to make a stick into a glow lamp anyway? Metal lasts longer since it doesn't rot or degrade like wood does."

"It was available," Anara muttered, feeling like a fool. She had not even considered what would happen over the years to the wood.

"Well, you certainly have the talent for it," Jocelyn said, handing the book back. "Given that you picked the right family of auras for a glow lamp *and* managed to make some useful solutions. However, I must advise you against enchanting outside of the *Enchantorium* proper. Alastair Lorne was not making an idle comment about it being dangerous. Students here have died because they weren't paying close enough attention."

"I understand," Anara said.

"But, seeing as how this is the best-supplied shop for enchantments I can offer you a vial of ichor, and some more suitable plates for glow lamps and the glass box, if you are still interested," Jocelyn said. The change of her tone was drastic. Mentioning what they sold, Jocelyn sounded like the fishermen at the docks. The sale was all that drove her. It was a little daunting to Anara as she stood there looking up at the two enchanters.

They must have been on a platform because they seemed too tall for their proportions.

"I am," Anara said, not wanting to hear the price.

"Of course, to contain the glow lamp, you'll need the saltpeter, boiled spring water, and azure salt to enchant the glass box."

"And how much will that cost?" Anara asked, looking at the floor.

"Three dragons and fifteen drakes," Jocelyn stated, sounding like she was enjoying herself. "Plus, a dragon more for the proper tools to engrave your materials with runes. Metal is a lot harder to etch into than wood." The cost was unbelievable. Two dragons—the highest denomination of Ilionan currency—could have provided *Wentworth's Home for Wayward Souls* with food for a week. Not the bland gruel that was actually served there, but good food.

"Thank you for your assistance," Anara said, steeling her heart with resignation to refuse when the sound of coins clinking on the counter drew her attention. A stack of seven gold dragons sat on the table. Gold, not silver covered in gold plating. Real, solid, thick yellow metal. Anara had some jewelry to be worn as a courtesan, but even that was silver. Roxanne had *gold*. Anara had never seen *real* gold besides the gold leaf inlay of her book, but that barely counted.

"This will cover the additional cost of *Advanced Enchantment Theory*, as well as *Basic Enchantment Theory*, and some vials of starter supplies as well, I believe," Roxanne said. "If I'm not mistaken, Alastair Lorne did a great deal better on his second text."

"You already have *Basic Enchantment Theory*," Jocelyn said, sliding a coin back. A single dragon was how much *Basic Enchantment Theory* cost! Anara felt even more childish for endangering the precious text.

"It *belongs* to our mistress's library," Roxanne said, shooting a disapproving glance at Anara. Anara shied away, knowing she would be washing pots again tonight. At least the soaps the courtesan house used left her skin feeling extra soft; Lena would enjoy that. "But she thinks Anara deserves her own copy, given her talent."

"Of course," Jocelyn said, gathering up the gold. Anara still could not believe how much money just exchanged hands. "Keep in mind, only a single drop of the binding ichor is needed. It was the priciest bit of this, so I doubt your master would approve of you wasting it." Anara nodded, watching as Jocelyn wrapped the supplies together in thin, crinkly parchment.

Anara left the *Enchantorium* with a considerably heavier satchel than before. When she returned to the temple, a full week's duty cleaning in the kitchens lay ahead, even on the days when she was to help with the cooking. Apparently, it was one thing to take a book out of the library, but something completely different to take it all the way to Aederon.

IX

CROWDED

"Miranda, stop slouching," Cassandra snapped as Miranda leaned her elbows against the dining room table, massaging her temples. She ignored her mother, her *slouching* was all she could do to keep conscious as she sorted a new batch of departed souls that came upon her.

I just want to go outside. If I go outside I'll feel better, I promise. Where is that bloody surgeon! If I die, I won't see Ishan's face again, the three still cried, but they had been joined by others.

I'm sorry, Mother and Father, another boy. The stupid fool was dared by his friends to go out on a frozen lake during the tail end of the Months of Frost. The ice had cracked and he had drowned. No one had found his body yet; Miranda could almost feel it still floating there. It was tangled in weeds now, suspended just a few feet beneath the surface. *Why haven't his friends told anyone?* Miranda wondered every time she heard him.

I had a good life, Miranda welcomed that voice, even though it still caused her a headache to hear it. It was one of the few who was not entirely depressing. The old woman had died, alone, as she held her long-dead husband's portrait in bed. Age had taken her, yet it still tugged at Miranda's heart to know she had passed away with little notice. So few people noticed the passing of every one of these souls.

So, this is the abyss, it isn't so bad. I should tell my priest, a man said. He had survived long enough to realize what was happening despite a fall that snapped his neck. Miranda had always thought such a death was instant since that was what the medical tomes in her father's study said. The man had slipped from his roof as he was working to repair the damage caused to the thatching during the winter.

Agh! It burns! Why! Why! It burns! Aaron, please save me! Miranda winced at the screams of a woman who had burned alive during the last snowstorm of the year. She was not alone.

Momma! Papa! Make it stop, it hurts! Make it stop! Miranda cried as she felt the mother and son die in an inferno as a crowd looked on. The father and, blessedly, the two other children had escaped with minor injuries. The father wept, being held back by citizens of Crossroads as he struggled to go back into the flames to find his wife and son. Miranda had watched the glow of the fire that night, it was all she could see of Crossroads through the flurry of white flakes.

They had all died during the Months of Frost, but luckily no others had fallen victim since then. None, that was, until today. Miranda's vision was growing dark with pain as she struggled to breathe over her midday meal.

What was tha– the voice had come suddenly, ending abruptly from the arrow that had driven deep into the back of his skull. The tip of the arrow split his eye as it came to rest. The man was not alone either. A caravan was being attacked by bandits and Miranda felt her stomach threatening to empty at what came next.

Papa! A girl thought, looking at her father seated beside her on the wagon as the man fell off the bench. She watched her father with horror, a black-shafted arrow sticking from the back of his head and blood streaming down his face from his eye. Her father fell out of the wagon and beneath the wheels crushing his already lifeless corpse as another arrow lodged in the girl's heart.

Ambush! a mercenary hired to protect the caravan began yelling, but the word was silenced in his throat as a rusted blade opened his neck and sprayed a fine mist of blood on the guard in front of him. The second man managed to give the alarm before he died as well.

Bastards attacked us from behind. I'm not a real soldier, why am I here? The second guard thought as a sword took him. Miranda could feel the cold steel slide between his ribs as the wide blade cut his heart into two pieces. She grabbed her chest, gasping from the pain.

"Miranda, are you listening to me?!" Cassandra yelled in anger, but Miranda barely heard her.

Quick, run, I can escape if I run! A woman fell, her head separated from her body by an axe that swung out from behind a tree.

The attack was disjointed. People she saw from another's perspective hopped around as if teleporting from place to place. It happened so quickly as the caravan scattered. She saw some people get attacked but never heard their voices while others fell dead in front of one person's eyes only to shift how Miranda was viewing the battle.

Mercy! A Priest of Fiel thought as he kneeled, holding his hands before him. They were covered in blood from the gut wound that stained his white and red robes.

I just want to go outside. If I go outside I'll feel better, I promise.

Where is that bloody surgeon!

If I die, I won't see Ishan's face again

I'm sorry, Mother and Father.

I had a good life.

So, this is the abyss, it isn't so bad. I should tell my priest.

Agh! It burns! Why! Why! It burns! Aaron, please save me!

Momma! Papa! Make it stop, it hurts! Make it stop!

What was tha—

Papa!

Ambush!

Bastards attacked us from behind. I'm not a real soldier, why am I here?

Quick, run, I can escape if I run!

Mercy!

The thoughts circled and circled, threatening to blur together again as Miranda struggled to keep them separate. K'Rania had told her to *see* the person the thought came from in their death, and that helped to keep them apart. But this new group, dying so close together and in close proximity, was much harder. *Please, let that be all,* Miranda's thought was nearly lost with the others. If the bandits killed many more she may lose her grasp of the voices. She waited, keeping them separate.

A boy in his bed. A lumberjack with a mangled leg. A woman, raped the night she was betrothed to the man of her dreams. A young boy that lost a dare and paid with his life. A woman who reached the end of her lonely years with grace. A young father, fixing his homestead who happened to slip and fall to his death. A mother and son burned alive. A, who was it? A daughter. No. A father beside his daughter in a caravan. The daughter of the man in the same caravan. A mercenary guard at the rear of that caravan, the guard in front of him. A woman walking with the caravan for its protection, fleeing when that failed. A Priest of Fiel.

Miranda slowly caught her breath and began quieting the voices. It worked best if she worked backward. The last voice she heard was always the hardest to drive from her mind. The priest, then the fleeing woman, followed by the guards. Next came the daughter and her father. After that, it was easy. She had quieted them before. Her skin felt sticky with sweat and her whole body ached from the ordeal as she shut her eyes and caught her breath.

Miranda looked up, leaning back in her chair with a sigh of relief, and caught Cassandra's open hand hard against her cheek.

"Pay attention to me when I speak!" Cassandra screamed and swung again. Miranda clenched her teeth, refusing to be goaded, and caught the blow that left her stinging cheek numb.

"What did you say, mother?" Miranda asked, keeping her voice calm even though she was shaking from the assault and mental ordeal. Several people had just lost their lives on a road as they made their way to Crossroads to peddle their wares and Cassandra squabbled about *manners?* She could barely look at her food. Miranda did not deserve her life of luxury. She knew real suffering now. *How did I ever consider my bedroom small?*

True, it was the smallest in the mansion but it was twice the size of the hovel where the boy died of a fever.

"Sit straight," Cassandra said, her voice at the edge of shouting or talking because she could not decide which to do. Ariel shied away from her sister-wife's rage. Ester was crying, she hated seeing Miranda get punished by Cassandra. Morgan was gone, again. He had been more frequently as if he were avoiding Miranda since she overheard them discussing what the tattoo on her breast was doing to her.

"If you'll excuse me," Miranda said, pushing away from the table.

"I said *sit!*" Cassandra swung her hand again but Miranda caught her mother's slender wrist. She squeezed, feeling the bones rubbing against each other beneath her grip.

"*I* said, excuse me," Miranda said through clenched teeth, keeping her voice level. Cassandra winced as Miranda's grip tightened. Miranda felt the power as she stood over her mother, the woman's wrist felt so weak beneath her fingers. "So, you *will* excuse me, understood," Miranda demanded. She could feel it now, just on the edge of her awareness. A great expanse of nothing was before her. Miranda knew she was a necromancer, and that at some point she would feel the power she had heard her father speak of on occasion but *this*. This sensation was thrilling to feel like she stood on the edge of a cliff of a never-ending chasm. This was the Plane of Shadow. Thade's realm. The emptiness of Thade's Abyss called to her, tempting her to touch it.

So she did.

A new world opened up to her. Not of day and night, winter or summer, or beasts and men but something *else*. Energy crashed into her, demanding she take hold of it from this new plane of existence she discovered and give it a way out into the physical plane she lived in. The raw power of it exhilarated Miranda as she let it flow into her even as her whole body was gripped in icy terror.

The room glowed with a sickly green light, giving her mother an eerie pallor as Miranda's veins flashed like luminescent vines crawling up a porcelain wall. Cassandra cried out and Miranda felt her mother's wrist withering beneath her touch. Miranda grinned. She could kill Cassandra right now.

Cassandra's screams grew louder, turning into a wail of pure agony. Miranda blinked and the intoxication of her power waned. Miranda's glowing green eyes met Cassandra's brown and she saw the pain in her mother's face. *This is wrong*, a voice in her mind—her own thought—whispered. She was killing her mother. *Killing* someone. Killing anyone was wrong. *Who am I to decide who lives and dies?* Miranda's stomach sank with guilt and the power she was channeling began slipping from her.

The guilt of knowing Cassandra's pain was her fault caught Miranda off-guard.

"I'm sorry," Miranda said, letting go and the room returned to normal with the last ebbing flow of the power from Thade's Abyss. Miranda staggered backward and bumped against a suit of armor against the wall. The full set of plate mail crashed to the ground with a tremendous noise followed by absolute silence. Miranda fell to her knees as she looked at her mother's arm with horror. Cassandra's wrist was little more than skin and bone. Her mother's pale skin had turned to shriveled gray where Miranda had held onto her. The shape was wrong too as if her grip had broken the bones in several places beneath the desiccated flesh. Cassandra whimpered, holding her arm close and cradling it against her stomach. Tears streamed down Cassandra's flushed cheeks. *I hurt her*, Miranda thought with shock and her stomach churned. *I* hurt *her*, Miranda felt shame welling up at the corners of her eyes. *Why did I do that! How could I do that!*

"Go to your room, Miranda," Ariel said timidly, her voice wavering with fear, and Miranda finally managed to rip her gaze from Cassandra. Tears fell down Miranda's cheeks, stinging against the warmth of them. Ariel stood against the opposite wall, Ester in her arms with Ariel's body between Miranda and her younger sister. Ester's face pressed against Ariel's belly. Ester was shaking with silent sobs of terror.

"Ester," Miranda said, reaching for her sister.

"Don't touch me!" Ester screamed even though there was a table between them. "You're a monster!"

Am I a monster? Miranda thought, looking back at her mother. Her entire hand had gone pale as if blood no longer reached it. It looked dead. No, it didn't *look* dead. It *was* dead. It just hung there limply on Cassandra's ruined wrist. "I *am* a monster." Miranda had planned to kill Cassandra with K'Rania. *I can't go through with it*, she realized, embarrassed that K'Rania knew as well.

"Your room, now!" Ariel yelled, finally finding the courage to stand up against Miranda. Miranda fled.

The halls of the mansion, the bars of her cage, flew by as she raced to her room. She slammed and bolted the door, anything to keep her away from what just happened, and threw herself onto her bed. She stuffed her face into her pillows, trying to blackout the world but it refused to go away. She could feel the cool spring air around her, the heat boxes had been removed for storage until the cold returned in force, and heard birds chirping outside her window. The world was still there. Cassandra was still there, her hand a withered appendage of what it had been only moments ago.

So, *this* was her power. A necromancer's power.

"I hate it," Miranda said, turning over and reaching towards a portrait of Driadra. Her skin crawled when she saw tiny, black flecks beneath each fingernail of her left hand. "*Thade's Grasp*," Miranda whispered in horror, the blight that was claiming her father's left arm. The mark of a necromancer. She had awoken it and begun her own slow decay. All sorcery had a price to balance its use; this was necromancy's price. A slow, agonizing, inevitable death.

"I never wanted to be a necromancer," Miranda said to herself.

You were born a dark one, K'Rania said. Miranda smiled in relief; she was never alone it seemed. *You will die a dark one, but soul rot is not that death.*

"How do I stop *Thade's Grasp* from killing me?" Miranda asked as she walked over to her vanity desk. She uncorked a lacquer for her fingernails, a gift from her cowardly father.

Finish the mark, K'Rania answered.

"I can't kill my mother," Miranda said, shaking her head as she carefully painted her nails red. "I feel terrible for the pain I caused her. How could I *kill* her?"

Finish the mark. I will guide your hand. Like my mark. An offered body for use. Link our bodies, K'Rania said.

"This will keep the rot at bay?"

Until the offered body is consumed, K'Rania answered. *Finish the mark,* K'Rania insisted.

"Lunarin returns in five months at the beginning of the Harvest Festival," Miranda said, holding up her left hand as the glossy liquid dried into hard enamel before painting the nails on the other. "Ester says the tournament is in Crossroads this year so my mother will probably wait until the competition is over before finishing the mark. It would not do to take my body half way through the championship, not when my existence is not known to anyone outside of the estate. She has to keep up appearances, after all."

The ink, it flows as blood, K'Rania uttered. The N'Gochen queen really was useless sometimes. It would be easy enough, Cassandra would probably keep the ink in Thade's enclave. Miranda would be home alone through most of the tournament as well, giving her ample opportunity to search her mother's room if she did not. Miranda set the vial of red liquid down, returning the cork to keep it from drying out.

"I just hope I'll be able to," Miranda sighed, but somehow, she knew K'Rania was gone again. There was still five months until the Harvest Festival. Five months of the dead assaulting her mind, haunting her with images of their deaths. A knock came at her door and she opened it to find Ariel and Ester standing outside it.

"I need you to watch Ester," Ariel said hastily without meeting Miranda's eyes. "Cassandra's hand needs to be amputated before its rot spreads, and I'll not bring my daughter to such a gruesome operation."

"I don't wanna stay!" Ester cried. "Mima's a monster! A scary monster!" Ester cried out.

"She is still your older sister, Ester," Ariel begged, kneeling in front of the young girl. "Please, Cassandra's not well. I knew something terrible could happen when those voices finally broke you Miranda," Ariel briefly looked at Miranda. "But Cassandra is needed by your father's side for-" Ariel paused and glanced at Ester as she realized she was speaking of things Ester did not need to know. Things Miranda usually ignored like her father's necromancy cult. "Cassandra can't die." There was fear in Ariel's eyes, not just from what Miranda had done but something else. "She needs a surgeon, Ester, I can't take you with me and see to mother Cassie's illness at the same time."

"She's a monster!" Ester screamed and Ariel looked on the edge of breaking down and crying. "A monster! She's an Abyssal!" Miranda flinched at the insults. It was all right if Cassandra hated her, or if Ariel feared her, but Ester... She was Miranda's only friend.

"Please, Ester," Ariel, said, wiping her eyes as she ran from the room. Ariel's longer legs carried her faster than Ester's could. "Just be good, and stop screaming."

"Don't leave me with her, momma!" Ester cried, stopping at Miranda's door as Ariel ran away. Ester turned around, clinging to her stuffed rabbit as she stared up into Miranda's eyes. It was quiet as the sisters just stood there, Miranda felt foolish but she was afraid to move and upset her sister even more. It was so quiet Miranda heard the front door close as Ariel and Cassandra left the mansion to see the surgeons in Crossroads. Miranda had no idea what lies Ariel would say to explain the death of Cassandra's hand. An accident where it got crushed might work, but how Cassandra could have crushed her hand was a mystery to Miranda. Or Ariel could tell the truth.

Miranda felt the blood drain from her face at that idea. Sorcery was forbidden by death in Iliona since the Last Necromantic War. *Now I know why*, Miranda thought, flexing the fingers of her left hand. Mortals should not be able to wield such destructive power; it belonged to the gods. If Ariel told the truth Miranda would be executed. Killed for a power she never wanted. It was enough to make her want to laugh out of despair.

If it were not for Ester she would have. Laughing now, while her younger sister was so frightened of her, would sever any relationship they might still have. So would a fit of departed souls.

Gods, please don't let anyone die until I can apologize to Ester, Miranda gave a silent prayer to any deity listening.

Miranda looked down at her sister, she wore a blue gown very similar to the one she had worn the day Miranda received her mark. The sleeves were shorter, and puffier around her shoulders, but the skirt was layers of frilly white fabrics beneath the blue-satin top-layer. Her rabbit was starting to look a little worn, no doubt it would be replaced by an identical one in a few more weeks. Ariel would claim to have cleaned the stuffed animal and Ester would believe her mother was telling the truth. The rabbit had a hole where cotton insides were coming out in little tufts of fuzz and the new one would not. Still, it was better quality than the ill boy's toys had been.

One of them had to talk or they would stare at each other all day.

"Ester, I..."

Ester started screaming at the top of her lungs. Miranda shut her eyes and pinched the shallow bridge of her nose at the screeching of her little sister, the sound plunging into her mind like a knife after the voices from earlier. Miranda felt famished on top of it because the deaths had happened before she had gotten to eat anything at the meal.

"Stop it!" Miranda shouted and Ester instantly switched to crying. "Please, Esty," Miranda begged, opening the drawer to her writing desk and pulled out a small box. She still had some of the chocolates from before, including the one her sister had given her. "I'm sorry about what happened, I didn't mean to scare you," Miranda said, kneeling as she opened the box and offered the chocolate back. "Will you forgive me?"

"But you hurt momma Cassie," Ester sobbed, cautiously taking the offered treat and a second that Miranda had not eaten. "That light scared me, your light."

"I'm sorry. I'm not a monster," Miranda lied. *Yes, I am.* "I'm still your sister."

"Then why were you glowing?" Ester sobbed around the chocolate she was chewing on.

"I'm just different," Miranda sighed, *I have no idea how to explain it to her.* Ester was not a necromancer, she never would be, she was just an ordinary girl. She was not cursed like Miranda was. "I'm sorry I scared you."

"It's okay," Ester said, finally the terror in her eyes lessened a little.

"Would you like to go for a walk outside?" Miranda asked.

"You aren't allowed outside," Ester said, frowning. Snot ran from the girl's nose, staining her upper lip with glossy liquid and her eyes were red with tears. "Remember?"

Ester bit her lower lip and looked over her shoulder. Of course, there was no one else in the mansion to hear. This was the first time, Miranda could remember when all of her parents were out of the house without a festival to attend.

"Father, mother, and Cassandra won't have to know about it," Miranda said, she sounded a little too excited. There would be no one to stop her from walking out the door right now. She could run away if she wanted to. *The ink,* K'Rania reminded her, as if Miranda could forget that. "It'll be our secret for today."

"Oh, alright," Ester said, grabbing Miranda's hand and pulling her towards the front door. "I've always wanted to show you my favorite places to play."

Miranda hesitated at the door, feeling *Soleanne's* light on her exposed face and bosom from the low-cut, red gown she wore. It was pleasing, the dark fabric soaked in that light and warmed against the chill of early spring. Her heart raced, as it always did when she looked out over the promenade that led to the mansion. Trees lined the wide cobblestone road all the way down to the iron gate at the estate's edge. A brown line beyond the gate marked the road heading south from Crossroads. The grass was green and still short this early in the season. The scene almost looked like a painting with how still it was. The world was vibrant and bright compared to the dark halls of the estate.

"Are you coming?" Ester asked, swaying back and forth impatiently.

"Yes," Miranda said and took her first step outside the Heath mansion. There was no screaming from Cassandra or whisk of a switch to punish her. Instead, her heel clicked against the marble porch and she was outside. It was rather disappointing that close to two decades of being afraid to leave ended so uneventfully.

Ester grabbed Miranda's hand and pulled her out onto the grass where she had trouble maneuvering over the uneven ground in her high heeled shoes. Her ankles threatened to buckle with nearly every step, they were too accustomed to the perfectly even floors inside and the ground beneath the grass was soft enough she could feel the slender support at the back of her shoe sink in with each step.

"Hurry up," Ester hissed, letting go to run ahead a little way. The young girl was leading Anara back behind the mansion. The mansion itself, seen from the outside, was *incredible*. The two stories were massive, yet from the outside it seemed smaller than she knew it was. The world just felt so *open* outside of the stone and wooden halls of that structure. Miranda looked around, ignoring the long wings of her family's home, to focus on the grounds surrounding it. They sprawled out for a league to each side, empty of anything but grass until pockets of trees from the nearby forest encroached upon their lands. Miranda had expected cultivated flowers and a garden, or something like mansions in Ariel's romance novels, but the grounds were left to grow naturally.

Ester continued leading, taking Miranda to the back of the home where the land sloped towards a stream nearly a tenth of a mile away from the structure. Tall plants, dead from winter yet still standing, stood stiffly along the bank amidst new growth. The stream was swift but shallow. The water rippled as it flowed around and over the smooth rocks in the streambed.

"My favorite spot is across the stream," Ester explained, pointing to a thicket of trees on the other side. "Careful, though; the rocks are slippery and the water is higher this time of year." Ester walked down the bank, her shoes and the hem of her skirt picking up dark brown mud, before jumping onto a large rock further into the stream. The young girl easily maneuvered across, using other rocks that seemed to form a path, and climbed up the steeper bank on the other side. Miranda sighed, lifting her skirts to avoid the mud, and did her best to follow her sister across.

Her first step onto the bank resulted in her heel sinking down into the mud; the second was the same. Miranda stumbled, her first shoe sticking in the mud, and quickly caught herself on the first stone with her nearly-bare foot. The stone was ice cold as she looked back at her defiant shoe. The glossy black leather of it was flecked with brown mud and the heel had disappeared completely.

"Hurry up, Mima!" Ester called out, waving to her from across the stream. "We have to hurry in case Momma or Mother Cassie come back!"

"I'm coming, Esty," Miranda said, placing her other foot on the stone. There was barely enough room to stand and she felt awkward with only one shoe. Miranda sighed, there was nothing for it and took off her other shoe. She tossed it back onto the west bank and stepped out over the flowing waters. Each stone was cold, but at least she had firmer footing in only her dark, sheer stockings. The last step was more of a leap, landing on a patch of damp grass. Then it was a puzzle to find the right places to step and avoid getting mud on her feet as she went from one patch of grass to the next and ascended the other side of the stream. Ester clapped once Miranda reached her and started running towards the trees.

Miranda walked quickly to keep the young girl in sight as they crossed the meadow. Shoots of wild flowers with their heads still waiting inside buds were more abundant on this side of the stream. Miranda jumped when a small rodent, a brown thing with black and white stripes down its back with a bushy tail, ran across her path. Its white face was narrow with chubby cheeks and a black nose. The creature's front paws had long, pointed fingers, almost claw like in appearance.

"It's only a squirrel," Ester said where she was waiting beside the patch of trees. "They're cute, and eat nuts."

Miranda laughed, sighing with relief. Of course, it was a squirrel. *What did I think it was?* Miranda frowned as she looked into the thicket of trees. There was no grass to walk on so she leaned against the closest tree, keeping one foot on the grass, as she pulled off her stockings before hanging up the thigh-length hosiery on a low hanging branch. "C'mon, Esty, show me your favorite place."

Miranda took her sister's hand again and ventured into the shaded woods. It was surprisingly dark inside the patch of trees, given the time of day. Miranda looked up, marveling at how something could grow so tall. Each tree had to be eight times taller than the mansion. The coniferous thicket had hardly any needles at her height, only broken branches, but the canopy above blocked out *Soleanne*'s light. The brown trunks looked gnarled up close, like old leather that had cracked from improper care. Sticky, brown goo leaked from a few of them where the bark had opened up. Dozens of bugs were stuck in the sap. Why the trees were wounded was something Miranda could not determine. Miranda nearly tripped over a root and her attention returned to the ground. The roots of the trees looked like serpents digging in the ground from where rains had washed away the topsoil to reveal them. The remaining dirt looked like steps leading up as the terrain turned into a hill.

"We're almost there," Ester declared after climbing for several minutes. The canopy opened up near the top, letting daylight shine down on the dirt floor in large patches. Grass started growing there, the thin patches a much darker green than those of the meadows. "Here it is!" Ester said, running to a tree where–to Miranda's horror–the young girl started climbing. Wooden planks had been nailed into the trunk of the leafless tree. Little brown buds were splitting with the green leaves it would grow as the tree awoke from its winter sleep. Nestled in the middle of the twisted branches was another plank of wood.

"Be careful," Miranda said as Ester climbed higher and higher. Miranda's heart raced; if Ester slipped she could break her neck like the young father who was only trying to repair his roof. Or a branch could break, tumbling her sister to the ground. "You shouldn't climb that."

"I do it all the time," Ester laughed, the boards grew less frequent as the branches turned into her hand holds. "Papa had some carpenters build it for me, you should come up."

Miranda walked up to the tree and placed a cautious hand on one of the boards. She looked up at Ester who was standing on a plank of wood nearly six feet above Miranda's head. From this viewpoint, Miranda could see another set of climbing boards that went even higher to another, smaller platform. Miranda felt dizzy and took a few steps back.

"I'll let you do the climbing," she said, laughing at her cowardice as she blushed. "It wouldn't do for me to fall and break my arm if I'm not supposed to be outside."

"Please, Mima?" Ester begged, leaning out over nothing by hanging onto the branch above her head. "We can see the entire valley at the top. It's beautiful." Miranda sighed, climbing a few boards until her foot slipped and she was forced to throw her arms around the trunk as far as she could. The rough bark bit into her cheek and arms as her heart raced. She looked down, trying to calm herself. "Don't be scared," Ester said as Miranda slowly lowered back down. "You're only a few feet up! Come on, just make it to the first platform..."

I wonder what was going to be for evening meal? a voice said and Miranda lost her concentration. She slipped from the trunk, falling backward with her arms flailing for *something* to hold on to. *I'm going to die!* she thought and laughed, she sounded like one of the voices that were buzzing around in her head again. Was there another person nearby who would hear that as her last words?

"Mima!" Ester screamed somewhere in the distance as time slowed. Miranda felt strange, the world beneath her seemed to have disappeared entirely and her stomach fluttered with apprehension at being away from it. Yet, somehow, being there with nothing to hold on to felt strangely familiar. Like she was floating in a void.

Miranda landed, catching a lot of her weight on her left wrist. She screamed in pain, curling up and holding her arm tight to her chest. The voices were becoming disjointed again, she had to find the one that let them in and see who it was. *If I die, bloody surgeon!* No, she knew those two already and their words separated. *Ambush! If I go outside, I'll feel better. I promise, Mercy!* Two of those were from the caravan earlier, the other was the boy who died in his hovel beside his parents.

I wonder what was going to be for evening meal? That was the one! Miranda winced, her wrist felt like it was on fire, and focused on the innocent thought. The soul was a man her father's age. He sat at home, eagerly waiting as his wife prepared supper in the room next to him but Miranda could not tell *why* he died. He was just dead. One minute he was happily whittling a flute out of wood, a gift for his newborn grandson, and basking in the aromas coming from the kitchen. He thought of his loving wife. How much he loved her. Then he heard a pop, and he was dead. The man knew he was dead, too, by how his thought suggested he would never know what dinner was.

Whatever the cause, he was dead now. The wife would be grieved by his sudden loss, but Miranda could not do anything about it but work back through the voices and quiet them again.

"Miranda!" Ester said, kneeling in front of her as the last of the voices left her thoughts. "Are you okay? What happened?"

"I slipped," Miranda said, wincing from the pain in her head and arm. Not to mention she would have a fresh bruise on her backside. Miranda's wrist felt stiff, she gasped at how swollen it was when she dared to examine it. "Is it broken? Am I going to die?"

"No," Ester laughed and gently poked her wrist. Pain flared up and Miranda nearly slapped her sister's hand away.

"That hurts!" Miranda hissed. "Stop."

"I think you sprained it," Ester said.

"Is that fatal? Am I going to die from a sprained wrist?" Miranda felt tears forming on the edges of her eyes. Ester was laughing, but Miranda could not see anything humorous about it. *They'll have to cut it off*, Miranda decided. *To save my life, I'll mirror Cassandra in having only one hand too.* "Stop laughing," Miranda sobbed. "It hurts."

"We should put it in the stream, it'll help with the swelling so we can get you back to the house and wrap it. I've fallen a few times, too, so I know it will help."

Miranda grunted as she stood, she felt sore all over from the fall and noted the mud stains covering her dress. Cassandra would find out she was outside after all.

"I'm sorry, Miranda," Ester said as they crouched beside the stream. The water was *freezing* and left her entire hand feeling numb as she let it soak. That helped since it dulled the pain of her wrist as well.

"It isn't your fault, Esty," Miranda said, taking in a slow breath to fight against the chill. Her skirts were covered in mud from the bank now. "I slipped and fell, you did nothing to cause that."

"I asked you to come up," Ester cried. "If I hadn't, you wouldn't have fallen."

"I wanted to see what was up there, Esty," Miranda sighed, pulling her hand from the water and gently drying it on a clean part of her skirt. Her wrist still throbbed but not nearly as much, and the swelling *had* gone down. "It was my choice."

Miranda retrieved her shoes after they crossed and carried them in her right hand as they made their way back into the mansion. Ester, who had experiences with sprains apparently, wrapped Miranda's wrist so tightly with a silk bandage that it could not bend. It hurt, as Ester put the strip of cloth on, but after she finished the pain lessened.

"I'll wash your dress," Ester said, her eyes cast down to the floor. "So mother Cassie doesn't find out. You can say you fell down the stairs for your hand, she'll believe that."

"Thank you, Ester, for showing me your tree," Miranda said, hugging her sister. "I've always wanted to go outside."

X

COURTESAN

Anara slowly walked the long path between the bath and the carriage house. She held a glow lamp with a blue-white flame ahead of her to light the way. The box was for Nicholas. He was old and needed a better light than the dim box he had been using for nearly a decade. That, and she wanted to sneak away from the temple for a little bit. It was her birthday. A year had passed since she was walking the halls of *Wentworth's Home for Wayward Souls* and so much had happened.

The tunnel ended at a simple, worn wooden door that creaked on rusted hinges as she pushed it open. She walked out into the warm evening air of early fall, trees and bushes obscuring the entrance from the view of passersby. Stones, almost natural in their arrangement, led from the door up the steep hill and back to the carriage housing. It had become a familiar path to Anara. She still received her copper and tin from Nicholas even though her enchantments had been bringing in enough gold to buy them from a proper enchantment supply provider.

The carriage house came into view after cresting the hill. It was not nearly as impressive as *Lussena's Temple*, but the cluster of structures was actually a small village. There were the barns to store the carriages closer to the courtesan house, but also several hovels where the drivers—and even some of their wives—lived. Smoke rose from several narrow chimneys as Anara made her way into the main street of the small town. Nicholas's house, the two-story structure in the center, was the largest one and looked more like an inn than a home. His own personal carriage, the one Anara had seen outside *Wentworth's*, was parked to the side of the house beneath an overhang to better protect it from the elements. Anara stepped up to the door, crafted from oak with an oval of amber glass at eye level, and knocked.

"Come in," Nicholas called and Anara opened the door that swung inward with little effort. The structure was considerably warmer than outside, not uncommon for the Months of Growth, but there were pleasing scents coming from inside that made Anara's mouth water.

"Master Brenton, I have something for you," Anara called out and made her way back to the kitchen. "I think it appropriate that I show my appreciation for the supplies you provided. Also, knowing how bad your eyesight has been getting, I figured it would help you..."

Anara froze, the lamp held out before her, as she turned into the small dining area and found Mistress Adair sitting across from Nicholas. She swirled a glass of wine in one hand before taking a long drink from it.

"Mistress Adair!" Anara jumped back, nearly dropping the device. "What are you doing here?"

"Good evening, Mistress Swift. I should ask you the same thing," Adair said, setting her glass down. She lifted her silverware and cut into a roast with the same refinement she expected of a courtesan while on assignment. "I'm surprised to see you away from the temple, given what tonight means to you. Lena has been gushing about your initiation for weeks, it would be unfortunate to disappoint her by getting yourself in trouble and ruining her plans. No, stay, Anara," Mistress Adair said when Anara took a step back to leave. "Would you like to join my father and I for evening meal?"

Anara's jaw dropped.

"Your father?" Anara took a step into the kitchen and set the glow box down on a counter as Nicholas cut a slice from the roast for her. "But your relationship with him... you take your own father to bed?"

Nicholas turned bright red, dropping the food onto the floor, and tugged at the collar of his shirt.

"By the gods no, Anara," Mistress Adair laughed as Nicholas tried to hide his bewilderment by cutting another slice. Anara awkwardly shifted her weight as she tried to focus on something other than the two people. *How could I think that? I always thought she was too young for him anyway.* Anara tucked her hair behind warm ears.

"But you don't have the same last name," Anara argued, they *couldn't* be father and daughter. She barely resembled Nicholas, but now that Anara knew she could see a few common characteristics. Adair and Nicholas both had a slightly dimpled chin and their eyes were strikingly similar.

"I was married once," Mistress Adair said as Anara took her seat. Nicholas kept busy by piling vegetables onto Anara's plate and pouring her a rather large glass of wine. "He died a little over fifteen years ago. Instead of taking another husband and giving him my late one's wealth, I decided I would leave for Aederon City in my pursuit of living Malef's teachings. After spending a year as a priestess in the Order of Flame, I discovered the courtesan house – what you know as *Lussena's Temple*. Back then it was *The House of Worldly Pleasures*. I joined their ranks and in five years I became headmistress of the house, renamed it and began catering exclusively to those who held titles to ensure a safer experience for my girls."

"And Nicholas approved of this?"

"By Fiel I didn'," Nicholas sighed, forcefully shaking his head. "But 'rin's always been one to live by her beliefs. I couldn' jus' le' her be taken 'vantage of by some of the less than savory folks in her line of work."

"So, my father volunteered to be the house's official driver and to find wholesome men to escort us to our engagements," Mistress Adair explained. "I've been grateful ever since, and I suspect since mother died he has as well. He is useless without women to protect."

"Am not," Nicholas argued. "Women folk jus' keep me in line with what needs to be done is all." Nicholas looked at his daughter and Anara recognized his adoration now. It was not the same as a lover's; Anara saw enough of that when Lena looked at her. Nicholas looked at Mistress Adair with pride. He may not agree with her career, but he was proud of what she had managed to make of it.

"I'm actually glad I caught you, Anara," Mistress Adair said while Anara chewed a slice of the roast. The beef was tender with savory juices flavored by a hint of juniper berries, carrots, and potatoes. It complimented the wine well, which Anara only sipped since her glass would have made her tipsy if she let herself drink too quickly.

"Why is that, Headmistress?" Anara asked after swallowing. One did not talk with food in one's mouth when in the company of her betters. That was one of the many etiquette lessons she had been given since becoming a novice, including how to set her silverware down, crossing over the center of her plate to indicate she was not finished eating whenever she stopped to speak. If she was done the silverware would be placed parallel to each other instead. Also, never lean against the table with your elbows. Sit up straight. Eat only after the head of the household had, unless given permission. Along with dozens of others that were discussed at nearly every evening meal in *Lussena's Temple*.

"I would like you to show me *how* you manage to sneak off the temple grounds. Master Brenton"–Anara frowned at how Adair still referred to her father as that–"has kept me informed of your visits and the several nights I've watched to see you sneaking beyond the Outer Sanctum I wound up falling asleep long after you had already left him and returned."

"I was hoping to keep it a secret a while longer," Anara sighed, testing the soft carrots that had been cooked with the beef. "But I'll show you the way once I have finished Master Brenton's delectable meal."

"This isn' *my* doing," Nicholas said, laughing deeply. Anara smiled, remembering the first time she heard his rumbling mirth. "This is 'rin's handy work in the kitchen." Anara stared at the headmistress who was trying not to smile behind her glass. Her cheeks were rosier than they should have been as well.

"I appreciate the praise, Anara," Mistress Adair said, putting one hand on Anara's. "And, of course, you're welcome to finish." She turned back to her father as Anara ate. The two were not discussing anything of real interest to Anara. There was a wagon that had a cracked wheel, and one of the drivers who Mistress Adair had hoped would be available that weekend had taken ill. It was all very professional until Nicholas's ale started taking its toll and discussions drifted to more personal stories. Even Anara laughed as Nicholas recounted, to Mistress Adair's embarrassment, tales from the headmistress's youth.

"She jus' stood there," Nicholas boasted to Anara. "All proud like she was the High Priest of Fiel 'erself or somethin' with 'er cheeks puffed up and crumbs falling out o' 'er little mouth. You know wha' she said, 'nara?"

"What?" Anara asked, grinning widely and giving a glance to Mistress Adair. Mistress Adair shut her eyes tightly as she readied herself for what was coming next.

"She said, pokin' me in the chest. Not jus' a little tap or nothin' either, but drivin' that little finger o' hers as hard as she could. She said, as 'er mother looked on with arms folded across her chest. 'rin said, 'paffa afe the cookies' as crumbs flew out o' 'er mouth with each word." Nicholas laughed, slapping the sturdy table hard enough their empty plates clattered. "An' her momma turned—as if believin' every word our little darlin' spoke—she turned on the spo' and said 'yer papa should stop givin' in ta his sweet tooth then.' O' course I just threw up my hands an' stormed out ta the shed. Silly girl eatin' my favorite treat an' blamin' me when they were all gone before I got home. I was so mad, I couldn' even speak to little 'rin for a week."

"Please, Father, no more," Mistress Adair squealed as they laughed. "Yer embarrassin' me!" Mistress Adair turned as red as her wine, covering her mouth from letting her speech slip. Nicholas only laughed harder at that. The laughter died down and Nicholas sighed as he slumped back in his chair. "I miss those days," Mistress Adair said, letting Nicholas take her hand in his.

"I do too, 'rin," Nicholas said, gently squeezing Adair's much smaller hand. "I miss Angelica the most."

Mistress Adair smiled, a tear in her eye, and squeezed her father's hand back.

"We should head back, Mistress Adair," Anara said, standing. She had only made it halfway through her glass, it was just too much for her. "My initiation will be starting soon and it would not do to have both of us missing." Mistress Adair let out a long, nostalgic sigh as she looked into her father's eyes.

"You are correct, Mistress Swift," Adair said and, with a peck on her father's cheek, stood to go. She swayed slightly from her drinks but otherwise was as composed as ever. "Until next week, Master Brenton."

"Next week, 'rin," Nicholas nodded and the two women left.

"I would enjoy your company again next week, too, Anara," Mistress Adair said as they made their way down to the tunnel.

"What about the rules? Courtesans are not permitted beyond the Outer Sanctum unless escorted by a driver."

"Thade take the rules," Mistress Adair said, taking Anara's arm in hers. Anara suspected it was more for stability than anything, her tipsy balance was no good on the steep descent. "Besides, technically you aren't beyond the Outer Sanctum. The carriage houses are behind the Inner Sanctum." Mistress Adair grinned slyly at Anara. "I can't very well punish you for being here if I don't punish myself, what sort of example would I be setting?"

"Ah, but you came here by leaving out the Outer Sanctum doors," Anara countered, which only made Mistress Adair chuckle.

"I didn't have your secret passage," they stopped outside of the tunnel after Anara opened the door. "You didn't bring a spare glow lamp with you, I assume?"

"I'm afraid not, Headmistress," Anara frowned and started to blindly make her way back by keeping one hand on a wall.

"I've told you before," Mistress Adair gripped tightly to Anara's arm as they went deeper and deeper. "Please, call me Erin."

"That reminds me," Anara said, recalling their first meeting at *Wentworth's*. "You said Nicholas had known you for twenty years, but if he's your father..."

"A lie, to shift suspicion. I'm afraid that number is closer to thirty than twenty, but that is all I'm going to say on the topic of my age. If all of you knew Master Brenton was my father, you would all know his stories about my childhood."

"Would that be so horrible?"

"How many of us speak about our lives before the temple?"

Erin had a point. Only Lena, who talked with Anara every night, had ever shown interest in her life before *Lussena's Temple*, mostly to learn about her rebellious days at the orphanage.

"Still, isn't the gossip worse than that?" Anara scratched her head but Erin just laughed lightly.

"Perhaps," Erin said after a little bit of feeling their way through the tunnel.

The bath was empty when the door, which had a latch on the opposite side as well, opened. It was far too late for others to be using the bath. Unlike Anara, they tended to keep to curfew. The pool of water was calm, letting Anara clearly see the glow lamps and heat boxes in each corner. Erin let go of Anara just before they left the room, regaining her own balance now that they were on even ground and out of the darkness.

"I will see you in the ballroom then?"

"Of course, headmistress," Anara nodded as she watched Mistress Adair ascend one the spiral staircase. Anara stretched and went down the hall to the other one, it was closer to her room and made her way up from the basements of the inner sanctum.

"Where have you been!" Lena gasped as Anara opened her door. Lena was sitting at Anara's work desk, one of her wood dowels in her hands looked like she had been working it for a few hours. The wood almost looked smooth and was stained dark brown with Lena's sweat. "You said you were going to get more metal shavings for another glow lamp, that was *four* hours ago!"

"I got caught," Anara sighed, falling into her bed. "Mistress Adair saw me go into the tunnel."

"Thade's Abyss! Leave it to Adair to punish you before your initiation," Lena cursed and sat down beside Anara. "Well, you can't sleep yet; get back up. They're waiting for you in the ballroom."

"Who?"

"Roxanne, Lisa and Helda, last time I checked," the three courtesan Anara was closest to other than Lena and Erin. "I think Tasha said she would be there tonight, at least she did when I spoke to her and her sister in the Outer Sanctum this morning. Of course, since you're so late they may have already gone to bed. I hope she was patient, you especially need another craftswoman to give you her blessing. Oh, and me of course. One from each chapter. So that makes five of us—other than you of course—to initiate you. Let's go!" Lena pulled Anara up out of her bed and back into the hall despite Anara's exhaustion.

The ballroom was darker than usual; the glow lamps had been covered up with only candles behind each of the other waiting mistresses. Mistress Tasha, a tall and slender woman with wavy black hair had fortunately shown up. Her sister, Sasha, had as well. The twins looked identical to each other except for the colors they wore and their hair style. Sasha kept her hair like Lena's, with one side shaved and the other side so short it did not even touch her shoulders. "Shorter hair is better for fighting," was Sasha's excuse. Probably a good choice since Sasha wore the black and orange of the blade dancers.

Sasha stood outside of the circle of five candles, however, because Roxanne was the blade dancer who would accept Anara. It was a bizarre ritual, almost religious, given that they were only courtesans instead of actual priestesses. Anara could see many pieces of the ritual were pulled from those described in the text of the Order of Flame. The incense in the air mixed with peppery spices, a scent favored by Malef's order, and the area at the center of the room lit only by candle flame were the most obvious rites from that religion's text. Even the dress (the sheer robes of the orders the women represented and nothing else) was reminiscent to the God of Fire's traditional ceremonies.

Lena took her place, standing in front of the last candle, and Anara made her way to the middle of them all. Erin stood on the edge of the candlelight as well—another witness to Anara's advancement.

"You finally showed up," Tasha said, her annoyance belied by her smile. "I was about to turn in with Sasha if you'd taken any longer."

"I apologize," Anara curtsied, embarrassed that she had caused them all to wait for so long. Not that it was *her* fault. Erin and Nicholas had just been more enjoyable company.

"She still blushes," Lisa-Mistress Cadence-whispered to Mistress Caidrill. Helda smiled, she was even more beautiful tonight because she had bothered with makeup. "Very rare with a novice at this stage in her life."

"Let's get on with it, shall we?" Roxanne said, shifting her weight to her other foot. "Tasha and Sasha may be up this late on a regular basis, but I've been on my feet all day guarding the Outer Sanctum. I detest guard duty; it's incredibly dull."

"Sasha said she would have taken guard duty today since she knows how highly you think of Mistress Swift," Tasha said. "I'm surprised you did not take her up on it, given you would have preferred being in the client rooms today."

"And truly been worn out for this? I think not," Mistress Ashton shook her head.

"Mistresses," Erin cut in and they all cleared their throats while standing up straighter. "If you would, Mistress Weston?"

"Yes, Headmistress," Lena curtsied and stepped forward. "As this novice's guide, I present her, Anara Swift, for the judgment of the chapters." Lena recited. "As an orderly, I have deemed her in good health both in body and mind. For these reasons, I accept her as one of our sisters." Lena said and Anara's heart raced at the familiar touch of her lover's hands on her chest and waist.

"As a scribe," Lisa said as she stepped forward. "I have a record of her resourcefulness in her studies as well as her already substantial contribution to the temple through her art. For these reasons, I accept her as one of our sisters." Anara refrained from shying away as Mistress Cadence placed her hand on Anara's back and waist.

"As a craftswoman," Tasha moved up next. "I have watched her art grow through her dedication to sustaining the temple. For this reason, I accept her as one of our sisters." Anara felt herself standing taller as Mistress Tasha placed her own hands next to Mistress Cadence's. Mistress Tasha, a career courtesan like her sister, was considered the head of the craftswomen chapter.

"As a caretaker," Helda said. "I have seen her diligence and skill to overcome obstacles in her art. For these reasons, I accept her as one of our sisters." Her hands went next to Tasha's.

"As a blade dancer," Roxanne said, smiling as she looked into Anara's eyes. "I have observed her advancement and pride in her art. For these reasons, I accept her as one of our sisters." She placed her hands next to Mistress Caidrill's.

Even the words they spoke, like the colors they wore, mimicked what little Anara knew of the gods. Fiel, the god of life and health was the path of orderly; Ezebre, goddess of air and mind, would cater to the calculating women of the scribes; Mertas, goddess of water and loyalty, gave the craftswomen great pride in their work when it aided the courtesan house; Duloreb, god of earth and strength, approved of those with the strength to dedicate themselves as the caretakers dedicated themselves to the house; and Malef, god of fire and passion, placed improving oneself above all other priorities like the blade dancers.

"Who are you?" Lena asked, slowly untying the pink sash at Anara's waist. Lena looked at her, her head slightly bowed, as if she were stalking Anara. It was the same way Lena looked at her before kissing her slowly from her feet to her lips.

"I am Anara Swift," Anara answered, almost breathless as the other four women pulled the sash free of her body. The robes she wore parted, revealing her body beneath it.

"What are you?" Lena asked, her hands slipping beneath the soft fabric around Anara's neck and pulling it down past her shoulders.

"A mistress of *Lussena's Temple*," Anara answered. "A courtesan."

The women pulled off her robe, leaving her naked between them as they all took a step back towards their candles. Lena had only desire in her eyes as she looked Anara up and down, a desire Anara knew was reflected in her own.

"Which chapter do you choose?" the five women asked in unison.

"I am a craftswoman, so that my art may support the temple and those around me," Anara responded and Mistress Tasha stepped forward, removing her own robe. *No wonder Lena wanted Anara to be an orderly*, Anara thought as Tasha dressed her in the thin white garment. Tasha's blue sash was still warm as she tied it around Anara's waist.

"I am honored to welcome my new chapter sister," Tasha said, kissing Anara's cheeks.

With that, the candles were extinguished, plunging them all into darkness. The room lit up again a split second later as the shades of the glow lamps were opened and the ball room erupted into cheers. *All* of the courtesans were present at the edges of the large, circular room. Anara covered her face as she laughed. A large cake stood against the back wall where Mistress Adair was standing with her arms folded. Erin beamed at Anara like Nicholas had over Erin's cooking. Anara felt her heart flutter with excitement. She had been successful at enchantments, fallen in love, and been welcomed by the others as one of their own. It felt like home here, more than any place had been before.

Each courtesan took turns kissing her on the cheeks as she went around the hall. The four oldest novices, each a year younger than Anara, went about the courtesan with slices of the confectionary like Anara had done at the young man's celebration where she had seen the sword. That flaming blade still came to the front of her mind if she let her mind wander. *Someday I'll make a sword like that*, Anara thought as she went by more and more women.

The names of all the women became a blur. Seventy courtesans lived at *Lussena's Temple* and Anara's schedules had never crossed paths with many of them. Lena walked up to her last and passionately kissed her; the jeers of the onlookers around them faded away with the scent and touch of the Borderlander so close to Anara.

"Tomorrow is your first day in the Outer Sanctum, I trust you had Moon Tea this morning," Erin said as Lena finally let Anara go. The reminder of the unpleasant tea created apprehension for her duties beyond the inner sanctum. Aside from Lena, Anara had never *been* intimate with someone, and tomorrow she would be with a complete stranger.

"Don't worry, the first one is the most awkward. It gets easier, just try not to let it show too much with Sir Edwin," Lena interjected, seeing the anxiety on Anara's face.

"Sir Edwin? Isn't he the champion of last year's Harvest Festival? He's returned from the skirmishes in the Borderlands, then? Is the fighting going that well?" Erin smiled, saying nothing and nodding as she handed Anara a slice of cake. "Did you make this too?" Anara asked, lifting a piece of the *chocolate* cake with her fork. Anara had never tasted chocolate before and she let the sweet, with a very faint bitter, morsel linger on her tongue as she savored the piece.

"Alas, I can only take credit for your dinner," Erin sighed.

"So, you did feed her then," Lena said, her hands on her hips. "It's because of your punishment for catching Anara... you know where... that she was so late to her celebration."

"You know of Anara's secret trips to the carriage houses, Mistress Weston?" Erin asked, smiling slyly at Anara. "It seems you'll be joining Mistress Swift at the weekly punishment for leaving the temple."

"You mean Lena can come too?" Anara excitedly asked.

"You didn't *tell* her I knew! You could have mentioned that, Anara," Lena growled as Erin walked away. Anara sighed as Lena continued to whine. Anara would just have to tell Lena what Erin really meant once they were alone. Erin had to keep up appearances after all. If Lena had just kept her mouth shut Erin may have invited Lena more discretely. "You don't have to be so happy about getting me wrapped up in your rule breaking again." Anara kissed Lena to get her to stop complaining.

The following morning Anara sat in the Outer Sanctum's waiting room. She had never seen this room before, but it was comfortable enough to sit in. A large fountain of Lussena stood between the two doors for the client entrance, that exited out to where the carriages picked up courtesans for assignments in Aederon City. Directly beneath the statue, one floor down, was the hall where courtesans waited to exit the temple.

Several identical couches, upholstered in deep reds that complimented the dark varnish of the wood, circled the large room. Several other courtesans were up as well, lounging as they waited for their own clients to arrive. None of them spoke to each other. It felt strange since inside the Inner Sanctum—even in the courtesan bath—they would have been chatting with one another about any number of topics. All of them were dressed in the gowns they would have worn if they had intended to leave the temple. The lowcut gowns showed off their cleavage, especially with how the underbust corset beneath the dress pushed them up and together. The thin fabric clung to their legs to show off the curve of their hips and waist. Anara took in a breath to calm her nerves—which would have worked better if the corset let her do so more deeply—and jumped when the side door opened. A young lord, Lord Fenrir, and his wife walked up the stairs and instantly approached the courtesan opposite Anara. Anara recognized the courtesan as Mistress Delayne. It must have taken her hours to manage her hair and it was already starting to frizz. Mistress Delayne stood, hugging and kissing Lady Fenrir before doing the same for Lord Fenrir. The three talked briefly in hushed tones and disappeared down one of the wings where the pleasure rooms waited. Where Anara would eventually end up. A room with her alone with a man. Unless Sir Edwin brought his wife too!

Anara laughed anxiously. *Sir Edwin doesn't* have *a wife,* Anara thought, trying to calm her nerves again. *Besides, Erin would have mentioned anything unexpected. Wouldn't she?* Anara felt like she was going to lose her breakfast, followed shortly by the cake from last night.

Anara shut her eyes trying to force the excitement she felt when she first lay with Lena, the strong desire with a serene foundation was too distant to grasp today. Today's excitement was different, anxious instead of aroused. She wanted to be a novice again – it was simpler then. Her nights were spent with

Lena and her days were spent only *talking* about what she was expected to do. She could be terrible at... *it*. Her heart raced and breath quickened. Her head felt light, too light. *Perhaps I'm ill,* Anara hoped, trying to feel a fever by pressing the back of her hand to her forehead. If anything, she felt cold.

Anara groaned internally, the wait was the worst part of this. Sir Edwin was due to arrive at noon, but Anara had been too antsy to stay in her room until then. Even worse, now that she was here, she would *much* rather be back at her desk working on her first set of geomantically enchanted glassware. Already the fragile medium had proven tricky to work with; a cup had already shattered after she carelessly bumped it off her desk while working on another. Even more so, glass did not carve like wood or metal did with the enchanter's engraving tools. Instead she had been painstakingly scratching away at the surface, making glittery dust as she went deeper and deeper into the thin, clear material. If she had stayed back in her room just a *little* longer she probably would have been able to mix the solution and enchant the cup the moment she got back. Now she would probably have to put that off until after evening meal.

"Mistress Swift?" an unsure, deep voice asked and Anara jumped to her feet.

"Sir Edwin!" Anara squeaked and cleared her throat. Sir Edwin was handsome, at least, and had no unsightly scars like soldiers often collected from their time in battle. His brown, almost blond, hair was cut short in the military style and his face still held the sheen of freshly used shaving oil. His attire would have been suitable for any ball and seemed a little overdone for a courtesan house but Anara suspected Edwin did so to stand out from the others. The military uniform was a long coat over slacks, all with crisp lines from ironing, and his sword hung at his waist from a baldric across his chest. "It is nice to finally meet you," Anara curtsied, offering her hand for Edwin. His hand seemed so large around her as he lifted it to his lips.

"A pleasure that is all mine, I am certain," Edwin said, a smile to match his dashingly chiseled features.

"And more will come," Anara said, standing up straighter as she linked arms with Sir Edwin. Anara feigned a smile, but Sir Edwin was very nearly her own height and with her heeled shoes she could even be an inch or two taller. Edwin did not seem to mind as his eyes explored her curves and the way her dress clung to them. "Shall we? I am yours for the time being."

Sir Edwin nodded, his eyes stopping on Anara's for a long moment. Even a knight, who had traveled around the kingdom, recognized the rarity of the color there. Anara blushed, realizing that the feature Lena cherished so much would be coveted by any who saw her. It felt like a small betrayal that another would look at them with such hunger as Edwin had in his eyes. Anara gently walked Edwin to the room assigned to her for the day. The excitement from before was still there, but now that someone else was sharing in it Anara could almost ignore the emptiness at its core as the two of them slipped into the room and the door shut.

XI

WARTIME NEWS

Joshua stared up from atop the *Academy of Enlightenment* outer wall as Gabriel leaned against it watching the girls. They were beautiful, like they always were, but none compared to the beauty of Mistress Swift's, the azure sky always reminded him of her. Joshua would be leaving Aederon for Crossroads today, in preparation for the Harvest Tournament, but he still could not get his mind off of the courtesan at his party a few months earlier. She enticed him in his dreams, a beautiful blonde with only a last name who blushed under the gaze of men. A courtesan who *blushed*. It was impossible and only proved to Joshua that Mistress Swift belonged elsewhere. Preferably somewhere with him. She was also a much better marriage candidate than Cordelia too, like Cynthia had been for Sir Echton, because they were already in the same social caste. It would be wonderful the day he earned his knighthood, he would race off on his horse, *Swiftstride*, and go to *Lussena's Temple*. He would force his way inside to free the beautiful mistress if he had to. Then, still wearing his polished armor he would ride off into the sunset to make a home with her in the countryside.

She would be grateful, falling deeply in love with him for ending her life as little more than a pleasure slave at the mercy of her clients' whims.

"You're daydreaming about her again, aren't you?" Eric groaned when he caught Joshua grinning like an idiot. "Forget her, Joshua, you can't have someone like her following you around in the Borderlands."

"Why not?" Joshua asked, sitting up. The home would have to wait for his revenge, of course. "I could protect her down there." Eric just gave him a flat stare that said *I don't put up with nonsense* and Joshua jumped off the wall.

"Why do we still hang out here if you don't even bother *looking* at them anymore?" Eric asked.

"I look."

"Really? What color is Cora wearing today?" Eric seemed thoroughly pleased with his conundrum. It was a stupid question to act like that.

"Blue, no wait... green?" Joshua guessed.

"It's violet, if you must know," Cordelia said right behind him. Joshua shrugged, trying to shrink, as he turned around. She was, indeed, wearing violet that was very pleasing to look at. So much so that Joshua was embarrassed that the cut might not keep her entirely decent if she moved the wrong way. Two spirals of gold embroidery radiated out from the center of the bodice, the long circles crossed again and again in a line down the center to the loose hem of the skirt around Cordelia's ankles. A decorative chain of gold and sparkling diamonds—which probably cost more than everything Joshua ever owned—decorated her neck and a large emerald pendant hung on the chain, drawing the eye to her supple breasts. He was likely to get slapped if he continued to stare, so he looked up into her light brown eyes. Her wavy, brown hair was pulled back, held in place by a hair band of more gold and diamonds, and fell to the small of her back. She was beautiful, of course, but the blonde hair and blue eyes of Mistress Swift were exotic to Joshua. He had grown up around brown and darker brown.

"Good afternoon, Cordelia," Joshua said, bowing slightly with a flourish of his hand. "I see you have learned your colors, this academy truly does provide enlightenment."

"Perhaps you should attend as well, I am certain you would fit in," Cordelia said, her arms folded beneath her bust. Her flock of girls giggled at her retort. "Then you might learn to think before you speak as well." Eric snickered and Joshua shot him his own no-nonsense glare. "You only need a dress of your own. Honestly, Joshua, eighteen and you still have no facial hair. Of course you would need a wig until your hair grew out. Aside from a little powder on your nose and some paint on your lips, you could be one of us."

"Not *all* men have to shave," Joshua defended, scratching his jaw. It was a weak defense; he was really struggling to quip words with Cordelia today as the girls laughed at him.

"Can't you tell he's been smitten, Cora?" Eric said, providing an even weaker defense than Joshua's was. "It isn't fair to attack a weaker opponent who has had his mind turned to mush by the wiles of another woman."

"Perhaps if he spent as much time sharpening his wits as he did his sword then he would have a better head on his shoulders and know a *real* woman when he sees one. From what I saw of the serving girl she was wanting. So what if she has blue eyes?" Cordelia sounded jealous, Joshua would never understand women. Cordelia would *never* be allowed to marry Joshua anyway; there was nothing for her to be jealous about. "Are we going to speak of lowborn pretties all day or are you here to escort me home? Certainly, news of the skirmishes has come since Sir Edwin returned to Aederon nearly a week back."

"The knights have returned for the Harvest Festival? I take it they weren't informed the venue changed to Crossroads?" Joshua asked, finally hearing *something* that interested him. "Did he bring word about Sir Echton? How about the war with the Ironeyes?"

"I can't say, I only found out he was back," Cordelia said, sighing like her entourage now that Joshua was genuinely paying attention to her. "Though you are welcome to our estate to find out, I'm certain our servants will have all the information you seek."

"No," Joshua shook his head, looking towards the tournament grounds. Sir Edwin, and any of the other knights would be practicing for the upcoming events. "I'd rather hear it directly from the source. Come on, Eric."

"Why do I have to go? I *was* here to take my sister home."

"They aren't likely to talk to me. I'm still just a squire even if I *am* able to compete now. You're the heir to the Lord Commander. They have to talk to you, or risk being punished."

"And leave me to walk alone?" Cordelia gasped as if that were the worst thing in all of Iliona that could happen. "Besides, if you had competed in the last two tournaments they would have talked to you out of respect."

"Gabriel can walk you home," Joshua suggested.

"Your half-giant friend! You'd have your oaf walk me home?"

"He's not an oaf, and *probably* not a giant," Joshua growled back. It was one thing to insult *his* intelligence, but Gabriel's was just rude. "And he isn't mine; he's his own person. Not to mention practically nobility with how rich his family is."

"I am an oaf, a little bit," Gabriel muttered, agreeing with Cordelia like a good peasant. If anyone needed sharper wits it was Gabriel.

"Then walk home with your geese," Joshua said, gesturing to the girls gathered behind Cordelia. Ignoring Gabriel, he started towards the arena. Eric was right beside him.

"Fine!" Cordelia screamed at them. "Come along, Gabriel," she said loud enough for them to still hear. "At least *you* are a gentleman, unlike my brother and Sir Echton's *honorable* squire."

Joshua did not care, or rather tried not to. Cordelia just got under his skin sometimes, like she knew where to prod to annoy and wound him. He was already leaving for Crossroads today; he did not have time to dally with Cordelia as they returned to the Ackart estate in Noble District. He wanted direct news, not some flowery tale spun by the Ackart servants with more than a little of their own opinions and assumptions tossed in. A soldier knew the horrors of war. Horrors Joshua knew. Servants painted those heinous acts like some glorified honor. As if glory could be won at the tip of a sword coated in blood like some tournament game. There was no glory in killing. Only a mess of entrails and blood. No, there was no glory. Joshua did not want glory, that was not his drive to return to the Borderlands. He wanted vengeance, and killing was the best way to obtain that.

"You two really should try getting along better," Eric said as the streets of Merchant's Row started becoming more and more crowded the further west into Cheapside they went to reach the arena.

"I don't see why, Eric," Joshua shrugged, testing his father's blade to make sure it was free in its scabbard. A soldier always made sure his weapon could be drawn at a moment's notice. *Vengeance* was back in his rooms at the Echton homestead and had not been drawn since his celebration. Cynthia had finally won the battle to have him move in. It was not practical to live on the other side of the city if Joshua was supposed to be protecting her for his mentor. "She's bound to marry some noble who is only interested in advancing his family's standing in the kingdom."

"I didn't mean for you to court her," Eric laughed, slapping the back of Joshua's head. "She's your friend."

"Since *when*?" Joshua rubbed the wound. It did not hurt, at least not physically. He would have returned the gesture if Eric had not been nobility.

"Since you were eleven years old, Joshua, remember? Since Sir Echton brought you back to Aederon City, the two of you had been as close as we are."

"We were younger then," Joshua sighed, doing his best not to run into anyone on the street. They were packed this far west in Merchant's Row where those from Cheapside could afford the wares. "She grew up and got... well... all womanly."

"And you're still a little boy, it seems," Eric chuckled. "Girls don't have some terrible disease that will infect you if you touch them."

"You don't understand," Joshua shook his head. "You're her brother."

"What's that got to do with it?"

"You don't understand," Joshua sighed, he could not explain it to Eric. Cordelia was beautiful and more. She was physically attractive, in the carnal sense of the term. It was hard to treat Cordelia like he had when they did not care about those things. They had been friends, but Joshua wanted more now and he could not deny it. "But what about you? Your woes with women are *far* more entertaining, Eric."

"What woes? I have none," Eric said. The arena came into view as the houses and shops turned into single level structures. The arena towered over them, four stories tall to provide seating for as many who could fit in as possible. Even more could fit in the peasant stands since there were no seats. "It is the blessing of frequenting whore houses. There's so many to choose from that you don't have to worry about meeting the same one twice."

"As well as the rashes you catch. I assume those are blessings as well. Remind me again about the diseases women *don't* carry?" Joshua snickered, receiving another, albeit well deserved, smack against his head.

The two walked out onto the arena grounds to t a horse's hooves drumming to a fast gallop. Sir Edwin—in his unblemished and decorated armor—guiding his horse towards a stationary shield set in the center of the run. Edwin's lance met the shield dead center, he was quite skilled-at least against stationary objects. The lance's shaft exploded as the shield was torn free of the post it stood on. Sir Edwin turned his horse around, raising his now much shorter lance to the cheers of the few other knights and spectators.

"Lord Ackart," Edwin said, raising his helmet's visor and reigning in his stallion. "You honor me with your presence. Have you received word from your father? Did he order me to return? I do have leave for the tournament if you are requiring that proof of me at this time."

"No, nothing of the sort," Eric said, patting the steed's nose and neck. "I am actually here for your word concerning the conflict in the borderlands. It seems I've yet to hear anything formally beyond your return."

"Of course," Sir Edwin said, hoisting himself free of his saddle with ease even though he wore a suit of plate and chain. A young boy of thirteen approached, probably Edwin's squire, and took the lance and shield from the knight. "Lord Commander Ackart succeeds at each front he visits," Edwin recounted. "His understanding of tactics and a battlefield's terrain is inspiring, though that is not to say Iliona is not sustaining any casualties. The women have been safely escorted to Ashfall, for the most part, but the Raykarn tactics changed once they realized that happened."

"What do you mean?" Eric asked; he looked concerned.

"Ironeye women have been in every skirmish since we arrived, I can't make sense of it. When our women were safely escorted, there were two Ironeye women for every man, as if they had run out of men to fight. It's absurd." Sir Edwin shook his head, the color draining from his face. "It's despicable, having our knights ride against their women despite reports of their overwhelming numbers of men. It is bad enough, seeing a woman speared by a lance or taken by sword while atop a horse, I cannot imagine what the footmen feel as they cut down so many." Joshua ground his teeth. What did it matter if they were men or women? Raykarn were still Raykarn. Clearly, Sir Edwin had not accustomed himself to war in his year-long absence.

"It makes sense," Eric sighed, his shoulders slumping visibly. "A soldier, raised to defend the virtue of women above all else, will be cut down by a woman willing to kill him. I would wager our losses increased when the Ironeyes sent those women into battle."

"Not just that," Sir Edwin said. "Many go missing as well as if our soldiers are being kidnapped now instead of the women."

"What?" Eric asked, his eyes opening wide. "Why, what purpose could that possibly serve? Capturing civilians is one thing but captured soldiers tend to attempt to break free, taking any large amount could be devastating if enough banded together. It's why we don't take Raykarn prisoners. Mobile prisons aren't sturdy enough to contain a determined prisoner and just five could tear a regiment apart in the night. Who has been taken?"

"Most the older knights too tired to fight. They leave our wounded behind."

"What about Sir Echton?" Joshua asked, grabbing Sir Edwin by his shoulders. Sir Edwin shook Joshua free, likely turning to Eric to hear his decision on Joshua's action.

"I'll not punish a squire for inquiring about his knight," Eric judged. Joshua ground his teeth at the formality. Grabbing Sir Edwin might not be enough to end up in the stocks, but it was enough for a public flogging. "Answer him."

"He was taken two months back," Sir Edwin said, sounding irritated at having to answer someone beneath him. "He's probably dead. Lord Commander Ackart refuses to declare it without a body, though he does nothing to find the old knight. If you'll excuse me, I have the run for another hour of practice, my lord."

Joshua fell to his knees, sinking a little in the mud of the arena. *Sir Echton captured*, Joshua thought and clenched his fists.

"You'll find him," Eric said, placing a hand on Joshua's shoulder. "Gods willing you'll find Sir Echton and free him."

"Damn the gods!" Joshua yelled. "I'll find him without their help. I'll find Sir Echton *and* kill every... single... Raykarn. I'll bathe the Endless Waste in their orange blood!" Joshua stood and left the arena with Eric on his heels. "Damn it all, I should never have stayed in Aederon."

"Joshua, calm yourself," Eric cautioned, Joshua smacked the noble's hand as he tried to hold him back. "The Borderlands are over two months away, what do you think storming off now will accomplish? You still have a knighthood to claim, and duties to keep Cynthia safe!"

"Cynthia is already safe! What soul from Cheapside would be desperate enough to venture to her homestead and rob her? He would be caught within a league of her street and escorted back to Cheapside... or a dungeon," Joshua fumed, he refused to look at Eric. Nobility or not, Eric did not matter. Nothing did. He needed to avenge his family. He *needed* to find Sir Echton. *Vengeance* would help him. All Raykarn would fear the bite of his fiery blade. They would all die by it as well. "I've fought and lived by Sir Echton's side in the Borderlands before! I should have gone south!"

"I gave you an order!" Eric yelled, grabbing Joshua by the nape of his neck at the same time his boot tripped him. Joshua found himself sprawled out on the road, his face pressed against the cold, muddy stones of the street as Eric held him down. "Calm yourself, squire, before you defy your liege lord and wind up in the stocks. You cannot win a tournament or rescue your mentor if you're chained to a block of wood!" Joshua turned red with anger and shame. Eric had taken him down so easily in his rage as the citizens of Cheapside parted to make way for the scuffle. More than a few murmurs of Eric's heritage broke the silence. "A reckless abandonment of your duties to charge south will only get you killed," Eric said, lowering his voice. He sounded like Sir Echton. "You swore to protect the weak," he said, beginning the vow every soldier took when they graduated the *Academy of the Watch*. "To uphold Iliona's values. To rise above the common man with dignity and honor. You are the shield and sword of the kingdom, sworn to serve her before your own ambitions." Joshua ground his teeth as tears came to his eyes.

Eric kneeled over him, letting the words sink in as Joshua was unable to do anything to get away. Joshua took a few deep breaths, each one smelling of musty dust and a hint of dung as he calmed himself. It took longer than it should have because everything the Raykarn took from him kept surfacing. Sir Echton, Father, Mother, Elisa... It hurt to think of them as he lay helpless on Aederon's streets. *Reckless things get you killed, son.* Sir Echton's words finally rang true. Eric was a decent fighter—not a good one but decent—but Joshua's haste to charge after his mentor had left him vulnerable.

"I'm going to let you up," Eric said and Joshua felt the young lord's grip lessen. "And forgive you for your lapse in judgment... this time. Next time I *will* exercise my right as the heir to the Lord Commander of Iliona to punish one of her sworn protectors. Now get up, you have three weeks until the start of the Harvest Tournament in Crossroads. It is time you participated and proved your worth to the kingdom beyond being a protector within her borders."

"Thank you," Joshua said, rising to a kneel. "My lord," Joshua hastily added and stood up. Both Cordelia *and* Eric had changed since they were children. Eric clapped his hand on

Joshua's shoulder and they walked towards Echton's homestead as if nothing had happened. Eric tried to be the same boy, but he *was* his father's son.

Cynthia was outside hanging laundry on the clothesline that draped from the house to the single tree. She still insisted on doing all the tasks a servant could, even though with Echton gone it meant she was doing all of them. Joshua walked up to her and she immediately knew something was wrong.

Cynthia did not take the news of Sir Echton's capture any better than Joshua had. She fell to her knees, clinging to Joshua's muddied tunic with her clean, delicate hands as she wailed. Tears streamed down her face as she looked up at him with pleading eyes. *Find Malcolm* they said, and Joshua would. Eric was correct, though. As a knight, he could lead any soldiers willing to go with him to rescue Sir Echton once he reached the Borderlands. He may *want* to kill every Raykarn, but that would be impossible without help. Joshua could only stand there, keeping the fire he felt towards the Raykarn at bay as Eric watched from the edge of the property. Joshua felt like he had failed Echton. He had stayed behind, true, but he had been unable to protect Cynthia from the only threat she faced in the safety of Ilona's capitol. Losing Echton would mean losing her world and Joshua could do nothing to prevent it.

His departure was quiet that afternoon, neither Joshua nor Cynthia said any words of farewell as he used Echton's mule to carry his armor, and slowly rode *Swiftstride* to the ferry in Cheapside. Sir Echton's horse was probably dead now. The Raykarn considered horse a delicacy and would have eaten the animal the night Sir Echton was captured. Gabriel, Eric, and Cordelia were waiting at the ferry to travel to Crossroads with him when Joshua arrived but he found little comfort in their company.

XII

HARVEST FESTIVAL

Opening Week

Nicholas's carriage bounced a lot as it journeyed south and Anara bemoaned silently as yet *another* field of amber grains swayed outside the window. Lena slept with the shaved left side of her head in Anara's lap. Erin sat reading, she had been doing the past three weeks as they journeyed to Crossroads. Anara had tried, but even the information in *Advanced Enchantment Theory* had been unable to keep her attention focused enough to avoid motion sickness. Roxanne sat beside Erin painting her nails. Another impossibility for Anara, she lacked the coordination it required to do anything other than putting lacquer splotches on her fingers with the constant motions of the cabin. Only four courtesans were going to represent *Lussena's Temple* at the Harvest Tournament this year because it had been pushed back and moved to a different city at the last minute.

Ultimately, the three of Erin's closest friends were heading south for a month long appointment; Roxanne was a fellow blade dancer while Anara—and Lena by association—had grown close during the dinners with Nicholas. It felt wrong to Anara since there *were* more experienced courtesans to choose from. Anara sighed again as yet another field rolled by.

"I had forgotten you were asleep for this part the first time we came through," Erin said, smiling from behind her book. "It was a little more exciting back then since I was worried you would die at any time."

"She was in no danger. I told you that the moment you got back... a week late," Lena said. Anara smiled, placing her hand on Lena's back. Of course she was only *pretending* to be asleep. "Mistress Caidrill was furious when you told her about the additional expenditures you paid, by the way."

"Really? She didn't say anything about it to me. How odd," Erin sighed. "Though it could not have been helped. Anara was really very little help when we had to set up camp and break it down every night, wasting time in hibernation."

"Sounds like how it has been this trek," Mistress Ashton chimed in with a chuckle. "I love the heat box she made right before we left, but I'd think she could help contribute a bit more when there *isn't* a tavern to spend the night in."

"It wasn't my fault," Anara pouted, glaring at Roxanne. She helped plenty those nights, Roxanne just liked to rub in how much more she could do. Anara could not physically lift as much as Erin or Roxanne since they focused on physical strength and agility for their chapter. "I was ill."

"No you weren't," Lena laughed, sitting up just long enough to kiss Anara. "I don't know what you were, but Erin's suggestion of hibernation seems the most likely. Your body just seemed to be frozen in time, you lost no weight and needed no food for four weeks. When I'm a famous orderly I might have to do a case study on you to see if I can reproduce the results."

"I'm not a bear who sleeps off the winter, nor a rodent to experiment on," Anara said, poking Lena in the ribs.

"More like a phoenix of the endless waste," Roxy said. "They hibernate in the summer, to be reborn in late fall. I always thought it strange that Malef's birds of prey sleep when it is warm."

"That is a better image, too, but still not right. Bear is a closer fit since they go to hibernate around the same time Anara did." Lena said, rolling over so she could see the other courtesans. "Anara doesn't look like a bear but she could be my phoenix."

"I don't look like a bird, either," Anara stated, starting to braid Lena's half head of hair.

"You can, I could get a craftswoman to make you some wings," Lena smiled at the attention Anara was giving her. "I heard Joshua Kentaine will be in the tournament this time," Lena said, winking at Anara.

"What is that supposed to mean? It isn't as if I fancy him, Lena," Anara said. "You're the only one I need."

"He is, is he? It's about time that twat joined a competition," Erin added, tapping her lips thoughtfully. "Pity he was not the one to approach me and request you for the Harvest Festival."

"Someone requested me?" Anara raised her eyebrows at that.

"Why did you think you were coming?" Erin asked. "No, Sir Edwin requested you to accompany him for the nightly celebrations as he advances through the ranks again to claim his tenth win at the Harvest Tournament. If he succeeds, he'll not have only earned his knighthood in this manner but a title of nobility as well. The first one in Ilionan history."

"Impressive," Roxanne said, blowing lightly on her finished nails. "Most men fail at that; they take too many injuries that age them too quickly to win ten in a row."

"They say he's never had a lance broken against him, Edwin the Untouchable," Lena said, grinning at Anara with another wink. "Apparently you made *quite* the impression on the man. Perhaps he is not so untouchable after all?"

"Don't remind me," Anara groaned. The unpleasantness of her first day as a courtesan still lingered. It had not been terrible, just men tended to be a lot rougher than Lena was. "I'm just glad you were right for once. It was easier the next time, not much easier, but a little."

"Oh, only once? I seem to recall saying you'd wear my colors when I first met you, and then you did the morning after *our* first night together."

"By the gods, Lena," Roxanne gasped, seething of sarcasm. "You must be a prophet. When did you unlock the ability to commune with the gods? I knew the myth that only the Xulesi witches could see the future was a farce!"

"When I was eight," Lena said, playing along. "I prayed for wisdom, but only to Ezebre and Mertas. The two goddesses came down to commune with me. We made love all night, and the next morning I could see the future. Don't be jealous of my past, my love," Lena said patting Anara's leg. "It was a forbidden affair that ended too soon with ecstasy that lasted far too long."

Roxanne laughed with Lena as Anara paused, disgracefully losing her concentration of Lena's braid. Roxanne brought out the worst eroticism in Lena.

"Now I'll have to start all over again," Anara sighed, pretending not to feel the heat of her face.

After days of riding in the carriage, Anara was growing anxious to wander a city's streets on her own legs. Not that Anara spent much time wandering Aederon City—apart from buying supplies for her magecraft and the occasional appointment—but even *Lussena's Temple* was larger than some of the villages they had stayed in. They would arrive in Crossroads today and she was anxious to compare Crossroads to Aederon. Anara looked out the window again at yet another field.

"It'll be after midday meal when we arrive, Anara," Erin said, still not looking up from her book. Anara absently let her fingers trace the Raykarn runes around Lena's neck band, it was impossible to decipher them since they did not even remotely resemble Ilionan runes. Lena had not been able to provide insights either, she may have learned to speak Raykarn but not read their own ancient writing. Lena closed her eyes, enjoying the attention, and shifted her weight against Anara as if she were a cat.

"I know," Anara said, watching the tall, swaying stalks of golden grain. "I was just hoping to at least catch a glimpse of the city. We should be able to see it by now, shouldn't we?"

"The road alongside Eastfold Forest is too snake-like," Roxanne said. "But we are still a way off yet."

Soleanne was setting when Crossroads finally, and quickly, came into view as they rounded one last finger of Eastfold Forest at the top of a low hill. Crossroads sprawled out more than Aederon City, growing denser in the middle where a single stone tower rose above the rest. There were no towering walls or bodies of water to divide and reign in the city's outward growth or separate the lowborn from the high. Crossroad's streets were nearly identical and Anara lost where they were in the grid-like design of the city by the time they reached a side street that ended at the fence of a two story structure.

"*Lussena's Rest*?" Lena read, glancing at Erin. "Don't tell me you own this place as well?" Erin smiled, pulling a key from her handbag that matched the building's lock.

"I have not used it in a few years," Erin said, opening the door for them "I meant to with Anara on the way. It would have given me a way to ease her into the transition to her new way of life. Her condition made me reconsider."

Anara entered, each step leaving a footprint of her heeled shoe in the layers of dust. It smelled musty like no one had entered to let the air circulate since it was last used. The furniture of the inn was covered by large white cloths that had been stained brown by dust. Mistress Adair pulled the sheeting off of the couch in the study and sat down with a long sigh.

"Finally," Erin said leaning back in the seat. "Something *comfortable*." Anara sat with Lena and Roxanne in the open spaces of the long bench with sighs of their own. Nicholas and one of the driver's hands, Gerrol, brought their luggage in and waited in the hall.

"Anara, Roxanne, and Lena's room is on the first floor behind the kitchen," Erin said, motioning to the room across the hall from the study. "Sorry girls, but there are only three rooms and the one upstairs is only big enough for one."

"Anara and I could make it work," Lena said suggestively.

"There's another room behind the study for you and Gerrol to share, Master Brenton," Erin continued without acknowledging Lena's suggestion. Clearly, she did not want to give up the private room upstairs.

"If you want some time alone with Anara, Lena, I suggest you go break in your bed while I'm luxuriating on this marvelous couch," Roxanne suggested. Anara's heart raced, as it usually did at the prospect of being alone with Lena. Lena pulled her out of the couch and back toward the hall where the drivers had disappeared. Lena undid the lacing of Anara's traveling dress as they walked through the cramped kitchen, forcing her to hold up her bodice when the two men appeared from the room and the four squeezed past each other.

"Apologies," Anara said uncomfortably as Lena giggled and disappeared into the room. Nicholas shook his head, disappearing back out to grab Erin's luggage, but Gerrol hesitated, spellbound by Anara's state of undress.

"Boy, leave 'nara 'lone," Nicholas called a moment later as Anara made it around the helper and into the room she would share with Lena and Roxanne.

The room was barely large enough for two, four poster beds and a single wardrobe. Lena had already claimed the one closest to the door as theirs where she was laying seductively with her skirts pulled up to the hip of one of her legs. Anara smiled, climbing into bed, and eased into Lena's embrace.

Anara awoke feeling refreshed, if not a little more famished than normal for skipping evening meal with Lena. She rolled over to find herself alone in the cramped room. Roxanne's bed was already made and her sword rested against the wall beside her bed. The weapon would probably not be needed—like usual—while they stayed in Crossroads but the blade dancer insisted on bringing it. Mistress Adair had brought her own as well.

"It's all the more reason to have it with me," Roxanne had said when they were waiting for Nicholas and Gerrol to load their cases back at *Lussena's Temple*. "If none of us are armed, we'll wind up in a situation where we need to be." Of course that was not entirely true. Gerrol and Nicholas both carried swords of their own in case a weapon was needed; the two men could actually be seen with them in public. Notably, Roxanne had left the sword in the room with no intention of actually having it on her in public. She had a long dagger for that.

Anara stretched and threw on her craftswoman's robe before walking out of her room and directly into the kitchen. Lena ate standing up at the table because there was no room for chairs. Breakfast looked to be of Roxanne's cooking – burnt toast and runny eggs. Lena ate it eagerly even while Anara wrinkled her nose at it. It had been a long time since Anara ate something similar, not since she left *Wentworth's*. Erin's plate looked like the eggs and toast had just been pushed around, turning the black bread soggy. Roxanne, of course, was busy adding more to her already dirty plate. Nicholas and Gerrol were not in the kitchen, Anara doubted the kitchen would be able to fit Gerrol with the four of them, let alone Nicholas's much larger build.

"When do the events start?" Anara asked, pushing her plate away. She would eat later.

"The sword has already begun," Erin answered, her nose still in the same book she had been reading the night before. "Joshua, it turns out, is competing in that as well as jousting. The lad barely squeaked by with a two-point lead during his first match. Hopefully, he does better on a horse in the afternoon. I can't imagine so; he took more than one solid blow today."

"I can't believe I slept through them," Roxanne sighed between mouthfuls. "I had been looking forward to those since leaving the temple. Damn travel fatigue."

"They run all day, Roxy," Lena laughed.

"And Edwin?" Anara inquired before Roxanne could say anything back.

"Only in the jousts," Erin said. "He will be tilting today as well. The lowborn usually face each other first so I doubt we will ever see Edwin matched against Joshua."

The courtesans changed into more appropriate attire to attend the tournament and were soon back in Nicholas's carriage as it rolled along towards Crossroads arena a little way outside city limits. Hundreds of tree stumps surrounded the oval stadium. Many of them so freshly cut Anara could smell the sap. She even spotted a tree trunk that had what looked like the remnants of a shrine—similar to those at the orphanage if a child died of illness—as they walked around the edge of the grounds to find the spectator entrance. Anara blushed when she noticed Sir Edwin waiting beside the door.

"Mistress Swift," Edwin said, bowing and taking Anara's hand to help her up the stairs into the stadium. "I am delighted you managed to make it. Tonight will be our first of many nights during the festival. Each night I win you will decorate my arm. I guarantee it."

"I expect that to be true, Sir Edwin," Anara said, slipping back into her role. "I have heard of your prowess with a lance since we last met," a lie. She knew back then; she just had no reason to mention it. "Nine times the Harvest Tournament champion, I will cheer for you. It would be impressive knowing a man who claimed nobility through competition alone instead of blood and gold."

"Then you shall know that man," Edwin said as the four women took their seats at the edge of the box. The nobility boxes were a little further back and above where Anara's group sat. In the middle of the nobility, and raised even higher, was the royal box where three women—Iliona's queens—were watching the field and fanning themselves. Their dresses were decorated with so much gold and so many gemstones Anara had to squint to see any fabric. The king, due to his age and frail health, was unable to attend and why the venue switch at the last moment was unexpected. It was traditional that the king see the start of each Harvest Tournament. "Originally, I was to tilt against Lord Ashton, but he seems to be having a spot of bother with his armor this morning so I agreed to let him face a later opponent instead of force him to forfeit. I tilt against Lord Egmont today instead. The man is rather useless on horseback, so I hope the event is not too disappointing for you."

"Each victory of yours is a victory of mine," Anara said, gently squeezing the knight's hand. "I will be excited, so long as you are triumphant."

"I must get going now if you'll pardon me, my ladies," Sir Edwin bowed and left them to their watching.

"Ashton?" Lena asked, elbowing Anara and nodding to Roxanne. "As in... Mistress Ashton? As in Roxy?"

"It is a common name, now hush," Roxanne hissed, pointing out to the field as a parade of horses entered. Anara recognized all of the knights and nobles by their coats of arms.

The nobility came first with soldiers carrying their coats of arms. The young Lord Ackart—whose crest depicted two lions crossing swords beneath a plumed helm—looked even more dashing in his full plate than Anara remembered from Joshua's party. Behind him came Lord Morgan Heath—two olive branches framed a red phoenix above a banner stating the family name—who waved to the crowds and blew a kiss toward two women sitting beside the royal box. The lady with brown hair so wavy it was almost curly caught it and pressed it to her lips. The other just stared coldly out over the competitors with little interest.

"Oh, dear! When did that happen?" Erin asked, looking at the two women. "It appears the first Lady Heath has been in some sort of dreadful accident."

"What do you mean?" Anara asked curiously. Looking over the stern woman made Anara uncomfortable with her own appearance. The Lady Heath—with straight, blood-red hair—was the most beautiful woman Anara had ever seen.

"She's missing her hand!" Lena gasped, pointing quickly to the golden hand in the woman's lap. "How *did* that happen? I've never seen a prosthetic for nobility, it seems a bit... ostentatious if you ask me. Kind of draws attention to it. I'd think she would want it to look more real so as not to draw attention to it." " Anara did not really care. The rumors would eventually find their way back to *Lussena's Temple* and Anara could pick one to pass along to her clients then.

Lord Barnum, the reagent of the Fertile Vale, in a suit of armor that made him look like a steel onion with his gigantic green plume and large belly entered next. The horse he rode must have been miserable carrying so much weight. Barnum's coat of arms had two sprigs of grapes—one red the other green—both held by a naked woodland nymph, a not-quite-human female creature that represented fertility in ancient Iliona. Lord Barnum was followed by the young Lord Ashton. He barely even looked their way as he passed, choosing that moment to fuss with the straps of his armor instead as if they did not exist. Had Anara not gotten Roxanne's lineage from her back at *Aederon's Enchantorium* she would not have even noticed the slight. Then came Lord Quill, followed by Lord Darren and his son, then Lord Farhold.

"There are so many of them," Anara said, losing track of the nobles following Farhold.

"Most won't make it to the second round," Roxanne said, shaking her head. "Don't these men realize how much of an embarrassment it is to lose that early? They're supposed to be nobility. In theory, they're the best of us all, yet most can't even stay seated on a horse." Lena laughed when the last lord, Lord Io, nearly toppled off his saddle as Roxanne spoke.

Next came the knights, who had disappointingly plain coats of arms compared to the nobility. Very few had full sets of plate, but rather had plate and chain mixes and even fewer had the delicate decorations that covered the nobles' armor. They also typically carried shields instead of the reinforced, larger left pauldrons the nobility wore.

Sir Stanson was in black armor atop a black stallion with black swords on a red and white field on his squire's marker shield. It was not a real shield like the nobility used for their coat of arms but just a simple, thin wooden shape to signal who was tilting during each match. Behind him was Sir Coldsworth whose marker had two doves on a green field. Then Sir Barton with a black crescent on white for a marker. Barton's armor was even painted to match his marker. Sir Matheson's marker had an orange sphere on an even brighter yellow field. His coat of arms left bright spots in Anara's vision and she missed the next three. Sir Edwin came by, blowing *her* a kiss, in his full plate. He almost looked like a noble already. Even his squire wore armor, unlike all of the others who looked more like peasants than knights-in-training.

"Those'll be the ones to watch," Roxanne said as the tail end of the knights approached. "They actually know how to fight, unlike the lords they serve or the peasants they protect."

After the knights came the men who sought to earn their knighthood by rising above each competitor in line ahead of them. Farmers, craftsmen, and soldiers—men from the lowborn caste—of a competing age made up this group.

Anara wanted to hide behind something as they came by; each one gawked at the four courtesans as if they had never seen a woman before. Since they had no squires they wore their marker shields on their backs. Instead of a coat of arms, the commoners' shields were simply painted one or two colors. Every now and then there might be a shield with three. Anara had no way of knowing who they were. Very few of them had any armor to protect them. Instead, they wore chain or boiled leather with simple, open-faced steel helms and the plates they did wear looked like they were a poor fit. Very few had their own horses. Those who did not would be expected to use horses provided by the Heath estates, which meant they would be using old and decrepit steeds. No noble would grant the use of a prized horse to a lowborn. Altogether, the odds were stacked against these men.

Anara yawned, hiding it with her fan, as the procession went on and on. Five hundred and twelve men came to compete each year, and it turned out that the vast majority of them were these ragtag hopefuls.

"Mistress Swift!" a voice called out and Anara's dazed eyes focused on a man atop a horse between a long line of walkers. It was Joshua Kentaine. He still looked like a boy without any stubble on his lip and chin. It made him surprisingly pretty, despite showing off his square jaw. Anara had just assumed he kept it clean shaven, but the tournament would be a time to show off what he could grow as some sort of badge of manhood. Apparently, Joshua just could not grow any facial hair. "It *is* you, I would know those eyes anywhere," Joshua said, sounding giddy and slowing to a stop below their box. Some of the other hopefuls grumbled, moving around him as they presented themselves for the crowds. Nearly everyone looked to be asleep now. "How have you been?"

"Pardon me," Anara said, watching in horror as peasants and nobility had their attention drawn to the disturbance in the procession. "But now is not the time to socialize, one would think."

"I asked a simple question," Joshua shrugged, frowning slightly and sounding hurt. *The fool does have an infatuation with me*, Anara thought and looked him up and down. He actually wore plates as well. No doubt he was spoiled by the Ackarts or Sir

Echton, though he was still an untested jouster. Two tournaments had passed since the man's celebration, yet he had not participated. "I will have to find you after if you refuse to answer now. Or is a simple answer too long for you to utter in my presence?" Anara furrowed her brow at the man. He had practically insulted her. And his tone was too familiar.

"Mistress Swift is doing well, Master Kentaine," Lena answered waving her hands to move him along. "Now if you would kindly stop blocking our view, I believe I can still see Sir Edwin on the field." Joshua tugged at his armor's collar as he turned bright red. His lack of facial hair made his flushed skin more noticeable even though his skin tone was a blend between Anara's and Lena's.

"Still looking out for your pupil, I see, Mistress Weston," Joshua grumbled dejectedly, guiding his horse back into the parade.

"I could have answered him, Lena," Anara said watching the young man go. She frowned at her love, it was slightly annoying that Lena had spoken for her.

"Of course, you could have, but you were toying with him instead. If Sir Edwin caught wind of you flirting with him... your time with him probably would not go well. Besides, now he'll probably still find you after to get that answer."

"And catch me with Sir Edwin? Joshua is infatuated with me, Lena, that would not end well either."

"I know! It would be exciting," Lena said, leaning over as if to kiss her. Blessedly Lena thought better of it considering how public they were. Unfortunately, that left Anara longing for Lena's lips as the fighting began.

The first several matches were between a handful of the lowborn. Even from what little Anara understood of jousting she could tell they were not that good. Nearly half the time the men missed each other completely, their lances bouncing as much as the men were in the saddle. Most of them looked like they had never even ridden a horse before the tournament. That changed when Joshua was paired with another peasant. It seemed unfairly one-sided as Joshua's lance drove into the man's shield and knocked him from his horse.

"That's it?" Anara asked as the crowd, for the first time in the evening, had cause to cheer. Mistress Ashton was cheering louder than most people around them.

"Of course," Roxanne said after retaking her seat. "The goal is to break three lances against your opponent, or at least strike him six times, but if you knock him from his horse you win the round. Joshua advances. He won't have to ride again until next week as the numbers are culled. Unlike the sword, where you fight nearly everyone and climb up or fall down the ranks, jousting is elimination based. The week after, if he wins twice to advance again, he'll be able to tilt twice more. Then four more times the final week of the Harvest Festival when the tournament wraps up. Assuming he is not defeated in any of the maximum nine matches he will have earned a knighthood. Everyone you've seen lose today will most likely be in the stands or on their way home for the rest of the festival. Honestly, how much attention did you pay during your lessons?"

"That may have been my fault," Lena confessed. "I often visited with her when they were teaching Iliona's sports."

Roxanne rolled her eyes, looking at Mistress Adair who was playing ignorance to their discussion. Now was not the time to dole out punishments for breaking rules; that would wait until they returned to *Lussena's Temple*.

A few more matches between lowborn occurred and then the knights and nobles faced off against each other. Sir Edwin had a proper match. His blue enameled armor seemed to make his opponents lance glide off him as they clashed. Each time his blue-striped lance hit firmly, exploding in a shower of splintered wood. Each of his three runs left him unscathed, but his opponent looked like he could barely stay upright on his horse as the two contestants cantered off the field for the next pair.

"Looks like you'll be busy tonight," Roxanne said, nudging Anara in the ribs. Anara reluctantly smiled at the teasing. It had become easier to pretend not to care about her duties as a courtesan, but that did not mean she had learned to enjoy it. She simply tolerated it by letting her mind go somewhere else. Tonight would be different from her first encounter with Sir Edwin. She would at least be able to smile after he had finished, even if the actions and words were hollow. As if summoned by Roxanne's suggestion, Sir Edwin joined them in their box several minutes later as two lords rode against one another.

"Well done, Sir Edwin," Roxanne said as she made room for him between her and Anara. "Though I would have expected you to unhorse the man in the first pass, given your skill and your past success."

"Where would the spectacle be in that? If I knock a man to the ground just because I can, the crowds would grow tired of me."

"They seemed to enjoy it when Joshua managed to unhorse his opponent that way," Lena said, very un-courtesan like to bring up a rival in front of Sir Edwin—if Sir Edwin even considered Joshua a rival, but that was because Lena was not Sir Edwin's courtesan.

"Joshua's strike was savage," Anara said, using the obvious opening to come to the defense of Sir Edwin's honor. "Not only does Sir Edwin have greater skill, but he shows mercy in that he allows his opponent to actually compete with dignity. Besides, Joshua rode against a farmer better equipped to walk behind a horse guiding a plow than riding atop one. I doubt he would do well against a properly trained knight such as Sir Edwin."

"Quite right," Edwin said, and his arm went around Anara's shoulders. He kissed her, much more deeply than Anara expected, but that was why he had requested her to be there.

"I would like to see one of your lances," Roxanne said. "If you are not too busy showing your favorite to Mistress Swift, that is. I've often wondered what it feels like to hold one."

"A strange request from a woman," Sir Edwin said. "Though you may need assistance to lift it; a lance is not as light as you might think from how slender they appear at this distance – especially a blunted lance."

"Why is that?" Anara asked, leaning lightly against Sir Edwin's chest as his hand wrapped around the side of her waist.

She gently pressed her cheek against him as she kept her gaze focused on the matches, it was still difficult to be like Roxanne could in public.

"Lances for competition are different than lances for war. In war, the lance is sharpened at the end and reinforced by a spike of steel. In competition that spike is replaced with a broader, heavier tip. Not only isn't the wood narrowed to a point, but a fist of iron or steel is added to disburse the point of impact and reduce the chance of injury. A man unaccustomed to that much weight, like the hopeless—the peasants I mean—have little control of the weapon. The result usually means that both competitors get to walk away from the battle. The loser gets to leave with little more than his pride damaged."

"Usually?" Anara asked, leaning her head against Sir Edwin's neck so she could still watch. He smelled musty, his neck and hair dampened by sweat. It was an unpleasant odor; Lena's perfume was much more enjoyable.

"Accidents do occur," Sir Edwin said, sounding as if he wanted one of the men who had just spurred their steeds into a gallop to have one of those accidents. Anara held her breath, half afraid she was about to see a man wounded, maybe even killed, in just a moment. The two struck, but nothing more than splintered lances flew through the air. Edwin leaned back in the seat once the opportunity for him to see another man's blood had passed. Sir Edwin clapped for the victor who had just claimed his third broken lance. Anara smiled, dreading when it would be time to satisfy Edwin that night.

XIII

VISITOR

Ester sat quietly as she pushed her vegetables around her plate. Cassandra, Ariel, and Morgan had left her behind since she had grown too disruptive during the matches of the tournament after the first week. Miranda sighed; no doubt men crashing weapons against each other must bore the young girl, but Miranda would have given anything to see them. That was until the competitors started dying. Then she saw too much of it.

But, my glory, was the first man to fall victim to a stray bit of lance that caught him hard enough in the eye that it pierced his brain. He was a young man, younger than Miranda, with blonde hair and only a hint of a beard. No doubt he was lowborn since he wore only chain and hardened leather against a noble in full plate. Miranda almost felt he was better off dying. For someone so low to beat nobility... that would have only earned the man punishment unless he somehow managed to beat everyone else he faced. That had been on the third day.

I can do this, was the next man, the following day. The peasant who rode against him struck his head instead of his shield. The blow instantly broke the man's neck, wrenching his head to hang off his shoulders like a scarecrow. Luckily both competitors had been lowborn so no punishment would be given for the accident. Accidents between the peasantry were allowed, accidents against those of a higher station than yourself were intentional. It was hypocrisy, but Miranda—to her frustration and detriment of her emotions—had no way of fixing that. To the rest of the world, to those dying in her mind's eye, she did not exist.

A hopeless peasant! was the knight's thought a day later. He had died, bleeding out with a piece of a lance through his neck. A few hours later the victor of the match joined the knight. *I'm sorry, I'm sorry! I swear it was an accident*, the peasant who killed the knight plead to the void as his head rolled off the executioner's block.

Competitors were not the only ones who were dying either. Disgruntled thugs who lost a bet either killed or were killed by the people who came to collect the winnings. It was a ridiculous reason to kill someone over a few copper wyrms, but Miranda had seen it now. Fortunately, people only died a few at a time, never like what happened with the attack on the caravan, so Miranda had been able to silence them with relative ease. Either way, Miranda had over one hundred souls to sift through each time someone died and the number was only ever increasing.

He comes, K'Rania said and Miranda let out a yelp of surprise.

"What is it, Mima?" Ester asked, looking up from her plate. A knock sounded at the door and Miranda jumped again.

Can't you be a little more descriptive? Miranda wondered as she stood. "I just heard the door is all, Esty, finish your vegetables and I'll see what I can do about making you a treat."

"I'll make the treat," Ester said, biting down on an undercooked carrot. So what if Miranda's first attempt at making a meal had gone a little poorly. At least they were not hungry again tonight.

Who's coming, K'Rania? Miranda asked though she suspected the answer.

The old one.

Miranda paused with her hand on the door's handle. She was not supposed to answer the door, no one was supposed to know about her. She shrugged. There was little Cassandra could do to her now. In fact, since Miranda killed Cassandra's hand, Cassandra had been very docile to Miranda. Not civil, but at least the arguments were few and far between. *Cassandra's rules be damned*, Miranda thought with a victorious smirk.

Miranda opened the door.

A single man stood there who lowered his hood as he stepped over the threshold. Miranda instantly recognized the man's race, he was a Dristelli, by the long, violet and green feathers that grew out of the top of his head instead of hair. His eyes were too large for an Ilionan's with a predatory glint you might see in a bird of prey. Dristelli were a fascinating race, at least from what she had read from her father's library about Archavia. Miranda longed to see their floating cities over Fathen Forest. *Anywhere* really, but Archavia always seemed to draw her more than most.

"Cassandra, I don't have much time... you aren't Cassandra?" the man said as he got a better look at her. "You must be the daughter, yes... I can see the mark of a necromancer in your eyes."

"How, uh," Miranda paused, *no one* was supposed to know about her outside of her parents' cults. *Have I heard his name before? A Dristelli in that group would stick out, wouldn't he.* "How can I be of assistance, uh..."

"Lunarin," the Dristelli said as he set a bag down beside the door. "I have no other name, just call me that. Would you go fetch your mother for me?"

"I'm afraid I cannot, Lunarin," Miranda sighed, clicking the door closed. *The ink*, K'Rania urged. "But she told me to accept the ink from you when she arrived."

"Conniving woman," Lunarin grumbled with a frustrated sigh. Miranda was shocked that the Dristelli spoke such eloquent Ilionan. He sounded like anyone else she had ever spoken with. He stood beneath the family portrait, looking at the life size mural with interest. Miranda was missing from the painting since anyone at the door would have known of her existence that way. Cassandra was taking great risk to be out of the mansion while expecting visitors, even if that visitor did know about Miranda. "I'm afraid your mother owes me for ink, and it is something only she can provide me," Lunarin said with a subdued, excited tone that reminded Miranda of her father when he was flirting with his wives. "Would there, perhaps, be a place for me to wait for Lady Cassandra's return?"

"Of course. The study is across the hall," Miranda said motioning to the spacious room branching off of the receiving area. "Could I bring you something to drink while you wait, she probably won't be back anytime soon."

"She knows I'm arriving today," Lunarin said as Miranda escorted him to the study to make sure he actually went there. "I'm certain she will return before much longer. I would gladly take that drink; an aged scotch if you have any on hand."

"I'm afraid not," Miranda sighed, there probably was some in her father's study but that was always locked when Morgan was not home. "But I can offer you red or white wine."

"Very well, a glass of Vallish Red if you would," Lunarin said, still holding his bag as he sat down in a chair near a glow lamp. "I have always enjoyed the vintages from the Fertile Vale." He removed a book from the bag, barely giving Miranda another glance. Miranda frowned and made her way back to the kitchen.

"Who was it?" Ester whispered, sneaking a peek out into the hall. Of course she would not see Lunarin, unless the Dristelli had left the study.

"A visitor for Mother Cassie," Miranda said, pulling two glasses off the shelf. She filled them from a dark bottle wrapped in a gold label. She set aside her own glass on the counter before taking Lunarin's to him.

Lunarin had made himself comfortable. His dark travel robe was draped over the back of his chair. He wore a robe made from draped, white fabric that left the right side of his chest entirely exposed. A wide leather belt covered the majority of his waist and pinned the toga to his body. Bonding tattoos decorated more than his muscular right breast. One was on his shoulder and another on his forearm. Something about how Lunarin's muscles were defined even at rest beneath his skin made Miranda bite her lower lip. She had never seen a man so exposed before and an unexpected amount of embarrassment tinted her cheeks red.

"You're a Dristelli bonder, aren't you?" Miranda asked as she set down the guest's drink.

"Cassandra told you about the Dristelli magecraft?" Lunarin inquired. He sounded amused.

"No," Miranda paused, K'Rania's ramblings and what little her father's books of magecraft had been enough to deduce what her unfinished tattoo meant. "I read about them," Miranda hastily covered, hoping Lunarin did not notice her hesitation. "I haven't much else to do with my time."

"No, I supposed you don't," Lunarin said, sipping from his glass. "Yes, I am a bonder." His smile unnerved Miranda as if the mirth of his lips did not reach his large, violet eyes. "Nothing like Aethelia of the Senate Guard, nor her twin sister Ethaelia, but I am decent at the craft." Miranda blinked at Lunarin, wondering if she should be impressed by the two names.

Before Miranda could ask more, the door to the mansion opened as Cassandra—alone and a little out of breath—swept into the room. She glared disapprovingly at Miranda but that changed drastically for the Dristelli. She smiled at the man, more lovingly than she ever did for Miranda's father, with a touch of color blooming in her cheeks. Cassandra removed her long, white gloves—using her teeth to remove the right one. Her stump was covered with a beautifully cast, gold hand that mirrored her natural one perfectly.

"You've arrived, Lunarin," Cassandra sighed, draping her gloves on top of Lunarin's coat. "You're excused, daughter. I will see to my guest's hospitality from now on."

Miranda curtsied, bowing out of the room and hesitating just out of sight.

"What caused your delay?" Cassandra asked.

"I was held up in Kindor, my love," Lunarin responded. "The mortiallus are restless, they sense power shifting in your kingdom. Something ancient stirs in the world."

The ink! K'Rania hissed.

Not now, not while they're both watching! Miranda thought back.

Flowing like blood over porcelain skin, the ink is coming, you must *take it,* K'Rania hissed back. Miranda ignored the N'Gochen. She would have to find a time to search Lunarin's belongings later. That could wait, but Lunarin had referred to Cassandra as his *love*.

Does father know? Miranda wondered. *Cassandra is having an affair, that bitch! With the man who provided my mother the means that nearly drove me insane. That is* driving *me insane...*

Not important. Hollowing you out, K'Rania hissed, at times Miranda wondered if she was actually like the other voices. Just saying things in a loop. Miranda still had not seen the way the N'Gochen had died. *Making room.*

"I know," Miranda responded. K'Rania felt pleased as if winning an argument.

Miranda stopped in her tracks as she turned into the kitchen. The room was a disaster.

"Ester! What did you do?" Miranda gasped, looking around the room in distress. Flour coated a large portion of the counters, table, and floor. The paper bag, probably too heavy for the ten-year-old, had split and lost most of its contents when it had been dropped. Empty egg shells sat on the counter, more than a few were just cracked and leaking their clear and golden insides out over the powdered surface. Ester turned around, a mixing bowl of white batter barely held by her short arms.

"I'm baking a cake, you said I could make the treat!" Ester whined. Miranda rubbed her temples. The room smelled of vanilla and Miranda wondered how much her sister had used. It seemed wasteful, knowing some of her voices had never tasted vanilla or chocolate in their lives.

"You're right, I did," Miranda said, *at least by not refusing anyway.* She carefully stepped around the flour to avoid dirtying the hem of her dark skirts. Ester was coated in the fine powder. The front of her violet dress looked closer to lilac and her face and arms, normally dotted generous freckles, were as pale as Miranda's. Miranda groaned as she slowly exhaled her displeasure. "After you finish mixing you have to take a bath. I'll draw water from the well while you get the cake ready for the oven." Miranda hesitated at the door. "*I'll* be the one to put it in. It is too dangerous for you to do. Understood?"

"Yes, Mima," Ester said, rolling her eyes.

Miranda was sweating profusely by the time she filled the tub and, after looking all over in the basement, brought the heat box up the stairs. Ester climbed into the water without complaint as Miranda returned to the kitchen with a sinking feeling in her stomach when she looked at the cake. The batter filled a pan large enough to feed a family three times the size of the Heaths. Miranda opened the enchanted steel door to the oven, the strong heat box stored inside welcoming her with a blast of sweltering air, and carefully slid the pan inside on top of the grating held a few inches above the top of the heat box. She turned around and looked at Esters mess with a sigh.

"I'm *not* leaving this for Ariel," Miranda muttered and went to work cleaning up the counters and floor.

Miranda stood and took a long breath before she sat down and took a slow drink of her nearly forgotten wine. The sweetness and sensation of floating that followed a few moments later were a worthy reward for her work and the liquor seemed stronger for it as well. Miranda cleaned Ester's mess to the growing strength of vanilla wafting from the oven, taking brief pauses to sip her wine.

I'm sorry, Father, A voice echoed in Miranda's head as the sound of breaking glass in the distance startled her.

The voice, a young man—a boy really—who died while surgeons bickered about the best way to remove the large piece of lance jutting from his ribs, had died without pain. His body had become numb to it and cold as educated, older, higher-born men wasted hours deciding how their actions could cause the boy's death. Their inaction left him in agony until his mind could not take any more. The surgeons stopped bickering as a knight staggered into the tent, kicking over the boy's orange and gray, toy shield. The knight had a dislocated shoulder and a half empty bottle of golden spirits in his good hand. They left the peasant's side as the boy quietly died amidst the knight's protestations of the formality of seeing the surgeons for an injury his squire could have set.

Miranda forced the despair she felt for each of the souls aside as she worked her way back through them all. There were *so* many now, she nearly lost track of them with each new soul and the struggle to keep control of her own mind was growing more and more urgent. K'Rania was right, she *needed* to fix this problem soon. Miranda stood and went to investigate the breaking glass before turning back to the study.

The ink! K'Rania hissed, she sounded angry. *It spills!*

"The ink is in the waiting room," Miranda whispered, peeking into the room to make sure. It was empty. Lunarin's robe still had Cassandra's gloves on top of it and his travel bag sat open beside the chair. Disturbingly Cassandra's prosthetic rested on the side table.

The bag was full of letters in what looked like six different forms of writing; she only recognized those in Ilionan. A brief read yielded nothing of significance so she dug deeper. Several pouches clinked with various coins, again each pouch showed a different kingdom's denomination and Miranda only recognized the copper wyrms, silver drakes, and gold dragons of Iliona because of the Ilionan writing above and below the embossed runes to mark them for what they were.

Miranda bit her lower lip, pouring some of the Ilionan coins out into her hand. She had never actually *held* money before and had no idea how much it was or what it could buy. Holding it, knowing it was money, gave her a strange sense of power. It was odd that such a simple thing as a few metal coins would do that and she doubted that she would feel the same if they were not valuable. Miranda split the copper, took several of the silver, and a single gold and tucked them into her bodice between her breasts.

"I'll need to eat when I run away," Miranda said to herself, rationalizing her theft. "I hope that will keep me fed for a while."

Aside from the letters and coins there really was not much to the travel bag. There was a spare toga but other than that Lunarin seemed to wear most of what he owned. After searching Lunarin's robes, and carefully placing Cassandra's gloves back on top when she found nothing, Miranda resigned herself to return to the kitchens where she removed the now finished cake from the oven using a wooden stick with a wide paddle on one end. The cake steamed as Miranda sat back down and poured a second glass.

The ink, it spills! K'Rania screamed and Miranda nearly dropped her glass. *Like blood over white porcelain.*

"There is no ink," Miranda grumbled, downing her glass in one go. "It didn't spill anywhere."

The shadow sees the ink spill, K'Rania countered.

"Shadows can't see..." But the shadow to Miranda was not the same thing as it was to K'Rania. "You mean the enclave," Miranda said, standing up with a slight head rush. "Thade's idol, the ink is there!" Miranda inched towards the back of the house, feeling the influence of her hastily consumed wine on top of the glass she already had. Grunts coupled with wet smacks sounded from the enclave as Cassandra's sharp moans of pleasure steadily rose in urgency. Miranda looked around the wall to see.

Lunarin's bare backside, just as well toned as the bare side of his chest, excited her as she watched the Dristelli's muscles flex to thrust in between her mother's legs. Lunarin's long crest of feathers stood on end, fanning out around his head as his body quickened to Cassandra's persistent gasps of need. Cassandra cried out, arching her back as she looked up at Driadra's mural with both arms outstretched. Her good hand reached for Thade, touching the sculptures featureless, black face as her stump reached towards the ceiling.

The ink! It flows, K'Rania said, distracting Miranda from the shock of her mother's dalliance.

What are you talking about? There is no ink only... something I'll never be able to un-see! Miranda blushed, realizing how private the scene she had just witnessed should have been.

The ink! K'Rania insisted and Miranda had the vague impression the N'Gochen wanted her to continue looking. Miranda hesitated at K'Rania's perversion. *The ink!*

Miranda clenched her jaw, sneaking a look inside again. Her mother held the vial she had used before against her bare, undulating breasts as Lunarin groaned with a final thrust. His legs shook as he stepped back and moved to Cassandra's side. The Dristelli's seed leaked from Cassandra's folds as her mother crossed her legs and rolled to look at Lunarin. He picked up the dagger on the cabinet beside the altar and cut his palm and clenched his hand tightly over the vial until dark blood dripped into it. After a few drops, Cassandra closed the vial with a stopper and held her mouth open beneath the Dristelli's palm. Drops of Dristelli blood landed on Cassandra's flushed cheeks, leaving trails of yellow behind as they ran down her jaw and neck, before Lunarin pressed the wound to Cassandra's lips so she could drink more easily.

Miranda fled, her stomach roiling at the display and nearly collided with Ester as the young girl, her hair damp against her skin and wearing a fluffy pink robe, left her bath. Miranda felt sick not knowing if she would vomit if she were to speak. The ink was *Dristelli* blood. Miranda felt her skin crawl at the idea of having Dristelli blood, *anyone* else's blood, in the tattoo on her left breast.

"What's wrong, Mima?" Ester asked, combing her damp hair with her fingers.

"Nothing," Miranda managed to say before being forced to swallow back sick. "I just have a stomach ache."

"I *told* you the food wasn't cooked all the way," Ester groaned, rolling her eyes. "Why do you think I only ate the vegetables, improperly cooked meat can make you sick. Didn't Mother ever tell you that?"

"No," Miranda said, fighting the urge to look back towards the enclave. "Mother has not told me a lot about growing up."

"Well, the cake smells like it's done," Ester said, taking Miranda's hand and marching off to the kitchen. "Should we save some for Father, Mother, and Mother Cassie?"

"I think Cassandra may be too busy for cake today, but I'm sure Ariel and Morgan would love a slice."

"What about the guest?"

The kitchen looked much like it did before Miranda's attempt to cook a meal. Ariel would probably find it out of order, but Miranda could not tell a difference. She filled her glass again, drinking from it as she reached for the bread knife. Miranda wrapped her fingers around the hilt, pausing with the memory of Lunarin's dagger sliding across the Dristelli's hand, and pulled it free from the knife block.

"He's had his fill already," Miranda shook her head as she cut into the soft, golden fluff of the cake. "I hope he'll be leaving soon, he got what he came for."

XIV

DUELING

Joshua tightened his grip on the dueling sword. It was heavier than his father's, and even a little heavier than *Vengeance*, but he was used to the weight. He had trained with the sword for seven solid years. The dueling sword felt more like a friend than a force fighting against him.

Unfortunately, being lowborn, Joshua's opponents all week had not provided much of a challenge. Each of his victories, however, had increased his rank and now he stood across from his first *real* competitor. It was fitting that Sir Stanson was the knight he faced. He would finally prove to the knights, and even all of Aederon—given the screams of the crowd—the skill he truly possessed with a blade.

"Natural talent, boy," Sir Echton had said the day after Joshua was rescued. "Not many men would stand their ground against that monster; even fewer would have survived. You have it, boy, natural talent with a sword. It'll carry you far one day."

"Will it let me kill them all?" Joshua asked, earning a disappointed sigh from the old knight.

"A blade is not just about killing," Sir Echton explained, adjusting Joshua's pose as he held a wooden sword. "Your blade can stop another as easily as a shield or sturdy plate, you mustn't forget that."

Joshua never did.

Stanson's strike came from above, he still favored swan stance to start. Joshua met him with boar stance, using its center strengths—as well as the deceptive reservation Joshua showed—to block and lure Stanson in. Another strike came for Joshua's helm, nearly invisible because of the narrow slit of his visor, but Joshua felt it more than saw it. Their swords met again and again as Joshua blocked each one. Joshua could almost see Stanson's grin in the knight's eyes. He thought Joshua was beaten, struggling to keep his ground from Stanson's fury of swings.

There it was, his opening.

Stanson swung. Joshua bent his neck back, feeling the wind through his eye slit from Stanson's blade as it flew harmlessly in front of his vision. A step forward brought Joshua's sword up and into the ribs of Stanson's armor. Sir Stanson staggered back as he regained his balance, only to take another strike from Joshua's sword to his arm and back of his helm. Joshua danced back from a wild swing and they faced each other again. The smirk in Stanson's eyes turned to rage when he caught a glimpse at the score. Stanson had three. Apparently the judges saw Joshua's dodge as a strike. Most knights would have cried foul about the judgment, but Joshua knew his move could have been seen differently from a distance. Especially in the middle of battle. Also, he was no knight. Joshua pulled away with six points in the brief exchange.

The crowd had even gone silent for a moment, as if they could not comprehend what had just happened. The sixth flag was slid into the hole above Joshua's color—an unfortunate green that reminded him of vomit mixed with feces. Realizing *that* had been on his back after speaking with Mistress Swift had been one of two very good reasons to stay away for the time being. Seeing Sir Edwin in her box, with her on his lap, had been the other.

The crowd shook with roars even greater than could be heard in the jousting arena as Joshua and Stanson began circling around the arena. Joshua had caught the knight's attention.

"You aren't going to argue the points awarded me?" Stanson said, barely audible over the crowd. "I don't recall feeling my blade make contact. I'll not argue the fact if you wish to do so."

"I don't care about points until this is over, Sir Stanson," Joshua said back, shifting his stances to counter what the knight switched to. The two circled again, adjusting their blades. Stanson *did* have skill, since he could see Joshua's counter moves and adjusted to match and force Joshua to change as well. Even more surprising was his comment indicated he had at least a shred of honor.

The crowd had quieted, most of them could not understand the exchange between the two competitors. In a real battle, this never happened, but Sir Stanson was waiting for Joshua to make the first move. He was on the defensive. Joshua had hoped to be defending the entire time, keeping a watch for an opening was easier if you only had to block, but Stanson had seen through his ploy now. Joshua clenched his jaw, changing to wolf stance, as he prepared for his attack. The leather palms of his steel gauntlets creaked against the wood of the dueling sword's hilt as Joshua made his advance. Sir Stanson switched to dragon stance, hoping to utilize wolf's wide strikes to throw Joshua off balance as he had done with Sir Echton a year earlier.

The crowd renewed their cheering as Joshua charged. Joshua swung, the image of Sir Echton's last attack replaying in his mind as Sir Stanson's deflection met Joshua's blade. *Gods! He's strong,* Joshua thought, feeling the tug of his blade and vibrations through his arm as Stanson's strike threatened to loosen Joshua's grip of his own sword. Instead, Joshua let the blade's momentum pull him into a spin, switching into a dragon stance strike half way, while he ducked. He heard Stanson's blade whistle harmlessly a foot over his head as Joshua started to rise. Sir Stanson was still turning, the knight's eyes widening at his miss as they caught Joshua rising. The knight faced him, his sword useless for protection in his right hand, as Joshua's blade crashed against the left side of Stanson's helmet. Stanson tripped over his own legs, twisted during the middle of his spin, as the force of Joshua's strike sent him backwards and to the side.

Somehow, as Joshua stood over Stanson and the cacophony of the spectators thundered in his ears, he could hear the three pegs sliding into their place above his putrid marker. Joshua exhaled slowly, letting the world—which had seemed so slow as he fought—come racing back in.

"Nine to three, favoring Squire Joshua Kentaine!" Someone shouted above the din as the fighters returned to the ready room. "Joshua Kentaine progresses in rank, Sir Wallace Stanson falls back." Joshua grinned, thankful his helmet covered his face, and offered his hand to help Sir Stanson back to his feet. The knight took it, nearly pulling Joshua down as he stood up with a slight sway to his posture. Joshua could face Sir Stanson again if Stanson won enough of his next matches, but given how dazed the knight's eyes looked that was unlikely. Sir Stanson, much as Sir Echton had done, would probably have to forfeit too many matches today to ever catch up.

The ready room of Crossroad's arena was nearly identical to the one at Aederon City. The only difference was the tent's dirt floor was a little darker here since it was more fertile land. The walls were plain, beige canvas that glowed orange from *Soleanne's* light and the only pieces of furniture were a few, simple, wooden benches. If it were not so blasted hot, it would have been enjoyable. The ready room treated everyone equal; lords, knights, and peasants seemed to lose their stations there before stepping into the ring.

"Well fought," Stanson said, clapping Joshua's shoulder. Stanson pulled off his helm, wincing as the metal brushed a large gash on his temple. "Bloody useless, these are," Stanson said, throwing the helmet to the ground.

"I wouldn't say that," Joshua said, removing his own helm with ease. "A strike like that would kill a man without a helm, blunted sword or not." Stanson laughed, falling a little hard as he sat on a bench.

"I wondered why Sir Echton staggered so badly last year," Stanson laughed again. "I can't say I'm entirely pleased being beaten by a squire, Joshua. Especially since I'm your first victim with a knighthood. But, by the Gods you're a quick bastard. As quick as Ezebre herself. Heir Lord Commander! Lady Ackart!" Sir Stanson nearly fell over as he stood up, saluting. Joshua turned around to see Eric and Cordelia—thankfully without her entourage—walk into the tent.

"Brilliant fight," Eric said, saluting Stanson back. "I guessed Joshua was the one fighting when we heard the cheers at the jousts."

"No; *I* guessed it was Joshua's match against a knight, brother," Cordelia sighed. "I believe you owe on a bet you made about it as well."

"You bet against me?" Joshua gaped as Eric gave him a half smile.

"Not exactly. Just whether or not you were fighting. The bet had nothing to do with the outcome of the match."

"Joshua won, my lord," Stanson said. He looked perplexed as if his mind were having troubles keeping up with the conversation. He really *was* acting like Sir Echton. Apparently even a young man could not take a slap to the head like that.

"You should see a Priest of Fiel," Joshua said. Stanson looked at him, blinking slowly before nodding in agreement.

"By your leave, my lord, my lady," Sir Stanson bowed his head.

Joshua sat back down, unlashing his armor after Stanson had left. Out of the corner of his eye he could see Cordelia watching with a little more interest than was appropriate in a ready room. After the armor came the lining. Joshua swore he heard Cordelia sigh when the chest lining came off, leaving his chest bare, and decided he would wait to remove the rest.

"Guess you'll have to really step up now," Eric said, sitting beside Joshua. "Stanson probably hates that you effectively removed him from the running this year, or probably will once he realized *who* just beat him after he is forced to forfeit a few matches to recover. Stanson took the sword last year, to be beaten by a lowborn..." Eric whistled, leaving the last unsaid.

"I'll be a knight soon enough," Joshua shrugged as Cordelia sat down on his other side. *I should have sat on the end,* Joshua thought as he caught a whiff of Cordelia's perfumed hair. It smelled sweet, almost like fruit. *Nobles and their luxuries,* he marveled, secretly taking a slow breath of her aroma.

"I doubt Stanson will see it that way," Eric shook his head. "If you claim a knighthood, that is. You still beat him as a squire."

"*If* I claim a knighthood?" Joshua raised an eyebrow at that. *Did Cora just move an inch closer?* Joshua swallowed. It was his imagination; It had to be. "What do you mean *if*?"

"Sir Edwin is still undefeated, not a single lance broken against him either. Just like last year."

"You don't find that odd?" Joshua asked. "When was the last time you remember a lance *breaking* against Sir Edwin?"

"Are you accusing a knight of cheating?" Cordelia asked, acting shocked as she covered her mouth but her tone suggested otherwise.

"Of course not," Joshua shrugged. "Or rather, of course not because I can't. But Eric could."

"True. If Sir Edwin were disqualified it *would* make things easier for you. But I'm afraid he really is that good with a lance. At least from the reports of his accomplishments in the borderlands would have me believe. Beat him and we'll see the first lance break on him, but until then keep your conspiracies to yourself," Eric scolded.

"But he's about to become nobility," Joshua started but cut off. Eric had meant it; no more voicing his suspicions. Joshua ground his teeth, the ready room made them equal only in discomfort of course. Besides Cordelia *was* closer now. Her soft, bare arm brushed against his. Instead of inching towards Eric, Joshua stood up and sat down across from them. Clearly, she did not like the way he ended her game because she frowned at him. "Are they still tilting? I'd like to watch some of the victors in case I go up against them."

"They should be," Eric said and the crowd outside the ready room cheered for the end of the match after Joshua's. Joshua did not recall his fight with Stanson being so short, though it probably was. "We'll see you there then?"

"Of course," Joshua answered as Eric moved to leave.

"Coming, sister?" Eric asked at the fabric door as the two competitors walked into the room. The two lowborn gawked at Cordelia as they looked around for a place that would be appropriate to strip before the highborn woman, which was nowhere in the now cramped space. Cordelia sighed, looking

Joshua up and down one last time before following her brother out of the tent.

Gabriel was waiting outside when Joshua emerged from the ready room in fresher clothing. He still felt grimy from sweat, and the chill of early fall felt good now that he was not wearing thick lining for armor. The giant blacksmith grinned widely as he strode beside Joshua, basking beside Joshua's newly won glory. Everywhere they went, people pointed at Joshua and whispered or cheered for his victory over Sir Stanson. Even a few knights congratulated him, thanking him for effectively removing Stanson from the running. At the same time, the praises of his competitors felt forced; Joshua was, after all, an unexpected contender. The short walk between the sword arena and lance arena turned into a fight against a tide of spectators who congratulated his victory. Lowborn from every part of the kingdom came forward to see, speak with, and touch one of their own who was *winning*. It was the same every year when lowborn were victorious against their betters in the arena. By the time they reached their destination, two more matches had already passed.

The lance arena was a large, long oval six times the size of the sword pit. The heavily used floor where two horses charged each other was divided by a low, colorful fence that the two opponents stretched their lances across to crash into each other. The long, wooden shafts of the weapons erupted to the joy of onlookers. When the cloud of splintered wood settled, one had been unhorsed, but both had broken their lance. Surprisingly, even unhorsed, the two men were tied and would tilt for a fourth time.

Nobody congratulated him inside the lance arena. None of them had been at his match or, if they had been, were too engrossed in the tilts. Eventually, his victory in the sword would reach these people and, if by rough description, they might recognize him as the squire who bested a knight. That recognition would grow when his victories in the sword continued. When he continued to win in the joust, though, he would become this year's legend among the common folk. Joshua grinned, folding his arms at that idea. He would claim his knighthood by the end of the

Harvest Festival and inspire countless other hopefuls to enter these games to do the same.

The very next thing Joshua noticed every time he entered the arena was the box where Mistress Swift normally sat. Sir Edwin was already with Mistress Swift today, thankfully not with her in his lap. Joshua would have preferred the blonde-haired and azure-eyed woman leaning against him instead of the knight. If only she had seen him at the sword arena today, she might be more willing to talk to him, putrid shield or not.

Beside Mistress Swift was Mistress Weston. Mistress Adair, who had been in the box every day until now, was higher up beside Lord Barnum. Whatever she was saying must have been hilarious because the man's face turned purple and his laughter reached Joshua across the stadium. The red-haired courtesan who had been sitting with Mistress Swift the first day had been in the crowds at the sword arena. She might relay Joshua's victory to Mistress Swift in enough detail to earn him her ear at least, though Joshua would like civility as well.

Joshua looked away, finding Eric and Cordelia instead. Joshua waved, and Eric nodded his head in acknowledgment. It would not do for a lord to be waving his arms about where everyone could see. Cordelia, though, waved back until Eric said something and they started arguing with each other.

Joshua turned to the match as horns blared and the familiar sound of hooves thundered towards each other. Lances snapped with a loud crack that echoed faintly in the oval structure. The two men were not that bad, especially since one was a farmer's son and the other a knight. Nearly half of the lowborn had been eliminated already, Joshua could not help but feel sorry for the poor boy who had faced him earlier in the week. He had felt so light when Joshua's lance struck him. Hopefully Joshua had not hurt the lad. The boy had walked off the field under his own power, and his armor *looked* intact, but the joints—particularly the arms—could hide splinters that had found their way through the loose-fitting plates of a man who was forced to borrow his armor. His competitor *had* been having trouble carrying his orange and gray shield though which was never a good sign since the lowborn markers were considerably lighter than the rest. The markers were more like a toy shield really.

"How's the armor holding up?" Gabriel asked after the matched ended, as slow as he was it seemed like he could read Joshua's mind sometimes. "It looked like it was helpful against Stanson in your fight, but I couldn't tell if any of the straps are wearing out from where I was watching."

"It is performing admirably," Joshua said, he had not checked the straps. He would have to before his next sword match tomorrow. "I was just thinking how lucky I am that I have a blacksmith for a friend who could craft me my own set of plate and chain."

"It isn't free," Gabriel said, smacking Joshua's back and nearly toppling him onto the field. Gabriel rarely had the awareness to control his blacksmith's strength, which may *actually* be giant's strength not that he would admit those thoughts to Cordelia or Eric. "But I know you'll pay me back when you win the sword." Joshua nodded, sword matches ended a week before the jousts. Fortunately for Joshua, that meant he would be fully committed to winning only one event the last week of the festival. *Soleanne*'s light began to shift to brilliant orange as the jousting matches wrapped up for the day and the arena slowly emptied of spectators.

Joshua stepped out onto the field as the last stragglers looked about for any winning slips discarded by the gamblers they could find. Instead of words, the slips were marked by the color or crest of the chosen competitor. Joshua's fecal color was probably worth a fair bit of silver today. Of course, a winning slip was never left behind. Only a fool would do that. Joshua scooped up a handful of the arena soil and dusted his hands with it. He sighed as he looked out over the heavily worn run. The events had torn up the soil from the hooves of horses thundering across the field towards each other in lines on either side of the fence, the area surrounding the run was still relatively compacted and even. Joshua stretched, it was time he went back to the inn.

The first week was over.

XV

HARVEST FESTIVAL

Second Week

Joshua grimaced as the surgeon went about resetting his shoulder. Unfortunately, this meant a lot more hand wringing and prodding the wound than actual work as the Priest of Fiel worried about which way to best pop his shoulder back into place. The wound from his last tilt would hinder him in the sword arena, but tournament champion was the only way to earn his knighthood and go rescue Sir Echton. He could not drop out of the joust to save his limbs for the sword.

"Maybe I should forfeit the sword," Joshua said.

"But I *love* to watch you in that arena!" Cordelia exclaimed. Every day since his victory over Stanson she had come to the ready room, he doubted she was even *in* the stands for his matches since the brutality of sword seemed to be more popular with the lower class. Every day she played her inching game too. *Bloody woman,* Joshua thought. *Can't she just realize I'm too lowborn for her?* Even now she was actually holding the hand of his dislocated arm like some doting lover.

"Nah. If anyone here can do both, it's you," Gabriel, as usual, added his support to Cordelia's.

"Oh, shove off!" Joshua snapped at the priest, pushing him back with his good arm. "Cora, hold tighter."

"If you say so," she blushed, tightening her hands around Joshua's. "Is the pain really that mu—" Joshua jerked his chest away from Cordelia, lifting the woman out of her seat as his arm slid back into his socket with a loud pop. Cordelia gasped in surprise and fell onto Joshua. She stayed there, lingering with her palms against his bare chest a moment too long.

"By Fiel's mercy!" the priest exclaimed, he looked ready to pass out. At least Cordelia seemed to have a stronger stomach. "The damage you could cause!"

Eric laughed in the corner, he had been unusually silent for the whole ordeal. The young lord had even gone a bit pale when Joshua told him to fetch a surgeon. *He probably had a wager on me for today's match in the sword*, Joshua thought with a little resignation.

"Feel's just fine. If you would give me back my tunic I can let you waste time fretting over your next patient," Joshua said, rolling his shoulder as he helped Cordelia back onto her feet.

"Insane peasants!" the priest puffed out his chest as he threw Joshua's shirt back and stormed out of the makeshift hospital room. An entire tent had been set up right beside the jousting arena just for treatment of wounds expected during a tournament. Joshua rolled his shoulder again, it hurt more now than when it came out, but he had to see the rest of the matches before he was due in the sword. He had just barely beaten his last opponent, Lord Causeworth, in jousting and could not afford to miss any more chances to watch his future opponents. "I was wondering, Eric, why do nobility compete in the joust?"

"To increase their lands," Eric said as they left the surgeon tent. "I do it for fun, which is probably why I'm not all that good at it, but some of the lesser lords are eager to expand their holdings in any ways they can. They bet against the other lords and, if they face one another, the victor takes what is owed out of the loser's holdings. Unfortunately, that makes people hard and brutal like Lord Causeworth. No doubt his unsportsmanlike behavior after being unhorsed with only one lance to break is preventing him from seeing his wager through. Or, he may have even lost something, betting he would beat you and remove one of the last lowborn competing."

"And because he *was* beaten by that peasant. No noble would take kindly to that," Cordelia added, blushing furiously. "Not that *you* are a peasant, Joshua. You are Sir Echton's squire, but to nobles like Lord Causeworth there is no distinction really between anyone who is not a knight or nobility."

So, she does *know we are different rankings in society,* Joshua thought. He found it more amusing than annoying that Cordelia would point out his low birth so obviously as she grabbed his hand again.

"Yes, I suspect that has a great deal to do with it as well. Pity, I wonder who he wagered against. I would have liked to see if I could have gained a few more acres for the Ackart estate," Eric sighed. "Guess we'll never know."

"Father does not approve of your gambling, Eric. Better you didn't," Cordelia sighed, she sounded annoyed. Very annoyed. The nasal tone put Joshua on edge as Cordelia glared at her brother.

"Father doesn't approve of my whoring either. Or the way I wear my hair. Or the way I go through scotch. Or the way..."

"We get it," Joshua cut in before Eric made Cordelia explode at him. "Lord Commander Ackart is a very disapproving father. Just be glad you have one." Joshua looked downward as Eric silenced and hung his own head out of shame.

"Squire Kentaine!" someone in the crowd outside the hospital tents yelled, preventing the awkward silence Joshua's words would have caused. Everyone always went quiet when Joshua alluded to his dead family.

A boy, wearing the blue and gold of Iliona's colors and no older than seven years, stopped short of their group. Taking a brief knee before Eric and Cordelia, though his expression looked up at Joshua with greater respect. "You're wanted in the sword arena, Squire," he said the simple title like it meant something.

"But my match with Sir Pendal isn't for another round or two, at least!" Joshua growled as they started for the sword. "They have to have gotten it mixed up. Sir Irvine and Sir Trent are in battle right now." Joshua had long stopped referring to any of his opponents by anything less than Sir in the sword arena. Stanson, despite his injury, had finally climbed above the lowborn but he was several wins short of ever catching Joshua. Stanson *was* a good swordsman, even better from his short tour in the Borderlands last year. Only poor luck had pitted him against Joshua in the first week. Stanson's few short months in the Borderlands was nothing compared to the time Joshua spent fighting by Echton's side against raiding parties as they fled north, gathering refugees, nine years ago.

"Sir Trent was taken by a lance splinter in the neck yesterday, Squire Kentaine. He is unable to fight today," the page said. Joshua winced, and heard the same sharp intake of air come from Eric.

"Will Sir Trent recover?" Cordelia asked. "I did not see him in the surgeons' tent."

"I'm afraid the knight bled out, milady," the page looked at the ground. "Died before the Priests of Fiel could reach him to administer any healing. The lowborn who faced him has already been executed."

A moment of silence weighed on their shoulders. Deaths were not unheard of during a tournament, but nearly twenty had already been claimed this year. An unusually high amount so early and not *just* the lowborn but knights who knew what they were doing. No, not just twenty, dozens of others had died in brawls, bar fights, and gambles gone sour throughout the city as well. There was nothing he could do, though. The deaths in the Borderlands would always outweigh any that could happen north of Ashfall. That would not change until Joshua could cut his way through the Raykarn oppressors, and to do that he had to have a knighthood.

"Very well," Joshua said, tossing a silver drake to the page. "I'll be there; inform the master of games overseeing the sword."

"Yes, Squire," the boy said, bowing his head before running off.

"You're becoming quite the hero to them," Cordelia admirably stated. She linked her arm around Joshua's as if it was normal. Cordelia's attentions were not the only he had received lately from highborn either. If Cordelia had been the only noble to give him unwanted attention, Joshua would have been happy, but

Lord Heath, who was eliminated from the joust by Sir Edwin the day before, had called him up to the nobles' box for a brief talk.

"From what I've seen, Joshua," Lord Heath had said, his two wives flanking him, as Joshua kneeled. "I think you may have what it takes to finally knock that smirk off Sir Edwin's face. Though, I pray to the gods you can knock him off his horse instead." Lord Heath sounded a little bitter for being defeated.

Joshua, too stunned to say much other than thanks for the compliment, had wandered away. Not only had the wealthiest noble—who did *indeed* have green eyes—known his name, but his wives were gorgeous. One rivaled Mistress Swift in beauty, with wavy auburn hair and a slightly freckled face, but the other—Lord Heath's first wife—was divine. The one with straight, dark red hair looked more like royalty than nobility, if looks alone earned a person their rank. It did not; the king's own appearance was proof of that. Her only blemish was the forged gold hand covering the stump of a misfortunate accident.

"Alas, now is not the time to think of women out of my reach, Cordelia included," Joshua muttered to himself after leaving Cordelia at the ready tent. A brief time later he walked out onto the field and looked at his opponent.

Sir Idris Pendal was held in high regard, even by Sir Echton. Idris, a son of one of the knights that rode with them nine years ago, had just come of a competing age a week before the tournament started. Idris's skill was not *too* surprising since his father had been one of Sir Echton's sparring partners. Joshua had been just as taken aback by the young knight's consistent wins as the other knights had been of Joshua. As Joshua tightened the last of his bracers, Sir Pendal turned to him with his visor up. The knight's face lit up, hopefully seeing Joshua as a worthy opponent instead of an easy one, and slammed the visor down.

Joshua took in a long breath, closed his own visor, and drew his dueling sword. Sir Pendal favored the Ilionan shield stance. The stance required a shield, obviously, but since those were not permitted in the sword arena, his arm would do. It left him open for striking but, if he timed it right, he could bash away an opponent's blade and open them up for a quick chest or helm strike. Of course, if you were desperate enough to use the stance in a real battle without a shield you would lose an arm unless you were lucky and caught your attacker's wrist. Then you could kill them without mercy.

Joshua instantly slipped into swan stance. If he was going to have his sword bashed away by Sir Pendal's arm, he might as well try to break it in the process with a solid overhead strike. Sir Pendal yelled his challenge as the horn blared and they clashed. Joshua's sword struck hard against Pendal's gauntlet. Unfortunately, it did not break, but swan stance was not just for that. The down strokes let Joshua pull back instead of letting Pendal bash it aside so Joshua was able to meet the knight's strike. Their blades rang as they danced apart. Seeing his usual tactic fail, after Joshua gained a four-point lead in similar fashion, Pendal switched to his own swan.

Pendal was leagues ahead of Stanson in skill. Even if Joshua had not humiliated the last year's victor, Pendal surely would have if they faced one another. Which also meant, unless Joshua could disable Pendal as he had done with Stanson, Joshua could easily face Pendal again at the end of the following week.

Their blades crashed against each other again and again and Joshua could see some of Sir Echton's influence in Pendal's skill. It only made sense that the knight's father taught Idris everything Sir Echton had taught him. Pendal's strikes were just slightly off, as if designed to counter Sir Echton's. They stepped apart to catch their breath and think through their opponents next move. Joshua still lead, five to four, but Pendal could easily take the lead.

"Stanson said you were quick," Pendal called across the small circle. "Show me your speed!" He charged, spinning into Joshua with a hasty dragon strike. Joshua cursed under his breath and spun back and caught the strike in his arm instead of his chest, renewing the pain from his dislocation. Pendal's next strike clipped his helmet and sent him staggering the rest of the way across the field. Pendal intended to end it quick now. The tables had reversed, Pendal now had the four-point lead with only one point to claim victory. Just one mistake could end this fight in Pendal's favor.

Joshua took his sword in both hands, stepping sideways to catch the spinning strike of Pendal's blade dead center. The stadium roared to the echoing ring of their blades as Joshua successfully caught Pendal's powerful blow. His palms cried at the vibrations the idiotic move caused as the two froze. Joshua barely managed to stop the knight's strike and every muscle in his arms cried out. Pendal stared at their swords and Joshua could see the shock in them through the man's visor.

Now! Sir Echton's voice screamed in his head and Joshua side stepped down the length of Sir Pendal's blade. The metal squealed as Joshua pushed up, turning Pendal's blade aside by his sword's cross guard and crashed his blade into the top of Pendal's helm. Joshua panted as he leaped back, giving them distance again.

Sir Pendal looked at his sword where a deep nick had been carved into the dull blade by Joshua's block. Joshua's own sword probably mirrored the dent. Sir Pendal charged again, still using dragon stance, and Joshua moved in. He would win or lose with this exchange. Joshua caught the strike against his sword, turning and lifting it over his head as he spun. He could feel the worn steel of each blade grind against each other until Pendal's blade left his. Joshua caught a glimpse of Sir Pendal's spin end with the tip of his sword in the sand as Joshua finished his own. Bringing the weapon up high, but not as high as Sir Echton had done to the Raykarn so many years ago, Joshua's blade crashed against the back of Pendal's cuirass an inch below the gorget around his neck. Pendal's curse was audible above the noise that shook the ground they stood on as the crowd's vigorous fervor bellowed out at the end of the match.

"What *was* that?" Pendal shouted as he pulled his sword free and flipped open his visor. He was not angry; his raised voice was the only way he could be heard even a foot away from Joshua.

"Something I once saw an old man do," Joshua shouted back and Pendal laughed, clapping a hand on Joshua's shoulder.

"Sir Echton does have a few tricks he kept to himself, it seems. A shame my father missed that one," Pendal roared back as they made their way into the ready room.

Cordelia was waiting there and ambushed him with a kiss. Eric's jaw dropped after his sister intercepted Joshua before him. Joshua just smiled at her and kissed her back, stations be damned. It was foolish, Joshua knew deep inside his mind, but he was still acting on instinct after the fight.

"Malef's fires," Sir Pendal cursed as he watched them.

"Enough of that!" Eric finally managed to say, pulling them apart. "You aren't a knight yet, Joshua."

"Can I kiss her then?" Pendal asked. "Cause, the gods be damned that looked enjoyable." Cordelia grinned at Joshua, tucking a lock of her wavy hair behind her ear while looking at the ground.

"No, you may not!" Eric shouted.

"By your command, my lord," Pendal gave Eric a halfhearted salute. He turned to Joshua, grinning at him and Cordelia. "I'll be ready for you next time we face, Joshua," Pendal said. Joshua did not doubt the young knight would be facing him again at the end of the sword competition. No one had been able to stand against the two of them so far. "I'm afraid I'm due to tilt now. How did you fare against Lord Causeworth?"

"Dislocated my shoulder, in the second. I unhorsed him in the third without his lance splintering."

"Damn, you did *that* after a dislocated shoulder," Pendal growled, pointing to the sword pit. "I might be facing you in the lance too. Damn it to the Abyss!"

"No, that isn't what we're talking about right now," Eric protested, jabbing his finger against Joshua's cuirass. "We're talking about what you just did to my sister!"

Pendal, laughing over his shoulder at Eric and Joshua, disappeared as Gabriel entered with a grin to match his size. The blacksmith also carried an entire keg of something wrapped with a gold label beneath one arm.

"What did Joshua do to Cordelia?" Gabriel asked, looking back and forth between the three of them.

"I seem to recall kissing him first," Cordelia said, linking her arm with Joshua's.

"Damned woman," Eric said, throwing up his arms in futility. "He could be flogged for kissing you back."

"Only if you order it, Eric!" Cordelia narrowed her eyes and Eric flinched. "That's what I thought."

"A little early to celebrate, isn't it Gabriel?" Joshua asked, slipping free of Cordelia and trying to move the topic to something else. "What's with the keg?"

"Oh, this? Seems you have an admirer on high. Lord Heath sent this pending your success in the sword."

"Great," Joshua groaned, rolling his eyes.

"It is," Eric said. "This is Vallish Wine; this cask is worth more than that little village you grew up in."

"New Barrow had a high price, I doubt as much blood has been spilled for this wine," Joshua sighed, but even that did not dampen their moods much. Joshua was set to win the sword, and he only had seven more bouts in the joust to win there as well. Of course, having only won two jousts and the last one just barely, that looked a lot further off than it seemed. Joshua rolled his shoulder; it felt like it was on fire. He moved to unlatch the straps only to find Cordelia's hands already working on them.

"Really? One kiss and now you think you can undress him too, Cora?" Eric grumbled. "It isn't proper."

"I recall two," Cordelia replied, ignoring her brother's unspoken rebuke.

"Lady Ackart finally kissed Joshua?" Gabriel asked, his head perking up to the sounds of cheers outside the tent.

"I'm certain the lecher did the kissing, *not* my sister," Eric argued, sounding annoyed with a furrowed brow and frown. "And don't let Sir Pendal tell you otherwise."

"Stop whining, baby brother," Cordelia stated offhandedly, rolling her eyes.

"I'm older than you," Eric said, though his tone was softening.

"So says father," Cordelia shrugged. "He wasn't actually in the room for our birth, you know. Our family's midwife on the other hand..."

"Father's word is enough, at least for this."

"There isn't anyone father could marry me off to, the Heath's have no male heir, just that girl Ester," Cordelia informed. "She is... an awkward girl. Dianne says she still has an imaginary friend even though she is around ten years of age, if you can believe that. It is a girl called Mima, though she speaks of her friend as lovingly as I do you, brother."

"So, not at all?"

Gabriel laughed.

"Only when you deserve it. I meant as I speak of you when respectable company is around. My point, however, was that I am free to pursue who I want."

"We aren't respectable company?" Joshua asked but Cordelia just smiled and kissed his cheek. Of course, that was not *really* an answer, but Joshua chose not to press the issue.

"One kiss and she treats you better than her own flesh and blood," Eric shook his head. "Tap that keg back at the tavern, Gabe, I could use a good drink."

"It was two," Cordelia reminded.

The match had been late and *Soleanne* was already on the western horizon when Joshua finished cleaning and storing his armor in the lowborn equipment tent. It had held up surprisingly well, not even a dent in the plates yet. *Luminara* had risen early, as she did in the later months, to catch only a glimpse of her lover as he set. *Night and day*, the echo of his mother's voice said. *Everything be in balance, so* Soleanne *must be setting at night to give way when* Luminara *be rising*. Joshua thought the story was sad, to love someone but never be with them in exchange for an eternity of their sight.

It would be his and Cordelia's fate as well. Joshua grinned, remembering the sensation of the young woman's lips on his. They had tasted as wonderful as Cordelia smelled. It was a pity it meant nothing. A pity he could not let himself return the love Cordelia felt for him. No matter what Cordelia said, there was always political gains to be had between houses if one house had a daughter and the other a son. Lord Commander Ackart would find a suitable match for Cordelia someday.

Joshua exhaled noisily, kicking a stone across the dirt road as he wandered back towards the heart of Crossroads. Crossroads had no wall, which meant no real checkpoint to go through as he sauntered back within the city limits. No Ilionan city, aside from Ashfall, Fort Stern, and Aederon City, had a wall. Kindor, a fortress city like Ashfall, had one as well but no one ventured near the place anymore. Not since the Last Necromantic War claimed it for foul beasts. The other cities had no need for a wall. Still, it felt unprotected. Joshua could be *anyone* just casually walking into the heart of the kingdom. Crossroads was at the center of it all. The town of Iliona north of Ashfall had always seemed so weak to Joshua compared to the forts that dotted the Borderlands.

"Not that New Barrow had a wall back then," Joshua said to himself as a man and his escort stumbled out of a tavern. She laughed at his stumbling without reserve from her inebriated state. "Would it have saved you, mother? Would I be walking these streets with my own sister if stone had stood between us and the monsters?" Joshua stopped and faced south with clenched fists. "You'll know my wrath soon enough," he promised to the distant Raykarn clans. "I'll bathe every grain of sand in the Endless Waste with your orange blood. Then I'll finally be able to rest."

XVI

CONSUMED

Miranda whimpered in pain, her head aching so much she could not even rise out of bed. The festival brought a cesspool of crime to Crossroads unlike anything Miranda had anticipated. More and more peasants lost bets they simply could not afford. With that came desperation and bred violent crime. By the end of the first week there had been several murders a night. That night there were so many, happening so close together all over the city, it was ripping Miranda's mind to shreds.

So, it ends, like a candle's flame in Ezebre's tempest, a bard, stabbed in the back after his performance for the small amount of coin he had earned, thought as his last breath left him. But he had not been alone. A woman in a wool shawl wrapped around her exotic dancing garb screamed as the bard died.

Call the Watch! the dancer had thought, dying when a club struck her head and she was dragged off into an alley to be raped. Her shawl was left behind in the street as the men grew excited by her exposed flesh. A small mercy of Thade was that all thought and feeling had left before the thugs began violating the mound between her legs.

I wasted it all, a formerly wealthy merchant thought after leaping from the Tower of the Watch as people celebrated in the heart of the structure. He had just lost the deed to his way of life after losing a bet.

Maybe he can help, a beggar child thought as a man and laughing woman stumbled out of the tavern next to his alley. The young boy had tried to cling to life, watching the street in silence as a tall man walked by without even glancing towards him. The stranger held himself with a sense of furious duty, possibly a knight but at least a soldier, as he looked south with clenched fists.

His dark hair was matted from a day's exertion; given his age, he was probably in the tournaments for the first time. His eyes, though, were unlike any Miranda had seen. They were narrower than most Ilionans' as if he came from some exotic part of the kingdom. He had a satisfying build as well; his shirt and slacks tight against the strength in his arms, chest, and legs. He was remarkably handsome with a strong, smooth, square jaw and dark eyes that seemed to see beyond great distances. Miranda's fancy turned to disgust given *how* she had chanced to see the man.

The child's life left his body before he could ask the man for a scrap of bread. The boy, dark and grimy from living in the streets, went unnoticed by the stoic man and stumbling couple. At night, he was invisible. Not that a seven-course meal could have saved the boy anyway.

They took everything I had, I have nothing left, another gambler muttered moments later even before Miranda could make sense of the four before. He sat in a cheap tub with his forearms split open by the bloodied knife on the floor. A paper with two boxes, a light blue one with a white dove and the other a sickly greenish-brown, was crumpled beside the knife. The light blue square was circled with an amount of silver written beneath it.

I just want to go outside. If I go outside I'll feel better, I promise, the cycling began again. But it was more like the first time now. Everything jumbled together.

They took Ishan's face again... I'm sorry, surgeon... But, my bastards, attacked us from behind. I'm not a real soldier, I promise... I just want to run; I can escape if I run!... I wonder what was a good life. If I go outside, I'll see Ishan's face again... If I die, bloody surgeon!... I had a good ambush!... If I want everything I'll bloody the Watch in Ezebre's tempest... Mercy!

Miranda was astonished that the last thought had been her own instead of the priest in the caravan though his cry came soon enough. The cycling went faster, spiraling into an incoherent buzz as Miranda sobbed against her pillows. It hurt, it all hurt. Their anguish. Their lives. Their deaths. All of it digging tunnels inside her skull. It all *hurt*. Miranda pleaded for release as a new voice— now indistinguishable—joined the others. The words of her prayers were lost in the racket of her mind. K'Rania yelled at her, trying to get Miranda to pull it under control again but even that was lost.

Miranda screamed out loud, hoping to hear *something* other than the voices but all she heard was the buzz. She screamed until her throat grew hoarse, and crushed her head between two feather pillows as if they might drown out the intruders. There *had* to be a way to find relief from the dead.

The ink! K'Rania slipped in during a brief lull in the storm as Miranda's mind was trying to focus on a way free.

The ink, Miranda thought, though the words spiraled into the whirlpool of souls. Miranda forced her eyes open, tears blurred her vision as she rolled off her bed and crawled to her door. She was alone today, Ester finally promised to behave at the tournament. Miranda's stomach growled; hunger pains were unimportant compared to the migraine demanding her attention even though she had not eaten at all the past few days.

Miranda pulled on her door's handle, whimpering as the latch refused to lift. "OPEN!" she demanded as if that would force the door to obey her. The door was a stubborn bastard; it refused to budge. "Please, just let me out," Miranda begged, putting all her weight onto the black iron grip. Fear gripped her heart, fear of losing her thoughts in the maelstrom inside her mind again. She whimpered against the door, pulling with all her strength and straining against whatever was keeping it in place. The steel bar clicked up with the sound of shearing metal and the door swung open. Half of the black key to her room lay on the floor outside. "That *bitch*!" Miranda screamed, cursing Cassandra, in unison with one of her many voices. She had no idea who had thought that in death. Probably the new one. "That cunt locked me in here," Miranda growled, wrapping her fingers around the key tightly and letting her anger fuel her strength to keep fighting against the terror that would consume her if she took a moment to think. Miranda could feel a steady flow of necromantic energies as she stood, clutching the key. The voices grew quieter against the world of power she was connected to but still remained. The iron in her grip rusted beneath her fingers.

Finish the mark! K'Rania insisted and Miranda stumbled forward on bare feet. Miranda lost her footing on the stairs, falling hard against the wall. She barely felt her bruised knees and battered shoulder as she pulled herself back to her feet at the bottom. The key in her hand snapped in half again, the long stem corroded entirely through, and the two ends rang as they clattered against the stone floor. Suits of armor crashed to the ground when she pushed them aside to use the wall as support while she walked to Thade's enclave.

The ink! Finish the mark! K'Rania urged as Miranda pulled open the drawer of her mother's cabinet. Miranda threw everything onto the floor that was not the ink. A mirror smashed against the stone, sending fine silvery shards of glass everywhere. Thread bounced on the ground, trailing a line of black as the spool rolled out into the hallway. Hair brushes and incense came next, followed by the drawer itself when it proved not to be where the ink was.

The next drawer was the same, each odd keepsake inside useless as well. Naturally, the last drawer only held the single, gray vial crafted from stone. Miranda opened the vial, setting it carefully on top of the short cabinet. Dark ink that had a faint, yellow shimmer greeted her. Miranda picked up one of the needles she had thrown to the floor, cutting her fingers on the broken mirror, and crawled onto Thade's altar. Miranda cried out, tugging at the neckline of her dress until it ripped to expose her left breast and the unfinished hex.

"I don't know what to do," Miranda cried, her strength failing her. The needle slipped in her fingers, slick with her own red blood, as she held it against her chest. The voices grew louder, taking over her resolve.

Let go, for a time, K'Rania whispered as her mind was consumed by the buzz once more. Miranda had lost sensation in her limbs and panic chipped at the voices driving her towards unconsciousness. She was dying. She welcomed it and passed out.

Miranda blinked back her tears, staring up at Driadra as her arm went limp and the needle clinked against the stone floor. The voices were still there, but they no longer assaulted her mind. Instead, they seemed to be attacking each other, ignoring her entirely. Thade's sculpture looked down at her as she struggled to sit up. Her body ached as if she had been lying on the slab for hours. Miranda shivered, seeing her supple breast coated in her own blood and the vile ink. Jagged marks, nothing like the ones Miranda saw on Cassandra or Lunarin, decorated the wheel around her nipple. One at each tip of the six spokes and one in the six sections of the wheel. The writing was *not* Ilionan and it was *not* Dristelli either.

N'Gochen, K'Rania explained, her thoughts were so close now it sounded like K'Rania was sitting right next to her. *I'Mirana, we are one,* K'Rania clarified.

"We are one?" Miranda furrowed her brow. K'Rania was there, inside her, right beside who she was. She could *feel* the N'Gochen now, the second source of memories and experiences that did not belong to her. K'Rania *wanted* things. Her strongest desire was revenge against her brother but even as Miranda tried to look into the other soul's desire they seemed to become blocked off. It unnerved Miranda, knowing that another soul was sharing her body. Even more, K'Rania had taken *control* of her body when she gave into the despair of the voices, meaning K'Rania *always* had that ability. *Will she do it again?* Miranda wondered.

Not while you choose to continue, K'Rania answered and Miranda shivered. *We are one.*

"And the others?" Miranda said out loud, resisting the urge to claw at her skin like something was squirming underneath it. Miranda could not undo what had happened to her any more than she could ignore K'Rania's presence.

Contained, but not gone. Open to the void too long, K'Rania thought.

"How do you know so much? How could you..." *take control of me?*

I studied, K'Rania felt the same adoration she had when Miranda first tried speaking with the spirit. *Learned of the void, how to travel it. Use it. Interact through it.*

"That's how you found me," Miranda said, carefully stepping off the altar to avoid the broken shards. "This place is a mess."

You cannot stay here, K'Rania had a sense of urgency to her thought, fueled by a deeply seated fear for Lunarin.

"If he sees the markings..." Miranda started, realizing why Lunarin would cause K'Rania to be afraid. Lunarin was a Dristelli bonder, he would know of N'Gochen bonding.

The old one will know them. Rip your soul from you by force and steal your power. You must not *let the old one use you. You must flee, I'Mirana!* Miranda hurried. *You must leave, the old one returns. A web in the void approaches.*

"He isn't *that* old," Miranda said, trying not to focus on K'Rania's terror as she hopped over the toppled armor and raced back to her room.

His soul is ancient, K'Rania said anxiously. *The body is a shell, hollowed out by his bonds. Hopped from one shell to the next over a millennium for personal gain.* K'Rania felt like Lunarin was blasphemous for what he had done, but the anger over that was lost in the terror of what it meant as well. *Flee from this place, get away.*

"You mean, like what you did to me?" Miranda asked. K'Rania did not need to answer, she knew she was right. Miranda felt sick, K'Rania seemed to respect the bond—even felt ashamed of it when Miranda called her out—but she had a feeling that Lunarin would not. A feeling supported by K'Rania's understanding of Lunarin. If K'Rania was right, Lunarin would have been around during the Last Necromantic War. His support for her father's cult suddenly became *much* clearer to Miranda. He wanted the Undying to return.

Flee, K'Rania repeated, the N'Gochen's anxiety feeding into Miranda's now. *There is no time, the old one approaches.*

Miranda groaned, grabbing her shoes and making a quick stop in the kitchen for a loaf of bread and some apples.

The old one touches many shells a web in the void. his plans are vast, you must stop them.

"I'm hurrying; can't you see that?"

Flee, there is no time.

Miranda groaned, she preferred K'Rania as a distant voice that only said two or three words at a time. She sounded like her mother now.

I am not your V'laski, K'Rania sounded offended. *Hurry, they approach. You must escape, seek safety.*

"Like Dwevaria?"

Yes, the great sanctuary city will do, but it is a great distance. Unfathomable to you, K'Rania stated.

"I can pay my way there," Miranda realized, turning back around from the door. K'Rania's anxiety turned into annoyed rage at not being listened to. "I'll leave, don't worry. We'll need something. I have plenty to sell to obtain the means to travel." Miranda ran back to her room. She opened her jewelry cabinet, putting on her favorite lattice necklace and gloves of gold and rubies before dumping most of it into a satchel. She had no idea what the trinkets were worth, but they should be enough to buy what she needed. First, she needed to go to Crossroads and buy those things. The last to go into the bag were the coins she stole from Lunarin. She turned to her wardrobe to change. She had no coats—she had never been outside in late fall before—and none of her dresses were really suited for the weather at this time of year but... *No time!* K'Rania insisted. *You've wasted enough already for those trinkets. Go!*

Miranda ran to the door and paused, pinning the tattered neckline of her dress together with one hand. Miranda started down the road, holding her torn dress closed. She froze at the sound of wooden wheels crawling against the stones of the path. A carriage was approaching.

The old one, K'Rania warned, sounding like herself again. K'Rania was none-too-pleased by that comparison, but let the thought alone as Miranda darted towards the north wing, hoping no one aboard the coach had spotted her in the dark.

"I have to say goodbye to Ester," Miranda said, hiding behind the sharp edge of her family's mansion as she watched five people disembark from the carriage. Two women, Ariel and Cassandra, with Ester between them walked in front of Morgan. Lunarin was the last one out and followed several paces behind the family before the carriage started back down the driveway. "Ester..."

Find another way, K'Rania suggested as the five people disappeared into the structure and the carriage rolled away. It would not be long before they discovered Miranda missing. Especially since Cassandra had locked her into her room. No doubt the woman was heading directly for Miranda's chambers this very second. Miranda moved to say goodbye to Ester to let her sister know she was alright despite the mess she had left behind. *The mess is good; you could have been taken. Find another way.*

"Cassandra will notice the missing ink," Miranda said, reluctantly continuing towards the stream behind the house. "I'll leave something at the top of Ester's tree, then head to Crossroads."

Avoid the road; they will search it for you, K'Rania said nothing about leaving the token. The N'Gochen almost seemed to wish she could have done the same. *You did not look into my death,* K'Rania said about her remorse. Miranda wondered why she regretted not leaving a message. *Now you never can.* Miranda smiled at the woman keeping secrets in her own mind. It was perplexing to think too hard about it so she focused on crossing the stream without losing a shoe this time. The water was shallower and the banks were dryer, given the late season, so it was considerably easier to cross and climb up. The thicket of trees came soon enough, followed by the dirt path through them to her sister's favorite place to play.

"I wonder what was going to be for evening meal?" Miranda smiled as she ran a hand over the first rung that climbed the tree house. Somewhere the question was echoed by a man deep inside her mind. "Such a stupid thing to be startled by." Miranda climbed. It was hard work. Her skirts tore slightly as they caught on branches in her ascent and her arms ached from pulling her own weight up and holding onto the tree, but she made it to the first platform and looked around. All she could see were branches and beyond them more trees. She looked up and smiled, spying the path to the next platform. "The best view of the valley, Ester said. It is time I saw what the fuss was about."

There is no time, K'Rania urged as Miranda started up the narrower path.

"They're busy searching the road, *remember*?"

Miranda climbed higher and felt a little dizzy when she looked down with nothing beneath her but the branches. A fall from this high *would* kill her, she knew, but she continued climbing. Vertigo made her grab tightly to the branches, pressing her body against the coarse texture of the bark. Now that she had run away life seemed so open, she had no desire to join K'Rania in the void. Miranda pulled herself up the last rung and sat down on the much smaller platform. The red, orange, and yellow leaves of autumn obscured her view but she needed to catch her breath.

"Why is everything so exhausting outside of the mansion?" Miranda asked.

You have no strength, K'Rania answered, feeling just as amused as she had been when she informed Miranda about her eyes. *You must grow stronger, I'Mirana.*

"I didn't want an answer, Karina," Miranda grinned.

I am K'Rania, Queen of the Kanach hive!

"And I am Miranda...er... me! Not I'Miranamana or whatever you keep calling me."

I'Mirana. Is your hive not Iliona?

"I guess you could say it is," Miranda shrugged. "But Mirana is not my name."

Very well, I'Miranla, K'Rania thought and Miranda had the sensation that the N'Gochen was giving her a sarcastic bow.

"Now you're just doing it on purpose," Miranda sighed, stretching as she stood. She opened her eyes and her breath caught in her chest. You really *could* see the entire valley up here. It was night, so everything was obscured, but the horizon was still spectacular. *Luminara* was full, casting a pale light on the gray stone peaks of the Cinder Mountains far to the south. To the east was a sprawling forest that reached as far as Miranda could see. Her mansion seemed so small compared to it all, but she could see a glow lamp circling the structure as two others went up and down the road. Several more lamps were approaching, these had the distinct flicker of an oil light and bounced as if on horseback. Someone had probably summoned the Watch to look for her.

Westward was another forest against the foothills of the Iron Mountains that divided Iliona in half. These were much closer than the Cinder Mountains, letting Miranda see a great deal more detail by *Luminara*'s light. Gray cliffs jutted out of the dark forest below and a few lights twinkled on the mountainside. They could be mines where men burned oil to see the veins of precious metals in the ore-rich range. Or they could be camps of bandits or adventurers out to see the world. Miranda would never know unless she went there, which was the wrong direction to reach Crossroads or Dwevaria. Miranda slipped off the two golden webs around her arms and placed them on the platform. She had no note, but Ester would recognize the jewelry. Hopefully, the young girl would know they were meant for her as a farewell gift.

"Alright," Miranda said, beginning a much slower descent out of the tree. "How do I get to Crossroads without using the road?" K'Rania smirked again, as if the answer was obvious. K'Rania would make for an annoying travel companion.

The forest, K'Rania stated as Miranda's foot fell on the solid ground once more.

"Great," Miranda sighed with disdain, brushing her hands off on her dress. She could feel dozens of scrapes and bruises Ester's tree had given her already. "More trees."

XVII

CHALLENGE

Anara gasped, arching her back as she rose and fell on Sir Edwin's stiff shaft. The sensation of it was enjoyable but it was just a show of course. Shallow or not at least Sir Edwin seemed to take a great deal of pleasure from watching her tits bounce with each of his thrusts as she sat atop him in bed. Sir Edwin had won his match in the jousts for the week, three lances broken against two strikes. He really was Sir Edwin the Untouchable as spectators from past tournaments called him in the streets. *Untouchable, at least, by a lance,* Anara smiled, bending over and resting both palms against Edwin's sweaty, muscular chest. She rocked her hips back and forth until his seed spurted into her to the sound of Edwin's grunts of ecstasy. Anara shuddered at the sensation; not from pleasure, the sticky warmth made her feel sick and had since the first time at *Lussena's Temple,* but this was her life.

For now.

"Another prize for my victor," Anara said, slipping off Edwin's slick rod and crawling beside the knight. She ran her fingers through the short, blonde hairs on Edwin's chest. Another ugly thing about men that she was *supposed* to enjoy. How *anyone* enjoyed chest hair was beyond her. "I hope I will not tire you out too much when you win multiple times a week. I'd hate to see you lose the last match because your thighs were too sore from mounting me to stay atop your horse."

"A fate I may have to accept," Edwin sighed, kissing Anara's lips. She hated the beard he was growing now that he was no longer keeping to military customs. It was a curly mop that covered his chin, upper lip, and went up into his equally curly head of hair. *All* of Edwin's hairs were curly from his legs and short hairs to his eyebrows and locks, and as coarse as short dog hair too. "And, perhaps, a worthy exchange. In all of my life, I've not felt such lust for a woman as I do when I am deep inside your folds."

"I am delighted to satisfy your desires," Anara smiled as Edwin rolled to lean over her, his still engorged manhood cool and wet against her bare belly as his hands wandered over her breasts. "We should bathe, Sir Edwin, we still have a feast to attend for the week's victors."

"A woman who both speaks the truth and fulfills a man's desires," Edwin nodded, climbing off the bed. "You are a rare find, Mistress Swift."

Edwin disappeared into the bathing room off of their quarters. Anara folded her arms across her chest as she heard the knight slip into the bath. She walked over to where her gown had been discarded in Edwin's zeal to see her naked. Picking it up, she frowned at the creases and wrinkles. Unlike Sir Edwin, who was living in these quarters, Anara had no change of clothes. Those were back at *Lussena's Rest*. Anara did her best to straighten the skirts, hoping that letting them hang as she joined Edwin in his bath would be enough to let the wrinkles fall out. Anara anxiously bit her lower lip, took in a calming breath and stepped into the steamy, small bathing room to join her client.

The carriage ride was quick as Anara and Edwin made their way to the center of the city thanks to the grid layout of the streets. The Tower of the Watch—which doubled as a temple to Iliona's gods and as ancient as Ashfall—was where the weekend victory balls were held. The large, stone structure was at the heart of Crossroads and was as well-guarded as King Aegen's palace. Considering the reports of riots, thefts, and murders over the outcomes of the games the security was a blessing for Anara.

The streets of Crossroads were similar to Merchant's Row in Aederon City. They were packed with carts and stalls where tradesmen shouted above each other to attract customers. Unlike Aederon, however, the overall layout was more organized. Each block, packed full of houses, was the same acreage that the tower stood on. If you kept to the main roads it was easy to navigate, but the streets that divided the blocks—like those that lead to *Lussena's Rest*—could be as twisted and thin as those in West End. The quickest and safest way anywhere, by design, was to use the main thoroughfares. The winding side roads were growing more and more dangerous. Numerous reports of muggings and murders spread through the city even as the fervor for the tournament continued to build.

"Was Aederon as woeful to travel through during last year's tournament?" Anara asked, turning away from the streets to look at Sir Edwin. He wore a decorative design similar to his uniform. His coat covered him up to his neck without showing any of the tunic he wore beneath but the color was certainly *not* military regulation. The dark green fabric was ornamented by golden embroidery down the sleeves and on the knee-length hem. The buttons only went down to Edwin's sword belt, letting the garment split to show off the tight, black breeches he wore. His slacks showed off the exaggerated bulge of his manhood in a split-colored gold and green codpiece. The display was meant to draw the gaze of other women, not that Anara was jealous. The other women could have Edwin if they wanted.

"What do you mean?" Edwin asked.

"The crime rates... Was there this much in Aederon last year?"

"A bizarre topic to be considering, for a woman," Edwin shrugged. "I don't really pay attention to the low."

"Even though you used to be one? I would think you would understand their plight better than most of those you face."

"I'm nothing like them," Edwin spat. His eyes burned with anger, and a vein in his temple even throbbed at the suggestion that he was like the lowborn. It was frightening how swift Edwin turned to rage but Anara smiled, keeping her composure.

"My apologies," Anara said, bowing her head. "I did not intend it as an offense, just to put your great achievements into perspective."

"Understandable," Edwin nodded, leaning back against his seat's cushion but he looked at Anara with caution in his eyes. "I cannot speak on the difference, but it is understandable that it might be worse this year than last. Lord Heath has very little care for his citizens."

"But Lord Heath is the wealthiest noble in the realm, possibly even wealthier than King Aegen."

"Alas, money alone does not dictate who rules the realm. Lord Heath is a shut in, keeping to his mansions across the realm as if they were all that mattered to him. What happens in Crossroads is none of his concern. He amasses wealth from the taxes and tariffs placed on merchants passing through and hoards it. Since his majesty still has no heir, many nobles support Lord Heath as successor based solely on his wealth and judge him strictly on his successes without giving any weight to his failures. Nearly half of the nobility have already offered their sons to wed his daughter even though she is barely ten years old."

"Then the crime is rampant because he does not fund the Watch, as he should, to protect his lands?"

"He pays them, but the Watch is underfunded here for the amount of patrols needed in this densely populated of a city. Especially since the Watch Academy is located here and the bulk of the Crown's funds go to that establishment instead of the ones on patrol." Edwin nodded his head. "A peasant in Crossroads is virtually a slave and a city of slaves breeds crime faster than the Watch can keep up with it. Underfunded and overworked guards create two types. Crooked and apathetic men walk these streets."

"That's awful!" Anara cried out and Edwin shrugged.

"Politics should not concern someone with your beauty," Edwin said as the carriage came to a stop. He opened the door and helped Anara down to the keep's walkway. "You should be more concerned about the tournament. Once it is finished we can both leave the city behind, its woes will no longer be your concern."

Anara would have frowned but the Tower of the Watch, and her duties, prevented her from doing so. It was her second time at the Victor's Ball, held at the end of each week during the Harvest Festival, but the scale of the structure was still a wonder to behold. A massive central tower dwarfed the six smaller towers at each corner of the hexagonal palace. The smaller towers themselves dwarfed the ones where the courtesan chapters were held at *Lussena's Temple*. Each of the outer walls had been carved to depict one of the six gods and their twelve saints with massive double doors to let visitors and petitioners in. Notably, Thade had been defaced to the point that none of the reliefs resembled Ilionans anymore, Thade's door had also been covered up by a wall of brick. As was customary, people chose the door of their preferred god to enter through. Most of them were using Fiel's door, including Edwin and Anara even though Anara would have preferred Malef. As they entered the inner courtyard that surrounded the central tower Anara caught sight of Joshua entering through Malef's door with, to Anara's astonishment, Roxanne on his arm. Anara waved at the other courtesan, who waved back and pulled the young man towards them.

"Mistress Swift, it is good to see you here," Roxanne said once they were in earshot. "And you, Sir Edwin, of course. Have you met Joshua Kentaine?"

"Mistress Swift and I have had the pleasure, once before," Joshua said and Anara felt Edwin's grip of her arm tighten. "As for Edwin the *Untouchable*, we have met on several occasions." Joshua frowned as he looked at Edwin.

"What is it?" Edwin asked.

"I remember you being taller, to be honest," Joshua sighed and Roxanne laughed. "Guess looking up at you on a horse gave me unrealistic expectations."

"Hold your tongue, peasant; you speak to one of your betters," Edwin's grip tightened again. "A quip to impress your companion is a poor reason to spend the rest of the tournament in the stocks."

"Mistress Ashton isn't my companion, I am merely discussing the sword and decorating her arm until... there they are," Joshua waved over another couple and Anara saw the color drain from Edwin's face. Lord and Lady Ackart approached as Roxanne stepped aside. Lady Ackart even *kissed* Joshua before sliding her arm through his and leaning her head against his shoulder.

"I remember you now," Sir Edwin said to Joshua after saluting Lord Ackart. "You were that squire who lost it when I told you of Sir Echton's death. I heard the heir commander had to put your nose in the mud like a disobedient pup after that."

"Capture," Joshua said through a clenched jaw. Anara could see the turmoil of grief and anger at Edwin's comment in Joshua's expression. "You said he was captured."

"That is as good as dead, given how Raykarn treat their prisoners," Edwin laughed as Joshua's face grew darker. "I'm surprised to see you at the Victor's Ball, only jousters are permitted to attend. Weren't you against Causeworth? I swore you lost that bout, though I admit Mistress Swift may have been distracting me."

"Joshua beat Lord Causeworth," Lord Ackart informed. "Unhorsed him in the third tilt. Though Joshua has proven himself to be as unbeatable in sword as you are in the joust, Sir Edwin. That alone may have earned him a right to be here after twelve straight victories."

"The sword is a savage event," Edwin sighed. "It does not surprise me a savage from the Borderlands would be good at it." Joshua moved to strike Sir Edwin but he was hindered from doing more than stepping forward by Lady Ackart.

"Joshua, no," Lady Ackart pleaded, pulling back on Joshua's arm gently.

"You wish to fight?" Edwin said, finally letting Anara's arm go, to her dismay it was only to draw his sword. "Have you even faced a sharpened blade, boy?"

"Joshua," Lord Ackart said, stepping between Edwin and the squire. "You'll face him in the lists."

"Doubtful," Edwin said, sheathing his blade. "He's the last hopeless in the joust after this week, I doubt he'll win his first match in the next."

"I will," Joshua said, his hand tight around the short sword at his waist. Anara was surprised that it was not the enchanted blade he received at his celebration several months earlier. "And the four after that. Then I *will* face you across the arena, and I *will* win a knighthood."

"If you are so confident, care to make a wager?" Edwin laughed. "Who am I kidding, you lack anything of value."

"I'll be his stakes," Lady Ackart stepped forward.

"Cora!" Lord Ackart yelped. "Don't be stupid. Father would never agree to *this* arrangement."

"Listen to your brother, my lady," Edwin agreed. "I already have a woman to bed."

"You don't understand," Lady Ackart sighed. "I'll wed you if you beat Joshua, giving proper weight to your new lordship."

Please, take her, Anara thought, though she did not voice her opinion. Aside from being a true noble, the young Lady Ackart was so beautiful that even Anara had a hard time taking her eyes of the woman. If Edwin had the Lady Ackart he would never have a need to visit Anara again.

"And what would I offer in return to a peasant?"

"Mistress Swift," Joshua said and a brief frown flashed across Cordelia's face. "You'll never request her services again."

"Joshua," Lady Ackart whispered, she sounded grief-stricken. As if her heart had been crushed that Joshua would wager for another woman. Anara swallowed, imagining if Lena ever chose another person over her. It was unpleasant to be cast aside by someone she loved for another. She could understand the painful whine in Lady Ackart's voice.

"I accept your terms," Edwin said, holding out his hand with a wide grin. Joshua shook and the four others left Anara alone with Edwin. "Idiot boy," Edwin laughed. "Win or lose he just lost the easiest way to become a lord. Lady Ackart would have declared her love for that peasant the moment he became a knight. *If* he ever became a knight."

Anara remained silent, keeping to her duties of decorating the competitor's arm, as Edwin escorted her into the vast entrance hall of the *Tower of the Watch*. The militaristic decorations were minimal except for the banners of every lord sworn to King Aegen hanging from the vaulted ceiling, which meant there were dozens of them. Tables lined the two sides of the room, leaving a great deal of space for the spinning couples on the floor. A band played the usual songs for such a feast across from the entrance on a raised platform above the dance floor. Conversations came and went as Edwin walked with her towards the tables where the most honorable—meaning wealthy—lords dined with the three queens.

Notably, Lord and Ladies Heath were not in attendance today which left Edwin and Anara free to take their vacant seats beside the queens. The three queens smiled at Edwin lustfully, not mentioning his improper actions.

Each queen was five years apart in age. The oldest, considered to be the highest ranking of them, was Queen Delilah. The short woman was rather stocky with exceedingly wide hips that many men thought meant she was more productive than the soil of the Fertile Vale on the other side of the Iron Mountains. It was nothing more than superstition; Delilah had never produced an heir for the kingdom, despite nearly fifteen years of marriage to King Aegen. As was the king's custom in his ninety years of life, Delilah would be replaced soon. A fact mirrored in her Majesty's scowl that seemed to say her life was only a disappointment. No doubt she would still have that scowl when Aegen married his sixteenth wife and Delilah's head was removed from her shoulders. That was King Aegen's usual pattern. Every five years he took a new wife and the one he had been married to the longest was executed for failing to produce an heir.

Queen Janette happened to be the second oldest and had been married to King Aegen just short of ten years. She was as skinny as Delilah was round. Tall and thin like a beanstalk with an almost haunted expression in her gaunt face. Like Queen Delilah, it was a wonder *why* King Aegen had chosen her to marry when he could pick any of the women in the entire kingdom Somehow Janette had become a queen and had taken to her power like flies to honey. Most women would lose their head if they looked at her the wrong way, especially if they were considered to be more beautiful. The only woman who could get away with arguing against Queen Janette was Queen Navine.

Queen Navine was desire made flesh. Anara could see hints of Borderlander blood in her bright orange eyes, but the light freckling of her tan skin and fiery red hair so light it almost seemed orange were distinctly from the Fertile Vale. Where Delilah and Janette were at one end or the other of a woman's build, Queen Navine was perfectly in the middle—not too plump to be considered large, and not too slender to be considered scrawny. Navine was the kind of woman Anara had seen a lot of in the corridors of *Lussena's Temple*. In fact, Navine probably would have fit right in at the courtesan house with the low cut of her neckline and how little fabric covered her breasts from cutouts in the sides of her bodice. Anara struggled to keep from biting her lower lip the way she did when she gawked at Lena as she stared at Queen Navine. The sparkle in Navine's eyes when they caught Anara's seemed to understand what Anara was thinking. Her majesty was certainly nice to look at, but Lena was who she would rather be seeing right now.

"Sir Edwin," Janette said, setting her glass of red wine down beside her nearly empty plate. "I was hoping to see you in attendance, though perhaps a little earlier would have been more appropriate for the man expected to become the newest lord in the kingdom."

"I beg your forgiveness, your majesties," Anara said, bowing her head as she gave a low curtsy before sitting beside Edwin. "I'm afraid Sir Edwin's tardiness is my doing."

"Of course, you would be the cause," Delilah humphed, she had barely touched her food. Queen Delilah's diets were notorious for gossip and rumor in the courtesan house. No doubt her refusal to eat food in an attempt to look more like Navine would end with a binge that emptied all the pastry shops closest to Noble District when the festival was over.

"Be nice, Delilah," Navine scolded, she smiled at Sir Edwin briefly as she turned back to her meal. "Sir Edwin is the closest man to ever claim a title of nobility from the Harvest Tournament, only six more tilts and he will make history."

"I cannot take all the credit, your grace," Sir Edwin said, leaning back in his chair. As good as a courtesan was at putting air into a man's ego, a queen's simple comment really did swell the knight's head. Both of them, if the lines in Edwin's pants were to be believed.

"Then perhaps we should be giving a title to another? Who else but you could take the credit for your victories?" Janette asked, leaning a little closer towards Edwin.

"That is simple, your grace," Edwin grinned. "My horse deserves the title for he is the only one I trust to carry me to victory."

The queens laughed, and Anara forced herself to join in. Monarchs never laughed alone and a courtesan never failed to laugh at her client's jests. Her fake laugh had gotten surprisingly good from being in Edwin's presence so much during the festival. He had a knack for wedging himself near the queens and they had a knack of enabling his horrid, often lewd, sense of humor.

"I'm curious, Sir Edwin, but what do you think of this year's competitors now that we are entering the third week?" Navine asked. "I mean, now that you have seen what they are capable of from the matches over the past two weeks."

"I'm not too concerned about any of them," Edwin answered, taking a generous drink from his glass that was refilled as a servant walked by.

"Pride is a sin, of course," Delilah countered. "It would be Fiel's justice to see you fail for that, would it not?"

"Pride is one thing, your majesty," Edwin sighed, emptying his glass again. He tended to drink too much. "But I feel I've earned this as much as any man who has seen the horrors of the Borderlands. I have protected the entire kingdom in the name of the God of Light."

"Then, perhaps, the title should go to the man being called 'the Squire'?" Navine suggested and Anara could see the vein in Edwin's temple throb as he choked on more wine. "If what my cousin said is true, he had quite a hard time in his early life living in the Borderlands."

"You cousin is misinformed," Edwin shook his head. "I doubt this—this squire has seen much of Iliona south of Ashfall. True he has Borderlander blood in his lineage, but no proper Ilionan would chase after a Borderland woman to make a life down there. If anything, she would be brought up above the safety of Ashfall."

"That isn't true," Anara found herself saying. "He was born in the south and brought to safety by Sir Echton during the skirmishes nine years ago." *What did I do!* Anara shut her eyes tightly. She could feel Edwin's disapproving stare on her.

"That is what my cousin, Lady Jocelyn Chase said about the celebration Sir Echton's wife threw for the man when he came of a competing age." Anara sighed, silently thanking Queen Navine for distracting Edwin from her slip up. He could not be cross with her, at least not in public, if Anara had the support of one of the queens.

"So, he was a child in the Borderlands," Edwin laughed the argument off. It sounded more forced than Anara's had felt. "That is not the same as being on the front lines, seeing their hatred up close. I'm sure Lord Commander Ackart evacuated his village long before any fighting began back then."

"Of course," Navine said, sounding unconvinced.

"Leave the man be, Navine," Janette sighed, actually leaning against Sir Edwin. Apparently, she shared his vice for wine. "He is as untouchable in the lists this year as he has been in the last nine. If that fact alone is not enough to show that Fiel has blessed him, Delilah, then nothing will."

The meal continued with very little excitement since queens had surprisingly very little to gossip about. After a few unsteady dances, Edwin drinking during each one, Anara was escorted back to Edwin's lodgings. He had not forgotten Anara's slip up. He thrust painfully into her sensitive slit while pulling her head back by her hair and gripping her throat so tightly it was difficult to breathe. Anara found no sleep, crawling into the empty tub and quietly coughing at the scratch in her throat. Anara curled up, terrified that Edwin would awaken and silence her sobs for good if she returned to the bed. She gently rubbed her throat and prayed he had not left a mark while crying for the first time since arriving at Crossroads.

XVIII

HARVEST FESTIVAL

Third Week

Miranda walked through the underbrush, her skirt snagging on *every single* twig or branch as she cut across the country. K'Rania's solution to avoiding the roads was idiotic. She was a *lady*, not some bandit or highwayman. Her skirts were practically rags now, not to mention the terrible state of her shoes and stockings. Even worse, the extended time and effort wasted on traveling through the untouched forest was exhausting. Miranda could not think of a reason why anyone would choose to go this way instead of along a well-worn path or road.

It is safer, K'Rania explained.

"Thade's Abyss, no it isn't," Miranda cursed back, nearly tripping over a particularly gnarled bit of root jutting up from the ground. "I've been walking for *hours*. How much farther until Crossroads?"

The north is unknown to me, K'Rania said. Ignorance was her usual excuse when it came to the terrain of Iliona. Miranda clenched her fists in frustration at the futility of arguing with the voice in her head. At least the other hundreds of dead were nice enough to be barely a whisper.

I am not loud, K'Rania growled back. Another root caught her unaware and she stumbled forward, twisted on the foot that caught her, and she fell to her knees.

"Damned nature! Why'd Duloreb make it so difficult!" Miranda yelled, examining her precious shoe, the heel was snapped cleanly off. She removed them both and tossed them away. Her sheer stockings were already a mess of rips and runs, dirt would be nothing compared to... "Thade's bitch!" Miranda cursed as her heel stung with something sharp being driven into it. She picked the thing from her foot and held the four-pointed seed in her hand. "What the bloody abyss is this supposed to be! Why would a plant ever *need* to make something like this?"

It latches onto the fur of animals. They carry it to other soil, K'Rania explained. She sounded amused. Miranda groaned, this venture into the outside world was turning out just as poorly as the first time with Ester. Miranda frowned, swallowing a lump in her throat as she thought of her little sister. How long would it be before Ester found her gift? Would it be days, weeks... years? Miranda stood up and continued onward, trying her best to avoid the traps Duloreb had for her in the dark of night. She could barely make out the shapes of enormous tree trunks in front of her and blobs of bushes where the tree cover opened to the sky. Miranda had not seen a single meadow or a clearing in the forest as she traveled northward towards crossroads. Each step made her heel hurt and she started hobbling about as she did her best to keep from putting her weight on the wounded part of her foot.

Every now and then she could make out the stars, broken by a light cloud cover, above her. That massive blanket of flickering lights was beautiful, but now that she had been in the world beyond her windows she wondered if the sky was just as hazardous. The forest and rolling hills had been just as beautiful before she was actually among them.

A wolf howled in the distance, sending shivers up her spine as she crouched against a tree. The coarse bark bit into her through the thin fabric of her dress. She owned nothing appropriate for this sort of travel. She shivered against the cold of mid-fall as the howling died down before starting on her way again. Her long hair caught on low branches, snagging and tangling against the rough patterns in the bark and causing her to cry out each time. More burs and stones assaulted her feet, and the rise and fall of the breeze continually bit against her skin.

"I'm never going to be free of this place," Miranda whimpered as yet another branch tugged at her lustrous locks, feeling and hearing the hairs ripping free. The next hill she crested, to her relief, spread into a dying field of grass where she spotted the orange flicker of a fire coming from a hovels window. "Finally," she gasped and sprinted across the softer, more even ground of an unattended field still full of crops. Miranda grew closer, her stomach grumbling at the scent wafting from the small home's pane-less window, and she froze.

So, this is the abyss; it isn't so bad. I should tell my priest.

She recognized the structure. The man who had broken his neck, a farmer and a father, had died where she now stood. The words of that soul seemed louder here. Miranda stood there, looking at the unremarkable spot just outside the window. She could see the farmer; he was a handsome man for his age with a full face of dark stubble peppered with gray. His neck, of course, was unnaturally bent where it had snapped to let his head hang free of his spine but at least there had been no blood. And it had been relatively painless for the man as well.

"By Mertas's bounty!" A woman gasped from the window, the farmer's wife was gawking at Miranda. Miranda's heart raced and she turned to run. "Wait, dear, you look terrible. Why don't you come inside, besides it's too late for a woman to be out at night in these parts."

"I couldn't," Miranda shook her head, even as her stomach argued with her.

"None of that, you don't look much older than my own daughter," the farmwife said disappearing for just a second before opening the door only a few feet from the window. She waved Miranda over. "What in Fiel's creation drove you to wander the forest alone?" The woman's jaw dropped as Miranda entered into the warm light of her home. "Milady!" she fell to her knees and Miranda stepped forward to pull her back up to her feet.

"I'm not a lady," Miranda lied, it was difficult to move the peasant. Her battle with the woods had been more draining than she knew and whatever the woman was cooking smelled *so* good. Miranda found herself glaring at the peasant who was shying away from her now that she recognized the difference in their clothing. Even as torn and muddied as her skirts were, they were still higher quality than what the farmwife wore. "My name..." *Don't use your own name,* K'Rania cautioned and Miranda cleared her throat. "My name is Karina," Miranda said. "A servant from the Heath Estate, if we could go inside I will explain."

"Of course," she said, looking back and forth as if someone was out there searching for Miranda. There might have been; she *was* important to Cassandra and Lunarin at least. Her value, however, may be lessened now that she had finished her mark. *The ink, black iron against porcelain skin,* K'Rania reminded. Miranda ignored the N'Gochen and marveled at how welcoming the woman was while crossing the threshold. *She seeks to claim a reward,* K'Rania said, as if she could read the peasant's mind as well. *She will turn you in, we must not stay long. Kill her before we go.*

I'm not going to kill her, K'Rania, Miranda thought, furrowing her brow out of frustration. K'Rania suggested that course of action too often.

The thin door of wooden scraps clattered shut as Miranda was ushered into the small structure. There was only one room, really, with what must have been sleeping arrangements in a loft above the dining area. All of it would have easily fit inside her room in the Heath mansion. "Have a seat, please, I was just sitting down for evening meal myself."

"This late?" Miranda asked, finally giving her legs a rest as she lowered onto a chair. One of the seat's legs was shorter than the other three and it wobbled so much she felt in danger of spilling out onto the floor. Miranda wrinkled her nose at what was beneath the stool and table. Calling it a 'floor' was too generous, it looked more like the dirt in the field had been trampled and beaten to be flat instead of tilled.

"I'm afraid so. Since Tyrone passed away it has just been me tending to the farm. I cannot get even half as much done as he did. I have been eating later and later, trying to save what I can of the fields I was able to plant." *So, this is the abyss, it isn't so bad.*

I should tell my priest. "Where are my manners, going on about my troubles without even giving you my name, I'm Idrid."

"What about your daughter? Doesn't she help?" Miranda asked as Idrid poured soup into a wooden bowl for Miranda. The soup looked more like hot water than an actual soup, but it smelled good enough so Miranda slowly drank from the rim of her bowl. The broth was delicious, filling her belly with a warmth that slowly spread outward.

"She helps how she can," Idrid sighed, eating from her own bowl. Each spoonful was only liquid. Miranda finished drinking, leaving the meager amount of vegetables and some unidentified meat at the bottom to be fished out with her own wooden spoon. "She is in Crossroads tonight working. Fiel be good if she makes it home unharmed."

"What do you mean?"

Idrid sighed, blushing and stirring her soup and looking like she had lost her appetite. "There isn't much work for a woman her age, or yours for that matter," Idrid said. "I'm not certain how you were treated by the Heaths, poorly no doubt since you fled, but you may have been better off staying. I mean, a servant in silk and jewels is unheard of."

"It is never better off staying with those who worship Thade," Miranda coldly said, pushing her empty bowl away and Idrid paused as she filled it up once more.

"*What?*" Idrid gasped, looking out her window again. There was still very little chance anyone had followed Miranda during the night. The gods would be good if they provided some rain to wash her trail away. "The Heaths... they worship the black one? Are they..."

"Necromancers? Yes," Miranda said, surprised at how easy her story was coming out. *Lies built on truths*, K'Rania mused. "They don't keep servants like regular nobility, I was to be sacrificed, I only found out tonight and managed to get away. I thought all the silk and jewelry were because they enjoyed my company and rewarded my efforts, but it was to distract me."

"I can't believe that. I know of servants who hate their lords... and that most of what they say *can't* be true but..."

Miranda let her tattered neckline fall, exposing the mark hidden beneath it on her chest and Idrid stood up and backed away against the counters behind her. The mark was not necromancy, at least not the kind Ilionans feared, but no one would know that. Very few nobility would recognize it as a bonding, let alone a random peasant.

"I fled when they finished this and overheard what it meant," Miranda said. "Please, help me." Idrid hesitated, holding a hand over her mouth as she kept looking out her only window. "I can compensate you," Miranda pulled out most of her silver drakes and placed them on the table. "I know you need help. Hire some. It isn't your fault Tyrone broke his neck."

"How did you..." Idrid gasped, trying her best to shrink back into the kitchen area even more. "I didn't say how Tyrone died."

Fool! K'Rania snapped. Miranda felt her gut wrench at the shock and suspicion blossoming in Idrid's eyes.

"It isn't your fault." Miranda hastily said. "Tyrone's death wasn't your fault, it was... I cannot say. I should not say." Miranda shut her eyes and bowed her head, hoping she had deflected Idrid's suspicion. *Unspoken words, false assumptions*, K'Rania approved of Miranda's attempt at subtle deception.

"Was it..." Idrid said, letting her hands fall to her sides. She clenched them as she glared towards the south. "Did they... I mean, necromancy needs death, doesn't it? Did they?"

Let her believe, K'Rania suggested, feeling like she was shrugging.

Miranda bowed her head and nodded. Idrid sat back down, placing a hand on Miranda's. She was kind, too accepting of Miranda's lies for someone who had known the horror of being lowborn.

So, this is the abyss; it isn't so bad. I should tell my priest.

Stillness filled the air, the only words coming to Miranda were Tyrone's as they cycled around in the loop with the murmur of the other ones. Miranda tried not to feel uncomfortable beneath the peasant's concerned eyes as she looked around the room. It really *was* tiny and every possible space was filled with something.

There were no decorations, at least not like the murals, rugs and suits of armor of her family. There were handmade knickknacks hanging on the walls that symbolized the five gods. They seemed strangely out of place to Miranda with Fiel's star rising above the other four without Thade's to balance it like the more elaborate ones at her home.

The cabinets were about the only places that looked a little sparse. Idrid and her daughter were running out of food without Tyrone there to tend the fields and keep collectors at bay. No doubt, if things continued this way, Idrid's family would die of hunger before the next planting season even began.

"I'll help you," Idrid said, smiling. "But I won't accept any payment. A woman like you deserves a second chance. First you need to look less stately and more like someone of your class." Idrid stood and pulled a set of shears from a cabinet drawer and moved behind Miranda. "No proper peasant woman would be caught dead with hair as long as yours. It is too much of a hassle to take care of. And, given your disheveled state, I think you must agree it gets in the way as well."

Miranda half laughed as Idrid went to work turning her into a proper peasant. She wanted to believe that a haircut and peasant clothes would make her look different, but her green eyes would surely give her away. If Idrid only knew what they meant, she would probably flee her own home in terror. If anyone she passed in Iliona knew only necromancers had green eyes, then Miranda would be executed.

Miranda rose late the following morning. The cotton nightgown Idrid had given her itched like she had slept in those four pointed seeds. Sleeping naked would have been a better option if the blankets had not been even more scratchy than the clothing. Her body ached all over from dozens of scratches and sore muscles thanks to her night's journey. Miranda slipped into the peasant dress Idrid must have altered for her earlier in the morning. Even with the alterations, it was still rather tight across her bust. Idrid's daughter must have been as flat as a board compared to Miranda; there just had not been enough fabric to let out. It appeared that Idrid's daughter had not returned home since one of the three, narrow cots above the dining area looked untouched. Miranda lowered herself down the ladder that went up to the loft and slipped on a pair of calf-high women's boots. They were well worn with soft, pliable leather. "My daughter grew out of them," Idrid had explained when Miranda tried refusing the boots and dress.

Miranda opened the silk pouch she kept her coins in to find Idrid had returned what she had offered and sighed. Miranda placed most of the silver on Idrid's dining table and slipped out of the hovel as she tucked her long bangs back behind her ears. The back of her hair was shorter than her father normally wore it. No doubt because of the clump that had torn on that last branch before finding Idrid's hovel.

So, this is the abyss; it isn't so bad. I should tell my priest, Tyrone said as Miranda gave her respects at his death spot before leaving the homestead on a muddy road. Apparently, the gods listened; it *had* rained enough to cover her escape. Miranda turned right onto the King's Highway and started for the bustling city she had only ever seen from a distance. She wanted to see what was so special about the Harvest Festival. Why so many would foolishly gamble their livelihood away on it. She had already missed the first two weeks; she would not miss the last two.

The walk into the city was a lot quicker than her hike through the forest had been. Very few people, other than men anyway, gave her a second look as she quietly made her way into the city. Her shorter hair bobbed with each step and swirled back and forth around her face as she looked up at all the sights to see along the road. A few directions from an elderly woman later and she was walking into a packed arena where two men fought at the center of a small circle of sand. It was a lot to take in between the roaring spectators and the men in suits of plate and chain fighting below. It was almost eerie, too, seeing those suits of armor moving. Miranda had only ever seen them standing in her halls and could almost imagine them being empty as their swords crashed against each other and off plates of steel. The match ended with an exciting flourish of one swordsman ducking beneath a swing and driving his sword against the other's ribcage.

"Nine to three! The Squire wins!" an announcer shouted, barely audible over the din of the crowd. The man removed his helmet after helping the loser up. Miranda froze, recognizing the man's smooth chin and narrow eyes. Her heart raced knowing that the man's face was no longer *just* the memory of a poor child's death. It was her memory now and she found her cheeks flushed with the excitement she felt over him.

He cannot see you, K'Rania grumbled but Miranda just wanted to hide. He was handsome, too handsome. Her heart raced and she was suddenly, painfully aware of the suffocating numbers of people around her. She slipped back into the jostling crowds who smelled of sweat, alcohol, and refuse. She escaped the Arena to stand beside a nondescript white tent and slowly caught her breath as another match started in the pit. *Silly girl*, K'Rania scolded but Miranda ignored her. She wanted to see the fighter again but there were just too many people there. *Stop wasting time.*

"What else would I do?" Miranda asked and blushed even harder, realizing she appeared to be talking to herself.

"Hoping to see someone?" a man—no, not a man—a *giant* asked as he walked up to the tent and Miranda nearly jumped out of her skin. She had never seen someone as tall as this one. He was enormous, with a sword easily as tall as she was strapped to his back. His grimy face made him even *look* like the sort of person who would rape her in an alley. He even had ash and sweat stains in his stubble and on his shirt. "Oh sorry," he said, wiping his face with a black cloth that did nothing but smear the soot around. "I've been in the forges this morning. Forgot to wash up. I must look frightening, I guess. Not many people actually jump like you did."

"What did you say?" Miranda asked, taking a step back and nearly tripping over a guide line from the tent. *Damned tripping hazards! I thought I was free of those.*

"The ready room, are you hoping to see someone?"

"The what?"

"Ready room, this tent," the man said with a lopsided grin. "It is where the competitors get ready for their matches."

"I... I think they called him the Squire," Miranda said and bit her tongue. *You say too much.* "Shut up," Miranda hissed at K'Rania, looking away from the giant man.

"I didn't say nothing," the giant said, scratching his head. "Anyway, Joshua's probably talking to Cora and Eric right now. They seem to be waiting for him inside after each fight." He sighed, shaking his head as he paused at the entrance to the tent. "He always catches the pretty ones. He'll probably say something to you if you are still here when he leaves. You're definitely one of the pretty ones." Miranda tripped over her tongue, unable to say anything else, as the giant disappeared into the tent. *Pretty ones,* she thought and hesitated at the door as well. *I'm one of the pretty ones?* Her father had always said she inherited Cassandra's beauty, but a stranger had never confirmed it before. Not that they could have; that would have required meeting a stranger. That and her father was a liar. He had always *been* a liar.

Liars do not only speak lies, no one would believe them, K'Rania stated. *You are beautiful.*

"You don't even know what I look like," Miranda argued and slapped her hands over her mouth. *Please, stop talking to me when I'm around... people.*

I will speak when I speak, and be silent when I am silent, K'Rania laughed. Miranda waited a moment more until two people exited, neither of them was the fighter, but they both looked stately.

The man wore a long, black coat decorated with gold cufflinks and buttons over a white silk shirt and sharp, military slacks. The woman dressed like Miranda usually did with a low cut, satin dress that showed off a considerable amount of her breasts. A white fur shawl covered her shoulders and draped around her embellished figure.

"You have to stop throwing yourself at him, Cora," the man said.

"I seem to recall Joshua was throwing himself just as hard towards me," Cora answered. "Besides you said he was a 'good enough' man. So, what if he's lowborn?"

"That was before last night, the way he was so eager to trade you," the man sighed. "I just don't want to see you get hurt." Miranda wanted to hear more, but she just stood there as they disappeared towards the larger arena. Her heart felt like it was being crushed from what the woman had said. The Squire, Joshua, was already courting another woman. And he was lowborn which meant he could only have one wife in Ilionan law. It should *not* have mattered, she still had not even spoken to Joshua but Miranda still felt devastated.

Silly girl, K'Rania sighed, sounding sympathetic. She had, apparently, known crushes as well. Miranda slowly wandered away from the arena grounds, the excitement of it all had dimmed so much from her crushed infatuation that she could not stand being around so many people. Even worse that they smelled bad, or leered at her, or nearly ran her over as they ignored her. She found herself walking the nearly empty streets of Crossroads and before long wandered into what she thought was an inn.

The Rested Lance sounded like an inn's name, like one from a novel, but when she finally looked up from her feet she turned dark red—a shade she had no idea she *could* be—when she caught her reflection in a mirror the size of a wall. Behind her reflection was a display very similar to what she had walked in on with Cassandra and Lunarin, only worse. More than a dozen couples were sectioned off in cubbies the same size of Thade's enclave.

"Can I help you, sweetie?" An aging woman asked. Her sagging breasts out for the world to see, as Miranda stumbled back towards the door. "Are you lookin' for a job?"

"I'm sorry, I thought this was..." Miranda turned and ran out of the brothel and down several more intersections of Crossroads streets before she stopped. She leaned against a wall and caught her breath but kept an eye on everyone in the street. Any of them could rape her. Any of them could kill her.

Maybe he can help. The boy's voice startled her as she looked past an alley beside a tavern. She walked down the narrow street before falling to her knees and emptying her stomach at the stench. Just a few feet away laid the boy's remains. The beggar boy had become a feast for the vermin of the alleys. His clothes were tattered and squirmed with the little rodents that dug beneath them at what must have been meatier parts of his starved body.

"Gods no," Miranda cried, covering her face with her hands. "He was just *left* here, gods *why*? Why was he just *left* here!"

She threw stones at the rats, causing them to flee before kneeling beside the boy. The vermin watched her from a safer distance as she cradled the boy's head, barely more than a skull, in her lap. People continued to walk by as Miranda mourned a boy who no one cared about. It was all so wrong. *Calm yourself,* K'Rania warned but there was nothing for it. Miranda tightened her grip of the skull, feeling her fingers slip against the remnants of flesh as she glared out towards the passersby. Each one was oblivious to the horror down the narrow alley. Each one ignored her and the grief she had for a stranger. Each one so wrapped up in their own lives that Miranda was easily forgotten. Easily ignored. Her fear took over. She could die here; she had seen so many die here. It was foolish to go to Crossroads where she could be killed, ignored and forgotten like the boy. *Calm yourself!*

They were nothing, those people who did not care about a beggar. They were lower than vermin, those who could ignore the passing of such a young soul. Those people who pretended to care about others as they gambled away their silver and copper trying to become wealthier than those around them. Those people who pretended not to question *why* the Heath estate had no servants or *why* the Heath's only showed up in the city for important events. Those people who had let her remain a prisoner while she looked out over them from her secluded mansion!

"I'll kill them all!" Miranda screamed, seeing the dark alley cast in a sickly green glow and felt the void flowing through her fingers and into the corpse.

You fool! What have you done! K'Rania screamed as Miranda watched in horror.

The boy's limbs started to move again. Flesh shook as bone scraped against bone and the boy rolled out of Miranda's arms, leaving a red and yellow stain on her peasant dress from his rotting flesh. A sickly green haze replaced the tendons and muscle of the body as it crawled towards the street. Each joint popping as more and more green haze gave the boy greater mobility. That fog seemed to fade as it crawled out into the *Soleanne*'s light and gained its footing to charge at someone. A woman screamed as the skeletal corpse leaped onto her back, tearing at her flesh and sinking its teeth into her neck. Blood spurted out through the bones and ghostly cheek of the boy's jaw as the woman fell to the ground. Flecks of red rain splattered nearby people as the creature's claw-like fingers ripped deeper and deeper into the woman after shoving her flesh into its mouth.

Oh, gods, it hurts! Thade has returned; Fiel save me! The woman's thoughts crashed into Miranda's mind as the stranger died beneath the skeletal remains. The animated corpse stood up, chewing on a large chunk of flesh from the woman's belly. The street turned into a flurry of panic as the monster crashed into another person, boney fingers and teeth tearing at thin cloth and soft flesh.

The darkness is upon me! Please, Fiel, save me from the jaws of Thade's Abyss! the man's final prayer echoed as the thrall ended his life.

Kill it! K'Rania hissed as Miranda backed further and further into the alley until she rounded a corner and started to run. *Kill the lifeless!*

"I don't know how!" Miranda cried, tears of fear for her own life streaming down her face as she ran out into a wider street amidst the others who were fleeing. *Why am I hearing their thoughts; this was supposed to be over!*

Connections in the void, sever the string that binds, K'Rania said but Miranda could not make sense of it. *Sever the string that binds!*

"I can't see a string. Why can I still hear them? I don't..." she looked back towards the street where her creation was causing havoc. A very faint, green line seemed to be flowing from her chest towards the monstrosity. Even as she watched the line jerked a distance and she could sense the creature crashing into another victim.

The end is nigh! a voice rushed towards her as another man's life ended. Without thinking, Miranda turned imagining that the line severed as she swiped her hand through it and it blinked out of existence. She continued running with the fleeing crowd, praying no one could tell what she had done and swearing to never return to that street. Miranda felt cold. Three new voices had joined her collection, but something far worse chilled her to the very core.

The beggar boy's voice was gone.

XIX

FALSE

Anara waited at the barricade set up by the Watch with dozens of others, trying to get a look at what was happening down the street with morbid curiosity. Sir Edwin was down there speaking with Lord Heath and the young Lord Ackart over a dark sheet with a distinctly body-like shape to it. Three other corpses were covered with similar sheets in the street not far from the first. Anara had never *seen* a dead body and wondered what the victims looked like and what happened to them. The reports said a feral boy had killed three adults – two men and a woman. Rumors, however, whispered of something darker.

"I heard it was a Raykarn," someone said beside her and she jumped. She turned to find Lena smiling and looking her up and down with her one hand on her hip and the other hanging by her side.

"Lena!" Anara squealed, throwing her arms around the woman's neck. "I haven't seen you in days. Where have you been?"

"I wandered into a Hospice of Fiel and have been applying my trade for most of that time, it is surprising how many people get injured during a tournament. Even those who *aren't* competing. So, was it a Raykarn?"

"I don't know," Anara said, kissing Lena before turning back towards the street. Edwin shook his head and waved his hands as if he were in a heated argument with Eric Ackart, his direct superior since he was a knight of Iliona. It was far from appropriate, but Lord Heath was agreeing with whatever Edwin was saying so Eric was unable to do anything about it. "Edwin is up there, maybe he'll tell me."

"I see you've finally taken to him then," Lena sighed, linking her arm with Anara's. She sounded jealous, even if she meant it to be in jest. "Have I lost my lover during this?"

"Hardly," Anara said, shaking her head. Her neck was still sore from when Edwin had nearly choked the life from her two nights earlier. She would never grow to like the knight. "You will be stuck with me forever."

"Well that won't do," Lena jested. "When your firm tits and ass finally sag, I'm afraid I'll have to find someone younger."

"Hey," Anara elbowed Lena. "You have more going on to sag above the waist than I do."

"But I'm a Borderlander."

"So?"

"So, my body stays like this forever. It's something about having a hard life. You'll see; hard lives breed firm bodies."

"Mistress Eezelle is a Borderlander too, and she's already sagging," Anara grinned as Lena furrowed her brow in annoyance. "I'm pretty sure a hard life means they sag sooner."

"Is this really an appropriate conversation?" Mistress Adair asked from behind them. "I mean, four people are dead."

Erin and Roxanne were both looking around Anara and Lena with interest at the macabre scene. Roxanne's hand rested near the thigh-high slit in her skirt as if itching to draw the dagger hidden beneath the fabric. Roxanne's gesture appeared as relaxed as ever, but Anara had noticed that she only reached for the dagger when she was on edge. Many of the courtesans showed signs of anxiety if you watched them enough.

"What of it? People die all the time. This is business as usual if you ask me," Roxanne muttered, her eyes darting about belying how on edge the murders put her. "You know, I think this may be the first time we've all been in the same place since the first night here."

"How is the sword going?" Lena asked.

"That Joshua kid's an artist with a blade," Roxy shook her head as Edwin started back towards them. "I've never seen someone move so fluidly in armor, except that one that nearly got him last week. Sir Pendal is actually chasing Joshua up the listings, just one rung below. Don't know if Joshua will be able to best that knight again when it comes down to it."

"Does that mean he won't be granted a title?" Anara asked as Edwin reached them.

"Who won't be granted a title?"

"The Squire," Roxanne said. "He is still probably going to win the sword, but Sir Pendal may prevent that." Anara could see Edwin's back stiffen as he puffed out his chest and pulled his shoulders back at the mention of Joshua.

"Gods be good if Sir Pendal does. That boy has an inflated ego if you ask me," Anara added, she could see Edwin soften in his posture. Anara would never defend Joshua in Sir Edwin's presence again. She rubbed her neck with one hand as she linked arms with her client.

"Sir Pendal will stop him in the sword and I will see him fail in the lance," Edwin said. "No, *The Squire* will not be winning anything this year. Especially not a title from the joust. I will see to that. Come, Anara, I'm due to joust in a few hours."

"But what happened up ahead?" Erin asked as Anara was escorted away.

"Nothing that concerns women," Edwin replied and let the matter rest.

It was an hour's walk to the arena grounds. Anara found her usual seat below the nobility box and hoped one of her friends would accompany her as she watched the jousts. Lena must have gone back to the hospice, and Anara could not blame her. Just thinking about a man touching Lena the way Edwin touched her caused her skin to crawl. Roxy was probably watching the sword again. Erin was most likely back at *Lussena's Rest* so she could enjoy being Nicholas's daughter without them watching. Anara sighed, feeling alone despite the seats filling around her, and toyed with the lace cuff of her sleeve.

Joshua tilted against a knight named Sir Odrich for the first match of the day. Anara had to at least acknowledge Joshua's skill. He rode a horse just as well, if not better than, Sir Odrich as they circled the arena to move to their starting positions. And he *looked* like a knight in his plate and chain that, despite a few dents, must have been crafted just for the tournament. He even possessed a great deal of skill with the lance as their horses broke into a gallop down the length of the field. Their lances lowered and plowed into one another, just like they always did, with a spray of splintered wood from both sides. The tournament was exceedingly boring at times. Anara could see why Edwin got excited about seeing a contestant dragged off to the surgeons; it meant something different had happened.

The second pass ended as Joshua's lance crashed into Sir Odrich with precise force and knocked the knight from his horse. Joshua only received a glancing blow from Sir Odrich. Most of The Squire's other matches had been won similarly, even the one against Lord Causeworth who had very nearly beaten The Squire. His other two matches, the one on the first day that ended so abruptly and another against a knight who had been beaten just like Sir Odrich, showed his prowess at adapting to his opponents form. A single strike had beaten the clearly untrained peasant. Two were needed to finish the others by learning each knight's strategy and adjusting to counter it. Causeworth had probably only been lucky to use three lances against Joshua. Joshua's opponents always landed on their back to end the match.

A few matches later Sir Edwin tilted against Lord Barnum. It was surprising that a large man like Barnum could manage to last this long in the tournament. The way his onion shape teetered on his horse threatened to dump him out of the saddle with each trot but he had lasted *because* his mass was too great to topple.

Unfortunately, like Joshua, Sir Edwin's matches were incredibly predictable. All three lances went the same way every single time. Sir Edwin's lance broke against Lord Barnum's plate and Lord Barnum's lance glanced off of Sir Edwin's plate. Anara preferred most of the other matches, they had more unpredictable outcomes. Those matches could end in draws where the victor would be determined by the toss of a golden dragon. A bizarre way to choose who was best, leaving it entirely up to chance, but at least the loser was given the coin afterward. It was a fair bit of money considering the person had lost, most lowborn could eat for a season off a single gold dragon.

Edwin's match ended and Anara stood, clapping emphatically so her knight could see her praise. Anara let out a long exhale of feigned delight as he trotted off on his horse, raising his freshly stunted lance to cheers, and disappeared to the staging area outside of the arena. He would be joining her again soon enough. It was all becoming rather routine by this point. She started each day by waking to moon tea at morning meal, followed by a day of watching men beat each other with sticks. Then there was evening meal or a banquet at the end of the week, all ending with intercourse before bed. It was all as boring as the matches themselves.

"Not enjoying yourself, Mistress Swift?" a soft, feminine voice asked. Anara turned to the speaker as Queen Navine sat down in the next seat. Everyone around Anara was suddenly looking her way. The lovely queen frowned towards the pit below as more men crashed their long poles against each other. "I find it is more enjoyable if you consider what the lance could represent in bed. Two women bedding each other is a private affair, but not forbidden. But two men? Now *that* would be something worth watching."

Anara could not resist laughing as both lances bounced off the polished cuirasses of the men, imagining them running against each other with their drawers down and manhood saluting.

"That is vulgar, Your Grace," Anara said but the queen laughed as well.

"It isn't unsurprising that vulgar humor would bring a smile to your face. Given what you are. Has Sir Edwin treated you fairly during your stay in Crossroads?"

"He has. He has shown me all the respect I deserve, Your Grace," Anara nodded.

"I doubt it," Navine said with a bow of her head towards Anara. "I doubt even you show yourself the respect you deserve, given what you are."

Anara blinked a few times at the queen. *I'm a courtesan, what respect does that earn me?* Anara furrowed her brow, rubbing her neck and still trying not to give too much attention to Navine's breach of protocol. She tried to make sense of what the queen was saying. As people started pointing towards them she could not ignore it any longer. "Forgive me, your grace, but why are you..."

"Sitting with a beautiful courtesan? Not in my proper place with my sister queens? I'm afraid I was given poor tidings concerning the king's ailing health and felt now would be a good time to return to Aederon City. I saw you sitting alone and decided I could spare a few minutes to keep you company," Navine said, sitting straight despite the discomfort she must be in sitting on a common bench. "It isn't very often I chance to meet a woman with eyes like yours. Have you noticed any strange things in your life because of them?"

"I'm afraid I don't understand what you mean, your grace," Anara shrugged. Now that Navine mentioned it, the queen had remarkable eyes as well. They were bright orange and seemed to sparkle knowingly about some secret. Amber was more common among Ilionans, but these were fiery orange without a hint of brown. "My life has been as ordinary as anyone else's, given how I was raised and where my path brought me, Your Grace."

"As you say," Navine sighed and stood. Edwin was approaching, still wearing his armor this time. "And Mistress Swift, I'm well aware I am a queen. You don't have to finish every sentence with 'Your Grace'. Perhaps I asked too soon, I hope you'll remember me when you realize just how precious you are to the realm."

"Of course, Your Grace."

"Your Majesty," Edwin said, bowing awkwardly in his plate.

"Sir Edwin," Navine nodded. "Is it not customary to *remove* one's armor before taking a seat in the stands?"

"Forgive me, but this late in the festival I do not want to miss more matches than I need to," Sir Edwin said, giving the queen his best grin. It would have been charming if he had bothered shaving more often, but his beard was turning into a bush. It was hard to see his lips through the curls.

"The best of luck, Sir Edwin," Navine nodded again, brushing her fingertips against Anara's shoulder as she stood. "I'm afraid I am needed by my king's side and will miss your triumph this year. Farewell, Mistress Swift and Sir Edwin."

"Farewell, Your Grace," Anara said, standing and curtsying, as Edwin groaned into his seat. Navine disappeared through the box's entrance and Edwin pulled Anara back down to place a heavy, armored arm around Anara's neck. The steel of the knight's armor felt cold, colder than it should be even with the chill in the air, but Anara fought the urge to squirm under the discomfort.

"Would you remove my gauntlet?" Edwin asked. "I cannot feel your tenderness beneath my armor."

"Of course," Anara smiled at him, wanting to roll her eyes in disgust. Anara fumbled with the straps of the armor for a little bit before figuring out the clasp to undo them. The instant Edwin's hand was free it slipped beneath her bodice to grip the tenderness he sought. Anara closed her eyes and clenched her teeth before examining the piece of armor. Edwin was engrossed in the matches, his grip tightening as his anticipation for carnage grew.

The gauntlet, aside from being enameled in blue, was unremarkable for armor. Segmented steel rings allowed the fingers to move naturally. Overlapping plates at the wrist let it bend there as well. Anara slipped her hand inside the large glove and her fingers brushed an indentation etched into the steel. She looked up at Edwin, who was nearly on the edge of his seat as the two contestants crashed into each other, before holding the gauntlet in her hands in a way to catch *Soleanne*'s light. She turned the glove and spotted what she had touched moments before.

It was a geomantic rune. More specifically, *Granite*, the same one used to make nearly unbreakable glass. To put that on *steel*!

272

Anara doubted anything short of a giant's strength could damage Edwin's gauntlet.

Anara quickly dropped the gauntlet to her lap to hide where she had been looking. The chill of Edwin's cuirass suddenly made too much sense. Pyromantic enchantments, even the internal boons, caused a material to feel warmer than it should. The reverse was true about hydromantic enchantments and some hydromantic boons caused material to be as slippery as wet ice, which would explain why all strikes against Edwin just seem to glide off him.

"What is it?" Edwin asked, turning from the fight to look at her.

"Nothing," Anara said, blushing as if she had been caught sneaking sweets from the kitchens back at *Wentworth's*. "It's just, my dear knight, your armor is so heavy I am finding it difficult to breathe with your arm around me and my waist in a corset."

"Of course," Edwin said and removed his arm. "I love how the corset shapes a woman, but given how often you lot complain about them I wonder if they're worth it."

Anara smiled, but said nothing, and placed both of her hands on top of Edwin's gauntlet. *Edwin is a cheat*, Anara thought, watching as two more wooden lances turned into splinters. Unfortunately, as the competitor who won the match rounded the field Anara could see a large bit of lance jutting out from the man's breastplate. Blood leaked from the punctured steel as he waved to the crowd while heading to the surgeon tent.

"Well, that looks good for whoever faces him next," Edwin said, he sounded too gleeful given the severity of the knight's wound. The victor was as likely to die from that piece of lance as he was to live and continue participating in the festival. He may even have to forfeit his next match if it was too soon to allow him any time to heal. "Hopefully it isn't me, I'd not want the trash and nobility to know I advanced just because a man had to withdraw."

It was sickening. Edwin fought in enchanted armor, he had practically no threat to receive a wound like that yet he was complaining about having to face the man. It was no surprise that Edwin never had a lance break against him. Anara slipped her hand into the gauntlet once more, tracing the rune with her fingertip and committing it to memory. She needed to find out *which* rune it was.

"Edwin, dear," Anara said, swallowing back her revulsion for the fake knight. "I'm actually not feeling all that well today."

"Your corset again?"

"No, it's... it's a woman issue," Anara hastily decided and could see the instant disgust in Edwin's features. His nose wrinkled and his brow furrowed as he tried to look anywhere but at Anara. "You do know what happens..."

"Gods! Honestly, you bring *that* up now? Of course, I release you from your duties to me for the day. Go, now, maybe I can enjoy the rest of the matches without thinking about *that*," Edwin said, practically pushing Anara out of her seat. Anara stared at him for a moment. He loved to see a man pierced by a lance but could not deal with a woman's bleeding. Anara bled a little every day because of the moon tea to keep up with Edwin's insatiable appetite for her flesh. "Take the rest of the week if you must, just come back to me when the last week begins."

"I am grateful for your understanding, *sir* knight," Anara said through clenched teeth and briskly walked back out of the arena. The nerve of a man who celebrated bloodshed to treat her like a leper at the idea of her own blood.

Lussena's Rest was a welcome sight as Anara found her way back to Erin's little, rarely-used inn. The streets were surprisingly empty because of the events still going on back at the arenas so it was a relief to find Nicholas and Erin enjoying a cup of tea at the kitchen table as she made her way back to her rooms.

"Nara!" Nicholas greeted her with a hug as strong as a bear's. "It's been weeks since I last saw you. Did ya hear abou' the deaths this mornin'?"

"I did, Master Brenton," Anara said, pushing her way out of his arms. "I'm here for a few days, there's something I need to speak with you both about but I need to research something tonight."

"Sir Edwin is letting you study your books on enchantments?" Erin asked, taking a sip from her steaming cup. "I'm surprised he would let you slip away from him."

"He is a bit... smothering in his affections," Anara nodded, putting how she truly felt in as polite of terms as she could, before slipping into her room. She grabbed her satchel from where it hung on the bed she shared with Lena. Unfortunately, Lena was not there waiting for her so she returned to the kitchen. "I have to check some stuff tonight, but I was wondering how much you knew about jousting."

"Well, one for a strike. Two for a broken..." Nicholas started.

"Not the points, the actual act. How does one joust?" Anara interrupted, to a disapproving glare from Erin. Nicholas burst out laughing.

"I don' see you takin' up that spor', 'nara, no offense," Nicholas managed to say through his mirth. "Not a pretty li'l thing like you."

"What is this about, Anara?" Erin asked, narrowing her brow suspiciously. Anara hesitated, looking between the father and daughter before sighing and joining them at the table.

Erin poured Anara a cup of tea as she explained how she discovered an enchantment on the inside of Edwin's glove as she thumbed through the index of runes in *Basic Enchantment Theory* until she found the rune she was looking for.

"I knew it! This one, *Granite*, that's the one on the inside of Edwin's gauntlet. It's used to reinforce the material—make it stronger than it naturally is."

"Good ta have in battle," Nicholas nodded, scratching his stubbly chin. "Though, no reason to have it in a joust. Guess it might help prevent injury. Aside from that, it wouldn't provide any real 'vantage."

"That is why I want to know *how* to joust," Anara sighed. "Are there pieces of armor you'd want to put *different* enchantments on? Like armor that a jouster is most likely to strike or aim at?"

"There's the shield pauldron," Erin answered. "Decades ago everyone used a shield to catch the lance, but it was too big of a target and too easy to apply maximum force onto. That's probably one of the reasons the lowborn rarely advance, they're easier to knock off their horse. Nobility switched to the shield pauldron, the large one that covers half of their helm when they were being beaten too often by the peasants. Knights who can afford it followed with their tradition since it added the protection of a shield while allowing more mobility in combat as well. You think Edwin has a different enchantment on his shield pauldron?"

"Probably, I'm going to sneak into the arena armory tonight to verify," Anara said, snapping her book shut.

"Why?" Nicholas asked.

"He's cheating!" Anara said, shocked that Nicholas and Erin just shook their heads.

"So what if he is?" Erin asked. "Only a noble or knight can call Edwin out for cheating in a tournament. And even they can't without proof."

"But I have proof," Anara folded her arms, it was not fair. The way Edwin treated her, he should be punished *somehow*. At the time she felt fortunate that he had not left a mark, but now it was the opposite. She had no *proof* of his abuse but she did for this. It would take one glance at his armor from an authorized enchanter to discredit Sir Edwin.

"Settle down, Anara," Erin said, standing up and putting an arm around her. "We are courtesans. We cater to nobility but remain free from their politics. Trust me, involving yourself in this will only end poorly for you."

"I don't care, I don't want to see a pretender rise to a title he doesn't deserve," Anara said, pulling away from Erin. "It isn't right that such a cruel man could be in charge of protecting anyone! It isn't right that he is given a pass *just* because he's a priest!" Anara stopped short, staring at them both.

"Anara..." Erin paused, glancing quickly at her father. Nicholas shrugged. "Edwin isn't Brother Mitchel," Erin reached out for her and Anara fled from the inn.

Erin is wrong, she thought, rubbing her neck. If Edwin had just gripped a little tighter, Anara would have a mark of his wickedness. Bruise, or death, Mistress Adair would know. Sir Edwin was worse than Brother Mitchel. Much worse.

Evening had come and *Soleanne* was setting as she stumbled back into the Arena grounds, still crying silent tears because Erin had not supported her. She felt even worse when she realized Erin *would* have supported her if she had been open about Edwin and her instead of trying to get him disqualified. Anara sighed, feeling foolish for letting her emotions over Edwin's cheating dictate how she behaved. She had the week off now, after getting more proof from Edwin's armor she could spend the rest of it with Lena.

Everyone but a few stragglers had found their way back to the taverns of Crossroads either to celebrate or share in each other's misery. No one even bothered looking up from their search through betting slips as Anara slipped through the heavily used pathways of the arena grounds. It was surprising how much room there actually was without it being packed full of spectators. Anara turned around the corner of the large tent serving as the event's armory and collided with a guard.

"Pardon me," Anara said, stepping back as the man grunted.

"You aren't allowed here," the Borderlander man said, brandishing a massive halberd and motioning for her to leave. He looked vaguely familiar but Anara could not place *where* she had seen him. "This place is off limits to anyone but a competitor."

"It's all right, Yondel," Joshua said as he stepped out from inside the tent. "I'll keep an eye on Mistress Swift."

"You sure Josh?"

"She obviously has a reason for coming here," Joshua said, taking Anara's arm with his. He wore his marker shield on his back but none of his real armor.

"Oh," Yondel said, winking at Joshua who only grinned back. "I get it."

"What do you get?" Anara asked as Joshua pulled her inside. Yondel and the other guard laughed about Joshua showing Anara his lance. Navine's observation about the joust suddenly came to her mind and she found herself with rosy cheeks. Joshua led her deeper into the suits of armor and stacks of weapons until the guards' whispers were gone.

"What are you doing here?" Joshua asked, barely louder than a whisper as he went about polishing a piece of his armor. "Shouldn't you be dining with Sir Edwin right now?"

"Shouldn't you be dining with Lady Ackart?" Anara asked, trying to keep the topic away from Sir Edwin.

"She's a little upset with me," Joshua shrugged, holding up the steel bracer to inspect it. "Something about betting her for you with Edwin. I thought she would be over that by now."

"She loves you," Anara said, placing her hands on her hips. Was Joshua really so ignorant of that?

"She loves what I represent; not me," Joshua shook his head and went to work on the next bracer. "She's a lot like her brother that way."

"What do you mean? I saw how she looked at you," Anara said, sitting down beside the hopeful squire.

"I'm lowborn. Even if I become a knight she is still too high-standing for me. Deep down she knows that. She knows her father would not approve, so she teases me anyway," Joshua said, the bitter spice of despair in every word. "Sure, we can have fun. I like her well enough that I could fall in love with her, but when it comes down to it she will do her duty. Just like her brother. A choice between me, their lowborn friend, and duty? Duty will always come first."

"So run away with her," Anara suggested.

"That won't work," Joshua shook his head as he inspected the bracer a little before continuing to polish it. "Running away never works. There's always *something* keeping you from actually doing it. If you're reckless enough to actually run off, then eventually that something catches up with you and ruins it."

"So you drove her away by showing you wanted me more? But you don't, not really."

"You are beautiful Mistress Swift," Joshua shrugged. He let that simple statement hang as he moved to polish his cuirass. His armor was well made for claiming to only be lowborn. The steel was expertly shaped to fit Joshua like a glove and decorated with bronze bands fastened to the hems of the armor by silver studs. Judging by the lack of wear on the leather straps that held it together, Anara knew it had been newly crafted for the tournament. Anara sat, patiently waiting for him to say something more.

"So you do only want to bed me? That's why you bet against Edwin, isn't it?" Anara asked. Joshua paused in his work to look at Anara. She could see the thoughts forming, disappearing, and reforming in his eyes as he contemplated what to say next.

"That isn't why I bet against Edwin," Joshua shook his head. "I just don't want you to be a slave to his whims. He has a reputation, you know, among the other knights and soldiers. If he doesn't get his way, he gets angry. If he drinks when he doesn't get his way, he gets violent."

"I know," Anara said. Joshua let *that* comment hang as well. He was not a very good at carrying a conversation. Then again, Anara was not certain she wanted to let Joshua know much more about her.

They sat in silence except for the sound of Joshua's brush and polishing oil scraping over the silvery steel armor in his hands. It was strangely relaxing listening to the patterned noise as the brush swirled around the metal.

The armory was a mess of shields, markers, armor, and weapons that would have appalled Roxanne if she had seen it. She insisted the blade dancers keep everything organized. The small closet in the blade dancer chapter was organized so that each woman's sword, armor, and dagger were kept together on wicker dress forms. Edwin's armor was probably in the pile, tucked away in a locked chest. Anara frowned, realizing that was probably true. It would take hours to find it, then she would have to break it open somehow.

"You never answered me, by the way," Joshua said.

"What do you mean?"

"Why did you come here?"

"I discovered something," Anara sighed. "I probably shouldn't tell you, since your Sir Edwin's competition."

"He's using enchanted armor."

"How did you know?" Anara asked, eyes widening as Joshua calmly continued with his work. "I found a symbol for a geomantic enchantment on the inside of his gauntlet today."

"I suspected as much. Lances seemed to flow off his armor like it was slick with oil," Joshua shrugged. "I'm not surprised to find out I'm right, though I didn't think a geomantic enchantment would cause that."

"I think his cuirass and shield pauldron have a hydromantic enchantment," Anara said, looking around and trying to find where Edwin had hidden his armor. "His cuirass, most definitely. It's too cold to the touch not to be enchanted. How do you know of enchantments? Well, I mean the differences."

"I have seen several kinds in my life," Joshua answered, not even pausing in his task. Again, he just gave a short answer and let the conversation die.

"Then let's find his armor, and prove he's a cheat," Anara suggested after getting frustrated with the silence between them.

"This armor isn't for knights and lords," Joshua said. "Only the lowborn use this stuff. Most of it is just collecting dust since all lowborn have been forced out of the joust and many have given up on the sword by now. Edwin's is probably locked away in the Watch's tower. How do you know about enchantments anyway?"

"I am an enchantress," Anara said, beaming with pride as Joshua looked at her as if she had just declared she was a queen. A look of simple skepticism would be giving her too much credit; absolute disbelief is how he looked. "Fine, *studying* to be an enchantress."

"But you're a courtesan," Joshua said like it was a revelation to her. The squire was rather blunt with his observations.

"I'm not always going to be a courtesan," Anara laughed. "No, L-Mistress Weston and I are going to go live together in some small village after I graduate. She'll be an orderly in a small Temple of Fiel and I'll earn money by crafting inexpensive glow lamps and heat boxes."

"That's good to hear," Joshua smiled at the breastplate, the reflection of him was distorted so much it was hard to make out the proper shape of his head.

"Why?"

"Because, when I become a knight I would like to court you," Joshua said, setting down the armor and beginning another piece. "I'm not interested in renting women."

"*When*? You do know Edwin is cheating, right. I know the Gods heard us just talking about that," Anara said, deciding not to immediately shoot down his idea of pursuing her out of love. It would be best to ignore his interests all together. Lena was the only person she wanted. "Besides, it would be much simpler if you just requested my companionship for a night or two. I'm certain you'll grow tired of me once my secrets are laid bare to you." Anara fluttered her eyes at Joshua, letting the sleeve of her dress slip from her shoulder as she leaned towards him.

"So he's wearing enchanted armor," Joshua shrugged as if that fact and Anara's obvious advances were meaningless. Well, at least Anara knew his reaction was mostly warranted.

"Enchanted armor designed to deflect blows. How will you beat him? You only get three lances." Anara sat up straight again, tugging her sleeve back to a proper position.

"You're assuming he's going to break each of them on me," Joshua smirked.

"Do all men have inflated egos? Or does it just reflect how aroused they are?" Anara asked, biting her lower lip. Part of her, a very small part that was buried by Lena's love, wanted Joshua to take her in the armory. Edwin's time with her in bed had been pleasing enough up until the incident, and she wanted to see how Joshua felt. The tent was private but had the excitement of the possibility of being caught. Joshua cleared his throat and inched away from her, far enough that his message was clear, he was too busy for her. Anara frowned. She needed more practice. Roxanne would have gotten Joshua to lie with her.

"I bet I can get four or five tries before I unhorse him," Joshua continued, ignoring Anara's other question. "If I don't do so sooner. Unless there's some sort of enchantment to make his lances more brittle. You are an enchantress, so you should know."

"None that I can think of," Anara sighed. "Maybe a Raykarn enchantment."

Joshua grew cold at that comment. His back stiffened and his shoulders slumped a little as if remembering a distant defeat. Anara had forgotten how he came to live in Aederon City for the moment. No doubt Joshua hated discussing the inhabitants of the Endless Waste, especially given the disturbing rumors about the tactics of the Ironeyes that had reached *Lussena's Temple.* Joshua probably feared Sir Echton to be among one of their victims. Either way, Anara knew any further practice of her arts would definitely go unacknowledged.

"Raykarn enchantments are... different," Joshua shook his head.

They sat in silence again, Joshua never stopping his efforts to keep his own armor ready for battle. Anara looked him up and down and found it odd that he was not wearing the sword he had been given for his birthday. He did wear a short sword, however, with a painfully plain hilt and scabbard.

"How do you intend to beat Sir Edwin then? You could use the sword you were given on your birthday. Shock him with it or something..."

"Swords aren't permitted in the joust," Joshua laughed. "I have another idea. Enchantments aren't perfect, no matter how good you are at making them," Joshua said and set down his helmet to draw his sword.

The wide blade rang as it left the scabbard and he handed it to Anara. Anara nearly flipped the blade, she had expected it to be weightier, like Edwin's gauntlet, and had readied her muscles for it. It *should* have been as heavy as one of the blade dancer swords. When she turned it over she saw an aeromantic rune etched into the flat blade near the hilt.

"It's enchanted," Anara said testing the weapon. It was so light she felt like she could have actually used it in battle if she needed to.

"This was my father's," Joshua explained as Anara swung it back and forth. She twisted her wrist to swing the blade in an infinity symbol through the air. She barely felt a tug on her tendons as the blade flipped from side to side, almost as if she were simply rolling her hand instead of a sword. If she knew how to fight with a sword, she could probably do any move with this weapon. "It makes for an excellent weapon in the hands of someone quick and agile, but it still isn't perfect."

"What do you mean?" Anara asked, looking at him out of the corner of her eye. "It's so easy to control. I bet I could beat even the *mighty* Squire if I used this." Anara caught Joshua grinning at her and she winked at him.

"I'm mighty now? I should listen to the crowds more often. Yes, it is easy to control but it is also easy to be controlled," Joshua said, suddenly tossing his shirt of chain mail at the blade. The flexible piece of armor wrapped around the weapon and ripped it from Anara's hand as it flew along its path. The armor and weapon quietly clattered to the packed, dirt ground a few feet away.

"I could hold onto it tighter," Anara pouted, folding her arms beneath her breasts. "Then that wouldn't have worked."

"And then you would be relying on your strength to deflect mine," Joshua said, retrieving the tools of war. "Suddenly the light blade would mean nothing."

"I could be stronger than you," Anara argued as Joshua gave her a sideways glance. It was obvious Joshua was stronger. Even if his sleeves had not been so short she probably would have seen the strength of his arms beneath them. Joshua had the build of a soldier; his muscles were for fighting, like Sir Edwin's. "Or not..." Joshua returned the weapon to his sheath and stuffed the shirt into a small barrel that he filled with white sand. "So that's the downfall of your sword, but how are you going to remove Edwin's armor? I doubt throwing your own armor at him will get the job done, no matter how much the women might enjoy the show."

"I just have to find his weakness," Joshua said, capping the barrel before rolling it back and forth between his feet. "You said his gauntlet only has a geomantic enchantment, which means he probably used others on other parts of his armor. I just have to hit the right spot where one piece of metal meets another that doesn't have a hydromantic enchantment. Not to make it sound easy, of course, since I don't know what pieces are enchanted and what pieces aren't."

"I could help with that," Anara said, looking down at her skirts. "I'm certain Edwin would enjoy me undressing him a little next time he joins me in the stands."

"And why would you do that?" Joshua asked, his tone suggesting he was skeptical of her plan, and opened the barrel again. Sand rained to the brown soil of the tent's floor as he shook the rings. Whatever the white grains were, they left the links of the shirt as shiny as the plate he had been working on. Anara had never seen the blade dancers clean their equipment and wondered if they put as much effort into it as Joshua did.

"Because, Squire, you're the first young man I've spoken to who has not tried to fondle my tits despite my obvious advances," Anara grinned, expecting Joshua to blush at the comment.

"Is that permission then?" he asked as calmly as he had said everything else and Anara felt her own face flushing instead. "I was only jesting... mostly. You should go back to Edwin; no doubt he's wondering where you are."

"He thinks I'm ill," Anara sighed, no need to go into details with what, but stood anyway. It was late, Lena would probably be back at *Lussena's Rest* now. "Good luck, Joshua Kentaine," she said with a low curtsy. "If you can last five or six lances against Edwin, I'd gladly permit you to at least court me once I leave Aederon City. Even if you are still just a squire."

"Thank you, Mistress Swift," Joshua bowed his head slightly as he continued his work. "I look forward to it."

XX

COMPETITION

Joshua steadied his horse as he stared across the field at his opponent. After this match in the lance, he was due in the sword to face his final opponent. The gods, unfortunately, had proven his prediction true. Pendal was his opponent in the sword today and the knight was focused entirely on that now that he had been bested in the lance by Edwin a day earlier. Pendal should have beaten Edwin, his form was perfect while Edwin's was the typical sloppiness Joshua had grown to notice. Edwin rode only to strike without consideration that he might be as well. Three more matches in the joust after this one, and Joshua would probably be facing Edwin. Joshua had to prove he could face the higher ranking jousters of last year's tournament instead of randomly being matched against them like he had been in the sword. Part of him felt like dropping out of the sword. It was pointless to waste energy on it at this point since the joust was the only event that could earn him a knighthood, but he was so close to claiming victory there he could not. Besides, it still meant he would have to face Edwin even if he did forfeit the sword.

Edwin was only at the top because of his blasted armor. Eric had refused his investigation, saying he had no proof. Especially since Joshua refused to name Mistress Swift as his informant out of fear of getting her—a lowborn without any ties to nobility like he had—in trouble. He had to end this match quickly if he wanted to get to the sword in time. Joshua suspected Edwin may have had a hand in the schedule of his matches given how close together they always seemed to be. Most likely it was just paranoia. Luckily he was against Sir Munroe. Sir Munroe was good but predictable and one of the few knights whose matches Joshua had been able to watch.

The trumpets blared and both horses leaped into a gallop down the length of the arena. The short, wooden fence between the competitors raced by to the steady drumming of his horse's hooves. Joshua felt the world slowing around him as he put all of his focus into how he would strike Sir Munroe. The distance between them seemed so great, but even as focused as he was it was not wide enough. Munroe's lance came into view, the steel fist at the end inching towards his breastplate even as Joshua's own lance drove towards Munroe's. A crack filled the air like thunder as they made contact. Joshua pushed against the force driving his lance backward as he did his best to roll his shoulder to let Munroe's lance glance off him. He felt the wood against his chest breaking, splinters of wood spraying outward as his own snapped at the same time.

The world rushed back into the roar of cheers as Joshua regained his orientation on the opposite end of the field from where he started and looked around to find Sir Munroe being dragged out of the stadium by his horse. Joshua sighed with relief as he cantered back to the staging area to dismount and get ready for his next match without any show to the crowd. It was customary to salute them, but he really was pressed for time today. Besides, if he saluted to the crowd he would probably find Mistress Swift in the stands with Sir Edwin. He did not have the luxury to be distracted by her today, or even for the foreseeable future since there still had not been any news of Sir Echton's fate. It seemed strange that the kingdom could be celebrating as good men gave their lives in the Borderlands, but no one spoke of that during this time. The Harvest Festival was the only news to be had.

Joshua quickly replaced his shield pauldron with a more flexible one for sword fighting and dashed to the sword arena to the cheers of the common folk who followed him. They expected him to win again, but Joshua had his doubts. Doubts about it all.

Pendal was good—too good—and Sir Edwin cheated. Mistress Swift had been right to doubt his bravado, he had no idea how to beat a man in enchanted armor. An enchanted blade was rare enough, but *armor*. A suit of it may as well have been as impervious as Ashfall's walls as far as the tournament was concerned. Not to mention ungodly expensive, which left Joshua wondering *how* Edwin obtained it nearly ten years ago for his first joust.

Joshua stepped out onto the field and was met by Pendal already in a non-Ilionan fighting stance. *No*, Joshua felt his teeth grinding together as he looked at Pendal. Pendal held his sword in both hands to the side of his head with the blade pointed down across his body. The last time he had seen this stance was nine years ago when a red scaled monster stepped through his barn window. The Raykarn style had been sluggish, impractical for a quick fight, but useful to cleave unprotected peasants in two.

"Malef's forge," Joshua cursed as he tightened his grip on the blade. "He'd dare taunt me with this?" Even the crowd, silent as they looked down at them, did not know what to make of Pendal as Joshua waited for the match to begin. The trumpets cried out and Joshua charged recklessly towards Pendal and his idiotic style choice. This would be quick.

Joshua's first strike bounced harmlessly off Pendal's sword and he was pressed to bring his own blade back in time to counter the knight's as it whipped around to strike at him. Each of Pendal's deflections smoothly transitioned into a strike as if the young knight was fighting with dragon stance. Unlike the dragon, though, the Raykarn fighting style removed the flourishing spins in favor of keeping an eye on your opponent. The sword was all that spun around after deflecting Joshua's strikes, whipping over Pendal's head with Ezebre's own speed. Joshua went as fast as he could, but Pendal was faster and Joshua was quickly forced into a boar stance to provide protection to his center. The Raykarn stance was boar combined with wolf, though, so Joshua had little opportunity to lash out before Pendal deflected and spun around to strike Joshua's arm. The first point was quickly followed by five more as Pendal pressed his advantage. Never a major strike on the head or body, just minor ones against his arms and legs that glanced off Joshua's armor without much force behind them at all.

Joshua was stunned to find out the stance was one of agility, not strength. This was not how Raykarn fought. They wasted their fighting style by using strength to wield massive blades. It was impossible to fight this quickly with those weapons. Sir Echton had never considered learning or teaching the style to Joshua.

Joshua was pinned against the wall as Sir Pendal's sword claimed another point against his leg. Joshua ducked and rolled to Pendal's side so he could gain some breathing room. Unfortunately, that was a luxury he could not afford. The move only provided retreating room, and Joshua needed more room to fall back. Pendal spun around with a dragon strike that nearly took Joshua in the chest and forced him to give enough ground for Pendal to resume his assault by jumping back. Pendal fluidly turned his strike back into the Raykarn stance and began pressing him across the field again.

Joshua cursed as Pendal scored his eighth strike. This would be a pointless fight if it were a real battle. The new style only ever slashed instead of thrust which would be useless against plate armor but this was not battle. Joshua had never seen it used in a tournament before. It was stupid to train in a fighting style that was useless against Ilionan armor. But this was a tournament and Joshua would be damned to Thade's Abyss if he let Pendal beat him flawlessly in the final round.

Joshua yelled, blocking Pendal's strike and ducking as Pendal's riposte swung towards his helm. The strike went wide and Joshua pushed his sword towards Pendal's breastplate. The dulled tip caught a dent and the sound of shearing metal filled the stadium as Joshua's strike pushed through the steel plate. Pendal jumped back, jerking Joshua's sword but he managed to keep a hold of it as it pulled free of Pendal's cuirass. Blessedly no blood coated the tip. Even a dulled blade would have skewered an unarmored man with how much force Joshua put behind his thrust. Pendal did hold his side as he backed away and two points were awarded to Joshua's bracket. Pendal, however, had managed to gain his last point from striking Joshua on the arm as he pulled away.

"I think you broke my rib," Pendal said, lifting his visor. He was grinning as he raised his sword for the crowd, though. "Damn, that was a strong thrust. Never thought a tourney blade could punch through plate."

"What gave you the idea to fight like a Raykarn?" Joshua demanded; he was furious. To be beaten so close to victory was one thing, but being beaten as if he were facing a *Raykarn*.

"The Ironeyes fight this way," Pendal grunted, ignoring Joshua's rage, as the two of them walked off the field. "They don't use the behemoth blades that the Redclaws do. Glad I didn't win nine to zero. That would have been disappointing given how you beat me last time."

"It's still disappointing," Joshua muttered as they stepped into the ready room. "You would have died fighting like that in battle."

"I wouldn't fight like that in battle," Pendal laughed. "I expected you to be a better sport about it."

"You fought like *Raykarn*! Why would I be pleased about that?"

"Calm yourself, squire," Pendal said, standing taller and wincing from his injury. Joshua ground his teeth at the gall of the man to pull rank. Joshua bit back his retort and fumed as he sat on the bench as far from the door as he could.

Cordelia was not there again. She had not visited him since shortly after his wager with Edwin. Obviously, Eric's droning about her duties because of her station had started to win her over. That or she was *actually* jealous about his wager. Either way, her absence just seemed to nail his defeat home. Eric, however, *was* there.

"What was that?" Eric asked as Pendal carefully moved over to the opposite side of the tent. "Are you injured, Sir Pendal?"

"I'm afraid your friend needs a lesson in fight etiquette. His ego may need more tending than my wound, my Lord Ackart," Pendal said, unlatching his cuirass first. Joshua ignored the rebuke, sighing a little out of relief when the cuirass was removed and no blood stained Sir Pendal's padding. Pendal winced as Eric prodded his side.

"Best see a surgeon. It may just be bruised, but no sense assuming as much," Eric said before moving to Joshua's side of the tent.

Joshua fumed to himself as he removed his armor, waiting until Sir Pendal left to do as Eric had instructed.

"He used a Raykarn style, Eric!" Joshua shouted as he threw his helmet onto the dirt floor. "It was an insult to me!"

"Fighting arts are not limited to the races that developed them, Joshua," Eric sighed and shook his head. "Dragon stance originated in the Endless Waste as well, or did you just assume it had always been an Ilionan style?"

"We've used *that* since long before the Last Necromantic War," Joshua argued. "It is as much ours as our basic shield or sword stances."

"And just as ineffective in a real battle against shield or sword stance as the new one Pendal used," Eric added. "So the Raykarn developed something to tire us in battle so they could focus exploiting the weaknesses in our armor. Unfortunately, that was only made clear recently against the Ironeyes who also switched to smaller weapons. So what if you lost in the sword? You were unsure about beating Sir Pendal a second time anyway. The lance is where you'll win your knighthood."

"And now I'll lose against Sir Edwin because he's cheating as well!" Joshua yelled and Eric pinched the bridge of his nose. Joshua did not just *lose* in the sword, he was humiliated.

"Pendal did not cheat, and Edwin *isn't* cheating," Eric repeated. "He is just good at jousting, but you're better. You have to be for Cora's sake. Stop finding excuses to disqualify your biggest threat."

"I should never have bothered with this," Joshua groaned, retrieving his helmet. "I have armor and swords now. I should have just gone to find Sir Echton a month ago."

"You need to be a knight—"

"No I don't," Joshua interrupted, throwing up his hands as he paced back and forth in the ready room. "I fought Raykarn as a boy nine years ago. The only difference now is that I'm actually capable of beating them in battle without Sir Echton's protection."

"Alone?" Eric asked, folding his arms as he stood at the door. He sounded like Sir Echton when the old knight was tired of Joshua's protestations. "Trust me, a mercenary's life does not suit you."

"You could come with me," Joshua said.

"I can't, I doubt I'll be leaving Crossroads for days because of all the cleanup I need to take care of. Honestly, some of the deaths in this city are unnerving. Especially the four from earlier in the week."

"Lord Heath assured you that it was just a cover up to distract investigators. Eyewitnesses all saw something different. The boy's corpse was a plant; necromancers aren't real. They were driven to extinction just like all the other sorcerers after the Last Necromantic War," Joshua groaned. He had heard too much about the skeletal boy who had killed three people at the beginning of the week. It was the only bit of so-called news going around other than the tournament. Superstition is what that was, nothing else. "I should just go south today."

"And leave my sister to wed Edwin? I doubt even your lust for vengeance would let her suffer that. You bet that you would beat Edwin to keep that courtesan away from him. Cora stepped up as your stakes, remember?"

Eric was right, Joshua had gotten Cordelia into a mess by challenging Edwin. Even if *she* had been the one to step blindly into that mess.

"Very well," Joshua resigned himself to stay for the final week. "But if I lose, I'm leaving, agreed?"

"Agreed," Eric said and shook Joshua's hand. "Cheer up, at least today you won't be required to show your face at the victor's ball. Technically you could since you won your joust, but I think a nice tavern with Gabriel, Cora, and me would help you get over the sting of your defeat today. There might even be some of the Vallish Red left over."

"Unlikely," Joshua managed a grin as he stood and followed Eric out of the tent. "Gabriel seems to have a taste for the stuff. I bet whatever was left over last week has found its way into his gut by now."

XXI

Harvest Festival

Fourth Week

Anara woke to Sir Edwin's weight shifting beside her.

Sir Edwin would be Lord Edwin soon enough. It was a strange sensation knowing that a man could so easily change his social status by cheating. Sir Edwin only needed two more wins in the joust. Of course, there was a simple enough way for a woman to change her social status too, at least if she was pretty enough. If Anara had *wanted* to be a lady, she would have to wed a nobleman who could easily have four other wives. It was not the same. Roxanne was right, it was nonsense to compete for a man's attentions like that. *Lena is the only attention I want*, Anara sighed, thinking of her lover. The last few nights before returning to Edwin had been a blessing.

"Pleasant dreams?" Sir Edwin asked as he fell back into bed beside her. "I hope they were of me."

"Of course, Sir Edwin," Anara lied, facing him as his hands began exploring her naked body beneath the bedding. Her heart raced with anxiety as they inched closer and closer to her neck. "I dreamt of your victory in the lists," Anara said, successfully shifting Edwin's focus. He smiled, his hand stopping between her breasts. "I eagerly look forward to watching today's matches. "

"Of course, you're right, I must focus on what is to be done now despite my desires," Edwin sighed, kissing Anara. She would never get used to the forest of hair he called a beard. The coarse hairs were darker than the curls on the top of his head, making his face look like it was heavier around his jaw and lighter at his scalp. "I'll celebrate *after* I have won again today. It looks like that peasant boy might actually make it to the final round. He should learn to bend a little, give the crowd a show. That brutal defeat made an embarrassment of Sir Munroe last week. He may be one of the best jousters I've seen ride, at least in his form, but that only matters in real battle."

Edwin rose out of bed and disappeared into the bathing room off of their suite. Anara sat up, swinging her legs out over the edge as she opened the drawer to pull a packet of moon tea from her satchel. Like every morning, a cup of steaming water sat on the bedside table for her to prepare it in. The servants of Edwin's inn were surprisingly attentive to the schedules of their clients – even their client's guests. The tea tasted as bad as it always did and made her stomach cramp a little as it settled inside her. The next few hours would be uncomfortable as the cramps spread down her belly and into her womb. Anara shuddered from the aftertaste and rose to throw on a dark blue robe before walking out onto the suite's balcony.

The inn was one of the taller structures on the northern edge of Crossroads and provided a beautiful view of the Iron Highway winding north towards the Iron Mountains, the tallest range in Iliona that ran from Fort Stern on the northern coast all the way down to the Cinder Mountains that marked the southern border of the kingdom. Barrowton, where Anara grew up, was somewhere over the western horizon nestled against those jagged, ore-rich peaks. Anara took another drink from her tea, shuddering again at the taste as she finished it, and leaned against the dark wood and marble banister. Down below the inn were stables where the customers kept their horses and a barn for storing carriages. Beyond that was the rolling hills of farmland surrounding the city.

Anara watched a woman around her own age scrubbing her dress at the washstand behind the inn. Anara smiled, letting herself get a good look at her beauty. Her long red bangs dangled around her pale face as she muttered to herself in nothing but the thin shift she wore beneath her dress. The hair at the back was the shortest Anara had ever seen on a woman, suitable for a warrior woman, a style Anara felt suitable for Roxanne. Beneath the shift was a figure that seemed sculpted by the gods themselves. Anara smiled, daring to imagine how the woman would feel against her, and frowned as thoughts of Lena and shame replaced fantasy.

The woman paused, pinching the low bridge of her nose as she left the dress to soak for a bit and began waving her arms as if she were explaining something to another person. She pointed back towards the city, looking up enough that Anara caught a flash of brilliant green in her eyes before dipping her hands beneath the murky water.

It had been over a year since she only had one thing to wear, and the woman's argument with the laundry reminded her of the times at *Wentworth's Home for Wayward Souls* when she would wash clothing with Sister Dawn as a punishment.

"When you're done with this," Sister Dawn said, setting another basket of dirty clothes down beside Anara. "You'll be tending to the kitchens as well."

"But isn't this enough?" Anara complained, she just wanted to get back to her dolls, Cassie was nearly finished. It wasn't *her* fault the fight started. Charles had been the first one to throw his food. Anara glared over her shoulder through the iron barred fence where the other children were playing. Charles was splashing in the puddles and getting mud on Tabatha's dress. Anara frowned; no doubt she would be cleaning *that* as well. "And I didn't dirty all these clothes! I do my best to keep my dress clean. You know I do."

"I'm afraid Overseer Wentworth insists, Anara. It was *your* food that hit Brother Mitchel in the back of his head," Sister Dawn sighed, but she sat down beside Anara and began helping her scrub the clothing. Sister Dawn was not *supposed* to be helping. It was not Sister Dawn's punishment. It was Anara's. Still, Anara smiled at the priestess as the aging woman splashed some of the water towards her. Anara splashed back and the two temporarily forgot the linens in their merriment.

Anara blinked, smiling briefly, as she realized she was still staring at the woman—a nymph really, if Lussena's daughters ever had a need to wash a dress—and stepped back into the suite. Part of her wanted to go down and help the washer just to get a closer look at her, but part of her felt guilty for the thought. Lena had been devoted to her, except for her duties as a courtesan. It would not be right for her to approach another outside of those duties as well. *It would not really be wrong to just give her company, not like I would be sleeping with her,* Anara thought, pausing at the door and hearing Edwin moving around in his bath, and sighed. She set her teacup and saucer down on the room's dresser and slipped out of her robe. She was a courtesan, still on duty, and needed to bathe for the day as well.

Later, Anara sat back down in her box, feeling a little sick from taking care of the tea's after effects, and continued watching the day's jousts. Luckily she had not missed Edwin's match. That would have been catastrophic given what he was paying to have her exclusively for the month. Edwin was just barely trotting out onto the field in his blue armor for the short parade before each match where the competitors did a single circle around the field to collect tokens from damsels. Edwin collected quite a number of them and, as he approached Anara, lowered his lance to let her drape a sheer scarf around the tip.

Anara smiled at him. A woman draping the lance fed into Navine's theory about men and their lances. It was considered the highest honor for a woman to do so during the tournament—a soft fabric to represent a woman's soft folds. Anara fanned herself slightly to help alleviate the sickness she was feeling as Edwin let the scarf slide down the lance and around his gauntlet. After the show, the two men lined up at either end of the short fence in the middle of the run. The stands shook with the stomping of boots and clapping of hands as the crowd showed their excitement. Now that the sword and archery were over the jousting stadium was packed beyond what she felt would be a safe capacity. The two knights saluted each other by raising their lances and waited for the trumpet to sound.

Roxanne sat down beside Anara, her face flushed and breathing heavily as if she had just run a great distance. The blade dancer let out a long sigh as she looked out over the field.

"Good, I didn't miss it," Roxanne said.

"Miss what?" Anara asked, idly looking around the stands to see if she might spot the red haired woman or Lena. Lena would be better, but if Lena were there she would probably be sitting with Anara.

"My brother's facing Edwin today," Roxanne said, pointing at the lord opposite Edwin. Anara barely even noticed that the man bore the Ashton crest on his shield and marker. The whole tournament had just become so repetitive that the details were lost on Anara.

Edwin and Lord Ashton raced towards each other as the crowd held their breath to see the outcome. Anara sighed, no doubt it would end the same way it *always* did with Sir Edwin. He cheated; of course it would end that way.

As predicted, Ashton's lance slid off of Edwin's armor and Edwin's lance broke on Ashton's plate. Roxanne winced, an odd reaction for a woman who claimed to have abandoned her family. Lord Ashton swayed in the saddle from Edwin's blow, nearly falling off to the side as his horse turned around to walk back to his starting position. A short amount of dressage with his horse had Ashton focused again and reaching for his next lance.

"He cheats, you know that, Roxy?" Anara said as Roxanne put all of her attention on the match.

"I heard that from Erin, yes," Roxanne sighed as the two struck again with the same results. Roxanne leaned back, much like a large majority of the crowd. The only ones who were still leaning forward probably had some stakes in the game, just a broken lance against Edwin would probably be worth a fair bit of silver if not gold. "I wish we could prove it."

"I can, if I could just get a good look at the armor," Anara said, sighing as the two men lined up again. "But, seeing as that is unlikely, I suspect the world will continue revolving around those who can get away with breaking the rules."

"Bitter much? Your life isn't so bad," Roxanne gave Anara a gentle push.

"Not now, at least not entirely, but before..." Anara shrugged her words trailing off as the two horses lurched into a gallop for the third time. As predictable as the game was, it was strange how the noise of horse hooves accompanied by the shouts of the crowd caused excitement to grow in her chest. It should have held no sway for her—it was barbaric—but with each charge of every match, Anara could feel that buildup of anticipation that hung thickly over the arena.

The knights crashed into each other in a burst of splintered wood as both lances shattered against their opponent. Anara blinked, almost unable to believe what she had just seen, as both Edwin and Ashton swung backward in their saddles and nearly tumbled out of their seats. Apparently, Joshua was right. Enchantments were *not* perfect. Roxanne jumped up and down, screaming with her hands on the railing of their box as the two men regained their posture atop their horses.

"Did you see that! Barty hit him! The *Untouchable* Edwin! Barty actually did it!" Roxanne screamed, lifting Anara out of her seat in a short celebratory dance.

"Barty?"

"Oh," Roxanne grinned. "Bartholomew, we just called him Barty growing up. Did you see it, though?"

"Yes, I saw it, but couldn't tell where he hit," Anara admitted and Roxanne showed her by giving a light tap to Anara's collar, a few inches above and to the right of her right breast, with her fist.

"There, where the gorget, cuirass, and shield pauldron overlap," Roxanne said.

"The what?"

"Gorget, the neck piece," Roxanne sighed, looking out over the field as the two men trotted out of the arena. Edwin still won, but many others were jumping in elation like Roxanne had been. They were probably the ones who had bet Ashton would score a broken lance. "Here comes Edwin; I'm going to gloat."

"I wouldn't, Roxy. He can be rough when he's upset."

"Barty did it, I have to. He is my brother, after all!" Anara could see Edwin making his way through the stands to his usual seat beside her and knew he was angry. His eyes and face had the same look after Anara defended Joshua at the banquet.

"Roxy, I wouldn't..." Anara gently grabbed Roxanne's arm. Roxanne slipped past Anara anyway. Edwin's face wrinkled with annoyed fury even as Roxanne spoke to him. Anara stood, trying to intervene and say something to temper Roxanne's words. Anara was too late. Edwin backhanded Roxanne, knocking her to the ground. Anara raced to Edwin and caught his arm as he was preparing to land a close-fisted blow to Roxanne's face.

"Edwin!" Anara gasped and he looked at her. "It was luck, nothing more," she said, doing her best to calm Edwin's ire while her stomach churned at seeing her friend struck so hard.

Anara looked down at Roxanne, her hand resting against the thigh exposed by the high slit in her skirt. If today was like most days, the blade dancer probably had a dagger hidden under those loose fabrics. A dagger would be more useless against his armor than the lances were. Her lip and cheek bled where Edwin had struck her with the hardened steel of his gauntlet and the skin around the split flesh was already swelling and turning purple with a bruise. Trails of dark red stained the left side of her jaw from the wounds as blood slowly crawled down the side of her face. The cuts were bad, especially for a courtesan away from the orderlies, and would probably scar.

"She meant nothing by it, Sir Edwin, I swear," Anara begged. "Lord Ashton only landed a lucky strike. The gods still smile upon your skill. You won. Let him have their merciful judgment. Can you not hear the crowd? It is good to show them you are still a mortal. It is a show you have never given them," Anara grinned, sliding her hand down Edwin's too smooth cuirass until she pressed harder between his legs through the chainmail around his loins. "Show me you are the better man both on and off the field, Sir Edwin. Show them all." *It's too late for that. Everyone saw you foolishly strike a woman*, Anara thought but could see Edwin's rage waning as his desire for Anara grew. Edwin took a deep breath even as Anara felt him stiffen beneath the links of his mail and the cotton of his breeches. Roxanne's hand slowly inched away from her thigh as she propped herself up. She was angry as well, but she could at least hold back that fury as she gave Anara a nod of approval. Men were so touchy.

"Seeing you struck, and yet still standing is more impressive," Anara said, lowering her voice to a whisper, forcing Edwin to lean in closer to hear. She bit her glossy, bright red, painted, lower lip and looked up into Edwin's eyes as she took shallow breaths that caused her bosom to heave inside the low neckline of her bodice. "My mound moistens, knowing even a wound will not stop you," Anara urged, pressing her womanhood against Edwin's thigh plate and his arm between her breasts. "None can defeat you," she lowered her voice even more, brushing her lips against Edwin's ear. "*My lord.*" The spark of lust she had seized on overpowered his rage and he pulled her into a tight embrace with one arm around her shoulders as his free hand eagerly squeezed her breast. The steel edges of his armor uncomfortably pressed into her body all over but Anara managed to force out an excited sigh before Edwin kissed her.

Anara looked down at Roxanne as Edwin's lips moved to her neck and mouthed 'tell Joshua' over the knight's shoulder. Roxanne raised an eyebrow, not understanding as she wiped her profusely bleeding lip. Anara pointed at Roxanne's shoulder and mouthed the words again with a surprised gasp escaping her lips as Edwin's hand slipped beneath her skirts. Not from pleasure. At this point Edwin would never do that again, the metal was bloody *cold*. Roxanne nodded and swept out of the box to leave Anara to deal with Edwin's idiocy at striking a woman in full view of the public. Roxanne nodded and disappeared. Anara did not care about Edwin's reputation at the moment, she was just glad her seduction training had helped spare Roxanne from Edwin's temper.

XXII

STAINS

The air felt so stuffy inside the pawnbroker shop as Miranda wandered around trying to find anything that would be more suitable to wear. Dozens of washings left her skirts a little threadbare and the dress *still* bore the stains of the young boy's corpse. It was a revolting, unwanted reminder of her power and the lack of control she had over it.

You will learn, K'Rania insisted like she always did when Miranda felt as if she were being tossed about in her life. She did not even know if she *wanted* control over the darkness within. It chilled her knowing that raising the corpse had silenced the boy in her mind as if his soul had been clinging onto this realm like a candle's flame in a storm. It had been so easy, yet it had cost so much. There were three other voices in the boy's place – voices Miranda had put there. Miranda sighed, stepping away from the display of clothing the shop had to offer. Most of it looked appropriate for a time forgotten by modern fashion – too much lace, not enough embroidery.

"Nothing to your tastes?" the broker asked as Miranda returned to his counter. The second to last of Miranda's jewelry was set aside pending her decisions. Pawnbrokers asked surprisingly little questions, Miranda discovered, so long as she did not try to pawn off too many pieces at once. The one piece Miranda had not sold, and would not, was the golden web that matched the sleeves she had left for Ester. Selling everything else from her cabinet, however, had proved to be considerably profitable. Seven more gold dragons joined the one she stole from Lunarin and dozens of silver drakes had replaced each one she had left for Idrid. Not to mention the hundreds of copper wyrms that would keep her fed. It was a comfort knowing she had a small fortune again. What was uncomfortable was the weight of all the coins.

"I'm afraid not," Miranda sighed as the broker, grumbling about being cheated, counted out the silver and copper they had previously agreed upon before he offered to let her look at his wares to reduce his losses. All pawnbrokers had made the same arrangement but Miranda rarely managed to find anything suitable in their offerings. It all just seemed so old to her.

A picky eater often goes hungry, K'Rania's grumbling joined the merchant's. *You waste time, the web in the void stirs. The old one's plans change and reform faster than you hasten to stop him.*

"I can't help it if I want to look good," Miranda sighed, completely forgetting she was in the company of another person.

"Might I suggest *The Golden Thread* then?" the merchant said as he passed the bag of coins to Miranda. "Best seamstress in the land."

Miranda quickly stuffed the coins into her brown, leather satchel – larger than the one she took from her house and one of the few things, along with a long dagger at her hip, that she had managed to find to her liking at other stores. She had no idea how to fight with the weapon, but just having one kept some of the more unsavory people in the city away from her. Why would a woman *have* a dagger if she did not know how to use it?

"Where can I find the shop?" Miranda asked. She had enough to buy what she wanted now. "And a stable where I might purchase a horse. I plan for a fair bit of traveling."

"*The Golden Thread* is five or six shops north of here. The best place for a horse is one of the stables at the edge of town along the major roads."

"Thank you," Miranda said, smiling at the man. He was ugly with a face that looked like it had been bashed in by a spiked mace several dozen times. Atop his head were a few wisps of orange hair that he had combed in an attempt to make it look like he had more. All *that* did was make it so the bald spots were more noticeable at the back. He smiled back, showing that his missing teeth outnumbered the ones remaining.

"Pleasure doing business with you," he nodded and Miranda went on her way.

The streets of Crossroads were considerably busier than the last few weeks. Now that the final week of the tournament was in progress, with very few matches remaining in the joust, most people had found their way to the vendors that lined the grid-like streets of the city. Miranda kept a close guard on her satchel, keeping one hand on the square bag to make sure the clasp that held the flap down was undisturbed and the other near the hilt of her dagger.

Miranda could not really see the draw of the street merchants; the wares they offered were normally very similar to the stall right next to them. Instead, her eyes drifted to the large windows at the storefronts. Permanent merchants had more varied options. Where one stall had simple breads and vegetables from the recent harvest, the stores would have frosted pastries and fruits from the Fertile Vale. If a stall had simple wooden shields or toys painted the colors of the finalists, a store had masterfully crafted wooden figures of knights in those colors or damsels complete with flowing ribbons fastened to their dated conical caps. Still, as Miranda wandered along, very few people went inside the stores. Those that did, looked like the sort who would not be caught peddling their jewels in a pawn shop. Nobility, like her family.

Miranda found *The Golden Thread* more than twenty shops north of the pawn shop and stood outside it for a moment as she took in the dresses on display. They were the kinds of dresses she would have worn at home. Elegant with tight bodices and flowing skirts cut from silken satin and embroidered with thread that glimmered like precious metals against the dark fabrics. Miranda sighed, picking at the brown stains on her skirts as she stepped inside the store to a welcoming chime of a silver bell above her head.

"I'll be with you in a minute," a woman called from the back of the store as Miranda made her way around the cramped front.

Bolts of all sorts of cloth, from coarse weaves even scratchier than Miranda's dress to the watery smooth satins of a noble's, filled the room from floor to ceiling except for narrow aisles between the stacks. Miranda let her fingertips grace the fabrics as she walked by, taking in the feel of the cotton and noticing how they were arranged. The weave grew tighter as she went further back, making the fabric feel softer and softer against her fingers until she reached the naturally finer silks. Even these went from having an almost sticky texture to smoother than a babe's skin as she continued her delving into the cavern of cloth. Finally, she exited the narrow walkways and entered a room where only three bolts of cloth sat atop their own tables as if on display.

The sheer fabrics shimmered from *Soleanne*'s light shining through the room's window. Instead of cloth, they looked more like woven gemstone. The middle was ruby, flanked by emerald on the left and sapphire on the right. Miranda touched the red cloth, luxuriating in the cool material that felt like she was touching air.

"It's beautiful," Miranda said.

"It's N'Gochen," the seamstress said, appearing in the doorframe at the back of the room. "Very few people actually buy any of it, since even nobility consider it frivolous. The queens usually requisition it in their dress, however. How can I help you?"

The woman was not much older than Miranda, but she held herself with an air of accomplishment only a master in her craft would be able to do. She wore a beautiful gown of tightly woven cotton beneath a white apron that served as a place to store spools of thread, needles and measuring tapes in the apron's numerous pouches. She had a common look about her, nothing that would hold the attentions of a man for very long by appearance alone. Three sets of sapphire studs adorned her ears.

"I need some new dresses," Miranda said, stepping away from the exotic fabric.

"I can see that," the woman nodded, her eyes lingering a bit on Miranda's stains. "Don't think I can help you. You don't have the look of someone who could afford me. I *do* make dresses for queens after all."

"I recently came into a considerable sum," Miranda said, holding out a hand as the woman turned to go.

"Won some coin off the gambling, eh?" she asked, sounding more interested.

"Yes, at least for some dresses, maybe some frivolity too," Miranda said, glancing at the N'Gochen silk. If she was going to buy a horse, or two, *and* supplies to get to Dwevaria, however, she would have to keep an eye on her money. No doubt horses would cost a lot, hopefully not too much.

"Well, then, if you've got coin, perhaps introductions are in order. I am Sophie Icon," she held out her hand towards Miranda. "Grand Seamstress of Iliona."

"Karina," Miranda said and shook. Luckily Sophie did not ask for a last name as Miranda realized she had not come up with one yet.

"A pleasure to meet you, Karina," Sophie said, walking out into her selection of cloth. Miranda followed her into those narrow stacks as she talked. "What types of dresses did you have in mind?"

"Two for traveling..."

"Atop a horse, in a wagon, or on foot?"

"A horse... or foot. I don't know how to ride one, yet, but I doubt I would walk all the way," Miranda admitted. The horses would be for carrying her belongings more than riding.

"A dress with divided riding skirts then," Sophie said, pulling a quill and parchment from the pouch of her apron. "Anything else."

"Something nicer, not quite suited for a ball but would not feel entirely out of place if I had to wear it to one," Miranda said.

"Planning on attending the gala at the end of the week? No doubt you've caught the attention of at least *one* knight if you've been attending the fights. Stain or not you would catch any man's fancy."

"Perhaps," Miranda said, realizing she was smiling and turned that into a frown.

"Not the *right* one's fancy?" Sophie asked, catching Miranda's expression.

"He has affections for another, but a woman can dream, can't she?" Miranda sighed. She had not caught a glimpse of Joshua again since she fled the tournament grounds.

"Then I will do my best work," Sophie said, smiling over her shoulder as they stopped midway through the stacks. "With your face and my dress he will fall for you without fail. Now, if you're traveling I suggest a winter cloak for each of your riding dresses and a lighter one for your celebratory dress. Not to mention sheer stockings, if you have ever worn those." Miranda nodded before Sophie continued with a skeptical look. "Now, given your figure, I assume you would like to embellish that. So an over corset for each dress as well."

"I don't understand," Miranda said. "They can be worn over the dress?"

"Not if your nobility," Sophie laughed, untying her apron and hanging it off one of the stacks. Sure enough, Sophie wore a beautiful, blue corset with black, floral embroidery over her white dress. "It is common for wealthy lowborn women to wear fashion such as this. It helps separate us from the nobles by sight, not to mention excites our men. Another reason why he'll be falling for you by the end of the ball." Miranda caught herself grinning, thinking of Joshua abandoning Cora on the dance floor to take her arm instead.

Foolish girl, K'Rania sighed. She sounded impatient.

"Now, I know a cobbler who can make you some better shoes. For traveling, your boots will work well enough but those won't do at all in more civilized company. After that will be a few pairs of gloves. A belt or two, I mean that ribbon holding your dagger is quaint but will not last very long. Good, strong leather with a gilded buckle would look much nicer. A leatherworker will have to be commissioned for the corsets, along with a cobbler for the shoes. Then there's..."

Miranda started feeling a little dizzy as Sophie added one thing after another which included everything from her underskirts to scarves and headbands until Miranda finally held up her hand to stop the woman's suggestions.

"Those all sound wonderful," Miranda said, not knowing *where* she would be storing all of those things. "But if we could pick out some fabrics?"

Miranda left *The Golden Thread* with six of her eight gold coins missing, somehow Sophie had convinced her to include some of the N'Gochen silks on her attire. All of it would be sent to her rooms in *The Rested Jouster*—not to be confused with *The Rested Lance* even though they were only two blocks apart—when it was finished. The only thing Miranda left the store with was a simple, brown leather corset that she wore over her dress to hide some of the stains as she made her way to a stable.

"Ten dragons," the groom said as he brushed a horse down. The horse handler had excessive blubber around his middle that caused his belly to extend out over his too-tight breeches. Despite the girth of the man, he stood on scrawny legs and had scrawny arms that made him look like one of Ariel's pin cushions.

"*Ten* dragons!" Miranda balked as she did her best to avoid the piles of horse manure mixed with straw. That seemed as impossible as the man's price. The entire floor seemed to be straw and horse dung. "I asked for your *least* expensive horse."

"An' I said ten dragons, they're worth every piece of gold too. You'll not find finer horses than the ones I have," the man said, spitting some sort of brown juices onto the floor from whatever he was chewing on. The stench of the logy added an acidic air to the putrid stench of the stalls. Miranda doubted, given the messy way he kept his stable, that the horses were even close to being worth what he claimed. "You won't find any cheaper, neither, lest you choose from the pick'ns at the tournament grounds. Doubt those horses will last you long, though; it's hard puttin' a horse to the joust that isn't bred for it."

"They sell them afterwards?" Miranda asked. "Why?"

"Provided horses are usually on their last leg anyway. Make's 'em less likely to buck off an inexperienced rider, I'd guess," he said, returning his attention to his horses.

"Isn't that unfair to the participants?"

"Might be, don' really care, though. Only the hopeless use 'em." Miranda sighed, leaving the stable for the tournament grounds. Even if she had not spent money on clothing, she would not have been able to afford a healthy horse, it seemed.

"I should have just spent more on N'Gochen silk," Miranda mumbled and felt K'Rania agreeing with that bit of frivolity. The tournament grounds were incredibly muddy since it had been raining all day. With only three more matches scheduled for the last two days of the week, the place was all but empty. As she walked towards where the tournament horses were kept it started raining again. Her hair clung to the sides of her face and her clothes to the contours of her body by the time she wandered into the temporary stables.

"Excuse me," Miranda called out, carefully pulling down the length of her long bangs to squeeze out as much water as possible. Part of her enjoyed the short hair in the back since it did not retain nearly as much liquid, but she still missed the long locks she had cut off. It had taken *years* to grow them out. She walked up to a man who hoisted a saddle over his shoulder with ease, something the groom at the last stable would probably have struggled with. "Excuse me, groom, but I'm interested in purchasing one of these horses." The man turned around and Miranda froze. The Squire—Joshua was what that giant called him—looked down at her. "I, uh," Miranda said, looking up into his dark eyes. *He's so tall*, Miranda thought, unable to see much else. "I mean, um, I'd... I'm Mir-Karina." He smiled at her, actually *smiled* at her. *Her* a girl in a soaking, stained dress.

"Not another one," Joshua chuckled lightly as his eyes locked with Miranda's.

Foolish girl, K'Rania sighed. *You must hurry, the web.*

"Thade take the web," Miranda cursed and blushed as Joshua's smile turned into a boyish grin.

"I don't believe I'm familiar with that one," the man said as he adjusted the saddle on his shoulder. It looked heavy, and with how his muscles bulged it probably was. Miranda wanted to reach out and feel how hard those muscles were as they flexed to hold the seat in place.

"I'm, uh," Miranda muttered. "I mean, my name's..."

"Mirkarina, you already told me that," Joshua said. "An unusual name, I must admit. But it is appropriate given your unusually vibrant eyes. I'm Joshua Kentaine," he said offering his left hand to her since it was free. Miranda took it with her right, shaking it awkwardly. Joshua's hand felt rough against hers. Her shaking stopped as Joshua raised her hand to his face and kissed her knuckles with soft lips. Her entire body tingled at the man's gentle touch. "A pleasure to meet you, Mirkarina. As far as buying one of the horses, well that is up to Lord Heath."

"What!" Miranda blanched at the reference of her father, instinctively pulling her hand away. "Why is it up to *him*?"

"He owns all the horses provided for the tournament. It is customary for the lord of the hosting city to do so," Joshua explained as he moved to the front of the stable and placed the saddle with a dozen others just like it. "Do you not like him? I'm certain he would be willing to part with one for a beautiful woman like yourself."

"I, uh," Miranda swallowed. *Joshua called me beautiful*, she thought and felt an odd sensation like K'Rania was rolling her eyes. "I'm, uh, well. I'm just not comfortable around nobility."

"Well, Mirkarina, I'm not nobility so try to relax," Joshua said, making sure the saddle was in place before returning to a stall.

"I know that. You're *The Squire*." Miranda gawked at him as he stepped up to a young, white stallion. A quick glance at the other horses showed what the groom had said, they looked on the edge of the void. Their manes were ragged and skin sagging. They all probably already had at least one hoof in the void as it was, but not Joshua's. The horse was beautiful. It looked *much* healthier than those at the stable on the edge of the city, as well as the others left for the lowborn contestants. It's mane and tail, dark black against a white body, were glossy and full and the horse's strength was visible beneath the short, coarse hairs of the rest of the beast's fur.

"*Swiftstride* is my closest friend," Joshua explained. "A gift from my mentor's wife on my twelfth birthday," Joshua explained. "I cannot afford to keep him in the stables at my inn, but Lord Heath was gracious enough to let me keep him here for the duration of the tournament."

"Right, gracious," Miranda absently muttered as she watched the man groom the beast. *Father just likes to keep pretty things in cages*, she thought as Joshua went about caring for the animal, it was a much more involved task than the groom at the stable had been doing but Miranda did not really notice all of it. Her attention quickly fixated on Joshua more than what he was doing. The way his muscles flexed as his arms brushed the animal's coat. The way he was so much taller than her and his dark hair and penetrating gaze as he focused on his task. She sighed, fixating on Joshua's lips and fantasizing how they would feel against her own. Joshua's eyes met hers and she cleared her throat. "Perhaps his charity would let me just take a horse or two. Gods know he owes me."

"I find it hard to believe Lord Heath owes a servant girl much of anything," Joshua said, raising an eyebrow at her. He sounded playful. "Though, perhaps he does not pay his tab?"

"What is that supposed to mean?" Miranda asked and Joshua just grinned at her. He had a handsome smile that caused her mind to stumble. *Of course, he owes me; I'm his daughter*, she thought but managed to keep from saying. Other than that, Miranda could not figure out what tab Morgan Heath might owe her. Walking out of the stall after brushing down his steed. He leaned against the tall, wooden post a few feet in front of Miranda and folded his arms.

"I just mean there isn't much work for a beautiful lowborn woman, so either you're a servant or a..."

"Whore?!" Miranda gasped and instinctively slapped Joshua.

"That was warranted, I admit," Joshua said, pressing his lips together. His cheek turned red where Miranda had hit, but he barely seemed to register any pain. Miranda, however, felt the sting in her palm and checked it quickly to make sure it would be all right. "But if you aren't a whore, then what are you? No lowborn woman has hands as soft as yours."

"I'm a... I'm..." Miranda said. *No last name, and no profession,* K'Rania scoffed at Miranda's realization that she had nothing really to talk about as Karina. *You will learn.* "I'm a seamstress, not that you need to know." Miranda folded her arms as she looked Joshua up and down. His eyes slowly drifted down her face until they fixed on her embellished bust. *Foolish girl,* K'Rania chuckled.

"You must be cold," Joshua said, clearing his throat uncomfortably and slipping off his leather coat. "I apologize for my assumption. But as far as your profession is concerned, I feel it is my business."

"Why is that?" Miranda said, shying away slightly and suddenly wary of Joshua. She knew very little of Joshua; he could be a member of the Watch. The Squire was just his nickname. *Does he know I ran away? Did Father tell him about me?*

"Because, I don't get to speak with many lowborn women as beautiful as you. At least none who are interested in me," Joshua said. Miranda's heart fluttered, it was foolish but every time Joshua complimented her it made every reservation about him disappear.

"Who says I'm interested?" Miranda asked as he placed the coat around her shoulders. She realized she was shivering as the warmth of the garment covered her. "I didn't say I'm interested."

"Because you didn't leave when I told you the horses would have to be bought from Lord Heath," Joshua said, leaning against the stall again. "Even though you clearly hate the man."

"It's raining," Miranda said, looking out the pane-less windows and pulling Joshua's coat tighter. It smelled wonderful and felt incredible from Joshua's residual heat. Miranda tucked her bangs behind her ear with the hand not holding the coat.

"You're already wet," Joshua informed and she rolled her eyes. She already *knew* that. "You should join me for dinner. I'm certain my friends would welcome you for the evening as well.

Besides, Mirkarina, I'd like to learn more about you." Miranda felt her heart racing. She wanted to say yes but her stomach fluttered about with anxiety as she took a step back.

"I, uh," Miranda said, retreating a few more steps. She felt flustered. Joshua was *actually* interested in her! Why? Her dress was stained with the boy's rotting corpse. She could *not* go eat with Joshua now. Not when it would be so easy for that beautiful woman, Cora, to make fun of her. Maybe once her new dresses were done, if she ever saw Joshua again, but not *now*. "I can't," Miranda blurted out and ran away.

"Wait, Mirkarina!"

"My name's just Karina!" Miranda yelled back over her shoulder, fleeing out into the rain so thick that it was hard to see more than several feet in front of her.

XXIII

PRIORITIES

Joshua brooded over Karina at the inn. It was just his luck that this would happen. Cordelia was highborn; they could never be together. Mistress Swift—despite being cordial enough—seemed to have no genuine romantic interest in him at all. But Karina was perfect, except for her running away and keeping his coat. That had been an unpleasant walk back to the inn after searching the tournament grounds for the woman for the better part of two hours. He doubted his clothing would ever dry, that would have been worth it if he had seen Karina's emerald eyes one more time.

Even worse, he had missed Edwin's match where Lord Ashton had managed to break a lance against him. He had seen Edwin ride so much that he did not want to bother watching another predictable match. He should have known better, he should have been watching Edwin's opponents to see what *not* to do and then he would have been there at Lord Ashton's small victory.

Joshua sighed, leaning back in the cushioned chair as he sat beside the fire in the private dining room where Eric, Cordelia, and Gabriel were enjoying a meal. Joshua, drenched to the bone, had ignored the food and gone straight for the wine as he let his head tilt back with a drawn out groan.

"I know that sound," Gabriel said around a mouthful of food. "You met another one didn't you?"

"Another what?" Cordelia asked. She still was not as affectionate as she had been before Joshua's idiotic wager with Sir Edwin. That was for the best, it showed she was willing to do what needed to be done and step back. Especially since by the end of the week, Cordelia would be engaged to Edwin. He needed to find Karina again.

She was perfect.

"Girl," Eric answered after swallowing a shot of whiskey. "And he says I chase too many women."

"I at least remember their names," Joshua huffed, taking a drink from his wine glass.

"Honestly, Joshua, why couldn't you just be happy with Cora?" Gabriel asked and got a glare from all three of them. Cordelia's, to Joshua's mixed relief, was at least a little sympathetic to the comment even though most of her stare was fueled by resentment at having yet another woman chosen over her. He did not really think of Mistress Swift that way; he did not even know the courtesan's first name. He could see a future with Karina, if only she had been willing to join the dinner that Joshua was ignoring.

"It all doesn't matter," Joshua said, standing and finally joining them at the table. "All women will have to wait until I'm done in the Borderlands."

"All women?" Cordelia did not go so far as to reach out towards Joshua, but the way her hand twitched showed and the hurt tone of her voice showed she wanted to.

"All women," Joshua stated. "Sir Echton is my priority the moment I claim my knighthood."

"Speaking of which," Eric said, stretching as he yawned. "We should all be heading to get some rest soon. Eat Joshua. Women can wait like you said. You face Sir Gunn tomorrow. After him, you only have Sir Edwin standing in your way."

"Right..." Joshua said after filling his plate, Eric made it sound so simple. Sir Edwin, the untouchable cheat, would probably end his bid for knighthood. He pushed the food away, suddenly losing his appetite again. "That."

"Cheer up," Eric teased, clapping a hand on his shoulder. "Even if you never find this one again, you can always come back to my sister and we can bicker about social castes again... Assuming Sir Edwin does not marry her because he knocks you from your horse in the lists."

"Eric, that isn't helping," Cordelia groaned as the young lord grinned and rose from the table.

"Don't worry, Cora," Eric said, yawning again. "Joshua will forget all about this new woman when he beats Sir Gunn tomorrow. Probably that courtesan too." Eric left the room as Joshua stirred his food about on his plate. Gabriel left next, humming terribly off key to a tavern drinking song as he stumbled up the stairs to the inn's quarters. Cordelia sat down beside Joshua and leaned her head against his right shoulder.

"I know why you don't want me," she said and he could hear the grief in her voice.

"I do want you," Joshua was shocked that it came out so easy. He stuffed food into his mouth to keep from saying anything even more foolish.

"But I know why you can't let yourself have me," Cordelia said. "Father would not care about your station, I know he wouldn't. He knows the kind of man you are."

"It isn't just that," Joshua sighed and kissed the top of Cordelia's head.

"I don't care about you charging into the Borderlands. I think it is brave," Cordelia cried. "To avenge your family like that takes a lot of courage."

"Stupidity is what Sir Echton would call it. You *should* care," Joshua sighed and rubbed his left temple. He was cold, wet, tired, and hungry. On top of that, he really did not want to deal with the confusion of women right now. Especially since it was tricky enough dealing with Cordelia and Mistress Swift. Karina just mixed it all up even more. "Charging towards an entire kingdom of enemies will most likely get me killed. I don't want you to be burdened with my death."

"Oh, Joshua," Cordelia cried, throwing her arms around his neck. "Don't speak like that. You won't die that easily." Her denial of Joshua's truth just made him want to slap her. That urge alone was the best reason to stay away from her. He needed to stay away until his vengeance had been satisfied and his rage tempered.

"*If* I survive, I'll consider your offer," Joshua said.

"Promise?"

"You have my oath."

Joshua was extremely agitated the following afternoon as he went about fastening his armor in preparation for the day's match. Edwin had already bested his opponent, unsurprisingly, in the morning and was gloating about it with the other knights. It felt all so futile knowing that Edwin was cheating and waiting for him in the final round. It may just be easier to lose against Sir Gunn on purpose, and get it over with. No matter what he had told Mistress Swift, he had no idea how he was going to best Sir Edwin's enchanted armor. If he lost he could do as he threatened to do – ride south with the armor Gabriel made him, his enchanted blades, and the horse provided by Cynthia. He knew how to reach the Borderlands, anyone did if they just followed the King's Highway south long enough.

"You have a visitor," a guard said as he approached with Mistress Ashton just behind him. The courtesan's face was bruised beneath a bandage on her cheek and her lip was scabbed, most likely a token from more aggressive clients. Just looking at the wound Joshua knew her beautiful face would always be marked by the cruelty of that man. "She insisted she needed to speak with you." Joshua clenched his jaw, and closed his eyes, feeling the same headache from the night before. Or it might have been a headache from the wine the night before, he lost track of how many glasses he had before retiring.

"Very well," Joshua said, waving the soldier out of earshot. "What is it Mistress Ashton?"

"I've been trying to talk to you for days, Squire," the courtesan fumed in quiet tones, putting her fists on her hips. "I had no idea it would be so hard to speak to a man. Do you have any idea what I had to offer that guard for this opportunity?"

"Probably not, and I don't really want to either, Mistress Ashton," Joshua said, slipping his arm into his shield pauldron. The mockery of having a proper suit of knight's armor when he would probably never be one disheartened him.

"Three dragons! Honestly, gold! I had to offer him gold. No doubt because he has gambling debts. But still, a quick tug behind the sword arena should have been enough. Yet they all seemed to value gold more than what I could offer them," Mistress Ashton went on anyway, wincing as she spoke and gently prodding her cheek. "Almost makes me wonder if they prefer plowing the manure field of another man more than the fertile soil of a woman. Not that I wouldn't approve of that. It is one of the sights I have yet to experience in my life."

"Which I did not care to know either," Joshua grunted. "Why are you here, Mistress Ashton, or is it just to make lewd suggestions towards me?"

"Prickly much? Spurred by a lover, perhaps?" Mistress Ashton barked, closing her eyes tightly and hissing in pain from too much expression in her speech. She must have had a cut beneath the bandage as well if too much stretch of her cheek hurt her.

"I'm afraid I'm the spur," Joshua sighed, sliding his full helm on and raising the visor as he grabbed the reigns of *Swiftstride* and began walking him towards the arena floor. "Please, I haven't the time for your gossip, mistress, if you could tell me why you are..." Mistress Ashton punched him in the shield pauldron and nearly caused him to lose his balance. She was surprisingly strong and Joshua looked at the woman's slender arms more closely. They were well toned for a woman, kept slender by physical exertion instead of a strictly controlled diet.

"There," she said. "Mistress Swift wanted me to give you that."

"Go!" Joshua shouted, waving the guard back over. Joshua had enough of women. Unable to pursue the woman he really wanted to, ignored by a woman unlike any other, and the last one fled from the mere thought of spending time with him. Mistress Ashton's attack, harmless as it was, was the last straw. He was done with it all. The moment the tournament was over for him, whether he won or not, he would race to the Borderlands and finally find peace. "Be gone from my sight! Relay that to your *precious* Mistress Swift," Joshua snapped as the guard took Mistress Ashton's arm. "I've nothing to do with the lot of you anymore."

"What of your wager?" Mistress Ashton asked, struggling against the guard's insistence. She was skilled at evading the single guard as another approached. "You promised to free Anara of her contract with Sir Edwin if you won." *So Anara is her first name,* Joshua thought as he watched the guards grab the courtesan. No doubt Mistress Ashton had let the name slip on accident.

"It still stands," Joshua reluctantly answered. "But I do not want to see her if I am so lucky. Keep her as far away from the final ball as you can."

"Remember what Anara had me give you," Mistress Ashton called out to him

Joshua slammed his visor down and mounted his steed to travel the short distance on horseback. He grabbed the lance offered to him as he rode into the arena to the cheers of the crowd.

The trumpets blared and Joshua urged his stallion into a reckless gallop. The ground flew beneath him as his lance lowered and he crashed into Sir Gunn. Splinters rained against him as his horse continued forward, his body bending backward from Sir Gunn's blow but not out of his saddle as he pulled *Swiftstride* back and reigned in the steed's savage pace. Joshua breathed heavily, his heart racing as adrenaline coursed through him from the attack and looked around at Sir Gunn. He was leaning against his stirrup with one hand as the other arm, his lance arm, hung limply at his side. Joshua recognized the wound, he had dislocated the knight's arm. Unlike Joshua who had his shield arm dislocated, Sir Gunn was unlikely to be able to finish as he was escorted off the field to see a surgeon. They were tied, but if the knight was not able to return within the hour then Joshua would advance by default.

Joshua paced *Swiftstride* back and forth as he waited for the outcome of the match. The crowd murmured as the spectators questioned what was going on and why the match was waiting. They had seen this before, but still, they just wanted to watch Joshua and Sir Gunn joust. Joshua raged at his actions. His form had been sloppy, in part to his haste, and he had landed the blow against the wrong arm. Not intentionally, of course, but Sir Gunn must have seen the attack as if Joshua intended to kill. Sir Gunn had only crossed a third of the arena by the time Joshua struck him he had pushed *Swiftstride* to go so fast. Nearly three-quarters of an hour passed before Sir Gunn rode out onto the field and approached Joshua. The man raised his visor with his good arm, exposing the battle-scarred visage of a seasoned warrior. Sir Gunn, nearly triple Joshua's age, nodded as he looked Joshua up and down.

"That fury is best left on a battlefield, son," Sir Gunn said, though he did not sound too angry.

"I apologize," Joshua lowered his head, it was the best bow he could do atop a horse and in armor. "I've had... difficulties with women lately and let my ire for that join me in the lists today." Sir Gunn chuckled at that with a long sigh.

"I can understand," he said with a grin and twinkle in his eye as he looked over at the spectator boxes. A woman with graying hair waved to him with a lace handkerchief. "I'm not going to raise a stink about it, son," Sir Gunn said, patting his horse's neck. The crowd was buzzing with discussions, probably gossiping over whatever the two competitors were talking about. "It would do me no good since my arm is useless. More than dislocated, it's broken. Guess I'm getting too old. I'd never beat Sir Edwin like this, and I don't much enjoy the thought of seeing the git rise to lordship either." Sir Gunn placed his gauntleted fist against the same spot Mistress Ashton hit him. "Aim here, tomorrow," the knight said and Joshua realized *why* Anara sent Mistress Ashton. "I saw a lance break against Sir Edwin there a few days back, I doubt many people were anticipating it to happen so they were not looking close enough. I intended to beat Edwin that way tomorrow, thinking I could best you as well, but apparently the gods had other plans for me." He sighed and waved back to the woman. "It appears I'm to retire from this game without one last victory to boast about to my grandchildren. A shame really."

"I am sorry," Joshua bowed his head again. "You are an honorable knight, Sir Gunn."

"Don't be sorry for winning, lad," he said and tugged his horse towards the spectator boxes. "Regrets are something an old man makes peace with. Sir Echton knows that as well as I do. He raised a fine boy." He waved to his squire and the young man unfurled the withdraw flag over Sir Gunn's crest. The stadium erupted into cheers as Joshua was declared the victor somewhere in the cacophony. A few more days and he would be facing Edwin at the end of the Harvest Festival.

XXIV

CLOSING

Joshua woke hours before dawn, not unusual since nights were longer now at the end of the Third Month of Gathering. He had a restless night, leaving him fatigued yet unable to fall back to sleep. When he did manage to sleep he had an uneasy dream. The only memory was of riding atop *Swiftstride* as six people pursued him across the dunes of the Endless Waste. He had not feared the six people, at least not physically, but he did know they had been the source of his headache. He sat up, pinching the bridge of his nose as his skull felt like it was trying to split open. He crossed the room to take a drink of cold water from the basin before splashing himself in the face in an attempt to wash away his grogginess.

"This is *not* how I wanted the day to start," Joshua sighed, squeezing his eyes shut against the migraine. His body ached from the toll of the month-long tournament and every muscle felt stiff as he dressed. It was the last day; rest would come soon. He could let his body heal as he traveled south. He would just ignore the pain one more day.

Gabriel, still asleep in the room's second bed, snored loudly as Joshua tightened his father's sword belt around his waist and walked out into the front room that joined the three sleeping chambers of the suite. Joshua quietly slipped through the room and made his way out of the inn and onto the streets.

Crossroads was eerily quiet and coated with a thin layer of frost as his boots crunched the dry grass on the side of the road. Even vendors and merchants, who normally woke first in a city to prepare for the day's sales, were still asleep. Windows were dark, chimneys still, and the quietest of sounds carried great distances to echo off the stone buildings.

The muddy path to the arena was uneven with every wheel track and footprint from the day before frozen in place. Joshua stopped near the armory tent at the sound of two people talking, little puffs of condensation escaping his lips as he silently listened.

"You know she raised the boy, Morgan," someone hissed around the corner of the tent and out of sight. "Miranda slipped through your fingers and is now exposing us too soon."

"I'll fix this, Lunarin," Lord Heath's voice snapped back. "Miranda is *my* daughter, I can bring her back."

Lord Heath has another daughter? Joshua thought, eyebrow raised and craning his neck closer. He crept into the armory tent and inched towards the wall where the two men spoke.

"You let her escape," Lunarin said. "I have no confidence in your little cult any longer."

"How else do you hope to raise the Undying? You need us, *all* of us. You'll fail without the six of us."

"You lack Miranda's raw power, she was a gift from Thade and you squandered her," Lunarin snarled viciously at the lord. Joshua balked that Morgan Heath, perhaps the most powerful man in Iliona other than the king and Lord Commander Ackart, took the stranger's defiant treatment. "She *was* your strength. Do not take me for a fool, I have other... plans to complete my master's goals."

"If Cassandra hadn't..." Lord Heath started, sounding like a child arguing with a parent.

"*If* Cassandra hadn't opened your daughter's mind to the void, she never would have awakened. You would have coddled her until the end, she would never have experienced the pain required to access her power. No, Lord Heath. Cassandra is *not* to blame. You should have beaten the girl into submission, then the bond never would have been required to break the girl and she would have followed orders."

"There *has* to be a way for us to fix this. I'll do whatever it takes. Just do not cut me from your schemes, Dristelli."

"There is always a way, but it will require *true* sacrifice on your part," Lunarin answered, he sounded more thoughtful and sympathetic to Lord Heath's plight, whatever the Lord's problem was.

"Anything for him," Lord Heath vowed. "Lest my mind, body, and soul be given to Thade's Abyss freely."

"Gather the six of you and your six thralls, *all* of you," Lunarin instructed. "I will meet you in Kindor in two months' time. Fail at this and you will pay severely. I *will* see my master obtain his goals. I will be with him again."

"And we will be rewarded? As promised?"

"For all eternity, Lord Heath," Lunarin chuckled. "For *all* eternity. Now go. Your tournament will begin soon. Abandon your search for Miranda. It is futile. Just focus on being in Kindor."

Joshua sat down on the dry, dirt floor as the two men went their separate ways. He was perplexed by the discussion, but he knew one thing. He had to warn Eric, no one decent went to Kindor. The vile fortress of the Last Necromantic War was cursed. If Lord Heath had a reason to go *there* it could only mean one thing. Lord Heath was a necromancer.

Joshua pondered the implications as he equipped his armor in silence before making his way to the tournament stables. *Swiftstride* shook his head in greeting as Joshua gently placed a hand on his horse's mane and attached the horse's feedbag.

"Impossible," he muttered, beginning to brush *Swiftstride* down. "Sorcery is a myth. No one has that magecraft anymore. It died out with the last sorcerer hundreds of years ago. Lord Heath is probably just looking for artifacts," Joshua tried to shrug off the conversation. It had not sounded like an archeological discussion. "I can't get wrapped up in the dealings of nobility like Lord Heath. Eric wouldn't believe me anyway; he refuses to believe Edwin is cheating. Why would he believe me about Lord Heath?"

Swiftstride just blinked at him as the horse chewed the oats in his feedbag.

"See? Even you don't believe me," Joshua sighed and checked his saddle straps for wear. The sky outside of the temporary stables slowly turned from dark blue to gray and gray to the orange of *Soleanne*'s dawn before Joshua was satisfied with the condition of his gear and he mounted his horse to warm the stallion's muscles before the match. The frosted ground glittered under the new light of day as the white icing slowly turned to dew.

The jousting grounds were coming to life as peasants, eager to get a good spot to stand and watch, made their way to the stands. Joshua watched them, circling *Swiftstride* around the arena's exterior and hoping he might see Karina among them.

Edwin arrived a little while later in his enameled, enchanted, blue armor. Across from the staging area and Anara took her usual seat. She wore a beautiful white dress. The cut was similar to the flowing silver gown she had worn at his birthday. The only difference was the lace accents on the bust and hems. It must have been cold because she pulled a blue, cotton shawl around her shoulders. A light blue scarf covered her slender neck and fell behind her. No doubt she wore it only for Edwin's sake.

"She *is* beautiful, isn't she?" Edwin said as Mistresses Ashton and Adair sat at Anara's sides. The three women were all beautiful, but Anara certainly stood out. Her golden hair glittered and even from across the arena Joshua could see her blue eyes.

"She is," Joshua admitted, grinding his teeth as Edwin trotted up beside him.

"I can't count the number of times I've plowed her mound. Are you certain you still want her? Not that it matters," Edwin laughed as Joshua tightened his grip of *Swiftstride*'s reins. "Soon she and the Lady Ackart will be mine, perhaps at the same time if Eric's sister is agreeable to that. A pity you had eyes for the whore when you had the heiress on your arm."

"Only the past is set in stone, Edwin. I wouldn't boast so grandly if I were you," Joshua grumbled back and Edwin laughed. His boast was well founded; he was a cheat. Overconfidence in battle could mean death, but cheating on a tournament field warranted Edwin's boastfulness. "Don't forget you're no longer the *Untouchable* Sir Edwin. Just Sir Edwin now."

"Better to be a *sir* than a squire. I'll be lord when this is over, peasant, and I'll not forget your slights to my honor." Edwin snapped his horse's strap and the two set off in opposite directions to circle in front of the stands.

Joshua just rode, keeping his eyes on Edwin across the grounds as they trotted past the spectators. Edwin enjoyed the show of the tournament too much, letting any number of women drape his lance with their tokens. It was disgusting and annoyed Joshua to no end as he was forced to match Edwin's sluggish, distracted pace. The two met beneath the royal box where both saluted the two queens and continued around the edge. As predicted, Anara removed her scarf when Edwin offered his lance. Anara's token joined dozens of others tucked into Edwin's cuirass. *Not like he needs the extra padding*, Joshua thought, smirking as he turned away from his opponent for a second.

"Squire!" a pleasant voice called above the rest as Joshua neared the staging area again. He pulled his horse to a stop as Karina elbowed her way to the front. She cast a wary eye to the noble boxes where Lord Heath and Lord Ashton were deep in discussion and pulled her hood up to hide her face. Joshua could not help but wonder if Lord Ashton was involved with the conversation he eavesdropped on earlier. It was more likely the two nobles were agreeing on a wager. Hopefully, the one who bet on him would not lose *too* much of their holdings.

"Squire! I have something for you," Karina said and Joshua returned his attention to the woman. Her blush was uncomfortably obvious against her porcelain skin as she removed the turquoise scarf from around her neck. Joshua let the beauty drape his lance with the fabric that glimmered like a calm, forest lake at sunset, the fabric that Joshua had never seen before looked more like liquid gemstone than cloth as it fluttered down the length of his lance to rest around his wrist.

Karina was much cleaner today when she pushed back her cloak and leaned against the banister to look up at Joshua atop his horse. The dress she wore beneath her white, fur cowl was tailored to fit her figure perfectly with a green bodice beneath her black, underbust corset to match the vibrant green of her eyes and more of the strange, sheer fabric—dark red instead of green—- clung to her like a second skin from just below her jaw to the sleeveless neckline of the bodice. A stunning lattice collar of gold held a large, ruby pendant between the cleavage of her generous bust. The sight of her alone was intoxicating to him, and the coy smile she gave him when their eyes met again seemed to convey that she knew it. His heart raced and the dour mood was replaced in a heartbeat. As quickly as the excitement of seeing Karina again appeared, it was replaced with disappointment. Edwin cheated; Karina had come to see Joshua lose. Joshua tightened his grip on the reigns, trying to muster up defiance at the inevitable.

"Good luck," she said as the trumpets blared to get the contestants to their starting positions. Joshua turned his steed to the staging area opposite the royal box and looked over his shoulder but Karina had already disappeared back into the throng of spectators.

"Gods take me," Joshua grumbled, lifting the lance offered to him by Gabriel.

"What now?" Gabriel asked as he walked beside Joshua to the start.

"She's here."

"Of course Cordelia's here, she wouldn't miss this," Gabriel laughed and patted *Swiftstride*'s neck. "I doubt anyone in the whole city would miss this. Don't worry about women, just focus on Edwin."

"Right... Focus..." Joshua groaned, searching for Karina's hood. Hundreds of the lowborn had their hoods up against the chill of the morning. He sighed, but the memory of Karina—a nymph to tease him when he needed his mind to be elsewhere— proved too distracting. He missed the short blast and dropped the flag to signal the start of the match. *Swiftstride* slowly raced towards Edwin out of reflex from what was supposed to happen at that noise instead of Joshua's orders.

Joshua fumbled with Karina's scarf, stuffing it into his breastplate even as he wobbled atop his stallion without a hand on the reins. His lance swayed wildly as he managed to secure the token and get a handle of *Swiftstride* again, but it was too late. He completely missed Edwin as they passed, it made no contact at all against his enchanted armor. Edwin, however, hit Joshua squarely in the chest. Joshua watched the shaft of Edwin's lance bend against him and felt the force driving him back just before the weapon shattered and sent splinters flying in all directions. Joshua closed his eyes, jerking his head back away from the flying debris, and pulled *Swiftstride* away from the center fence that divided the competitors. Joshua's stomach churned as he took his place back at the staging area as he kept his eye on the score. Two flags went up for Edwin, Joshua had nothing. The crowds hissed and jeered around him.

"I said *focus*, Joshua," Gabriel said as Joshua took his place again. "I haven't seen you joust this poorly since you first rode a horse."

"I know," Joshua growled at the man who easily kept pace with his horse. "I didn't mean Cordelia, Gabe. Karina's here somewhere."

"So you're losing for her? I doubt she'd much appreciate that," Gabriel laughed.

"Thade take you, Gabriel," Joshua snapped and the large man only laughed harder. Joshua ground his teeth together as Sir Edwin did a victory lap. The crowd cheered hardest at the wealthier side of the arena and the lowborn sneered as the knight went around. The difference between the calls of the wealthy and the poor was drastic. The poor were offering support for Joshua even though it was weakened by disappointment from the results. The merchants and nobility, however, seemed delighted as they cursed and yelled derogatory statements at Joshua. It was normally like this, but today *felt* different. Gabriel offered up a new lance and Joshua raised an eyebrow at him.

"I don't need a new one," Joshua said and Gabriel slapped his forehead.

"Right, I just... it's habit," the blacksmith laughed again. "Going to focus this time?"

"Yes," Joshua said, sitting straighter in his saddle as he tested the weight of his lance. He could imagine Edwin thinking this would be easy as the pretender stared at him from across the field. The trumpet sounded and the flag fell. Joshua urged *Swiftstride* forward, taking the stallion almost to the brink of its speed as he had done against Sir Gunn, and aimed his lance for the spot Mistress Ashton and Sir Gunn indicated.

The carved, wooden fist at the end of Joshua's lance struck and he felt it stick but as the lance bent from the impact it slipped off the spot and slid over Edwin's armor. It was a strange sensation, having it hit so hard only to roll along the too-smooth surface of Edwin's cuirass. It felt more like he had slapped water only to let his arm slowly sink through it after. Edwin's lance bent against him and he rolled his shoulder back, praying the gods would be merciful and spare the wooden shaft as the two of them passed each other. The lance creaked loudly under the strain as the shaft pushed past Joshua's shoulder without breaking; he would have sighed with relief if the blow had not winded him. Edwin only had a two strike lead from the first broken lance, so Joshua could still beat the knight. Edwin unhorsing him seemed as unlikely as Joshua's ornamental broad fist catching Edwin's armor. Joshua lifted his visor and spat as Gabriel offered his next weapon. His current one was fractured, not broken.

"Not that one, Gabriel," Joshua said without looking at the blacksmith. "Get me one of the Hopefuls' lances."

"But I spent weeks carving all of these for you before we left," Gabriel whined. "It'd be a shame not to use them all."

"And they're very good, but the fist is too broad," Joshua argued, he needed his own real squire. A squire would have done as Joshua asked without delay. The flag bearer to start the tilt stepped up and raised the signal. "Quick, Gabe, no questions!"

Joshua was forced to spur *Swiftstride* the moment Gabriel exchanged his weapon. The white stallion raced towards Edwin and his blue armor. The fence whipped by his foot as the gap closed and they struck. The unornamented Hopeful lance held. Joshua felt Edwin fighting against the strike by leaning into the blow, a rookie mistake, as Joshua rolled his own shoulder back and down to deflect Edwin's lance up towards the sky. Joshua forced his lance forward even more as he turned the other side of his chest away from Edwin and the shaft of unpainted wood split before splintering in two, slivers of wood littering the arena. Nearly ten years of being undefeated. Ten years of facing off against nobility and knights who ornamented their lances to show off. If Edwin had ever faced one hopeful with even a little skill it would have been over. Edwin's blue striped lance fractured but was still in one piece when Joshua turned around beneath the royalty box.

Edwin tossed his weapon down as the crowd cheered. The knight leaned forward in his saddle and raised his visor to yell at Joshua, but this far away he only heard the spectators. More than a few nobles and merchants joined the enthusiasm of the lowborn. Edwin at least *looked* furious, Joshua saw that in the man's eyes and flushed face even though Edwin still led by one strike. Edwin would win with his next broken lance, but his strikes were incredibly predictable. All tournament long Edwin had never needed to adapt, he probably never had for the past ten years given how he was fuming across the arena.

"You cheat," Edwin hissed at him as they passed each other to take their starting positions. "It is the *only* explanation a squire could break a shaft on me."

"How?" Joshua asked, grinning at Edwin's ire and raising one eyebrow. "That last strike was a lance provided by Lord Heath's weapon smiths. Do you accuse him of providing me with a weakened lance?"

Edwin ground his teeth and pulled sharply on his steed's reins. Joshua delighted in his small victory. A knight would not dare accuse a lord, doing so was as taboo as Joshua accusing a knight of cheating. Joshua let *Swiftstride* trot to Gabriel where the blacksmith waited with another simple lance. Gabriel was a quick learner no matter how slow others said he was. The large man leaned on the long weapon as he scratched his chin with opened mouth and gaped at Joshua.

"How did you do that?" Gabriel asked as Joshua took the weapon.

"A flaw in his armor," Joshua shrugged, raising his visor to look down the field as Edwin backhanded his squire before picking his own lance. Joshua suspected *this* lance would be weakened to ensure Edwin's victory with this final pass. No doubt Edwin was aware of the dent where Joshua struck him, forcing him to cheat even more. Joshua knew he would break every lance against Edwin now and Edwin probably did as well. Joshua sighed. Anara said he needed to last at least five rounds before she would consider courting him. That would have stung a considerable amount if Karina's fluid cloth was not still tucked into his breastplate. Karina would probably lose interest in him when he lost, however, and Cordelia would be married to Edwin too. *Why did you get yourself into this mess? You should have kept quiet, Cora,* Joshua thought, narrowing his eyes at Edwin.

"You're thinking of women again, aren't you?" Gabriel whined and Joshua turned his glare to the blacksmith.

"If he wasn't cheating, Gabe, this would be easy. Edwin is a terrible jouster. I'm shocked other knights haven't spoken out against him."

"How can he have gotten this far then?" Gabriel said. He sounded disinterested. The oaf clearly believed Eric's opinion that Edwin was not cheating. The realm was full of fools apparently, only he and Mistress Swift knew the truth.

"I have to unhorse him," Joshua said and patted *Swiftstride*'s neck before lowering his visor. He dug his spurs into the horse's flanks and the horse reared as the flag dropped. Edwin had done the same thing, his own brown steed rising up on its rear hooves before they both charged at one another with speeds best left for real battle.

Joshua could see the fury in Edwin's actions and suddenly realized how Sir Gunn must have felt watching Joshua come at him the day before. The aging knight must have thought Joshua intended to kill him. Joshua certainly had the sensation that Edwin intended to do just that. Joshua let his anger for the knight fuel him; not the same he had felt when he faced Sir Pendal a week before, but the anger of someone slighted. Instead of letting the anger consume him, Joshua poured that anger into his focus as Sir Echton had taught him. The world slowed to a crawl and his lance steadied despite the breakneck gallop of *Swiftstride* beneath him. Edwin was furious. Joshua could see him putting pure brute force behind his strike. Edwin could not even *ride* well; he bounced wildly in his saddle at this speed as if he had never pushed his horse this hard before.

Edwin tried leaning into the force as he bounced in his saddle but all that did was let him vault backward in a seemingly insignificant moment of weightlessness as Joshua's lance, creaking with the strain of Edwin's weight, snapped and tossed Edwin clean from the back of his horse. Joshua lifted his lance, barely disoriented from the light strike Edwin's weakened lance gave him. He slowed *Swiftstride* and trotted over to the humiliated knight. Six flags joined Joshua's three, putting him three points above Edwin.

Edwin groaned, rolling his helmet against the heavily worn soil, as he clutched at his shoulder. Edwin's cuirass and shield pauldron were dented deeply inward, the gorget—probably geomantically enchanted—looked unscathed and a long, thick splinter from the tip of Joshua's lance was pinned between the gorget and dented plates with a small amount of blood flecking the armor's cracked, blue enamel. Joshua dismounted as Edwin struggled to sit up and pulled the long, azure, silk cloth Edwin had taken from Anara at the beginning of the match from where Edwin had tucked it into his breastplate.

"I win," Joshua said as a very loud groan sounded from Edwin's helm. "Mistress Swift is no longer in your service, as per our agreement." Edwin fell back again and his helm rolled off showing he had fallen unconscious. The poor fool was probably unaccustomed to any amount of pain. His wound looked minor all things considered.

Joshua walked back towards the royalty box as the two queens, flanked by the Ackart siblings and the Heath family, walked out onto the field. The queens, Janette and Delilah, looked at Joshua with their arms folded beneath their breasts. They looked none-too-pleased that Edwin had lost, but they only came out onto the field for one reason. Either to knight the victor or, if Edwin had won, raise a knight to a title of lordship.

Cordelia was smiling widely as Joshua looked at her. The fire in her eyes reminded him of the day she ambushed him after beating Pendal the first time, but she managed to hold herself back in the presence of the queens. Eric was just as delighted, probably because he had stakes in the match. Lord Heath nodded respectfully and his wives fanned themselves as they looked him up and down. The second Lady Heath even blushed slightly under Joshua's eyes. The first just sniffed as if the whole event was beneath her.

"Kneel, Joshua Kentaine," Queen Janette ordered and Joshua gladly fell to one knee and bowed his head to the queen. "Young Lord Ackart, your sword," she said and Joshua heard the familiar sound of Eric's weapon being drawn.

"In recognition of your skill, young squire," Queen Delilah said as the crowds around them began to hush. "It is with great honor that I, the First Queen of Iliona, and the Second Queen of Iliona, grant you with this year's winnings. One thousand dragons," she said and a heavy chest was placed and opened beneath Joshua's gaze. His eyes widened at the fortune. He had forgotten all about the monetary prize. It had never been his goal and seemed so unimportant until the glimmering pile of gold stood in front of him.

"And a knighthood," Queen Janette finished as a long blade touched Joshua's left shoulder. "Rise," Queen Janette said, moving the blade to his right shoulder. "Sir Joshua Kentaine, knight of Iliona and protector of the realm."

The noise of the arena's crowd followed Joshua—along with Eric, Gabriel, and Cordelia—all the way back to their rooms at the inn. Karina, either unable to elbow to the front of the throngs or too quiet to be noticed in the cacophony, did not show again by the time they reached the relative quiet of the sitting room outside their sleeping chambers. The tavern downstairs could be heard, even felt when laughter rose too great, but the four of them were able to sit and enjoy an evening meal in relative peace.

"I should have listened to you," Eric sighed as he held a glass of wine in both hands. "Edwin was clearly cheating, though not the way you assumed. That last lance was clearly rigged to break."

"He used enchanted armor, Eric," Joshua snapped, the merriment suddenly left their little party. Eric *still* refused to believe Edwin had enchanted armor. "I'm a knight now, you have to look into this."

"You beat him, Joshua," Eric shook his head, finishing his glass and setting it on the short table between their seats. "Even *if* his armor is enchanted, you accusing him now would seem petty. Let it be, enjoy your victory."

"I don't care how it looks. He cheated and nearly claimed a lordship because of it," Joshua argued.

"And now he can't," Eric folded his arms. "He'd need to win ten times in a row to do that. He'll be an old man by that time."

"An old man who still cheats," Joshua sighed.

"So call him out on it next Harvest Festival," Cordelia suggested with a light touch on Joshua's arm. "You personally shamed him already by beating him, even more so if he is cheating as you say."

"I thought you would take my side after this," Joshua leaned back in his seat and pinched the bridge of his nose. He was getting that headache again. They *still* refused to listen to him. "Especially you, Cora."

"You may hate the man, but Edwin... He's done a lot of good in the war with the Ironeyes. Not just that, but he has done a lot of good keeping the Crown's peace in the realm. I don't care if that was because he has enchanted armor, in war and on patrol things like that don't matter. I'll not strip him of his knighthood which he would have earned in the Borderlands by now anyway."

"He doesn't deserve any of it! I should have just..."

"My father needs your help with something else *here*," Eric interrupted. "If you had been allowed to earn your knighthood through blood in the Borderlands you would have stayed down there. We need you here," Eric sighed, giving his sister a long look.

"Tell him," Cordelia frowned, but nodded.

"There are rumors of a necromancy cult, and with what happened a little while back with that boy I'm afraid they might be more than just rumors," Eric sighed and leaned back in his own chair.

"You never intended to let me go south, did you?" Joshua ground his teeth, his glass of whiskey shaking because he was gripping it so tightly. "You only wanted me to be a knight so you could avoid questions as to why I was investigating a rumor that might involve nobility?"

"I am sorry, Joshua," Eric said and the glass in Joshua's hand shattered.

"Joshua!" Cordelia squealed and instantly crouched at his knees as she cradled his hand. She carefully cleaned shards of glass and winced as she inspected the cuts. "I'll get bandages." Joshua leaned back and tried to calm himself for Cordelia's sake.

"And after *this* errand?" Joshua asked, closing his eyes.

"You can go south," Eric said. "I swear on my family crest." They sat silently as Cordelia carefully tended to his wounds. "How do you know it involves nobility?"

"I think Lord Heath is involved with them then," Joshua said, recalling the conversation earlier that day. He had nearly forgotten it between the tournament and Karina's gift. He wore the scarlet cloth around his neck to Cordelia's disapproval. At least it was not Mistress Swift's that he took from Edwin.

"Lord Heath?" Eric asked, his eyes widening as he looked at his sister. *Here it comes*, Joshua thought and took the wine Cordelia offered him. They would never believe that about a noble, especially since Lord Heath had given them another cask of Vallish Red. "How did you know that? My father has suspected Lord Heath for years. What proof do you have?"

"I don't care if you don't believe..." Joshua stopped as what Eric said set in. "You already suspect him?"

"Why wouldn't we?" Cordelia laughed. "The Heath family is a reclusive lot. And our rivals, not that it matters. I'd love to storm their estates to find *something* that links them to illegal activities."

"You'll get your wish then," Joshua said. "I doubt the Heaths will be home if you went right now."

"Why's that?" Eric asked. Joshua told them about the conversation he overheard before dawn.

XXV

 Awakening

A beautiful doll, fit for any princess or young lady, sat atop a wardrobe in a comfortable room. The dolls fabric was clean and rich with a pink satin dress and peach cotton for the arms and face. Golden yarn fell to each side of the doll's head, each end tied off to keep from fraying and the cotton stuffing inside the fabric made it clear what the toy was supposed to be a young woman. The wardrobe was dark, earthy red and held a high polished gloss beneath the doll and the red satchel it rested against. Gold paint decorated the fine detailing etched into the wooden surface near the smoothly curved edges.

Anara relaxed near the window of her cramped room at *Lussena's Rest* as she looked out into the narrow street behind the inn, *Advanced Enchantment Theory* sitting on the table beside her. She was not really watching the street. There was not much to see in the alley, but without having to worry that Sir Edwin would call upon her made everything seem beautiful. Even the sleet would not dampen her spirits today. It had been so long since she last opened the book. It was comforting to know that it was still there waiting for her, even if Lena was out tending to the sick and injured at the Hospice of Fiel again. Anara suspected Lena had only joined them because Erin let her, for Anara's sake, and not because anyone had requested her. Lena has performed little courtesan duties—if any—done during the tournament. Erin was here for her own break from being a courtesan. Roxanne had kept busy; she happily found new clients nearly every day. Anara sighed, turning back to the text which read more like a journal than a scholarly work.

> On the topic of multiple enchantments, as far as any Ilionans have been able to achieve, seem to be impossible. It is true that the Raykarn, who were given enchantment as their magecraft by their dragon gods, can place multiple enchantments on a single object but Ilionans cannot. Unfortunate, really, as this limits what we are able to do with our materials.
>
> The Raykarns (at least according to the scholars of magecraft among the other races who are on speaking terms with the serpents) speak of connector runes when they try to describe how they accomplish multiple enchantments on a single material. I have yet to discover what these may be for Iliona. If I had only a chance to observe a master enchanter in the Endless Waste make a channeling rod, I might be able to deduce how to copy the results in an Ilionan enchantment. However, as of late, I have not heard back from any of my petitions to the Ironeyes. I must pursue this somehow, but until then I will continue experimenting with what I have.
>
> A promising theory occurred to me today as I watched a blacksmith at work in Merchant's Row. I will report back concerning this in my next entry.

Anara marked her place at the sound of the front door opening. She returned the book to her satchel with her doll and *Basic Enchantment Theory*. Erin and Roxanne were not due back until *after* the celebratory ball to close the festival. In fact, everyone was off in more popular parts of the city than the block where *Lussena's Rest* was built, so it was very quiet. The person arriving could only be Lena. Anara stood patiently beside the door and waited for it to open. Anara threw her arms around Lena's neck the moment the woman walked into their room and pressed her lips against Lena's.

"What was that for?" Lena asked, grinning widely as they embraced.

"Joshua beat him," Anara said, kissing Lena again, letting it draw out this time and deftly undoing the laces of Lena's dress before slipping the tight bodice down. "I'm free for the rest of our time away from *Lussena's Temple*," Anara whispered, gazing at Lena's bare torso as she pulled the woman to their bed. The only thing decorating Lena above the waist was her slave bands; the polished steel stood out against Lena's dark skin. The sight of Lena's firm, bare breasts with dark, stiff nipples aroused Anara like nothing else ever could and she felt the folds of her mound moisten.

"I just got back, Anara," Lena teased, resisting Anara just enough that Lena fell on top of her with a tug when Anara lay back on the mattress. "I've not had anything to eat all day. It is surprising how time gets lost as I apply my healing skills to others. Even more surprising is how little the Priests of Fiel in this city know about basic anatomy."

"I know your anatomy very well. Let me show you," Anara toyed, untying her robes and pulling them apart to feel Lena's skin against her own.

"Still," Lena sighed, pressing her bosom to Anara's. "I'm certain you could find *something* else to occupy your time until I've had something to eat."

Lena smiled, weaving her fingers through Anara's hair. Anara's skin tingled at the warm touch of the other woman's mouth with each kiss as Lena slowly traveled down her neck, between her breasts and below her navel until the Borderlander kneeled on the floor between her legs. Anara moaned as Lena's lips and tongue found her womanhood and ignored everything else, letting her entire world become the pleasures Lena provided.

"Satisfied?" Lena asked. The excited pleasures were gone and replaced with a calm relaxation and a longing to just be beside the

Borderlander. Anara smiled and moaned her approval. "But now I need something to eat."

"Don't be gone long," Anara said, moving to lean against the headboard and watched Lena, mesmerized by the sway of her hips, walk out into the kitchen without anything on.

Anara stretched out in bed feeling refreshed – something Edwin or any man would never accomplish. Anara threw on her craftswoman robe and reached over to the bedside table for her book to begin reading about Alastair Lorne's idea of giving a single piece of metal more than one enchantment. His theory was fascinating. It involved enchanting two metals separately then forging them together at a single point.

> *After several attempts, and a considerable amount of wasted time, I was disappointed to discover that my theory was incorrect. It was impossible to re-forge a blade that had been geomantically enchanted, as the steel was too tempered against anything that might damage it, including heat. It would take dragon's fire, or Malef's own forge, to do so by my estimation. Something, unfortunately, that would not be happening unless I found myself in the Eye of Gods, a place I have yet to discover. It may actually be a myth, as my peers say, but someday I will find the Eye of Gods. Unfortunately, I cannot get into detail about that as my thesis regarding the mythical place can be found in a different tome. To understand that one should read Whispers in the Void first, a fascinating book I found in my travels.*
>
> *An attempt with other enchantments yielded similar results. A pyromantic enchantment made the sword too hazardous for the blacksmith to handle, at least according to him. I don't care about the aprons it burned or blisters he received as he tried to work on a fiery blade, I just wanted*

results. Unfortunately, there was nothing I could do to make the man see reason and those tests were abandoned even before they truly began.

Finally, I thought I may have found some luck with trying to combine an aeromantic and hydromantic enchantment, but this ultimately led me to my conclusion. This is not the way to achieve multiple enchantments. True, the metals could be forged together, but for one reason or another, the energies within the enchantments were incompatible. It is unfortunate what happened to the blacksmith's shop. Hopefully, the man will make a full recovery, but how was I supposed to know that it would react so violently?

I'm afraid that is all I can say on the matter for the foreseeable future as the guards are only being merciful enough to let me write for a few minutes before I'm confined to a cell for the next year.

Anara snickered at the idea of a stuffy scholar, very similar in appearance to an elderly man with a gray beard that dragged on the floor, being thrown into a prison cell for an experiment gone horribly wrong. Anara closed the book, leaning against the headboard as Lena began singing a song in her native dialect as she went about preparing a meal.

"I be singing against Ezebre's storm. Love be lost by Thade's own grasp until my heart be forgetting warm. Till I meet my love, so sweet at last. I be singing against Ezebre's storm; I be singing..."

The hairs on the back of Anara's neck stood at the abrupt end of Lena's melody.

"Lena?" Anara called out, slipping out of bed. She hesitated at the door for Lena to answer. "Lena, what happened, are you alright?" Anara reached for the latch and jumped back as the door burst open. Sir Edwin pushed Lena forward as he held her mouth shut with one hand and the blade of his sword against her neck with another.

"There you are," Edwin snarled, tugging slightly on his weapon and leaving a shallow cut across Lena's neck just above her slave collar.

"Lena!" Anara screamed as the other woman tumbled forward into Anara's arms. Lena held her wound with a quick, terrified look at Anara before glaring at Sir Edwin.

"You bastard!" Lena screeched, looking at her hand where a line of her blood reached from the tip of her finger to her wrist. Luckily, the cut on her neck was barely more than a scratch. "What are you doing here?"

"Claiming what's mine," Edwin snarled and stumbled a little as he brandished his sword at the two of them. "I paid for that bitch; she's going to fulfill her duties."

"You gambled that away, Edwin," Anara said, stepping back a few steps even as Lena went forward.

"Get out of here! You don't belong..." Lena's shout ended as something slender and tapered to a point punched through her back. The long protrusion was coated in red that slowly ran downward, revealing the polished steel beneath.

"Lena! No!" Anara screamed as Edwin pulled the blade free and Lena fell to the floor.

"I lost *everything*! I should be a lord! I should be the second most powerful man in Iliona with Lady Ackart by my side!" Edwin bellowed, stepping over Lena. Anara scrambled back, wanting nothing more than to go to Lena's aid to comfort the panic in her lover's eyes, but instinct drove her away from Edwin's sword. "Spread your legs for me, Anara, or I'll stick you like that other whore. You owe me one last fuck before you can scurry back to that den you call home." Edwin reeked of liquor and stumbled with each step, copious amounts of wine stained his tunic and coat.

Lena dragged herself to their bed, pulling her dress from it and pressed it against the wound in her slender belly even as blood leaked from the gash in her back. Her hands and dress quickly turned red from Lena's futile efforts to stem her own bleeding. Anara stepped forward to help Lena, but Edwin moved between them and swung his sword. The razor tip flecked Anara's chest and face with Lena's blood as it passed less than an inch away from her skin.

"Get on your knees," Edwin said, undoing the laces of his breeches with one drunken hand as he rested his bloodstained blade on Anara's shoulder. All Anara felt was the cold of the steel and the sick slickness of Lena's blood as she slowly lowered to the floor with one hand on the post of Roxanne's bed. Tears fell from her eyes as her hand brushed the scabbard of Roxanne's blade dancer sword, barely registering the weapon had been at hand if only she had drawn it before seeing why Lena had stopped singing. "That's right," Edwin sneered as he stepped closer with his lance of flesh stiff in front of her face. "Show me what your whore school teaches you to do."

"No," Lena muttered weakly from where she leaned against the foot of their bed.

"Quiet or I'll cut your tongue from your head before you die," Edwin spat and Anara let out a sob. Lena was pale, incredibly pale and she was having a hard time keeping her head up as she weakly reached out towards Anara. Tears rolled down Lena's face to match Anara's. "Hush, Mistress Swift, I'll not have you sobbing on me tonight."

Lena needed Anara to get help. She needed to get away from Edwin. She walked her hands slowly up the drunken knight's chest until she reached his shoulders and slipped a hand beneath the wraps of the bandage there. She dug two fingers into the wound on his shoulder, hooking them as she went deeper into his flesh. Edwin screamed in pain, reflexively stumbling back and ripping free of Anara.

"You bitch!" Edwin roared and wildly swung his sword; his attention was focused on his fresh and re-opened wounds so he missed as Anara pulled Roxanne's blade free from the scabbard. Edwin was bleeding profusely from his shoulder.

Anara held Roxanne's sword out in front of her with both hands as far as she could to keep Edwin at bay. Edwin laughed, a forced one through the blatant pain on his face that turned into a cough. Blood seeped through the fingers of the hand held tightly against his shoulder.

"Thade's cunt! What did you do! You fucking, demented bitch! What in the abyss would drive you to do that!" Edwin stepped forward, tripping on the breeches around his ankle and swinging his sword. He knocked the weapon from Anara's clutches with ease, just as Joshua had done in the arena armory. If not for his loss of balance the blade would have passed through her neck. Edwin regained his balance and inched forward with sword raised in one hand.

Anara whimpered, finding only the wall behind her, as the sharp tip of Edwin's sword rested against her throat. "No," Edwin shook his head and abandoned the weapon and his wound. He wrapped both hands around Anara's neck and pushed her to the floor. Anara tried to breathe, panic growing to fill her mind. Her vision started growing dark as she gasped for air that could not reach her lungs. She kicked in futility with Edwin's weight straddling her and pressing down on her slender neck. She was going to die. Her hands were useless as they battered and scratched against Edwin. The knight's eyes bulged with insanity as he laughed over Anara.

"You see now? Your life was *always* in my hands!" Edwin bellowed even as warmth flooded Anara's body that turned into searing pain. Edwin's unhinged eyes widened even more as his features were lit by an orange light much like the aura of a common glow lamp. "By the Gods!"

"Get off!" Anara yelled as Edwin's grip lessened and she struck out. Her open hand seemed to move so slowly as Anara watched it crash against Edwin's face. Flames trailed behind her fingertips and her veins glowed bright orange. All of the light and fire disappeared in an instant as her hand made contact with Edwin's jaw. Energy from the plane of fire—the same energy pyromantic enchantments tapped into—used her as a conduit, flowing through her body and out into the world.

A flash as bright as *Soleanne* filled Anara's vision as her fingers passed through the open air where the man's cheek and jaw had been a fraction of a second before she slapped him.

Edwin fell on top of her, his face horribly disfigured. Half of his head was torn to pieces with charred flesh and bone, everything below his nose was just gone. Blood leaked out of the gaping hole in his neck and what remained of his tongue hung limply from his throat. Blackened brain matter could be seen where skull should have been. The scent of burning flesh stung her nose and her stomach churned. Anara screamed, pushing Edwin's bloodied corpse off of her, and crawled away to huddle against Roxanne's bed. Every inch of her body stung as if she had suddenly jumped into a boiling pot of water and she heaved out the contents of her stomach at the foot of Roxanne's bed. She nearly threw up again as she wiped Edwin's blood from her chin and neck with Roxanne's sheets.

"Anara," Lena said blinking where she lay. She seemed so still as Anara looked at her. It was as if Lena's limbs were already dead. Lena's dress just lay against her wound, her hand no longer had the strength to staunch the blood. Only Lena's chest moved with quick, shallow breaths as she watched Anara. Each rise was accompanied by a quick, awkward pant that sounded as if she was struggling to breathe as her bosom fell. "My... goddess... Anara," Lena said with each word interrupted by her unusual breathing.

"Lena," Anara gasped, refusing to give in to the pain coursing through her veins, and crawled to kneel beside Lena. She held the robe tightly to Lena's belly with one hand while caressing the woman's cheek with the other. "You're so cold, tell me what to do. Tell me how to make this better."

"Anara... I love... you..." Lena said, smiling so weakly it pained Anara to watch. "There's... nothing, I'm... sorry..."

"Don't say that, there's nothing to be sorry for. There has to be something I can do!" Anara demanded, her cheeks stung with the salty lines of tears though all she could focus on was doing whatever it took to make Lena better. "You aren't going to die. You can't! I love you too much to let you die!"

"My... goddess..." Lena smiled again, slowly lifting a hand to Anara's face. Anara pressed her cheek against Lena's chilling touch, trying in vain to give the woman her warmth. "Thank you, Anara." Lena's hand fell to the floor with a loud crack of her knuckles against the wooden planks. The light in Lena's eyes disappeared. In that instant, all five slave bands snapped open on invisible hinges and clattered to the floor. Anara stared into Lena's eyes horrified at being alone.

"Lena?" Anara whispered, kissing Lena's lips. "Lena, please," Anara begged, taking both of Lena's hands in her own. "Don't leave me like this. Lena? Lena! No! Lena! You have to wake up. You have to tell me how to make you better. I never studied as an orderly. I don't know what to do." Anara lowered their hands as her vision blurred with tears. "Lena, please don't go. Don't leave me alone, don't abandon me..."

Anara swallowed, trying to clear the lump in her throat, and stood to retrieve Roxanne's sword before standing over Lena again. She felt numb and quickly pulled the blanket from their bed to cover Lena's body. She needed to do something more. There had to be *something* she could do. Anara looked down at her free hand, the hand that had held the dress against Lena's belly. Lena's blood coated her palm.

Lena was dead.

An impossible breeze picked up and tugged at Anara's hair and bloodstained clothing as the whole inn creaked against the emotions Anara was trying to hold back as she stood over Lena's body. The air grew cold enough that Anara could see her own breath in her gloom even as her skin tingled with the smoldering warmth of anger. The pain from channeling pyromancy against Edwin was gone. Only a cold emotional numbness remained inside her from the overwhelming sensations in her heart.

Lena was dead.

Anara screamed towards the heavens, striking out with the storm that broke free of her. Anger turned to rage as fire erupted from her skin and burned away her courtesan robes. Gloom turned to despair as icy rains swirled about with the tremendous winds of her hopelessness. The structure shook with her shame of being unable to save the only person she cared about. The window of the room blew out, but even that was not enough of a vent to stem the pressure building inside the small inn. Anara's heart felt like it was imploding inside her chest with the cruel grip of terror.

Edwin's body darkened, every inch of flesh turned black as it decayed in a matter of seconds and left only his glossy, white bones behind as the winds kicked up the ash and added it to the ice and fire swirling around the room. The ground beneath Anara's feet trembled and the entire structure shook with the sounds of creaking wood and cracking stone.

Lussena's Rest exploded with Anara's final grief-filled scream. Everything went impossibly quiet before Roxanne's sword slipped from her hand and clattered to the floor. She fell back to her knees and wept over Lena's corpse. Anara caressed Lena's wound, watching as the split skin mended without a scar but still Lena did not wake up. She was dead, whatever had awoken in her had come too late. Whatever she could do was useless when faced with the finality of death. As the connection to infinite energies in her ebbed away, taking her emotions with them and leaving her body cold with nothing, memories returned.

She remembered everything.

Anara stood in Brother Mitchel's room.

Brother Mitchel's room was different from Sister Dawn's or any of the other priests really. Where they decorated their rooms and had luxurious furniture compared to what the orphans had, Brother Mitchel's room was even more barren than Anara's. The bed had no mattress, just a pillow and thin blanket and the wardrobe had no doors to show the few robes Brother Mitchel owned. Even his robes were different. Where all the other priests and priestesses had white robes with red accents, each of Brother Mitchel's were reversed. A single candle offered the minimum amount of light on the plain bedside table. There was no other furniture. No desk or chair, just the bed and a pair of manacles bolted to the wall across from the door.

"How many times have you fought with Young Master Charles while you've lived here, Anara?" Brother Mitchel asked as he slowly circled her. His red robes whispering with each step as he held a switch in both hands behind his back.

"He was hurting Piper's feelings. I had to stop him," Anara said, glaring at the floor between her feet. This was the first time she had been sent to Brother Mitchel's room. He was new at the home. She needed to stand up for her actions, try to get out of the punishment. This was not going to be like washing laundry with Sister Dawn.

"That was not the question I asked. Do you know how many times have you fought with Charles?"

"I don't know. How many?"

"Forty-eight, in nearly seventeen years," Brother Mitchel answered. "Clearly you have not learned your lesson. It is up to me to do that."

"He never gets punished. Why is it always..."

"Silence," Brother Mitchel yelled, snapping Anara's bare leg with the switch. The strike flared with a stinging pain and Anara whimpered. "Not another sound or I will double your punishment." Brother Mitchel pushed her up against the wall, pulling her arms up to the hanging chains and locked them around her wrists.

"But I..." another strike to her other leg silenced her.

"I'm giving you a lesson that you might remember. I'll break you for your transgression, child," Mitchel snarled, the worn fabric of her dress tore so easily as Mitchel pulled it from her body. The switch landed against Anara's exposed back. She cried out and he struck her again. "Hush, Swiftling. You brought this on yourself." Something stiffened against Anara's exposed buttocks and Anara looked over her shoulder to see Mitchel lifting his robes.

"No!" Anara struggled against the chains, the metal digging into her wrists. Brother Mitchel was a priest of Fiel. "Your vows!"

"I said silence!" Mitchel grabbed her hair, pulling until it hurt, and pressed her cheek against the rough stone wall. Mitchel forced his hardness into her and Anara's fear was replaced with pain and then anger. The light from the single candle flared as warmth and her first taste of the pyromantic plane flooded her. "Fiel's mercy!" Mitchel gasped as he staggered back when Anara's veins glowed a brilliant orange. "You're a... But they all... You heathen! You dare to use forbidden magecraft against me! You will burn for your sins, sorceress!"

Anara screamed at him for being defiled against her will. Her wrist pulling against the chains as the candle's flame bloomed into a serpent of fire that encircled Brother Mitchel. Panic filled the priest's eyes. He watched as the iron around Anara's wrist glowed orange against her skin until she pulled free from molten bonds.

"I was protecting someone!" Anara shouted and the circle of flames grew taller than the priest. "*You* are the sinner, Brother Mitchel, *you* will burn!" the tube of fire collapsed inward and burned the man to a crisp. The connection to the plane of energy ended, unimaginable pain filled her from head to toe, and she passed out.

Anara sat dazed by the flurry of emotions around losing Lena and the realization that she had *killed* Brother Mitchel. Not scared, or hurt, but actually taken his life. Wentworth had let her get away with it. *Why would he do that?* she wondered. Everyone knows the sorcery she did tonight and toward the lecher priest was punishable by death. *Why am I still alive to feel the anguish of losing Lena?*

"Why are you just *sitting* there? We have to go!" The red-haired woman from Edwin's inn, dressed in a beautiful riding dress, yelled and tugged with all her might. Anara snapped out of her memory, the strange woman had pulled Anara several yards from Lena.

"I can't leave her!" Anara screamed and scurried back to Lena's body.

"She loved you. I know," the stranger said. "You were *everything* to her."

"How do you know?"

"I heard her last thoughts," the woman said placing her hand on Anara's shoulder. The woman's touch was so warm against the cold of late fall. "People will be investigating what you did soon. Lena will be taken care of. You and she weren't alone, were you?"

"Erin and Roxy..." Anara mumbled as she brushed Lena's hair from her face and traced the tattoo on the side her lover kept shaved. *Were they here? Did I kill them too?* Anara thought but she remembered they were still out at the celebration when Edwin invaded their inn.

"We have to go," the woman urgently whispered. The sounds of feet crunching towards the small inn reached Anara's ears. She had caused a scene and drawn the attention of anyone who might have looked this way. "Sorcery has been banned since the Last Necromantic War," the stranger explained as if Anara had no idea about Iliona's history. "We have to go."

"You keep saying *we*," Anara mumbled, kissing her fingertips and pressing them to Lena's cold lips.

"I'm a sorceress too, like you," the stranger shifted uncomfortably. Anara wanted to deny the woman's accusation, but the ruins around her were proof of what she was. "This isn't the time for proper introductions."

"Fine," Anara said, picking up Roxanne's sword. The weapon and her satchel seemed to be the only things other than Lena untouched by the power she released. Anara stood, pushing the woman away when she tried to help.

"How can you *stand* after what you did?"

"You keep saying we need to go," Anara looked down at Lena, keeping her eyes on the Borderlander. She had no desire to answer questions, especially questions she had no answers to. "So let's go."

"I have a dress for you to wear back at my inn. We'll leave tonight, I hope you can ride a horse." The stranger said as they darted into the narrow maze of streets near the inn. Bells rang for the Watch when people finally stumbled upon the scene behind them.

"I have had some training, yes," Anara said, still looking back towards *Lussena's Rest*. Her stomach felt empty, more than it actually was, at having just left Lena lying there.

"Good, because I can't. No, it isn't funny, I just... I just don't talk to many people. Yes, I know Anara just lost someone, but could you please just be quiet."

"Are you all right? How do you know my name?" Anara raised an eyebrow at the strange woman. "Did Edwin send you?"

"Sorry, I just... shut up! I don't care what you say about her, I'm helping Anara," the woman argued, folding her arms beneath her generous breasts. The stranger caught Anara's cautious look and laughed uncomfortably. "I'll explain later. I'm sorry for your loss. She really did love you."

"I know," Anara said solemnly with one last look at *Lussena's Rest* before it disappeared behind some houses.

EPILOGUE

Joshua turned over the skeletal remains with his boot. The bones had no marks of fire except around the obliterated skull. The ruins of the inn suggested there should have been. Joshua crouched down to snap one of the bones in half and found the marrow still slick and red. The poor soul had been stripped of its flesh recently, somehow, without any marks being left on the bone.

He sighed as he looked over where the second corpse, Mistress Lena Weston, was covered by a black shroud. Mistress Weston's body was equally as perplexing. Lena had no visible wounds, yet the wood beneath her was stained red by blood. Her entire petite body seemed to have bled out, but aside from her too pale skin, she appeared unharmed.

This is a waste of time, Joshua thought and looked south. Sir Echton was waiting for him—if he had not died in the Ironeye prison—but Eric had roped Joshua into some sort of necromancy conspiracy involving Lord Heath and now *this*. Eric was checking the Heath mansion, delegating the investigation of the carnage that was Mistress Adair's inn to Joshua. This was to distract Joshua from immediately riding south to find Sir Echton. Joshua was well aware of *that* fact, yet Mistress Weston's death—and even worse Anara's disappearance—demanded his attention. At some point, he had actually decided to care about the courtesan, and now her disappearance was as troubling to him as Sir Echton's capture.

"There you go again," Gabriel muttered. "Thinking about Anara?"

"How couldn't I? This was her home for the festival," Joshua said and placed the broken bones with the rest. "This looks like the work of a Raykarn channeling rod." *For all I know, that's Anara!* Joshua frowned at the skeleton. *Did I just break one of her bones to see if it was a fresh corpse?* he thought, feeling sick in his gut.

"That isn't Anara," Mistress Ashton huffed, ignoring the guards and entering the ruins. Mistress Ashton's face was still greenish black, with a tinge of yellow at the edges of the scabs. Joshua looked at her, women always seemed to know what he was thinking, that or Mistress Ashton thought the same. Anara had been the woman's friend. "Too tall."

"You can tell how tall the person was just by looking at the bones?" Gabriel asked with surprise, he was easily impressed. Joshua almost laughed, he knew it was not Anara. He knew the bones were somehow wrong, but even the remote chance that it *could* be her was unnerving. They just did not look like what he thought woman bones would look like.

"It was probably male, too," Joshua guessed before Ashton could continue making him look the fool.

"A good eye," she smiled and patted Joshua's shoulder. "Broad shoulders, not very common for a woman."

"You really shouldn't be here, Mistress Ashton," Joshua said, waving back towards where Mistress Adair was looking over the wreckage of her inn. She was crying uncontrollably into her driver's chest as the tall man—not as tall as Gabriel, no one was as tall as Gabriel—looked at Lena with silent tears and a clenched jaw.

"You can call me Roxanne, knight," Mistress Ashton said, poking him in the shoulder. "I want to help catch him."

"Him who?" Gabriel asked, scratching his head.

"That rat, Edwin," Mistress Ashton barked. "It is obvious he did this. The bones are probably our second driver who tried to interrupt." She spread her arms to encompass the rubble. "I haven't seen the second driver today. I assume that's him."

"He could just be hung over," Joshua groaned. Everyone was. Even *he* was a little. "There is no reason to assume anything." He sighed and looked into Roxanne's brown eyes with a hand on her bare shoulder. Roxanne was probably correct, but a simple lie might delay the pain of losing yet another friend. She seemed unperturbed by the cold even though her dress had no sleeves or straps. In fact, it was considerably more elegant than anything Joshua had seen the courtesans wearing with pearls sewn into the hems and gold embroidery in the fabric. It almost looked like something a noble would wear. "Please, Roxanne. You aren't helping by disturbing the scene. Go back to Mistress Adair and help her."

"Erin's tough as iron. She'll manage," Roxanne said shrugging off Joshua's hand. "What other kind of bastard would do this? I know it was Edwin. I can feel it in my bones."

"Perhaps," Eric said and Joshua turned to watch the young lord gingerly making his way across the rubble. "No one has seen him since just before the Harvest Ball to mark the end of the festival."

"*Now* you suspect Edwin?" Joshua growled, throwing up his hands. "I doubt he could have done this. Look around you this looks like the carnage of..."

"A Raykarn channeling rod," Eric finished nodding. Eric carried what could only be a sword wrapped in black cloth. "Please, Lady Ashton, this is a crime scene."

"I don't want you guys messing it up," Roxanne put her fists on her hips and stared down Eric. Gabriel looked back and forth between the courtesan and young lord as if he expected one or the other to back down. "Besides, you're letting the blacksmith look around," Roxanne finally said as she seemed to shrink under Eric's gaze.

"Your brother is concerned about you," Eric said, motioning towards Mistress Adair and the elderly man. Roxanne's attire suddenly made sense. Lord Ashton stood at the edge of the rubble, talking with members of the watch as he waved towards Joshua and the other two with frantic eyes. "He cannot come onto the scene. He is not heir to the Lord Commander. Only knights and the Watch are permitted to investigate."

"Very well, I'll see what Barty is going on about," Roxanne said, raising her chin once more.

"Why do you suspect Edwin if this was a channeling rod?" Joshua asked once Roxanne was out of earshot.

"He came back to Iliona with souvenirs," Eric explained, uncovering the weapon in his arms. "And we found this lodged into a thatcher's roof a block away, the sod was none-too-pleased at the damage it caused." Joshua recognized the sword. How could he not? It was the same one Edwin had brandished the night they made their wager over Anara's contract.

"So he *was* here," Joshua clenched his fists. Edwin had gone back on his word and taken Anara by force, killing Mistress Weston and some boy named Gerrol in the process. "How did he get an active channeling rod past Ashfall?"

"I don't know. He brought dozens of spent ones back with him. I know that much. He showed them around in Aederon City by accounts of some of the other knights. Perhaps one of them was not as spent as they thought," Eric shrugged and recovered the weapon.

"I'll kill him," Joshua stepped towards the south and paused. He had no idea which way Edwin went, killing and south just went together.

"I'll worry about tracking Edwin," Eric said, putting a hand on Joshua's shoulder. "I need you to investigate Kindor. You were right. The Heath mansion is empty of people, it was eerie seeing such a large mansion void of life yet spotless and organized."

"But Anara..."

"If she's alive, I'll keep an eye on her until you return," Eric smiled.

"She'll be waiting a long time," Joshua said, looking south again. Sir Echton was waiting. Eric could save Anara even if Joshua would have loved to be her knight in shining armor. His mentor could not wait any longer than was necessary. A quick investigation in Kindor and Joshua would be on his way to finding his teacher.

"You really intend to go back to the Borderlands? Seek vengeance for your family?"

"Yes," Joshua said and pinched the bridge of his nose; he had that same dream again of six people chasing him across the Endless Waste, he had no idea who they were but aside from the headache they caused he had felt safe with them. "But it's more than that now, I feel like I'm being drawn back there."

"Because of Sir Echton?" Eric raised a curious eyebrow at Joshua.

"It sounds insane. 'Destiny is what you make it, not something the gods decide,' the old man used to tell me. But his capture. My childhood... I feel like I am *needed* there."

"Just don't die down there," Eric said. He sounded as concerned as Joshua imagined an older brother might be.

"I cannot guarantee that, my lord," Joshua said, shooting Eric with a very brief smile. "I will do my best, though."

"You'd best be off then, Sir Kentaine," Eric said and quickly gave him a hug. "Lord Heath has a full night's and day's lead on you and I doubt he's stopping at any one spot for very long if the ringleader of the necromancer cult has summoned him."

Joshua saluted Eric, crossing both arms across his chest, and marched off towards their own inn to gather his belongings. Eric went over to Mistress Adair, probably to speak with her about who he suspected was responsible, as Gabriel quickly joined Joshua.

"We off then?" Gabriel asked.

"I'm going to Kindor, yes," Joshua said and looked up at the tall man. Gabriel scratched his wide jaw as he looked out over the narrow streets of the block. Even though Gabriel had shaved in the morning he already had his usual rugged look from the re-growth of his beard. "You're staying here."

"No, I'm not," Gabriel shook his head. "You'll get yourself killed if I don't go with you, no doubt over a woman too."

"Women are the furthest from my mind right now," Joshua said, crossing his arms and turning his attention to the road. His mind wandered to Karina's scarf that was tucked away in one of his saddlebags. He had spent hours clutching the luxurious fabric the night before, it had smelled... good. It was hard to explain, really, he had smelled pretty women before and most of them were pleasant enough but the scent of Karina's scarf was just calming and untainted by perfumes.

"Right..." Gabriel chuckled as Joshua let his eyes wander over shop fronts without actually seeing anything for sale. "Furthest from your mind. Yeah, I'm coming with you."

"You don't know how to fight, Gabe, I can't..."

"Of course I know how to fight, you've been beating on me for years. I might not be fast, like you, but I can hold my own against someone," Gabriel said, thumping his broad chest with a fist to pound his statement home. "I'm your squire."

"You're a *blacksmith*, a good one too. The gods gave you an uncanny talent for it, I don't want you to squander that." Joshua shook his head. He *had* to convince Gabriel not to come. Joshua could stand dying in the Endless Waste, he had no one who really counted on him, but if Gabriel died Cole and his wife would be devastated, and that is not to mention what would happen to the finest smithy in all of Aederon City. Gabriel had a *real* future. Gabriel was important, even if he did not realize it. They argued about it all the way back to the inn, but it was decided by someone else.

"Of course he's going with you," Cordelia frowned at him as Joshua went about the room packing his belongings. It was incredibly improper for her to be in his room. If Joshua had been in hers Eric would have killed him, at least probably gone through with locking him in the stocks. "You may have a death wish, riding against the Raykarn without a thought in that thick skull of yours, but Gabriel can keep you safe."

"I'll probably be spending most of my time protecting him!" Joshua groaned and rolled his eyes.

"And thereby keeping your own neck safe because if you died who would protect Gabriel?"

"Hey!" Gabriel barked but Cordelia just ignored him.

"You *have* to come back, Joshua," Cordelia said and stopped his frantic packing by taking both of his hands in hers. She smiled at him and fluttered her long eyelashes and Joshua had the sense that she was going to kiss him again.

"Fine," Joshua said as Cordelia began leaning in. "He can come if it will ease your mind, Cora."

"Of course it will," Cordelia smiled and stepped back, letting go of Joshua's hands to clap them together. "When will you be back?"

"A year, maybe two," Joshua nonchalantly stated as he checked his father's sword to make sure it slid freely from the scabbard before sliding it into one of his bags. He checked *Vengeance*. The orange flame briefly bursting to life when it cleared the sheath before sliding back in and tied the hand-and-a-half sword to his waist. It was the first time he had worn the weapon and, compared to his father's blade, it was heavy. The weight felt good, like a knight's sword *should* feel. "Probably closer to four."

"*Four* years!" Cordelia gasped. An unwise reaction in her corset as she raised a wrist to her forehead and nearly collapsed before Gabriel managed to catch her. Joshua would never understand why Cordelia insisted on wearing her corset so tightly. Cordelia blushed as she cleared her throat and stood up after Gabriel fanned her with one of his massive hands. "Sorry, I just meant that... well isn't... isn't that a bit long for a tour in the Borderlands?"

"Eric's sending me on his little errand too. That will delay me at least two or three months—possibly six if winter hits the Iron Mountains in the next few weeks—before I even *reach* the Borderlands. Even without Eric's errand, I have *a lot* of business in the Borderlands. I have no idea where Echton is being held, or if he is even still alive, not to mention making the Raykarn pay for what they did to my family."

"Four years," Cordelia repeated and sat down on Joshua's bed.

"I'll understand if you don't wait for me, Cora," Joshua said and finally closed the last of his travel satchels.

"Four years is not so long," Cordelia smiled at him and stood up to walk him and Gabriel out of the inn to where their horses were waiting. Cordelia remained by Joshua's side as he went about attaching the satchels to the pack horse's saddle.

Swiftstride bumped Joshua with his head as the stallion watched Joshua taking care of a strange horse.

"You're still my best friend, *Swiftstride*," Joshua said, patting the steed's long, white nose and slipping him a carrot from one of the satchels. Gabriel mounted his own horse—yet another one Joshua had needed to purchase—and lead the pack horse towards the west, towards Kindor. Cordelia bit her lower lip and clasped her hands together as she swayed between Joshua and *Swiftstride*. "What now?"

"I just... want a kiss before you go," Cordelia blushed and looked towards the ground. "Something to remember you by."

"I doubt you'd ever forget me, Cora. We grew up together," Joshua chuckled and Cordelia frowned at him.

"Well if..." she started and Joshua lowered his head to kiss her firmly on the lips. Cordelia *was* a wonderful woman to kiss, even if Joshua knew it would never amount to anything between them. Cordelia smiled, brushing her lips with her fingertips, and stepped aside to let Joshua take his seat atop *Swiftstride*. "Come back to me," Cordelia said, loosely taking Joshua's hand in her own as *Swiftstride* walked around Cordelia to face westward.

"Of course, my lady," Joshua said, gently squeezing Cordelia's fingertips before *Swiftstride* started walking to catch up with Gabriel. Joshua refused to let himself look back. It would be best for Cordelia to move on and that would be easier for her if she did not know how much he wanted to see her one last time before leaving.

"Are you going to cry?" Gabriel gently shoved Joshua, which meant Joshua nearly tumbled out of his saddle. Had Gabriel been his opponent in the last round instead of Edwin, Joshua suspected he would have been the one to land on his back when his lance met the blacksmith's brick wall of a build.

"No," Joshua pushed back.

"She might," Gabriel said, looking over his shoulder back towards Cordelia. "I mean... not might..."

"I know," Joshua clenched his jaw together.

"You don't intend to see her again, do you? Even if you live through your crusade?" Gabriel frowned and looked down at his horse's mane. Joshua did not answer; Gabriel knew what he would say but Joshua just could not get the words out. Instead, the knight looked south, his real destination, and struggled against the pain from ignoring Cordelia behind him.

Joshua took in a deep breath. The air had a chill bite to it, winter always came too quickly this far north. In the Borderlands there would still be a month, maybe two, before the cool rains of the Months of Frost came. Still, the serene, chilled landscape outside Crossroads was beautiful. Rolling farmlands slowly blended with meadows towards the Iron Mountains before a dark, green forest swallowed the flatter lands and crawled up the sides of the jagged peaks. Unfortunately, without anything more to really say about their assignment, Joshua's mind wandered to Cordelia and the mess he had left behind. He exhaled and shut his eyes, this would be a *long* journey if they failed to catch up to Lord Heath before Kindor.

Made in the USA
Lexington, KY
08 August 2017